HAUNTINGS

A COLLECTION OF GHOSTLY ENCOUNTERS

*With contributions from
authors of the
Historical Writers Forum*

Copyright ©

Simon Turney, K.S. Barton, Paula Lofting, Stephanie
Churchill, Jennifer C. Wilson,
Judith Arnopp, Lynn Bryant, Kate Jewell, Samantha
Wilcoxson, D. Apple

THE HISTORICAL WRITERS FORUM

Who we are

The Historical Writers Forum (HWF), started out as a social media group where writers of historical non-fiction, historical fiction, and historical fantasy could come together to share their knowledge and skills *to help improve standards amongst this genre of writers, whether they be new or well-practiced.* The aim is to encourage peer support for authors in a field where sometimes writing can be a very lonely business. We currently number over 800 members and are growing. We have recently been busy organising online talks via Zoom and now have our own YouTube channel where you can find our discussions on a variety of topics. Our membership includes several well-known authors who regularly engage to share their experiences and strengths to help other members build their own skillset

We can be found on

Facebook:
https://www.facebook.com/groups/writersofhistoryforum/

Twitter: @histwriters

YouTube
https://www.youtube.com/channel/UCSsS5dFPp4xz5zxJUsjytoQ

Dedicated to Sharon K. Penman

One of the world's greatest historical fiction authors

Those who were lucky enough to have encountered a Sharon Kay Penman novel know what an incomparable author she was. Those who have been fortunate enough to have interacted with her know what a lovely woman she was. And those who had the privilege of being her friend know just how special she was.

In the early stages of the creation of this anthology, I asked Sharon to do an introduction for us. Sadly, it was not meant to be. She passed away only a few months later.

This is for you, Beautiful Lady.

Stephanie Churchill

September, 2021

FOREWORD

BY

SHARON BENNETT CONNOLLY

Since time immemorial, people have sat around the hearth, in the dark of night with storms raging outside, telling each other ghost stories. Even the fairy tales told to children over the centuries have bordered on horror stories, with a wicked stepmother here, an evil witch there and the candy-selling man who turned out to be a child-catcher; all just waiting to scare and horrify the unsuspecting. Many were moralising tales, told to scare children into being good. But the effects linger. As children become teenagers, they tell scarier stories, staying up late into the night on sleepovers and camping expeditions. The aim has always been to frighten and entertain with ever greater levels of horror, often shining torches into their faces at odd angles to create special effects.

The enduring need to push our fear to the limits has been with us since childhood.

Such camp-fire tales belie the fact that horror and ghost stories have a place deep in the culture of society. They have always been way to explain the unexplainable.

We have all had that moment, that sense of being watched. But when we turn around, there is no one there…

The most famous incident of this kind gave birth to not only the vampire but also what is probably the most famous horror story of all time. And it started, as it always does, with a gathering of friends, in their late teens and early 20s, trying to shock and scare each other as a storm raged outside.

Europe had just emerged from its own horror story. Over twenty-five years of warfare had ignited with the French Revolution in 1789 and ended on the battlefield of Waterloo in June 1815, raging across Europe, from the Iberian Peninsula to frozen Russia and even venturing into Africa. A generation had grown up with the shadow of war looming over them. This man-made tragedy had been exacerbated by volcanic eruptions, famine and epidemics; the volcanic ash would cause 3 years of darkness, crop failure and cholera outbreaks. It was a time ripe for dark and desperate literary endeavours.

In the aftermath of Waterloo, a young couple, Mary Wollstonecraft Godwin, her lover Percy Bysshe Shelley, travelled to Lake Geneva in May 1816, ostensibly looking for rest and relaxation. Their party included their four-month-old baby and Mary's stepsister, Claire Clairmont. At the time, Claire was pregnant with a child by Lord Byron, the ground-breaking poet whose personal affairs and love life had proved too scandalous for England. Most recently he had divorced his wife, abandoning his young daughter, Ada Lovelace, and, so rumour had it, pursued an affair with his own half-sister. Plagued by gossip and debt, he had left England for Europe. Claire, it seems, had decided to surprise her lover by following him.

Mary had fallen in love with Percy in 1814; the couple had run away together, despite Percy already being married, and travelled around Europe for the next 2 years. After Byron left England, a distraught Claire convinced Mary and Percy to travel to Geneva with her. A few days later, Byron—clearly unaware that Claire would be there—arrived in town. Mary, whose own love life not without controversy, sympathized with the scandalous poet.

With Percy and Lord Byron soon forming an intense friendship, the small party abandoned their various travel plans and rented properties close to each other along Lake Geneva. They would gather together in the long, dark, cold evening at the Villa Diodati, the stately mansion Byron had rented for his stay along with John Polidori, his doctor. They read poetry, argued, and talked late into the night. After three nights of the party being trapped inside by the raging storm, tensions were running high. Byron was annoyed by Claire's obsessive attentions, Mary likewise had to fend off the unwanted attentions of the equally obsessive Doctor Polidori.

They spent their evenings reading horror stories and ghostly poems to each other until one night, they were given a challenge. Byron proposed they each write a ghost story that was better than the ones they had just read. Inspired by a tale of Byron's, Polidori produced his novella, The Vampyre, which would be published in 1819. It is the first work of fiction to include a blood-sucking hero—which may have been modelled on Byron himself. Mary took a little longer to settle on the subject of her story but after a long, sleepless night she produced her offering, Frankenstein, or the Modern Prometheus. Considering what happens when men play gods, and perhaps with the upheaval of the last three decades in her mind, she would later call the story her "hideous progeny".

Frankenstein would be Mary Shelley's enduring legacy and the inspiration for so many hopeful writers.

Fast forward a little over 200 hundred years. It is now 2021, the world is in the midst of a pandemic of horrifying proportions. Travel to the neighbouring town is frowned upon, families are forced apart, the schools closed and writers the world over are sat in their studies, or at their kitchen tables, tapping away on keyboards, alone, solitary...

Well, not quite.

We now have the internet, so when you are alone, you are still not totally alone. Once again, with the storm raging outside, a group of writers have come together, not in a luxury Swiss mansion, but via the miracle that is the internet. Despite the miles and oceans apart, and across the continents, these ten historical fiction authors were given a challenge: to write a ghost story, to regale each other with terrifying stories of ghosts and ghoulies. Through history and legend, from the legions of Rome to a spooky hotel, from Tudor England to an asylum for the insane, those who have suffered injustice may finally be laid to rest, those who have sought loved ones across the centuries may finally be reunited and those who have suffered nightmares for past deeds may finally find peace.

A year after the idea first formed, those stories are set to be unleashed on the world.

Dare you read them?

CONTENTS

An Unquiet Dream
by Lynn Bryant

*

Here there were Dragons
by Kate Jewell

*

Among the Lost
by Samantha Wilcoxson

*

Hotel Vanity
by D. Apple

FURIES

BY

SIMON TURNEY

*B*ritain was in the charge of Suetonius Paulinus, in military skill *and in popular report — which allows no man to lack his rival — a formidable competitor to Corbulo, and anxious to equal the laurels of the recovery of Armenia by crushing a national enemy. He prepared accordingly to attack the island of Mona, which had a considerable population of its own, while serving as a haven for refugees; and, in view of the shallow and variable channel, constructed a flotilla of boats with flat bottoms. By this method the infantry crossed; the cavalry, who followed, did so by fording or, in deeper water, by swimming at the side of their horses.*

On the beach stood the adverse array, a serried mass of arms and men, with women flitting between the ranks. In the style of Furies, in robes of deathly black and with dishevelled hair, they brandished their torches; while a circle of Druids, lifting their hands to heaven and showering imprecations, struck the troops with such an awe at the extraordinary spectacle that, as though their limbs were paralysed, they exposed their bodies to wounds without an attempt at movement. Then, reassured by their general, and inciting each other never to flinch before a band of females and fanatics, they charged behind the standards, cut down all who met them, and enveloped the enemy in his own flames. The next step was to install a garrison among the conquered population, and to demolish the groves consecrated to their savage cults: for they considered it a duty to consult their deities by means of human entrails. While he was thus occupied, the sudden revolt of the province was announced to Suetonius.

— Tacitus: Annals 29-30

1

Aut non rem temptes aut perfice

(Either don't try at all, or make sure you succeed.)

— Ovid: Ars Amatoria I:389

W as there something ominous about the sky above the city of Rome tonight?

Gaius Suetonius Paulinus stood in the centre of his austere yet stylish atrium, next to the small square pool with its bronze nymph fountain, and peered up through the open roof into the inky evening. Try as he might to blot out the squawks of Roman matronhood and their portly, ambitious husbands busy drinking his wine and scuffing his expensive mosaic floors, he consistently failed. The sky helped keep their cackling at bay, at least. He'd seen such skies before, full of predatory clouds and a striped, feral moon, and they never boded anything good.

Good?

As if he had any concept of such a thing, as he had proven.

'Gaius, come back in. I did not arrange this lavish occasion so that you could land me with entertaining the world's most boring men in the triclinium while you stand in the atrium and feel sorry for yourself.'

For myself? He thought. *Hardly.* Paulinus painted a fake easy smile across his careworn features and turned to his wife, the love of his life, the only one who knew him and the only one who cared to do so these days. Too much, sometimes. But then, despite his erstwhile celebrity as the hero of Britannia, Paulinus's choice of emperors to follow in the last few years had damaged his reputation and made him almost untouchable. First there had been the despised Nero, to whom he owed so much of his career. Then the unfortunate Otho. Truth be told he *liked* the new one, Vespasian, and considered him by far the best candidate for the purple since the stammering Claudius, yet his connections to those other two had ruined his chances of being one of Vespasian's chosen. So while the new emperor's cronies, many of whom had never been closer to battle than reading Polybius, lorded it up around Rome, men who had forged the empire at the cost of their very soul sat on the periphery, overlooked.

Most of them, anyway, he reminded himself bitterly, watching the impressive young officer, Agricola, telling his tales of the civil war to a gaggle of adoring youngsters.

His own audience looked less enticing. A cluster of women with white faces and enough tightly curled hair to hide a lion, alongside their husbands with their puffy, red-veined faces and hungry expressions, waited to talk to the house's owner. He sighed. They only ever wanted to talk about two things, and neither of them gave him any joy. Still, his wife had organised all of this in the hope of rekindling his career, and

3

he owed it to her to try, even though he would rather kick them all out and spend yet another night alone in the silent dark, wondering why he hadn't already thrown himself on his sword.

He allowed Marcia to guide him towards that horrifying tangle of guests, and within a matter of heartbeats he found himself sitting among them, amid the stink of sweat and heady perfume, the brainless chatter and the inanity, holding a cup of expensive Falernian while some matron quizzed him on the subjects he most loathed.

'And did the red-haired bitch truly fight half naked? They say she was almost an animal on the battlefield.'

He turned a resigned expression on the woman. 'She was buried under half a ton of armour and wool when we found her, and I don't think she'd got closer than the very rear of her army. Don't believe everything you hear.'

'So you did not let the colonies burn?' another unwelcome voice chimed in.

There it was: the accusation. Yet again. He'd *had* to let Londinium and Verulamium burn in order to gather his army and face Boudicca with even a hope of victory. If he'd tried to save Londinium, the Iceni queen would have won the whole thing, and he wouldn't be here to be accused and demeaned so. In fact, his head would have bounced down the stairs to the forum for his failure. He'd sacrificed two towns to win a war.

He let out a noncommittal grunt and turned from the fat moron who'd spoken, only to find himself facing yet another brainless harpy with a pile of hair with more density than the brain beneath, who'd pushed in between.

'I'm more interested in the druids,' she said in excited, breathless tones. 'They sacrificed their own people, I understand, in brutal, horrifying rituals.'

Ah yes, the threefold death...

'They were the greatest enemy of Rome since Hannibal,' she went on. 'Even Caesar had failed to destroy their power. But that was before you.'

Ah yes. Hero worship. More familiar. Less warranted. Less welcome. And all because of the second of the two subjects he loathed.

'Won't this be your decennalia?' another idiot asked. 'Ten years since both the druids and the redhead queen? Your twin victories in Britannia?'

He looked past the senator. On the wall of the triclinium he could see the triumphal honours Nero had granted him for his victories: a golden shield, banners from the captured tribes, a wreath, a bust of himself in rich armour. A brightly-painted frieze which showed the Iceni queen kneeling at his feet. The sword he had worn in battle against her. No joy to be found there, with any of it. Hollow victories at best. Because for all his glorious victory in Britain, that was also the scene of his worst crime. He dare not look at the shrine of the household gods just visible along the corridor, for no god would countenance him now.

'Well, the world is better off without such creatures,' another senator with a nose like a stork said gaily. Something about his manner just nagged at Paulinus, and before he could stop himself, he had turned, his face twisting into a rictus.

'You think so, do you? You, who sit comfortable in Rome and pay your dues and give offerings when needed and are perfectly happy that the gods will watch over you, because you are Roman and therefore you are blessed and untouchable? You think I did a good thing? You think I did the *right* thing? That the druids had to be destroyed?'

He snarled, angry with himself. 'Yes, and perhaps they did. Perhaps Nero was right with his commands and the world is safer without the druids and their masters. But Nero did not have to walk into the lair of those gods, and neither did you. None of you had to commit sacrilege on a grand scale. None of you walked into the sacred forests of Toutatis and burned the druids' groves. None of you took a hundred heads in a morning and hung them from trees as a warning that their day was over. None of you watched temples char and collapse, feeling the presence of those hateful deities all around you as you imposed imperial will even upon the gods. The day you have faced down a god and bellowed the emperor's fury in his face, *then* you can lecture me on what is right and what is not. Until then, keep your fatuous comments behind the prison of your teeth.'

He sat trembling in the uncomfortable silence which followed. He could feel Marcia's disapproval even across the room. That one outburst had cost him any chance of advancement this entire gathering had offered.

'Well, the world is better off anyway,' the offended man said, rising and pulling his heavy toga around his sweaty, rotund form before stomping away to find a better conversationalist.

'Perhaps we should go out into the garden?' a hopeful harpy murmured.

'A shame, but not a good idea,' Marcia said, appearing from nowhere to try and save the evening. 'A sewer overflowed during the last storm and flooded our garden. We have a company of expensive gardeners, the same ones who have been working on the emperor's projects, dealing with it, and it's screened from view for now. Perhaps you could come and join us for an evening in the peristyle when it is finished?'

* * *

It was a dream. He could feel it. More than that: it was *the* dream. The dream that came with soul-crushing regularity to rob him of rest and to give him the gaunt look that most people took for over-work.

The men of the Twentieth moved towards the sacred grove, the *nemeton* as the enemy called it, a circle of trees around a pool of untouched crystal water. The clouds above raced past as though they had somewhere to be, each a dark stripe of omens, each threatening, yet never quite delivering. The black furies on the beach and their hordes of howling natives were behind him now, and just the heart and soul of the enemy remained.

Dozens of white-clad figures, some with bronze armour, some without, all with faces twisted in hate and defiance, waited at the entrance to the grove, seemingly calm. Paulinus shivered. He knew what was coming, for all his inability to stop things or to change them.

It was the emperor's abhorrent order, but the emperor's word was sacrosanct, and could not be defied. The druids were the very heart of tribal resistance in Britain. Just as the fastest way to win a battle was to kill the enemy general, so the fastest way to end resistance was to remove the white-clad menaces whose word was law to these people just as was the emperor's to Rome. But these were not just generals, and they were not just kings. These men were both those things and more, for they were also the mouthpiece and the gauntleted fist of their gods. They were tied to the native deities in ways that even Rome's priests could not understand. And no Roman wanted to anger a god, let alone the triad of them who controlled a whole culture – Toutatis, Taranis and Esus. In the whole history of Rome before that day no commander, no matter how brave or how mad, had challenged the gods.

6

Only him. At the word of Nero, only Gaius Suetonius Paulinus had made war upon gods.

The pantomime began as usual. His men, the Twentieth 'Valorous and Victorious', roared. The rest of the army was moving about the island under the command of competent men like Agricola, but he alone had brought the Twentieth to end it all, for this nightmare task was his alone, and he could put no other officer in the position of killing the chosen of a god.

And at the command, the Twentieth began to move, an inexorable stomp towards that circle of neatly tended trees.

The men in white began to chant, a moan in eerie low harmony, a last appeal to their triad of powerful gods to drive out these intruders.

Then it happened. The men stumbled to a halt. Confusion reigned in every face as the men of the Twentieth reeled, unable to comprehend why they had stopped. Even the centurions were standing there, bewildered. Men looked to each other for an answer, finding none.

As the druids began a new chant, a new spell to turn back the steel tide of Rome, Paulinus knew two things. He knew what he was doing was dreadfully, fundamentally, wrong. And he knew he had to do it regardless, and that it was all down to him.

'Forward, valorous and victorious, men of the Twentieth. For the senate and the people of Rome. One fight and it is done.'

And his words cut through the torpor holding the legion in place, as though snipping a cord that bound them. In a heartbeat the centurions were bellowing encouragement, and the legion was moving once more, stomping forward. Slaves came on behind with pots of pitch and flaming brands, ready to remove this place of power forever, and damning themselves alongside him in the process.

The Twentieth moved into the grove, roaring, shields up, swords lancing and cutting, chopping, and scything. The moan of choral magic became a moan of horror and disbelief, white robes flowering red. Such a spray of blood in the air that it felt like mist. Paulinus, standing in the front line as if he were a common legionary, bellowed his prayers to Mars and Minerva as he struck a man in white, his blade tearing through the wool and the flesh beneath, grating on bone as it speared vital organs. The druid's face contorted in agony, yet Paulinus was impressed to see it cling to a vestige of defiant anger to the last as the governor pulled his blade free. Roman generals did not fight in the front line like this, but now, doing this, how could he order his men to war against gods and not share their peril?

7

Recovering from his blow, and grateful that as well as honing his military mind he had kept up the practice with his sword, Paulinus paused to take stock as his men surged on, taking out the last resistance in the grove, ending Celtic defiance on this sacred isle.

He saw the man, then. One tall druid in a bronze cuirass which bore strange designs, a long sword in one hand, but a set of iron manacles in the other, the sort one might find around a slave condemned to the mines. The sort they had found around long-dead corpses in murky bogs all across this island. Amid the fighting no one seemed to notice that one figure, untouched by the fray, as its sword came slowly up to point directly at Paulinus.

He awoke in a cold sweat, muttering fear and shaking. He was not in bed. He usually emerged from the dream in sodden sheets, but to his shock, as his eyes snapped open, he was standing before those trophies and honours on the wall, the imperial confirmation of his 'victory' in Britannia. This was new. *Horribly* new. The dream had not changed, but it was changing reality around him. As the house slave Barates rushed to help him, he let the man, acquiescing to whatever he said. His mind was elsewhere.

Ten years. His decennalia.

* * *

The morning sun, freshly risen, was little comfort, the horror of the dream still with him, his skin still prickling, and the cold shivers occasionally rippling through him. He couldn't look at the sky, his habitual practice, in the atrium, for that was altogether too near his trophies and honours, of which he was giving serious thought to disposing. Instead, despite the mess, he strolled in his fresh-pressed tunic and best boots, through the atrium and out into the peristyle.

The gardeners were already at work, and had been since sunup. A tall wicker fence surrounded the work site, leaving only one side of the garden open for the residents, a colonnaded walkway which led to the small private bath house and the slave quarters beyond. The sky was a cold vault of blue steel, such solid, high and light cloud that if it had not been for the weak sun showing faintly through it, one might think the all-encompassing haze to be merely the blue of the sky. Paulinus knew it was not. He was familiar with the sky.

Strolling along the walkway, he felt he might be able to recover his senses and his poise. If the day held steady and good, he would be able to put aside the dream and return to the... well, to the dour and miserable man he had been anyway this past decade.

At the walkway's end, he contemplated using the baths. He would have no visits from clients this morning. He had few anyway, but the news of last night would have spread and he would hardly win any popularity contest. No. He had to do something more active. Lounging around would only allow moods to settle on him once more.

He turned to head back to the house, and stopped sharply. Here, the wicker screens had been lifted aside to allow the gardeners in and out, for their stacks of flowerpots and stonework, of cement bags and turf rolls, remained outside the barrier. His eyes widened as he peered into the worksite behind the screens. His heart began to race.

Stepping awkwardly forward, he realised he was stuttering in a panicked voice and tried to get a hold of himself, waving at one of the workers, who carefully replaced the marble lintel he was lifting, and hurried over. They were good gardeners. Very expensive and brought in from Tibur. They were one of the teams Vespasian had used to rework the site of Nero's palace he had demolished. The man stopped before him, head bowed respectfully.

'Domine?'

'What is the meaning of this?'

The man frowned and looked at their work, then shrugged. 'Sir?'

'Who told you to do this? Who put you up to it?'

The man gave a polite cough. 'You only gave the vaguest of orders, Domine. Repair the sewer, recover it, and replace the garden with something "quiet and understated, rural and calm." Your very words, sir.'

Paulinus stared at the manicured circle of poplar trees, beautiful and neat, perfect, and freshly planted. A circle of white marble gravel completed the surroundings beneath them, while small flower beds were strategically placed, each in the form of a magical animal or a scene from heroic myth, each with carefully chosen flora of specific colours and with a nod to each season so that they were never bare. And the centrepiece? A pool of beautiful clear water, edged with travertine, perhaps two feet deep and immaculate. It was all beautiful. It was, as he had requested, quiet and understated, rural, and calm. It was also an almost perfect reflection of his dream, so much so that he could all-but see the druids standing between him and the pool, obscured by the baffled workman.

'Who designed it?'

As he stared at the scene, the gardener called over a man who was busy marking off a list on his wax tablet. The man, dark complexioned and lean, bowed his head as he stopped before Paulinus.

'Domine?'

'You designed this?'

The man nodded. 'It is, if I say so myself, one of my more pleasing works. You are not pleased? The emperor himself commended me for my work on the Oppian Hill.'

'Who gave you this idea? Who put you up to it?'

'Why, the gods, sir.'

A chill ran through Paulinus again. 'Gods?'

'Of course, Domine. It is a representation of the most beautiful temple in the world, that of Vesta at Tibur. A circular shrine of travertine, with eighteen columns, here shown as trees to make the garden more rural and pretty. And at the centre, where the flame of Vesta would burn in the temple, here we have its reflection in peaceful water. Is it not everything you asked for?'

Paulinus stared. It was. It really *was*. And yet it wasn't. 'Tear it down. Make something square. And no pools.'

The gardener stared at him, but Paulinus simply turned his back and stomped away. All the way to the atrium, he tried to shake off the feeling that somehow that trio of British gods were taunting him, playing with him. As he walked past his trophies, he made a mental note to order their removal and storage before the end of the day. Decennalia indeed.

Marcia appeared from a side room, her face full of concern. 'Have you recovered, husband?'

'I... I may have irritated the gardeners, set them back a few days. You might have to budget a little higher for them. I didn't like what they'd done.'

She chewed her lip as though fighting the urge to enquire further, but nodded. 'You look a fright, Gaius. Tired and pale. You won't try and sleep some more?'

'It's the last thing I need right now.'

'Is this about Gaulish gods again?'

'British. Same gods, though, I suppose.'

'Then you need to remember that Rome's gods are stronger. If they were not, would we have mastered half the world?'

He let out a noncommittal grunt in reply.

'I've said it before, Gaius, this is all in your head. You are blameless, just a loyal general of the empire. This fear of what you have done? Of their gods? It is *all* in your head. Get yourself to the pantheon this morning. Make offerings and libations to all the gods, and beseech them for their protection and aid. Most of all beseech them for a good night's sleep and an improvement in your mood, my love, for I cannot hold up the façade that things are normal for much longer. You are in danger of becoming a pariah.'

'I am in danger of becoming a madman. Possibly a corpse,' he replied darkly. Then, seeing her expression, he bolted on a smile, one of the many masks he kept for the public, and patted her on the shoulder. 'It is a good notion. I will visit the pantheon, and I will make amends with the counsellor gods. Surely no harm can come from weakened foreign deities when great Jove and wondrous Vesta keep us in safety.'

Marcia nodded her agreement. 'Take a litter and a couple of strong guards. There has been trouble in the Campus Martius recently.'

Paulinus shook his head. 'I'll take men, but I need to walk. I need the air and the exercise.'

'It's not befitting a man of your status to wander the streets like a one-armed veteran.'

'Marcia, I know what I'm doing.'

Kissing her on the forehead, he found Barates in the cloakroom and had the slave carefully drape a new clean toga around him, winding it and settling it, adjusting the folds. The formal garment was a bit much for walking around the city, but it would add weight to the sanctity of any offering if he had the toga over his head in the traditional priestly manner.

Half an hour later, with four burly Germans armed with stout ash cudgels, two slaves following at a respectful distance, and his nomenclator at his heel in case he met someone he needed to remember, he passed through the forum. The nomenclator was probably unnecessary. He knew everyone he cared to talk to, but Marcia was still attempting to build him up, and being able to name peoples' children or their hometowns and their businesses always went down well.

The city was busy, but only pleasantly so, not over-crowded, especially for a man with four armed Germans forging a path. From their home on the western slope of the Palatine hill, the least crowded route skirted the southern edge of the Capitol and the periphery of the *Forum Holitorium* – the flower market – down towards the river. He tried to hold his breath as they passed the cattle market, then breathed in willingly the heady scents of the flowers, and was starting to feel more like himself as they passed close to the Tiber. Here, sweaty in the heavy wool toga, he turned north, heading towards the great Campus Martius, which had been naught but a field a century ago but now housed some of Rome's greatest imperial monuments.

At its southern edge, close to the Capitol and surrounded by scattered temples, rose the great semi-circle of Marcellus's theatre. Stalls had been set up outside selling souvenirs and sweetmeats, pastries and jewellery. Paulinus struck up a conversation with the nomenclator, quizzing him over the most important person he had ever worked for, and it took him completely by surprise when he walked straight into the back of one of his German guards while not looking where he was going.

Stumbling to a halt with a curse, he was about to harangue the guard over his clumsiness when he realised that all four of them had stopped, and their leader was holding up a hand, warning Paulinus to stop, though he had not noticed, having been looking the other way. Confused, his head snapped this way and that, trying to identify the cause for the halt.

His blood ran cold.

A group of figures in ragged black garb were cavorting wildly in front of the arcade of the theatre, women, he surmised from the clothes. The people around them stood spellbound, in awe.

In a flash, Paulinus was back on that flat-bottomed boat, crossing the waters to Mona, while the tribes and their druid lords waited for them on the lush grass beyond. There, on the beach, black-clad furies leapt and danced, casting their spells and bellowing terrifying encouragement to their warriors. Sable-draped monsters from the pits of Tarterus, choking the will out of the legions as they approached.

Back in the present, in the city, before the guards or the slaves could stop him, Paulinus was storming past them, pushing the Germans aside as he snatched one of the ash clubs from the nearest. They hurried on, carefully encouraging him to stop, for a servant could hardly issue an order. He marched with fury and icy horror towards the cavorting black shapes.

His arm came up and then down, the length of heavy ash smacking into the shoulder of one of the leaping figures. Despite their station, the guards and the slaves were on him now, trying to wrestle the club from his hand as he rattled off furious curses and tore at the black garb.

The figures had stopped their cavorting now, staring at this attack, even as a stunned and horrified hush settled upon the crowd of watchers. Paulinus couldn't stop it. First the grove, and now the British furies? It was a deliberate campaign against him. It had to be. Who would do such a thing? Who *could* do such a thing?

For a moment his mind furnished him with an image of Agricola, now a well-connected man with a solid military and civic record. He had been there on the island when it happened, as a young and talented tribune. He brushed the notion aside. Agricola was far too straight-laced and Roman for such a thing. No, this was the work of gods or of sorcerers.

He had torn away the black tattered robe now to reveal the pale and uninteresting face of a young man beneath. The man was howling with pain and clutching at his shoulder, and two other furies had thrown back their hoods and were demanding to know what he thought he was doing.

His toga had slipped awry, and he must look a state, yet still his pulse was racing.

'What is this? Who put you up to this?'

One of the black figures, his face a mask of confusion, coughed. 'Er… Pollentius.'

'Who is this Pollentius? What has he against me?'

'Nothing,' answered the man. 'He's the dramatist, the man in charge of the show. He said we needed to draw crowds, to pull in custom. He's the one behind it.'

Baffled, Paulinus shook his head. 'What? What show?'

'Euripedes. The Trojan Women? It's been running in the theatre since the Ides of this month, but the crowds are waning, and we needed to get more custom. Bums on seats, sir, bums on seats.'

'This is for a play?' He shook his head. Gods, but he'd seen the Trojan Women before, and of course he could see how this was part of that tragedy. How had he mistaken this for…

He shivered. He couldn't even think of the furies on the beach.

He was on the move again in moments, so fast the guards and the slaves had to scurry to catch up.

'Domine, perhaps we should return home?' one of the Germans said in thickly accented Latin. 'I fear you are not well.'

'As well as I'm likely to get,' he snapped in return. They walked on, hurrying, purpose and desperation in their step. The shape of Agrippa's baths and basilica came into sight, as well as the great square of the

Pantheon the famous general had constructed as a personal shrine to honour all of Rome's gods. After his death, his family had bequeathed it to the city, and it had become a favourite place to beseech all the gods. Thus it was that there you would find the most desperate. Those folk who were in such dire need that they needed *all* the gods on their side, or perhaps they just needed *any* god to listen and to help. That it should come to pass Paulinus was one of those desperate pleaders was astonishing, really.

His roving wide eyes continually strafed the streets, watching for the shapes of druids or harpies, of sacred groves or pools that should not be there. He was so prepared now for portents and signs he did not even slow as his gaze fell upon the puppet show. Dozens of children sat around watching the wooden figures acting out their scene. In silver and green, they had the look of auxiliary soldiers. Very familiar ones, too. They were the spitting image of Batavian cavalry such as he had led in Britannia. It came as no surprise to see that they were swimming across the water alongside their horses, using their shields as floats.

He remembered them well, crossing the waters to Mona, to the beach with the waiting tribes and their black-clad furies. The Batavians, strong and reliable, one of the few units not to baulk at what had been asked of them in that dreadful war. After the garden and the actors, that such a thing might appear in front of him was now almost expected. It was a scene from his life once more, and yet he knew this portent would have a ready explanation. Gods were like that: clever and devious. He pointed at the puppets and waved to one of the slaves.

'Find out what the story is.'

As they walked slowly on towards the pantheon, the slave made a quiet enquiry with one of the children's mothers, then rushed to catch up.

'It is the tale of Caesar in Aegytpus, Domine. The great general's German cavalry crossing the river to put a final end to the usurper pharaoh and settle Cleopatra on her throne.'

He nodded absently. Of course it was. Paulinus wasn't the only man who had ever relied upon the rather unique tactics of the German horsemen.

Still, three scenes now on his decennalia.

He made his way into the pantheon, adjusting his toga to a more respectable hand and draping a fold reverentially over his head, and there made twelve of the most expensive offerings he had ever made, overshadowing the gifts of anyone else in the temple by far and beseeching each of the twelve Olympian gods to support him in his hour of need. He poured libations to them all, dividing a flash of very expensive Chian into twelve equal portions. Let the gods feast on his behalf.

Having done what he could, he gestured to the guards and slaves, and they made their way back out into the cold morning. He took the same route back to the house. Though it made him feel queasy to pass the puppet show of his life and the leaping harpies of his past, at least he knew about them, and could face them. Taking any other route opened him up to a world of potential new horrors and omens. Still, he was relieved when he reached their door and the stout portal opened to admit him.

He walked through the house and turned his face aside so as not to see the trophies that would bring him no joy. Stopping on the far side of the atrium, he took a deep breath. Something smelled of smoke. The guards had gone to change and put away their clubs, and two slaves were carefully unwinding his toga now that he no longer needed it. The nomenclator had disappeared, and he could hear Marcia making her way towards him through the more distant rooms, her light sandals slapping on the marble as she hummed an old tune.

He definitely smelled smoke.

Frowning, he turned and made his way to the doorway which led out into the gardens.

His eyes widened at the column of smoke rising from behind those woven screens to mar the blue-grey sky above, black vapours coiling and reaching for the heavens.

'What are you doing?' he demanded as he half-ran along the colonnade for that gap where the workers went in and out.

As he reached the aperture and turned, his eyes danced with wild shock, and once more he was struck with the memory. The slaves smashing their pots of pitch among the trees of the sacred grove while their compatriots put flames to them all, turning the druids' most hallowed temple into an inferno, smoke signals going up to their gods proclaiming that Rome was here, and their people were to be no more.

He realised he was shaking wildly. Six of the poplar trees, so recently planted, had been uprooted and sawn up and were burning even now. A seventh was already leaning as the gardeners took it down. The perfect pool had gone grey, filled with ash and detritus. Gardeners had turned to vile desecrators. That same man with his wax tablet was hurrying over.

15

'Why have you done this?' demanded Paulinus.

'Domine? You *told* us to. "Change it all. Do something square." I'm replanning it even as we tear up what we've done.'

'You can't burn a sacred grove,' bellowed Paulinus, earning peculiar looks from the workmen as they did just that.

A hand touched his shoulder lightly, and he jumped, turning sharply, ready to fight.

Marcia stood behind him, her face troubled. 'Gaius, come inside. I think you need to stay out of the garden until the men have finished. It is doing you no good.'

He allowed her to steer him away and walk him like a feeble old man back to the house. As they left, she gestured to the gardeners. 'Go on as you need to. Just make it pleasant.'

What was happening? Did other defamers of temples suffer such decennalia?

* * *

'We should have had children,' Marcia said, pushing away her plate and lounging back on the couch, her scrutiny still on Paulinus.

'We would have, but you could not, remember?'

'There are other ways,' she said quietly. 'Adoption. Rome is not short of children needing a better start, especially after the last years of Nero and the civil war. Many good men left struggling orphans. We could still do it. I think that your lack of an heir makes you focus too much on yourself and your woes. If we had a child, you would by necessity be more optimistic.'

He sighed. 'You are not well, Marcia. For years now we've known that. And I? Well, clearly either madness or death is closing in on me now. I will never be the great figure in politics you hoped for. My popularity has atrophied with my spirit.'

'Gods, but you're more dour than usual, Gaius. What has happened?'

He brushed it aside. 'Signs and portents. Cruelty and trouble are coming for me. I think you should go and stay with your sister for a few days. My decennalia, as that idiot last night called it, is upon me, and I fear something is about to happen. If my offerings today were enough, then in a day or two the trouble will be past, and you can come back to a happier and more comfortable husband. If not...'

She shook her head. 'When we married it was a union of politics, but you know that despite that, I have always loved you, Gaius, and I know that you have always loved me. If you did not, you'd have cast me aside in search of a fertile wife long ago. I still firmly believe this is all in your own mind, Gaius, but I will not leave you in your darker hours, whatever the case.'

'Then I cannot protect you, Marcia, and I am sorry for whatever is coming.'

'You should add offerings to the household gods to your jobs today,' she advised. 'If you can find them. What did you have done with the shrine?'

He frowned. 'What?'

'The shrine. The household gods. I presumed in your troubled state today you hid them, or sent them to be cleaned or repaired or something?'

Pushing away his plate, he rose from his couch and crossed the room, emerging out into the atrium. The wall was now empty of his trophies and honours, gone into hiding somewhere, yet irritatingly they had been there long enough that their shapes remained in silhouette until the wall could be cleaned and repainted. He could still see them, even when they were not there. Grumbling to himself, he passed into the vestibule and there his breath caught in his throat.

The small shrine stood where it always did, clean and neat, overseen by the faces of his ancestors in the form of busts and death masks. The figures of the *lares* and *penates*, the spirits that protected the house and its occupants, were all gone. He waved over the door-slave from his alcove nearby.

'Did you see who took the figures from the altar?'

The burly African shook his head, brow folding in confusion. 'I've seen no one, Domine. I've been here since dawn, since before you left for the city.'

Paulinus chewed his lip. The gods had been there first thing this morning. He was sure he remembered seeing them. And the door slave might have missed something if he was deep in his alcove seat and paying attention to his duties, but it seemed unlikely that anyone in the house would remove them. He turned to see Marcia behind him, her expression ever deepening with concern.

'The gardeners haven't been inside?' Perhaps they had been irritated at his manner and orders and had taken petty revenge.

She shook her head. 'No. They spent the entire day trying to do your bidding in the garden.'

He looked up at the faces of his father, his grandfather, his uncle and many other luminaries of the line. Those cold, immobile visages must have seen it, if only they could talk. He waved to Barates, who was at work with a broom. 'Take a purse of coins and go to the forum, fast. Buy images of the gods and the divine genii loci for the shrine. Do not skimp. I want the best you can buy, and I want them immediately.'

The slave bowed and hurried away to find the major domo and secure money.

'All will be good, Gaius,' Marcia said soothingly, clasping his upper arm, yet she recoiled oddly at the look in his eyes as he turned.

'No, Marcia. No, it won't. A man does not declare war on the gods without consequences.'

'You are a good man, Gaius, remember that.'

'No, I am not. I saw scores of good men meet their end defying the commands of the madman Nero. And those who were left were not the good, but the pliable. I should have refused the emperor's orders and conquered Britannia the old-fashioned way without attacking priests and temples.'

'Then you'd be dead.'

'But honoured.'

Before she could argue any more, he pulled away from her grasp and pattered off into the gloom, looking for somewhere to think.

* * *

It had taken him far too long to get to sleep. The day had been a constant battering of the senses, filled with horrors and dark omens. He'd done what he could, attempting to secure the aid of the gods of Rome and replacing the missing spirits from the household shrine. He wished Marcia had left. He'd tried to persuade her to visit her sister again late in the evening as they'd seen the gardeners off the premises, but she insisted on staying with him. She didn't understand. She just thought he was pessimistic and gloomy, still insisted this was all in his head, all part of his own imaginings. She knew the facts, knew what he had done ten years ago, and she'd seen how it had soured him ever since, but while she *knew*, she did not *understand*.

He'd committed the worst violation imaginable. Never before had any Roman done such a thing. Even against the Carthaginians, the great enemy of the Republic, they'd never lowered themselves to burning temples and slaying priests. You just didn't do such a thing. Even the most minor of foreign gods was still a god, and often an aspect of one of Rome's own. Oh, it had happened *since* his dreadful campaign, for the emperor's own son, Titus, did much the same in Jerusalem, tearing down the Jews' holy temple along with the city walls and anything that spoke of their continued resistance to Roman authority. And Titus would surely pay the price for his impiety in due course. But still, Paulinus had been the first. It was all well and good Marcia saying that it was Nero who'd ordered the burnings, but it had been Paulinus who'd *done* it. He could have refused. He'd have died for it, on his own sword in his own room, but he would have died righteous. That would not be his fate now, and he'd drifted off slowly, tormented as he tossed and turned.

He awoke with a start, not entirely certain what it had dragged him from sleep. For a blessed moment he was grateful, for the dream had begun once again. He'd been standing on the mainland and looking out across the water to the dancing shapes on the beach. Then reality folded in on him, and that gratitude evaporated.

There was a dirge echoing through the house: a low, discordant moan. A non-melodious melody that made the hairs stand proud on the back of his neck. His skin turned ice cold. It was a sound he knew all too well, for all that it had been a decade since he'd heard it. After all, it had been a decade since *anyone* had heard it, for those responsible were all long dead, their homes and groves burned and torn down.

Slowly, he turned, hoping not to disturb Marcia until he knew what he was dealing with.

The other side of the bed was empty. His heart skipped. Where was she? Gods, but if a horrible fate were coming his way, surely**,** *she* must be spared it? She had ever been an innocent. Desperation arose now, clawing at his throat. He'd resigned himself, but not to this. Sliding out of bed, he felt his bare feet slap down onto the marble floor. He rose, his rumpled sleep tunic dropping straight. The low discordant moaned melody seemed to fill the house, suffusing it, leeching from every wall.

Slowly, he paced across to the door and pulled it open. The dirge's volume doubled without the door in the way, and he shivered at the sound of approaching death. Where was Barates? The slave slept on a pallet outside their door every night. After Marcia, he was the most important figure in the house, really.

The pallet was there, the slave was not.

19

Nerves twanging, he moved across the atrium. Damn it but he'd been short-sighted. He'd had the trophies and honours removed and not even asked where they would be put. Hanging on the wall amid them had been his sword. He could see its silhouette even now. Not that a sword would do him much good, he suspected.

The doorman would have his cudgel. It was no gladius, but it would be better than nothing. Turning from the missing trophies, he moved into the vestibule, calling out the man's name, loudly so as to be heard above the strange chanting. He felt relief for a moment as a figure emerged from the doorman's alcove, but that relief shattered in an instant. The shape that moved out into the corridor was no slave. Tattered black robes wisped this way and that as it moved with a strange lope into the hallway. A second figure followed it from the alcove, and then a third, until the three figures filled the vestibule from side to side, moving sinuously in a strange dance. He felt the panic set in at a flash of bronze. A sickle in the grip of the middle one. Then two more, each black shape wielding razor sharp bronze. They started to dance towards him.

He could not face them. Perhaps properly attired and with a weapon, but not in a sleeping tunic and unarmed. Women they may be, but he'd learned not to underestimate the women of Britannia at the hands of the rebel queen Boudicca.

Instead, he began to back away. He stumbled against the shrine now and looked down. It horrified him to realise that once more there were no gods or protective spirits on it, his new replacements just as absent as the originals they had replaced. No protection. His ancestors looked on with hollow eyes, disapproving.

Back into the atrium now. He was shouting. Shouting names. His wife. Barates. The major domo. The doorman. Any slave name he could remember. There was no one. Just that weird, unearthly chanting. He realised with a sinking feeling he was moving closer to the source of the chant, but he had little choice. Like all Roman townhouses, the only proper door was at the front, along the vestibule and beyond the black furies with their gleaming blades. There was a servants' exit from their quarters at the bottom of the gardens, though that should be locked and the major domo kept the key. Still, it was a slim hope, and perhaps he might find someone there. The occupants of the house seemed to have gone entirely, from Marcia right down to the lowest slave. Only he and the ghosts of his impious past remained.

He looked into the doorways as he passed, but every room was empty as he backed away continually, ever closer to the peristyle garden from which he knew the chanting to be coming. The black monsters were still following him, herding him away to the open, and he had little choice. He could hardly hide in any of those rooms, and he would die agonisingly on the edge of those blades if he tried to fight them. They would have no mercy for him, and he knew that.

He was in the open night air now. The singing, louder than ever. He turned to the peristyle and his heart leapt into his throat. The wicker screens had been taken down, and his ruined garden had never looked more like a scene of devastation from his wicked past. The trees that remained in a small arc around the pool were burning bright, coils of black rising from them into the night sky. A blazing grove, just as he remembered. The gardeners had removed the planters and flowers and the travertine edging from the pool, and with the murk that had settled into the crystal water, it looked like one of the bogs they had found on Mona full of bodies, ritually murdered. He shuddered again.

A dozen white shapes stood among the burning trees, watching him, faces as pale as alabaster, beards grey and straggly. And from the centre of the grove, a single white shape emerged, gripping a pair of iron manacles.

He turned as he stumbled to a halt. The black furies were still behind him. Now the druids were in front, and just as in the dream one was stepping forward, brandishing those manacles.

They'd seen the results of the druids' rituals all over Mona, and what this meant was no surprise to him. He'd puzzled over the submerged bodies they had found, drained of blood, garrotted and drowned – the threefold death. It was said that they were not just sacrifices, and not just murders, but offerings to the gods. Willing victims, giving themselves to their deities. At the time, he'd wondered, as they burned the groves and buried the dead, what might drive a man, even a barbarous one such as those they'd fought on Mona, to willingly submit to a torturous death.

Now, he felt he understood. In some cases, at least. In his, most certainly. It was atonement, pure and simple. And now they had come for him. The last echo of a people, an entire culture, that he himself had wiped out, come for the man who'd consigned them to history. A last sacrifice.

He looked at the white-clad man and found that he had stopped shaking. The fear had gone. He was calm. This was his fate. Atonement for his crime.

'The threefold death. I understand.'

As the black-clad harpies danced around him, and the silent white figures watched, he walked, slow and calm towards the gaunt spectre in white. Standing still, he placed his arms behind his back, and waited as the shackles were tightened. He was moved, then, steered forward and down until he was on his knees by the edge of the water.

'I hope your gods can forgive me,' he said, with nothing more than resignation and a little sadness in his voice. Perhaps it was better they'd never had children after all. It was something of a pull leaving Marcia, but he could not imagine how he would feel if there'd also been a boy or a girl to bid farewell to.

He knelt, leaning forward. The pool was dark and murky, full of ash and detritus from the gardeners' work, yet it seemed somehow a mirror into the past, showing many things. In it, he could see his reflection, of course, but what he saw was most definitely not what he expected. The face looking back up at him from the black water was a warrior, a Roman general of power and confidence. Not young as such, but still in that bloom of advancement and hope. A him of ten years ago, when he'd secured one of the most important positions in the empire, a governorship that made careers. A him who had arrived to discover the land in foment, with tribes requiring the steely fist of a true Roman general. A him who'd seen in that trouble a path to fame and glory. A him who had not foreseen the emperor ordering him to burn temples and defy gods, who'd not had all his good work undone by an Iceni queen with too much time on her hands. A him with a future.

Not the old, cold, haunted spectre looking down into the water. Not the man who'd assiduously avoided all possible glory and attention ever since, who'd tried to keep things going because Marcia deserved it, but who had seen this moment coming somehow since the day the last druid died before his very eyes.

He felt the cord drop around his head. He didn't fight it. Not now.

He could see the others in the water, all the strong and impressive tribunes and prefects and the grizzled centurions who'd marched across Britannia and fought the enemy into a corner, only to cross to the island and burn the gods themselves.

The cord tightened. He could feel it biting into his windpipe now. The end had begun.

He could see the enemy. Stupid really, risking so much to control them. With their druids and their strange practices so very far from the heart of Rome they were weird and otherworldly, barbarous and untrustworthy. But he could see them reflected in the dark waters, and that was not who they were. They were just farmers, poor people who worshipped their gods. Gods taken away by him. One day they might have been like the Gauls, so pro-Roman they might as well have been born on the Palatine. He suspected that what he'd done on Mona had destroyed all hope for Britannia ever truly accepting Rome. In exerting control, he had effectively prevented it.

Air stopped. The cord pulled so tight, he could feel his chest labouring for something it could never again have. His eyes bulged. His tongue lolled. He wheezed soundlessly.

He could see at last just that burning grove where it had all begun for him.

Before he could die of asphyxiation, he felt the razor edge of the sickle cross his throat. He felt the tearing pain and sensed the warm blood sheeting out and down to the ground beneath him. He was done for now, even if they let go of the cord, but he knew from the bodies they'd found that this was not the end. He would bleed out, but only if he had the time, and he felt sure he wouldn't have the time. This was, after all, the *three*-fold death.

He looked into the water, his ultimate fate, and a new image was gleaming back up at him from the rippling surface. His eyes widened to see he was no longer alone in the reflection. Marcia, on one side, looked sad and hollow, and Barates on the other edged on panic. He tried to cry out, but he no longer had a throat to cry with. He tried to move, but he was being held, pushed forwards even as he died. No. That couldn't be. That wasn't justice!

His head disappeared beneath the fetid, murky pool's surface and was held there even as the cord loosened, and the blood bloomed out from him to further darken the water. He fought if for a precious, desperate moment, but there was no way out. He was secured, and already dead. He finally surrendered, unable to hold it any longer, and let in the cold water, which rushed through him like a cleansing tide, filling every space.

Paulinus's world went black for the last time.

* * *

Marcia stood at the entrance to the gardener's worksite, peering between the wicker screens. Barates was crouched by the shape at the ruined pool. He rose slowly, his expression bleak as he turned, shaking his head.

Oddly, she'd known. From the moment she'd woken to find the other half of the bed empty, she'd known. It had not taken a lot of thought or searching to find herself in the garden looking at her husband's body. It had been in his head for a decade now, but she'd always suspected it would end like this.

'He was not attacked?'

'I don't think so, Domina. There's not a mark on him. It looks as though he simply lay down, put his face in the pool, and drowned.'

She nodded. He'd needed to find peace. He'd spoken of the bodies they had found on the island all those years ago. The image of them had haunted him ever since. Their gruesome, dreadful sacrifices. She sighed.

'Thank you, Barates. I think he was trying to sacrifice himself, his own version of the druids' threefold death.'

The slave frowned. 'Really, Domina? I'd heard that the threefold death was all about the trinity. Three endings for three victims for the three gods?'

She frowned. 'Then perhaps his sacrifice was in vain after all?'

She and Barates turned from the sight and made their way back into the house, ready to prepare all that needed preparing. Neither remained long enough to see the tattered black shapes moving among the ruined trees. A low, discordant melody began to rise…

* * *

Historical Note

Gaius Suetonius Paulinus governed Britain from 58 to 61. His destruction of the druids' groves on Anglesey is recorded by Tacitus, as are the descriptions of the battle, the druids and the black-clad women. He served in Britain with distinction, and won honours for his war against Boudicca. What happened later in his career is more vague. He probably achieved higher office, securing the consulate in 66. In 69, on the death of Nero, he backed the wrong horse, and was probably not in the favoured camp when Vespasian came to the throne. His fate is unrecorded, as is any family he might have had (Marcia is my own addition.)

Agricola went on to become the governor who completed the conquest of Britain, albeit only a brief control. His achievements would forever overshadow those of Paulinus, courtesy of Tacitus.

The Romans were surprisingly set against human sacrifice, considering how bloodthirsty their world was, and more than one Roman writer has described the vicious work of the druids. This might be considered fictional, but for the fact that so called bog burials seem to suggest that the infamous threefold death is more than a simple myth. Indeed, manacles had been found in pools on Anglesey. Voluntary sacrifice is attested in South America and in Viking culture as well as many others, so it is not too much of a leap of faith to make it real in ancient Britain.

The Romans were a very superstitious people. Wars had been started and ended because of signs, and woe betide a man who ignored them. And though Rome conquered the known world, their culture was religiously inclusive. All conquered gods were seamlessly folded into the Roman pantheon. The only times this system failed were with the Jews and the Christians, whose worship forbade them from acknowledging Rome's gods and the divinity of the emperor, and on the one other occasion when a Roman general marched into Anglesey, massacred the druids and burned the sacred groves, ending Druidry in Britain forever.

Paulinus has paid the price.

Happy Halloween.

Simon Turney

Simon Turney

Having spent much of his childhood visiting historic sites with his grandfather, Simon fell in love with the Roman heritage of the region, beginning with the world famous Hadrian's Wall. His fascination with the ancient world snowballed with interest in Egypt, Greece and Byzantium, though his focus has remained Rome. A born and bred Yorkshireman with a love of country, history and architecture, Simon spends most of his time visiting historic sites, writing, researching the ancient world and reading.

Simon's career meandered along an eclectic path from the Ministry of Agriculture to network management before settling back into the ancient world, returning to university to complete an honours degree in classical history through the Open University. With a rekindled love of all things Roman, he set off on a journey to turn Caesar's Gallic War diaries into a novel accessible to all. Marius' Mules was completed in 2003 and has garnered considerable, bestseller status and reviews, spawning numerous sequels.

Now, with in excess of 40 novels available in numerous languages, Simon is a prolific writer, spanning genres and eras and releasing novels both independently and through renowned publishers including Canelo, Head of Zeus, and Orion. Simon's varied series now cover numerous periods of ancient Rome, Medieval and Renaissance Europe, Viking Byzantium, and the Templar Knights. Simon writes full time and is represented by MMB Creative literary agents.

The Praetorian Series

The Great Game (2015)
The Price of Treason (2015)
Eagles of Dacia (2017)
Lions of Rome (2018)
The Cleansing Fire (2020)
Blades of Antioch (2021)

The Templar Series

Daughter of War (2018)
The Last Emir (2018)
City of God (2019)
The Winter Knight (2019)
The Crescent and the Cross (2020)
The Last Crusade (2021)

The Marius' Mules Series by S.J.A. Turney

The Invasion of Gaul (2009)
The Belgae (2010)
Gallia Invicta (2011)
Conspiracy of Eagles (2012)
Hades Gate (2013)
Caesar's Vow (2014)
The Great Revolt (2014)
Sons of Taranis (2015)
Pax Gallica (2016)
Fields of Mars (2017)
Tides of War (2018)
Sands of Egypt (2019)
Civil War (2020)
The Last Battle (2021)

Tales of the Empire

Interregnum (2009)
Ironroot (2010)
Dark Empress (2011)
Insurgency (2016)
Emperor's Bane (2016)
Invasion (2017)
Jade Empire (2017)

The Damned Emperors by Simon Turney

Caligula (2018)
Commodus (2019)

Rise of Emperors (with Gordon Doherty)

Sons of Rome (2020)
Masters of Rome (2021)
Gods of Rome (2021)

Wolves of Odin

Blood Feud (2021)

Legion XXII

Capsarius (2022)

The Ottoman Cycle

The Thief's Tale (2013)
The Priest's Tale (2013)
The Assassin's Tale (2014)
The Pasha's Tale (2015)

The Legion Series (Childrens' books)

Crocodile Legion (2016)
Pirate Legion (2017)

FURY OF THE CURSED SHIP

BY

K.S. BARTON

A Viking age tale of a long ago curse and one woman's destiny to break it. After a Norse woman shipwrecks alone on a night filled with spectral lights and eerie sounds, she learns of a cursed ship and its doomed men. As if called by the gods, she enters the ghastly barrow to confront the undead's fury.

"Alight!" I shout, although it comes out as more of a croak. My mouth and lips are parched and taste of bile. No one answers my cry. I am alone and have been for so long, I think for sure my boat has wandered into a world of the gods.

Rain batters my head and body, nearly pounding me to the boards, and the wind shrieks, tearing at me. It tore my sail to shreds ages ago. My small fishing boat bucks and yaws to the sea's thrashing swells.

The light looks like the bright thread I saw in the dream that made me flee my home. My breath comes in gasps from the cold and the terror of the storm. A wave slams into the boat and tosses me down into the bilge water that threatens to sink me. Some splashes into my mouth, and I gag on it. I drag myself up and push wet hair out of my face.

I stare at the light, willing my vessel toward it. I have no sail, no oars, nothing by which to aid my journey. All was lost to the god, Aegir's, vicious storm. Maybe the light leads me to Aegir's hall. Or to the hall of the sea goddess, Ran. I pinch myself checking for pain to see if I am alive. Nothing. Either I am dead or too cold to notice. I swallow down the fear. It will not help me. As my hand drops to my side, it hits something even colder than my skin.

I glance down at the silver glinting in the darkness.

29

"My arm ring," I breathe. The boat jerks, and I fall, my screams echoing in my ears. Sea spray hits my face. My heart skids to a stop as panic races through my limbs. I nearly plunge into the icy depths.

Water lashes me until I gain a grip on the hard wood and haul myself back. My chest heaves. I want to curse the water gods. I bite the inside of my cheek to keep from speaking.

I claw at my arm to pull off the ring. In my frantic dig, the metal tears the skin, making it bleed. Staring at it, I take the ring and cut it in even deeper to draw more blood, watching as if this body belongs to someone else. Goose flesh prickles over my arm and the fine hairs stand on end.

The blood is so vivid compared to the dark sea and sky; it is like a beacon of life. I drip it onto the ring.

Nausea roils in my belly as my blood darkens the silver. Despite the bucking of the boat, I keep to my feet and shout into the wind.

"Ran! Mighty goddess! Deliver me safely to that beacon of light."

As the words disappear into the howling wind, I throw the ring into the black, heaving sea. It reminds me of a hungry beast, snatching at its prey.

Grasping the edge of the boat so hard it cuts into my palms, I watch as the silver vanishes into the darkness, and I wait, barely breathing.

The sea shifts under me, like a cat gathering itself to pounce. I turn and a gasp escapes my throat.

A monstrous wave swells, growing and growing. It will swamp me. It rolls under the boat, tilting it so severely, it sends me scrabbling to hang on to something. I grasp what remains of the mast and cling to it with stiff, aching fingers in a grip that will not last long.

My stomach heaves as the swell flings the boat toward shore and the light. Or is it the silver thread? When my vessel smashes into land, I am tossed free. As I fall, I hear the wave crash and the boat breaks into pieces. I lift my head, spitting sand out of my already dry mouth, and watch as the sea grabs the remaining splinters and hauls them back, leaving me with nothing.

***

I huddle under an overhanging of rock on the side of a high cliff. My teeth clatter together. Surely, I will freeze before morning. After the pieces of my boat disappeared, I had searched for the light I'd spotted from the sea and did not find it. The walls of the bluff glowed in the moonlight, and that was where I'd taken refuge for the night. The storm finally blows itself out, and the quiet is like a sigh of relief.

Instead of sitting here freezing, I rise and carefully pick my way over the pebbly shore to the water's edge where I dip my injured arm into the salt water as the waves lick at my feet.

"I thank you, Ran," I croak. The sea goddess might have saved me from the storm, but where had she delivered me?

Everything goes completely still, even the shushing of the waves. The dark intensifies as if someone has lowered a hood over me. I brace for an attack. When none comes, I jump to my feet and stumble as the wet sand gives way beneath me.

A noise fills the darkness. A loud creak and groan of wood, the soft splash of oars carefully placed in water, and the indistinct murmur of men's rhythmic voices as they chant in time to their rowing.

I peer into the night and see only blackness. A bitter wind sweeps over me, like icy fingers, making me shiver.

The noise continues.

It does not come from the sea. I spin, searching for the origin of the sounds. My heart pounds so hard, I fear it will make its way into my throat.

The men continue their chant and the oars continue their rhythmic dips into water. It comes from above me, which is impossible.

Just then, a bluish-green light spreads over the night sky above the cliff under which I'd found shelter. It hovers, rippling like a sail in the breeze. The colors look like the sea on a bright day, the blue and green swirling together. An eerie sound, like a high-pitched squeal and a low moan mixed together, floats with the undulation of the lights while matching the rhythm of the men's chant.

The lowest pitch of the intonation touches my heart, making it skitter and jump. I clutch my still-damp dress against my chest, and my ears fill with the sound of my own racing blood.

I stand rooted in the sandy soil, afraid to move as I watch the lights dance and listen to the creak, groan, and chant of men aboard a ship—a ship that does not exist. The strange sounds and lights last until the sun's rays peek over the horizon. They disappear as if they had never been.

Then I collapse onto the sand. I am still shivering and staring at the cliff top when the fishermen find me.

***

It is now night, and I sit in the largest house of a village nestled on the cliff. This village is the source of the light that had drawn me to shore. Earlier that day, the fishermen who found me took me to their wives who then kindly fed me, removed my clothes to dry, and wrapped me in a blanket to warm before a fire where I slept.

At sundown, these women brought me to the home of the village elder and his wife. The other villagers brought food and drink that they shared with me. It was not much, but enough to fill my belly. After the meal, they questioned me about my identity. Over cups of ale, I told my story of a cruel, abusive husband and of how a dream told me I needed to flee that awful man. I told of my escape one winter night in a boat provided by a kindly family and of how the storm caught me until I'd landed on the shore of the cliffs.

"An auspicious night to arrive," the village elder, Thorleif, tells me now. Murmurs of assent ripple through his home. Everyone from the fishing village, not many people in all, is in attendance. Most keep their distance from me, as if Loki himself had arranged my arrival.

"What night is it?" I have lost track of how many days and nights I'd spent at sea; the days blurred together until the storm left me with no sense of time or place.

"Midwinter Eve," Thorleif says.

The assembled villagers grow quiet. When the fire crackles in the hearth fire, one woman jumps, and her husband puts a soothing hand on her arm. "It will be over soon. Two more nights."

A little boy, perhaps eight winters old, approaches me. "Did you hear *them*?" His tone holds both fear and excitement.

"Sh," his mother says. "We do not speak of them." His father grabs his arm and pulls him back into their family huddle.

I look at Thorleif. "I heard something last night." The old man stares at me with a slight nod. "And I saw strange lights."

People shift on their benches or on the floor, where many of them sit, while the little boy's mother clasps her hands over his ears. He struggles, and she murmurs something under her breath.

"What are they?" I ask Thorleif.

"We don't speak of it." A man rises from the floor. He has a deep voice and unfolds himself gracefully. From his clothes and the lines in his face, he looks like a fisherman. The others agree with the tall man.

"Birger, we must explain it," Thorleif tells him.

"She is a stranger," the tall man, Birger, says. He stares at me.

"She has already seen it."

"And survived the night outside." Thorleif's wife, Gislaug, rises to stand by his side. "In full view of the cliff."

"That's right," a village woman says. "Tell us what you saw and heard."

Before I can speak, an argument breaks out among those who want me to tell my tale and those who want no more said. The fear in the house grows thick and heavy.

"Enough." Thorleif does not yell and yet the word carries so much force everyone quiets immediately. "There is no point in keeping it a secret. Our guest," he emphasizes the word, "landed on our shore. Near this village." Before anyone can interrupt again, Thorleif raises his craggy hands. "It is the work of the gods."

A shiver trails down my back. An image of my arm ring swallowed by the sea appears in my mind. The goddess had accepted my offering. She had delivered me to this place. Thorleif is right; the gods are at work here.

The old man points a thick finger at Birger. "It was your ancestor who brought this upon the village. Him and those who followed him."

Birger blanches and recovers quickly. "They paid the price. We all have." They stare at each other for a long moment.

I step forward, deciding to speak my mind whether they like it or not. Facing Thorleif and Birger and speaking quickly so no one can stop me, I tell them what I'd seen and heard the previous night. I try to keep my voice from quavering as I recall the eerie lights and noises.

"I told you my tale," I finish, sweat forming at my hairline even though it is not hot in the house. "Now, tell me yours." I stare at Birger as if daring him to refuse.

"I will tell you," Thorleif speaks. When he feels several people wind up to argue, he raises his hand to stop them. "You have time to reach your homes while it is still safe. No one has to stay against their will."

"Make haste," Birger warns. He stalks to the door and flings it open, peering into the night sky. "All is quiet."

Most of the villagers gather themselves and hurry out, glancing back at me as they go. Several of them touch amulets they wear either on their necks or wrists and mutter words I cannot hear. By habit, I go to touch my arm ring only to feel the abrasions left behind when I'd cut it in offering to the goddess. A vision forms in my mind of my ring dangling from Ran's watery arm.

The locals think I will bring misfortune. I hope they are wrong.

"Come." Thorleif beckons to me.

A few villagers remain behind, including Birger. He stands at the threshold, legs apart, arms crossed as if on guard. When I look his way, he frowns, but he does not take his gaze from me. A tingling shoots down my back and through the soles of my feet.

I shudder. Birger's frown deepens.

"Aesa," Gislaug says. My name jolts me back, and I join the old woman at the table.

Thorleif steps into the center of the house and speaks, "Listen to my tale."

As if in answer to his words, I hear it. The groan of a ship on the water. The splash of oars. The rhythmic chant.

My feet move me to the door. Birger blocks my way.

"Move aside," I tell him. I do not know where my commanding tone comes from.

"No."

"I must see it."

"You have already seen it." Birger has angry eyes, like a stormy sea. But I am used to angry eyes.

"Let her go," Thorleif tells Birger.

"It is not safe." Birger speaks to the old man, but his gaze is on me.

Why should this man who I had not met until this day care whether I go out into the unsafe world? I open my mouth to ask him when he steps aside.

The chanting grows louder, and my shoulders instinctively hunch around my neck.

Birger's lips are at my ear. "They grow louder each night." His hot breath is on my neck. "If you go outside, you will not come back."

"Aesa," Gislaug calls out. "Listen to him. You made it this far. Do not risk what you have gained."

A wail rises in the air outside, followed by a flash of the bluish-green light. It penetrates through the tiny slits around the door and every crack in the walls, blowing in like bursts of winter wind. People cry out and cover their faces. All except Thorleif and Birger.

Birger's eyes reflect the light as they flash at me.

"Before you decide, Aesa," Thorleif says. "Let me finish my tale."

"Yes." Gislaug hurries forward and pulls me away from the door. I go, my feet dragging across the floor. Birger returns to stand guard.

Gislaug pours a drink and hands it to me. I push it aside.

"Many generations ago," Thorleif begins. As he speaks, the lights illuminate him from all directions. They waver around his body and make him sway as if he is on board a ship. The sight makes me queasy.

He continues with the story. "King Ale ruled this area. He was a generous ring-giver with loyal men. When any young man from the area came of age, he wanted to join King Ale's crew and go raiding in distant lands. It was a great honor to be part of this band of men. Many sons returned with great riches. Many sons left and never returned. And on it went, season after season. Then a rival king died and his son, now King Yngve, took his place. Not long before this, a mysterious woman arrived at King Yngve's household, so beautiful every man wanted her. They fought over her. But it was King Yngve who claimed her as his mistress and displayed her as if she were a treasured piece of his hoard."

At the words, the chanting intensifies, the pace speeding as if racing toward something. The lights dance their undulating dance. My heart races along with them both. I grab Gislaug's hand. It is sweaty but strong.

It is as if the men on that cliff top hear what Thorleif says, and it agitates them. Now I understand why the villagers had not wanted the elder to speak of it.

"At midwinter, King Yngve held a tremendous feast and invited King Ale. The two kings drank and ate together. King Yngve had his mistress by his side, bedecked in gold, silver, and jewels. In the mead hall, she glowed as brilliant and beguiling as the gold she wore, and every man in the hall jostled for her attention. It was as if the goddess had touched her to bring lustful thoughts to all men. When King Ale joined King Yngve at the high-table, the mistress had eyes only for him. No longer did she want King Yngve.

Enchanted by the young woman, King Ale visited her in the women's bower that night. She knew he would come to her and was waiting eagerly."

As Thorleif speaks of the king and the young woman, I can't help but snatch glances at Birger. Throughout this story, he remains by the door. I wonder what he can do to keep out whatever plagues the town if it decides to enter the house. What besieges us is no human, and although tall and broad through the shoulders and arms, he is only a man. Every time I glance at him, he is staring at me. He does not smile or give any indication of what he thinks. That strange tingling feeling in my spine grows stronger every time his eyes meet mine.

Thorleif goes on. "King Ale and the mistress shared a night of passion. But King Yngve's thrall, who was devoted to him, snuck out of the bower and informed King Yngve that King Ale was with his woman. King Yngve was as possessive of the mistress as a dragon with his treasure. He and a dozen of his men stormed the bower to kill King Ale."

Thorleif pauses and listens.

The house nearly shakes with the force of the chanting and the clap of oars in water. The voices vibrate through my body.

"They grow angry," Birger tells him. "Finish quickly."

"King Ale and the mistress were gone. She told Ale she had tired of King Yngve and his grasping, controlling ways. She would be owned by no man. King Ale took her and left quietly that night with his men."

When Thorleif mentions how King Yngve was a controlling man, I feel the blood drain from my face. I let out an involuntary, "oh." Escaping a brute like that was what brought me to this tiny fishing village. But why here? Why now?

A tremor I do not understand travels across my skin, making it prickly. I resist the urge to shake it off. Thorleif picks up the story again.

"In a fury, King Yngve had the thrall dragged before him. He killed her and with her blood whetting his blade, he thrust his sword into the bed where he believed King Ale ravished his mistress and there he swore an oath.

'By the blood of women
I curse King Ale and his men
When next you travel the whale-road
Your sea-steed will falter.
You will not feed Aegir's daughters
Or feast at Grim's hall.
You will be lost forever
In between.'"

As soon as the words fade away, the door bangs open, hurtling Birger to the floor. I jump, my scream of fright mixed with that of the others.

The lights enter, blinding in intensity. I squeeze my eyes shut, but it shines through my lids so brightly, I have to cover my face. A loud chorus of chanting follows the lights and this time, it is not unintelligible babble. The men chant the oath of King Yngve, ending with an echoing repeat of "lost forever, lost forever, lost forever."

36

A surge of cold bites into me.

The villagers scream, asking for the voices to stop and begging to be left in peace.

I hear scuffling and a groan, and I squint my eyes open and peer at it.

Birger struggles to his feet, the green-blue brightness surging around him like the sea at high tide. As he rises, the lights bulge like a wave, crash over him and recede toward the door. They unsettle him, and he falls again as the wave-lights swirl at his legs and tug at him.

The intoning grows so fierce and so loud, it makes my ears ring. This time it changes to, "King Ale. King Ale. King Ale."

"No," I shout and lunge at Birger. I do not know this man and do not understand what is happening, but I cannot let the horror take him.

The neck of my dress tears as Gislaug tries to hold me back. I rush to Birger and grab onto his arms as he slips out the door. I expect him to be wet as if he was truly in the sea, but his grip is dry and strong, and his eyes determined. He kicks at what has hold of him, but it is nothing but empty air.

The lights swirl around my ankles, as cold as ice, rising to my knees as if a tide tugs at me but without the wetness of the sea. The cold is so intense it burns my skin. I almost lose my grip on Birger.

"This man is not King Ale!" Thorleif bellows.

The lights waver and flicker, and the chant stutters. Birger exchanges a look with Thorleif and for a moment I think Birger will sacrifice himself to this menace. The old man shakes his head.

With a final heave, I help Birger free himself from the freezing lights that now recede out the door. They heave and thrash like an angry sea before retreating up the side of the bluff where they hover on the cliff top. The chanting subsides as well.

Birger lies on the floor, breathing hard. My breath comes in frosty gasps and I still have a tight grip on his forearms. I feel his blood racing at the wrist. Mine does the same.

Sobs and muffled exclamations come from the people in the house. Gislaug rushes to me and pulls me to standing. I'd fallen to my knees beside Birger without realizing it. I tremble so badly, I believe I will shake right out of my clothes. Gislaug takes my hands in a tight grip. Her warmth slowly makes its way up my arms and into my chest.

After a long time at which everyone settles and calms, Birger rises to his feet and strides toward the entrance as if nothing has happened, but when he reaches to close the door, I see that his hands are shaking.

"Finish the tale," I tell Thorleif. I cast a glance at Birger, who has given up on guarding the threshold. He accepts a drink from a village woman. "There is more to it."

"That has never happened before," Birger says. He is a little paler but looks mostly untouched by his ordeal.

"No," Thorleif agrees. He studies me thoughtfully. "They grow agitated. Angry."

"It is because you uttered the oath!" A village man cries. Others agree. Their eyes are wide with fright and their faces wan.

Birger interrupts their outburst. "No." He stares at me. "It is because of her."

"If this is what she brings upon us, we must throw her out." More shouts of agreement. Several men rise and take a few steps toward me. I match their movement backward.

Thorleif and Birger put themselves between the angry mob and me. Gislaug soothes the villagers by reminding them I am a woman far from home and a guest in her home. After a while, they quiet.

"Now, let me finish the tale." Thorleif continues. "The following summer King Ale and the men of his region, including this village, sailed out. With much reluctance, he left behind the woman who was now bearing his child. She glowed even more like a goddess, and King Ale could barely leave her. Her last words to him were, 'no matter what happens, we will always be together.'"

Birger's gaze is on me again. The silver thread I'd seen in my dream flashes in my mind. I shake my head to rid myself of it.

"After a successful summer, the men returned. The people of this village could hear their song as they rowed. We heard their cheers to people on shore about the bounty of riches they'd gained. But, a fierce wind cut their voices short. The sky turned black. The sea grew ugly. As the village watched, a swell rose as high as the cliff and swallowed King Ale's ship. There were no death cries, not a single crack of the boards. Nothing but silence. The sea and sky returned to normal. The ship and everyone on it had vanished. Our ancestors searched the beaches for days for signs of survivors, bodies, treasure, or any detritus. Nothing appeared. As if it had never been."

Thorleif looks at me and grimaces. "Until midwinter, when the nights are at their longest. That is when the locals heard the sound of a ship full of men. That was the first time the lights flashed across the sky. My grandfather climbed the path to the top of the cliff to discover what caused it."

He pauses. "He never returned. They never found his body. He had vanished, as did any man who ventured to that cliff top during the nights of midwinter. Those who climbed to the cliff after that first midwinter discovered a burial mound. It was … is … the same size and shape as King Ale's ship."

Thorleif looks tired and Birger takes up the story. "Every winter, two days before midwinter, it begins. On midwinter night, it is at its worst."

"And what just happened to you?" I ask.

"That has never happened in living memory."

"Thorleif said you were not King Ale. What did he mean by that?"

Birger looks to Thorleif, who nods. "I am a descendent of King Ale and the woman he spirited away from King Yngve."

"But why attack you?"

"King Ale was not on the ship when it went down."

That does not answer my question, but I do not push. His gaze bores into mine, making my skin erupt in gooseflesh. I do not understand why this man affects me in this way, and it unbalances me for a moment before I regain control of myself. "Where was he?"

"No one knows. The men on the ship are always searching for him, angry and hungry. That is why any man who approaches the mound vanishes. We think the cursed sailors take them. They want their king."

"What became of the woman and child?"

"She birthed a son and gave it to a family to raise. Then she vanished."

"Did she go looking for King Ale?"

"No one knows."

"The cursed crew." I shiver as I say the word. "Think if they get King Ale back, the curse will break?"

"Yes," Thorleif answers.

"My father." Birger swallows hard. "Thought if he sacrificed himself to them, it would stop. He went to the mound on the night of midwinter." The words come harsh and raspy as if hard to choke out. "He did not return."

"And the curse remains," Thorleif says.

"You." Birger starts to touch me. I flinch and his hand hangs in the air, his eyes sad as if he understands my reaction. "Arriving here must have changed something. You are the key." He says it with such surety, I feel it as if he's touched me physically.

"Come," Gislaug tells me. The serious look on her face tells us all the conversation is over. "You must be tired. Rest." She indicates a thin mattress made of grass with a woolen blanket on top. I do not resist. As I settle, I think about Birger's comment that I am the key. A dream led me to flee my home, the storm pushed me toward this village, and I made the offering to Ran. Perhaps my *wyrd* led me here. Or the gods.

As everyone sleeps, I stare into the gloomy room, only half-lit by the hearth fire. The chanting continues above us. An occasional flash of light enters the house and then disappears. I seek Birger, who sits with his back against the door. He watches me and that feeling spreads over my skin again.

I stare at him as the firelight flickers across his face. I grow drowsy and my eyelids droop. Jerking awake at a throb in my lower belly, I watch as a silver thread, the same one as in my dream before, works its way from me across the floor to Birger. It wavers and glistens like it is wet. I glance over wondering if he has seen it too. His head rests against the wood; his eyes are closed and his chest rises and falls in sleep.

I kneel and touch the floor; the thread feels like warm metal, only softer.

When I rise, Birger jerks awake. He examines me as I follow the strange appearance. If I move to the side, it follows me. No matter what I do, it continues to direct me to this man. I point at the floor, but he does not see it. He will think me mad if I tell him, so I return to my mattress and watch the thread to see if it will change or vanish.

It vanishes at dawn when quiet settles over the village.

***

It is midwinter night. I pace the house, my entire body tingling, my skin sensitive as if I have a fever. My mind races as I search for meaning in what has happened in the past two days.

I have just reached the door when I hear the clink and groan of the phantom ship louder than ever. So loud it makes me quaver.

"It will be a terrible night," Thorleif tells us.

I swallow down fear and reach out to the latch. Once I touch it, Thorleif says, "If you step outside, it will mean your doom."

I pause. Without turning, I say. "I know."

When I hear Birger's footsteps cross the room, the tingling in my back becomes so intense I shudder. "No one who goes to the barrow on midwinter returns."

40

"No men." I face him.

"What?"

"You said the 'men' who went to the mound vanished. I am not a man." I lift my chin in defiance.

Despite his fear, I see Birger's lip start to quirk into a grin. He clamps it down. He nods, his gaze heavy on me. The thread appears again, thicker and more vivid. An ache touches my belly.

"What will you do?" He does not see the connection.

"I do not know."

With a deep breath, I lift the bar on the door.

The wind nearly knocks me off my feet as I step into the night. The door slams behind me and the latch goes down, sealing my doom. It will not open again. I want to cry out to Birger and ask why he does not accompany me.

I turn to ask when the wind rips at me as viciously as if it is alive. Tendrils of hair escape my braid and blow around my head, stinging as they snap my cheeks. The bluish-green light flies in the storm, crackling like lightning. This is not like two nights ago when it undulated like a sail. Now it rages.

The wind pushes me away from the house so hard I stumble and fall to my knees. Pain sears my hands.

The cursed crew's chant is so loud it burrows into my mind, crowding out all thoughts. Between the chant, the lights, and the wind, I am kept in place like an animal gone to ground.

I finally rise and take a step, like a child first learning to walk, with great effort and concentration. Ahead of me, a winding path leads up the side of the cliff. Against the headwind, I trudge up, and it is like being underwater with every movement slow and thick. The light surrounds me and presses on me from all sides. It makes my head ache and my stomach churn. I stop halfway up the path, my breath coming in ragged gasps. As I look back, I see nothing of the elder's house or any of the village. As if they have never been. Only the silver thread links me to the world of men, like a beacon in the darkness, until it disappears around a switchback.

It takes so long to ascend to the cliff top, dawn must surely be coming. When I reach the summit, the wind knocks me over. The light grows dark and menacing, pushing me down. The depth of the men's voices resonates in my heart, making it skitter until it beats to their rhythm.

"Lost forever. King Ale."

The barrow glows ahead of me, as long as a ship and as wide. I push myself to standing and approach it. I am at a loss as to what to do, for I did not think I'd make it this far.

My toes touch the very edge of where the barrow rises. It sends a quiver up my legs.

Push forward comes from deep within me. I step onto the rising mound.

Everything stops. The wind. The lights. The chants. It all dies away while continuing to thrum in my body. The silence presses on me.

It is cold. As cold as Hel's realm. As cold as death.

A scream forms in my throat but does not escape.

At least forty monstrous men face me. They sit on their sea chests, oars in hand. One grasps the ship's rudder.

But that is not what makes me want to cry out.

They are gigantic, much bigger than human men. Their skin is the blue-black of the dead and gleams in the unnatural glow under the barrow, different and more unnerving than the lights that shone in the night sky. Their arms and necks are draped with gold and silver rings, some so encrusted with jewels they look like eerie dew drops covering their bodies. One man wears a woman's circlet that sits too high on his huge head. A ruby drips like a bloody teardrop onto his forehead. Another creature has piled so many chains around his neck, they ripple when he moves. The one closest to me wears a large Christian cross inlaid with jewels. He strokes it with one finger as he watches me with clear blue eyes. They all have the same eerie blue eyes.

It is a grotesque display of wealth that no one will see. None but themselves. Forever.

Stunned by my appearance, they do not rise at first. Then one of the monstrous men growls at me and others take it up. It reverberates through the barrow and into my body, making me tremble. That is when I notice the other figures, more than a dozen of them, sitting or lying in the hull. They do not have wealth and look like fishermen with desperation etched into their faces. The tallest of them resembles Birger.

The doomed villagers.

I open my mouth but cannot form words, only mumbling as if my tongue has been cut.

The steersman, his long blond hair lank across his shoulders, releases the rudder. His blue-black chest is bare, and he wears a thick, twisted gold chain on his neck. The gold glimmers against his dark skin. A woman's silk head linen with emeralds sewn into it sits daintily atop his immense head. His tread thuds on the boards of the ship as he makes his way toward me. Slowly.

He snarls at me, his teeth a shocking white.

"You are not King Ale."

"King Ale." The men chant. They stomp their feet to the words and the ship sways. More treasure is scattered on the hull and clanks with the movement. Gold chalices. Christian crosses. Silver cups and spoons. Coins.

I swallow down a whimper. "King Ale is gone," I say. I intend to speak strongly, but it comes out like a breeze.

"King Ale. King Ale." The men's chant becomes fiercer, louder.

"He is not gone."

I pivot at the new voice. Birger staggers into the barrow. As he does, the thread that connects us bubbles up from the ground. It does not look like the silver of the undead's treasure but gleams and shimmers like molten metal.

The sailors, their blue-black skin glowing, snarl and bite at the air. They rise as one and stalk toward Birger, surrounding him.

"Leave him alone," I squeak.

The steersman, their leader, his tread so heavy it makes my legs shake, looms before me. He smells like meat that has rotted in the sun. I gag and swallow down bile. As if I matter little, he howls in fury and shoves me aside. I tumble to the bottom of the ship, the wooden boards cutting painfully into my knees.

I try to rise, but the enormous monster's tread shakes the ground. Steadying myself, I glimpse the spot on my arm where I'd cut it when I made the offering to Ran.

Despite the din of the snarls and howls, I hear a whisper in my ears that sounds like "Freya." An image appears in my mind of a ravishingly beautiful woman entrancing everyone in a mead hall. In my vision, I see a handsome man, who looks much like Birger, going to the woman's bed and the two of them lying together. The image changes to a teary goodbye as the man leaves the woman who is heavy with child. A baby handed over to a family. That same stunning woman, now wearing golden armor and helm and astride a magnificent horse, snatching the man off a battlefield while his guard's attention is elsewhere.

The vision leaves me like a slap.

The undead swarm over Birger, pulling him down and pinning him like wolves on prey. They howl and gnash their teeth.

"Wait," I shout. "Stop."

They halt like dogs come to heel. Their snarling faces are ghastly, bloated and rotten, and they glare at me. I can just make out Birger's body at the bottom of the pile, but whether he lives, or is now doomed to walk this half-life, I cannot tell.

The creatures prowl so close to me, I can smell their putrid breath. My legs wobble and sweat beads down my back, even though it is more frigid than the coldest night I've ever experienced.

Two men grab me, and I shriek as their enormous hands touch my skin. I fight against their grip, but it is like trying to escape iron shackles. One caresses my hair as if he's never seen anything so pretty. He smiles, but it is a death grimace, his mouth black and rotten. My scream intensifies.

Birger jumps in and breaks their grip on me. They soon wrestle him to the ground again, pushing him to his knees, his arms wrested behind his back. The one with the ruby teardrop on his forehead unsheathes a dagger, and the blade glows in the unearthly light of the barrow.

They mean to sacrifice Birger.

He nods to me. He means to sacrifice himself.

The tingling in my back grows to such ferocity, it is like knives slicing into my skin, and the silver thread linking us pulses.

"What was the name of the woman in the tale? King Yngve's mistress?" I ask Birger, my voice frantic.

At the mention of King Yngve, the men grow so angry they roar his name and then King Ale's. The undead with the dagger pulls Birger's head back to expose his throat.

"No one knows her name," Birger croaks, showing no fear as the dagger threatens him.

"She was Freya!" I scream it so loud that everyone freezes. Even the monster with the blade. Forty sets of clear blue eyes stare at me like glowing orbs in the darkness. I shudder.

"You cannot know that," the steersman growls. With lumbering steps, he approaches me. He towers over me, and I put my hand to my mouth to keep from gagging.

I drop it to speak. "Freya was in love with King Ale. She took him from the battlefield to be one of her own."

He grabs my arms. His hands are so cold, they burn me. I cry out in pain.

"You lie," he growls.

I force myself to hold his gaze. His vacant eyes stare at me, and I feel them like fingers trailing down my spine. Similar eyes stare at me over his shoulder. I feel many more, cold, bloated bodies behind me.

"Aesa." Birger's voice reaches me. It is warm and human. "You must let them sacrifice me."

"Sacrifice. Sacrifice. Sacrifice." The undead chant this new word, their agitation returning. Their icy, putrid breath fills the barrow.

"No." The steersman squeezes my arms so tightly, I think he will break my bones. So close he could kiss me, he says, "*She* will do it."

I recoil and turn away from him. I catch Birger's gaze. He nods.

Crazed now, the monsters bump into each other and their teeth snatch at the air.

"I can't," I say to Birger. If I keep my gaze on him, I can remain standing. Every bit of me wants to collapse and hide my head in my hands. "I can't kill a man."

"*I can't kill a man*," the leader mocks me. The others take it up, their high-pitched voices screeching in my ears. They howl with laughter. It is like the cry of an osprey mixed with a dying man's screams.

Through the cacophony, Birger speaks to me, calm and sure. "It is why you landed on the shore of this place, at this time."

Is this true? Ran delivers me to this place to kill a man? To sacrifice him to the gods to break an old curse? It is a cruel thing to do. But then, the gods can be cruel.

"If you don't do it." Birger breaks into my thoughts. "He will." He turns his gaze toward the grotesque man standing behind him.

I want to tell Birger to let the horrible thing do it.

The bright thread pulses again and a deep knowing slides over me like calm made manifest. "I will do it," I say.

Telling the creature with the dagger to let go of the human, the leader steps aside to allow me to pass, and his frigid breath hits my neck. My heart skips frantically. "If you fail or if this is a trick ..." He lets the threat linger.

I nod, gulping. I focus on Birger. In his warm, soft, brown eyes, I see him tell me to make it quick, to make the blade hit its mark. I follow the silver thread to Birger. It throbs. Why would it appear only for me to snuff it out along with his life?

A dagger hilt is placed in my hand, and it feels like it has been retrieved from a block of ice. Steam forms in my palm where my human warmth hits the undead cold.

I stand before Birger.

"Sacrifice. Sacrifice. Sacrifice." The roar of the chant makes me dizzy. Their feet pound the ground in a ghastly rhythm.

I take a heaving breath and lift the blade. Birger keeps his eyes on me. They are steady and show no fear.

As if someone else controls me, I feel a pleased smile spread across my face at his bravery. His brow furrows.

"Stand," I whisper. The creatures grow so excited at the prospect of blood, they do not hear me. Still frowning in confusion, Birger rises.

"A trick," the one with the teardrop ruby shrieks. He reaches for me, but before he can yank me away, I drop the knife and grasp Birger's hands.

The warmth floods through me like I'd slipped into a hot bath.

The silver thread races up our legs and along our arms, twining around our hands. When it touches the rotten grip of the undead, a hiss of steam rises. He howls in pain and jerks away.

"Kill them," the leader growls.

A brightness glows around Birger, and his eyes, wide with surprise, reflect the light that surrounds me as well. As I watch, they change, the brown lightening to show a tint of amber, and his hair growing longer.

"King Ale! King Ale!" When they see the transformation, the dead sailors cry out. They crowd around us. My heart races, afraid they will rent us to pieces.

"Sacrifice. King Ale. Lost Forever." The crewmen's chant grows confused, like the sound of madness. The boat sways so furiously, I tighten my grip on Birger. Or is he King Ale? Panic spears through me. If he is no longer Birger, what will he do to me?

The crewmen are in a frenzy. A massive blue-black body appears next to me and an axe falls. Before I can even scream, the blade hits where my arms link with Birger's or King Ale's or whoever he is now. A great storm of sparks showers over all three of us in a blinding flash. The beast with the axe careens backward at the blow. The thread slips loose, and I fall to the ground, screaming in pain. My forearms hiss and blister where the thread had connected me to Birger. As soon as I hit the ground, one of the monsters leans over me, his blue-black skin shining even though there is no light. His bloated arms reach for me, a black tongue sliding over black lips.

"Men," Birger shouts. His voice still sounds like his and yet, there is an unearthly power to it, like it comes from everywhere at once to be focused through this mortal man.

With a look of disappointment, the creature about to abuse me rises and lumbers to face this man who is now King Ale. They all quiet.

"It is a trick," the leader growls. "Kill him."

I cannot see what is happening. All I can see is dark legs as thick as tree branches, and feet bound in tattered shoes. I can barely focus on King Ale through the haze of pain. Blood forms where the thread had wound around my wrist.

Blood.

Crawling on my knees, my head spinning, I push aside a gold cup and hold my wrist over the boards at the hull of the boat. A droplet of blood falls to the wood. I watch it as if it has a life of its own as it spreads and is absorbed.

"Freya." I want to shout so loudly that she can hear my words in the land of the gods. It comes out weak. It will have to do. "Accept this offering of my blood." I grasp onto my wrist and squeeze so more will flow.

As I speak to Freya, I hear a powerful male voice coming from above me.

"Men!" King Ale cries again, no longer my Birger. "King Ale has returned!"

His cursed crew shriek.

More of my blood drips and is accepted by the boards of the ship. I hope it is enough. The gods and goddesses are always thirsty for blood.

"Freya," I plead. "Accept my offering. Come to the aid of your kin." That is it. I can squeeze out no more. I search for the knife I'd dropped, but it is too far away, kicked by the clumsy feet of the dead.

"Where is the woman," King Ale demands.

The bloated bodies part and the king steps forward, his face hard as granite. The silver thread hangs shredded from his arms, swinging and glowing in the unnatural gloom.

"Sacrifice. Sacrifice. Sacrifice." The chant resumes. One monster kneels beside me and sniffs the hull where I'd dripped my blood, the thick Christian cross he wears around his neck banging onto the wooden boards. His black tongue snakes out and licks the wood. Crouching on his haunches, he howls in excitement. He turns on me, those ghastly blue eyes on my bloody wrists. He smacks his bloated lips.

I jerk away, shouting "Stay back." He pauses and cocks his head. Taking advantage of his confusion, I rise to standing.

When King Ale approaches me, the silver threads throw sparks as he walks. He is handsome, but not as much as Birger. My heart sinks to think he might be gone forever. The king's gaze travels over my shoulder, his face softening. I spin to discover a new threat.

A woman, much taller than any human, stands at the bow. She wears golden armor and helm. Her face, beautiful and terrible.

Freya.

"My doomed sailors and villagers." Freya's voice bores into my head, so enticing I crave to throw myself before her. She pins me with her gaze.

She says my name, Aesa, her voice smooth with an undercurrent of hardness, like every wonderful and awful thing in the world is possible. I cannot speak.

"You know what to do," she tells me, inclining her head toward the threads that hang in tatters at King Ale's wrists. My own burned skin aches at the thought.

I must reforge the bond. But I do not want to do it with King Ale. I need Birger.

"I—"

"Kill the human," the steersman growls. Freya silences him with a look.

"Men!" King Ale shouts. "You were brave warriors in life." They all cheer, raising their weapons high. The roar hurts my ears and I flinch. I slowly collapse and put my aching hands to my ears. I want to be inside a house. I want Birger back. He may be a stranger to me, but he felt safe, unlike this warrior chieftain who looks and sounds as if he could strike us all down.

"Are you brave in death?" The king asks his men. They roar their answers.

Through the din, I hear a ship slipping through the water. I peek to discover this new curse. A glowing ship arrives at the shore at the base of the cliff in the same spot where I'd landed. No one steers or rows the ship. It is empty.

"Freya calls you to her hall," King Ale tells the men. "Will you go?"

They roar like beasts and a small illumination enters the barrow as an archway. The monster with the Christian cross tries to take a step through the arch. As soon as his body touches the barrier, a flare sparks like fire and pulses inward, pushing him back. He howls with rage.

"To enter my hall," Freya speaks. "You must make an offering."

He spins to face me, whips out a knife and licks the blade.

That calm knowing travels over me again. "The goddess already has my blood," I say, staring at his golden cross.

He growls. Putting the blade between his lips, he pulls the necklace off with great reluctance and drops it at the archway. This time he steps through. One by one, the crewmen leave their most beloved treasure and exit the barrow. As an act of mercy, Freya does not require the villagers to make a payment. As they file out, my heart returns to beating normally. I let out a sigh of relief.

A huge, ice-cold hand grips my arm and lifts me to my feet. I stare into the face of the steersman, his silk head linen askew grotesquely. In his cracked palm, he holds a dagger.

"Your blood is my offering," he whispers, as quiet as death. The blade is icy as it touches my neck, and it starts to bite into my skin. I feel warm blood trickle down into the hollow of my throat.

"If you kill me, I will curse you to roam these cliffs forever." My voice is stronger than I think possible as my hand clasps onto his to stop the blade. I should not be able to stop him. He stares at me with those empty blue eyes, and he puts his face close to mine, his foul breath full in my face. I try to look away, but he shakes me until I meet his ghastly gaze. With a growl, and as if I weigh nothing, he tosses me aside, and I catch myself before crashing to the ground. At the archway, he snatches the silk linen off his head and drops it on the pile of treasure.

It is so cold, I cannot move. Blood slides down my neck, the only thing that feels alive in this place.

Blood. Sacrifice. The words form in my mind. I stand, knowing what I must do.

The undead are gone. Both King Ale's crew and the doomed villagers. I can hear them tramping down the cliff side. The archway vanishes, the goddess with it.

"Birger," I call. I do not want King Ale. I want Birger.

A man emerges from the darkness. Birger, not King Ale, holds out his arms, the thread dangling between us. I do not know how he returned to himself, but I sigh with relief. I rush to him and his hands clasp my forearms. Pain bites into me as he touches my burns. I welcome it, for it means I am among the living.

Light brightens the barrow as the threads knit themselves and wind around our arms again.

Once they are whole, I hear the ship slide into the water to take King Ale's crew to Freya's hall.

"It is done," I breathe. Birger tightens his grip on me.

The ground shakes, forcing us both to our knees. A cold breeze blows across my skin, bringing the fresh scent of the sea. The ground continues to buck and buckle, like a ship tossed in a stormy sea.

My body thrums and the earth trembles like a great beast rising from the depths. Birger and I cling to each other.

The darkness lightens, and I see stars.

The rumbling continues.

As we stare at the plain, the earth breaks apart. Something sprouts from it. All around us, boulders erupt, one after the other, the ground shaking until they finish.

After a long time, Birger and I rise. The burial mound is gone, replaced by a ring of stones and we stand at the very center.

"It is a ship," I say. The stones at the bow and stern are taller and bigger than the others, at least twice the height of a normal man. Beyond the stone ship to one side is an expanse of grassy plain. To the other side is an equally wide expanse of sea.

The first rays of the sun peek over the horizon, one ray illuminating the line of the vessel from bow to stern exactly. It shines through the ship made of stones, lighting the day.

Birger looks down at me. His eyes are brown and soft, human and alive. A single beam of sunlight shoots through us. The thread disappears, but our arms are still clasped, which reveal the swirls of where it bound us.

We remain silent. The sun continues to peek a little higher above the cliff. The waves crash below. There is no trace of the undead crew. Or King Ale. Or Freya.

Birger breaks the silence. He turns in a circle, staring at each stone before looking down at me. "What are they?"

We study the stones. He speaks first. "Fifty-nine of them. One for each of King Ale's men."

"And the doomed villagers," I add.

"My father."

We share a look and my skin shivers. "A work of the gods. A monument," I say.

He nods.

We remain in the middle of the circle for the short day, hungry and weary but unwilling to leave. We touch each stone and watch the sun rise and fall. Just before the sun disappears, the last rays touch the boulder at the bow. It spears right down the center of the ship.

A name comes to my lips. "We will call them King Ale's Stones."

"And we will call the curse of the doomed ship broken," he adds. As if a great weight leaves him, his face softens. "The others said you brought trouble. I said you were the key. I was right." He raises an eyebrow.

"I could still be trouble."

He laughs, and it sounds like he hasn't done so in a long time. It is deep, rich, and so very human. My face softens and breaks into a smile.

I walk to the massive monument that marks the bow of King Ale's stone ship. The burns on my arm throb, but I do not mind. They are a reminder of my connection to Birger. The gods directed me to this place. I turn to face him again and the silver thread spreads from the stone at the bow, through him, and out through the stern. Now I know why I was led here.

To break the curse of the doomed ship.

Historical Note

The stone monument on which this story is based is a real place in Skania in Southern Sweden. Known as Ale Stenar, or Ale's Stones, the henge was believed erected at least 1,400 years ago, but it could go as far back as 5,000 years ago. There is some evidence of a much older burial mound at the site. Legend has it that a mythical King Ale is buried there and the stones are symbolic of the ship that would have taken him to the afterlife. For the purposes of the story, I kept the name of King Ale and created a fictional legend for why the stones were on that plain overlooking the water. A cursed ship sounded like a plausible explanation and what better reason for a curse than a spurned lover. You can still visit Ale's Stones.

The undead/ghosts in Norse culture were not the ephemeral beings we often associate with ghosts. In that time, ghosts were more like monsters, and they were almost always malevolent. The undead were men who died in an unfitting way or who were unpleasant and mean in life; they came back to harass their families. The undead were also described as being exceptionally large, strong, bloated, and with blue-black skin. It took quite a bit of effort for families to get rid of the unwanted ghost. I had a great time creating the monsters for this story.

Author Bio

K.S. Barton writes historical fiction stories of love and adventure set in the Viking age. In addition to being a lover of Norse mythology and culture, K.S. is many things. A mother and a martial artist. A dancer and a tutor. A quiet reader and a rowdy old school video game player. A *Lord of the Rings* geek and lay historian. A drummer. A lover of heavy metal and classic R&B. Under the name Kim Barton, she wrote *Aikido: My Path of Self-Discovery*. She resides in sunny Southern Arizona.

Visit https://ksbarton.com/ for more details and where you can claim *By Their Wits*, a free prequel of the *Norse Family Saga* series.

Books:

The Norse Family Saga trilogy:

- ❖ *Warrior and Weaver*
- ❖ *Sword and Story*
- ❖ *Hero and Healer*

Visit her on social media:
FB: https://www.facebook.com/ksbartonauthor.
Instagram: https://www.instagram.com/ksbartonauthor/

THE HOWLING OF WOLVES

BY

PAULA LOFTING

A story from the Sons of the Wolf *saga.*
In the aftermath of a great battle during the 1058 invasion of England by the Norse, Wulfric and his father, Wulfhere, must cope with the untimely death of Wulfwin, Wulfric's twin brother, whose demise, whilst having been met on the field of slaughter, bears all the hallmarks of a murder rather than a battle killing. No one believes them when they protest that Wulfwin's death was suspicious and that the likely perpetrator of the crime is Wulfhere's arch enemy and nemesis, Helghi, with whom the Wulfheresons have feuded for many years.

The Howling of Wolves *is a little standalone spin off from the main books and incorporates elements of the narrative from the saga.*

June, 1058
Somerset

The battle was over. Wulfric stared at the body of his twin as it lay wrapped in its burial shroud, resembling a moth in its cocoon.

Had he just seen the chest rise and fall? He shook his head. *Surely not.* He'd seen Wulfwin's death mask as he'd washed and covered him and knew it impossible that he still breathed. He shut his eyes and moments later opened them again. The cadaver lay still, just like the line of other slaughtered warriors. Sadly, Wulfwin was quite dead.

He'd stopped counting the corpses at one hundred. He figured there must be at least the equivalent to add to it. So many dead, despite their victory. A large trench had been dug in which the bodies were lowered with as much respect as could be afforded. Father, badly injured during the battle and having his wounds tended to, was unable to say goodbye to his son. Leofnoth, his father's friend, stood in Father's stead and had helped Wulfric carry his brother to the death pit. They deposited him in the ditch with a companion on either side, so he would not be alone. It felt strange to touch the lifeless carcass, knowing that a soul no longer inhabited it.

The priest took some time to walk around the site, sprinkling holy water over the dead, and reciting the rites in Latin. When done, he made a sign of the cross over them, and the ceorls cast the earth back in. Prayers said, the corpses were left to start their rot in their earthly resting place. Leofnoth patted him on the back comfortingly and turned to leave. Finding that he could not, Wulfric remained, joining those who wished to stay and sing a lament.

The evening was still. Warmth clung to the air and the sun still held sway over the day like a watchful mother. Across the meadow of slaughter, Norse prisoners dug a hole for their own dead. Wulfric heard the huscarls barking profanities at them for being 'lazy sons of whores' when they didn't dig hard enough. Wulfric felt no anger toward the enemy, for it was not they who'd killed his brother, he was certain. Nay. It had been the hand of their family's arch nemesis, Helghi. Or someone close to him. His son, Eadnoth. Or their kinsman, Hengest. Or someone else in their pay, perhaps.

Neither Wulfric nor Father had been believed, when they'd protested Wulfwin's throat could not have been cut by the Norse Wícinga. The incision had been too clean to have been given in battle. A killing like that was hard to prove as murder, but they alone were convinced of the truth.

Wulfric, numb with grief, scooped up some dirt, sniffed it, threw it down where his brother's corpse hid in the soil. The pungent odour of moist, brown earth filled his nostrils. He would never forget the smell.

A warm breeze played with his fringe and caressed his cheeks. To his amazement, a gathering of twigs and leaves rose upwards, spinning like a whirlwind, picking up momentum as it reached the edge of the pit.

Whoosh! His hair whipped back. The wind roared; whistled through his ears and blustered against his blood encrusted tunic. He gulped mouthfuls of air trying to refill his lungs, and let out a loud gasp as his breath returned, and with it, the familiar odour of his brother seemed to envelop him before moving on.

Wulfwin had passed right through him.

The day after the battle, Wulfric did not rise at the sound of the morning horn. Sleep had evaded him, left him lying awake most of the night in the hope Wulfric might let him know he was still here. But nothing.

Surprised when the tent flap opened, he blinked. The sun streamed through, blinding him.

"What are you doing? Why haven't you risen?"

For a moment, Wulfric thought it his brother who stood before him, but it was his father, Wulfhere, eyes rimmed with red, the torn flap of his cheek stitched into a curve. His complexion was the same pallid shade of green of Wulfwin's just before they'd wrapped the shroud over his face.

"What is there to get up for? Wulfwin is dead and that bastard Helghi goes unpunished."

Father stood awkwardly in the entrance, clutching the tentpole as though he were about to pass out. "We break our fast. You should eat something. Come if you want to." Wulfhere turned to leave.

"Wait. I'll come," Wulfric said, crawling out of his bedding.

Noon came and at last the fyrd was ready to march back to Gleawecaester. Father, obviously in pain, waved away attempts to get him into the wagon with the other injured. "I will not ride in a litter like an old lady, but like a man," he'd insisted.

Why Father had to be so stoic, Wulfric could not guess. He'd always been that way.

Seeing he needed help to mount his horse, Wulfric clasped his hands together allowing Father to lever himself awkwardly into the saddle, his injured leg stiff and obstinate, hose stained with blood. A sword thrust had also gouged into the flesh above his hip. He was not in good shape.

Wulfhere rode in silence. Gloom wafted from him like a bad smell. His stallion, Hwitegast, was unusually subdued for such an animal often flighty around other horses, especially the mares. He and Wulfric made a melancholy pair but were not alone in their grief. The men of Súþ Seaxa lost many men to the Norse, and amongst those revelling in glorious victory on the journey, were those grieving for the friends and comrades who would never again join them in the warriors' meadhall.

Wulfric glanced at his father riding beside him. The sweat pooled on his face. "You should have gone with the rest of the injured," Wulfric told him sternly.

"Many are worse than I," Father replied.

A passing rider called to them, "Wulfhere, 'tis a great scar you will have there, ruining your pretty looks. Will your wife still love you?"

Father responded with an unenthusiastic smile. Wulfric scowled his offence, and the man, realising his mistake, rode on in awkwardness.

"Do they think they can jest when we have lost my brother?" Wulfric said angrily.

"Life goes on, Wulfric."

Wulfhere bit down on his lip.

"You are in pain, Father. You should have gone in the wagon."

"I am all right," Wulfhere told him.

"Nay, you are not."

"There was no room, and I can ride. Do not badger me."

Wulfric said no more of it. He was afraid of losing him as well as his brother, but Father's stubborn resistance to comfort defeated him.

Bruised and battered himself, Wulfric counted himself lucky to have come out of his first fight largely unscathed. As one of the younger warriors, he'd been protected by the older men. At only sixteen, he'd started out on the venture with excitement. Father had caught him and his friends acting out their boyish bravado, boasting about their supposed prowess, as if combat was no more than a game. Father, incensed by their foolhardiness, warned them, lecturing them that they should be fearful, not full of unqualified confidence, for without fear they would be like apples on a tree waiting to fall at the slightest gust of wind.

"It wasn't meant to have ended like this, was it?" Wulfric murmured. "We were to have returned together. All of us." He gulped, stifling a sob. "Half of me has died, Father."

Without looking at him, Wulfhere replied, "I know."

"Father?"

"Aye?"

"Do you think he will hate us for leaving him?"

"He will understand. Besides, he will not be alone."

"He wants vengeance. I feel it."

"He will have it, I promise you."

Father turned to him and their eyes locked.

56

"How? How will we avenge him? When will we avenge him?"

"We will bide our time, Wulfric."

"I don't want to bide my time, I want to kill Helghi now," Wulfric muttered.

Father looked away wearily.

The King's Stronghold at Gleawecester

Wulfric dipped the compress into the basin, squeezed it out, and dabbed at Wulfhere's sweat-drenched face. Father's closed eyes flickered, and rapid movement beneath the lids indicated that his sleep troubled him.

Tears spilled down Wulfric's cheeks. *God, please, do not take him from me too.* How could he go home without his brother or his father?

Æmund, his sister's husband, appeared beside him and handed him a bowl of stew. Wulfric put down the sponge, took the meal, and gazed at the unappetising contents.

Æmund enquired, "How does he fare?"

Wulfric put aside his supper, his stomach clenched.

"He should have ridden in the cart with the injured," he replied. "And he should not have worn his mail over the wound…" he paused, stared at his fevered father then continued, his voice increasing to an angry crescendo, "causing the stitching to undo and open the gash."

Æmund, a few years older than him, put a comforting hand on Wulfric's shoulder. Looking up, Wulfric asked, "Am I going to lose him too?"

"Nay, he will live. Wulfhere is a strong man, has taken worse injuries, or so my father says."

"He always did come back from battle wounded." Wulfric hesitated. "Your father does not. How so?"

"Father says that Wulfhere puts himself in the middle of the fight every time. Remember, he fought the champion fight 'ere the battle had even started. My father, well, it has become his custom to keep himself out of the way as much as he can."

The tent opened. A tall fair-haired man, his woad-dyed tunic partially concealed by a rich scarlet cloak, stood with the light behind him. It took Wulfric a moment to realise who it was. Astonished, he attempted to stand as Earl Harold entered with his huscarle, Tigfi.

"You will excuse me for intruding," the earl said, "Please, stay seated. I came to see how Lord Wulfhere is. We are all sorely anxious for him…. And –", he turned to Tigfi who rummaged in his satchel, "I wanted you to have this."

The earl, crouching, stretched out the money pouch handed to him by Tigfi, across the tormented figure of Wulfhere. Wulfric took it silently.

"It is your brother's wergild. Your father left it in my chamber when he collapsed."

Wulfhere made a groaning sound and muttered some incoherent words before quietening again. The earl gazed at him, his face etched in sympathy. "I will pray Lord Wulfhere recovers soon," Harold said.

As Tigfi drew aside the tent flap for the earl, Wulfric got hurriedly to his feet. "My lord," he said, "I must ask of you something."

Harold paused. "Aye, lad. What is it?"

"Did my father speak with you about my brother's death?"

"He did… He mentioned it. And I have told him he should bring the matter up with the hundred moot. If what he says is true, then the truth will out."

The earl exited the tent and Tigfi turned to Wulfric and said, "It is best to leave it to the king's law, Wulfric. If your brother was killed by Helghi, then as Lord Harold says, the truth will out."

The truth will out…

Wulfric doubted that it would.

August 1058
Home

Wulfric shivered as he entered the gates of Horstede feeling as though he'd stepped into a cloud of misery. The homestead was usually so full of life at this time of year. It was *haerfest monath* and the steading should have been alive with celebrations. Something did not feel right. It was as if the place already knew that Wulfwin was not with them. Or perhaps it was something else that brought the shadowy atmosphere to them.

Father and Wulfric walked at the head of the group who were just as gloom-ridden as the place they'd walked into. Leofnoth, his son, Æmund, and Wulfhere's standard bearer, Yrmenlaf, followed behind.

Mother appeared from inside with Sigfrith, her maid servant, on her heels. Both women were beaming to see them. They could not yet have heard of Wulfwin's death.

His younger sisters, Winflæd, and Gerda, faces full of eagerness to get their hands on Father, scurried past them. Wulfhere held them as they clung to him, kissing and embracing him almost violently.

After them, his eldest sister, Freyda, appeared briefly on the porch before rushing back inside as though fearful of seeing anyone. Wulfric expected her to be big with child by now. It had been all that Æmund talked about on the journey home. Yet the girl was as slender as ever. If the babe had already arrived, then it must have come early.

"Freyda?" Æmund, her husband, pushed Wulfric aside, and leapt up the porch steps.

Catching Wulfric standing some feet behind the others, Mother smiled at him, then looked around. "Where is Wulfwin?" she asked, her face suddenly grave. "Why is he not here?"

Sobbing, Wulfric put his arms around her. A great scream came from her. She wriggled from his embrace and ran up the porch steps wailing.

*

"Could you not have brought him home?" Mother demanded when she had recovered a little.

Too busy berating Father about leaving Wulfwin in a ditch, Ealdgytha failed to properly greet Wulfric, the son that was still alive, and inquire of his wellbeing. Nor did she inquire into Father's injuries either. When Wulfhere walked silently away, leaving her scolding the air, she then turned on Wulfric.

Unable to stand her complaining any longer, Wulfric escaped outside to seek peace on a grassy patch behind the chapel. As he hurried there, her wretched sobbing echoed from the hall until the distance was enough to no longer hear it. He leaned against the stone wall, and after a while he took out a piece of whittling he'd been working on, something for Wulfwin – a wolf perhaps.

"Does she never stop?"

"You know how Mother is," his dead twin said.

Wulfric spoke with him for a while as tiny pieces of shaved wood fell about him.

"No one comes to see how *I* am. Not even Mother. Not even to continue her damned chiding. Does anyone care that I have lost you too?"

"They only care about themselves, my brother. You should know that by now."

Wulfric smiled. So used to having his life-long companion always there to talk to, it seemed only natural that he would answer. "It is all they ever cared about."

About to walk back to the hall as the sun was going down, angry voices caught his attention. He looked across the small expanse of meadow. Framed against the orange glow of sunset, his sister Freyda walked with Æmund. They stopped in the shade of an old oak. Æmund crouched to look at something on the ground. Behind him, she stood with her cloak about her, shoulders moving, crying. Neither had seen him.

He watched silently, curious as to why they were there. Was that a grave marker? A little wooden cross?

Freyda touched her husband's shoulder. Æmund put a hand over hers, then moments later withdrew it sharply. He stood and turned from her, and she reached out to grab him. His brother-in-law shook her off, turned and said something in an angry tone before storming away. The tension between them reached Wulfric across the meadow. Wulfric stood, instinctively protective, the sensation strange. The only person he'd ever felt protective of was Wulfwin.

His sister sank to the ground, and then came the sound of her tears. He paused and thought before deciding he would go to her.

"Was he being unkind to you? Æmund, I mean," Wulfric asked as he approached.

Freyda turned, a look of surprise on her tearstained face.

Wulfric sat down and gazed at a little burial mound, covered in picked flowers. "What is this?" he asked, yet he knew the answer before she gave it.

"My baby," Freyda answered in a low voice, not looking at him. She sniffed and wiped away tears.

Wulfric's heart missed a beat. Now he knew the reason for the misery that had greeted him on his arrival home. He ventured an arm around her. A hint of surprise glimmered in her eyes. When she did not flinch, he pulled her to him. Freyda looked up and stared at him questioningly, then allowed her head to rest against his chest.

"I know. This is unlike me," he said.

As small children they'd played together, but in their adolescence, Wulfric's sister thought herself too high and mighty for her younger siblings. Now that she'd seen eighteen summers and he sixteen, would things be different?

More tears fell and he held her closer. He did not know why, for he'd never comforted anyone, not even his brother. And yet it felt right. She cried for some moments before abruptly withdrawing. "Wulfric, I am so sorry about Wulfwin."

Her words hit him, his chin trembled, and it was his turn to weep. She comforted him this time.

"What happened to your child? Why was Æmund angry?" he asked after a few moments.

"We called the babe Eadric. I am to blame for his death. It was my fault he was not baptised! My fault he could not go to be with God!"

"Why? What did you do?"

Freyda pulled back and wiped her face on her sleeve. "It happened just after you all had gone with the fyrd, I worried about Winflæd being here, what with Mother and Sigfrith both unwell, trying to cope with everything on her own. Father sent for me, but Æmund forbade me to leave our homestead. Said it was not safe for me or the bearn to manage the journey. I just couldn't bear to be in Hechestone without Æmund there, and thinking about poor Winflæd here in Horstede, so I disobeyed him. He was right. I should not have left... The child came early. Too early. He didn't have the strength to live, and he died." She burst into tears again.

"God, Freyda. You should have done as you were told, girl."

"I know. You think I'm a bad wife, don't you?" she wailed.

Wulfric shrugged. In the last years, they'd not had much to do with each other, but there he be, comforting her, feeling her pain. He wondered if this was what it was to be a man.

"You've not always been good," he said, tentatively. "All that trouble with Edgar... Promising to marry him and then marrying Æmund."

"And you? The things you and Wulfwin used to do to Winflæd and Tovi..."

"I-I know," Wulfric said. "We were not very good to them. But – sometimes, well, they asked for it."

Freyda giggled through her tears and gave him a playful smack on his chest. "You terrorised them. I remember when you put poor Tovi down the well! And when you threatened to hang Winflæd as a witch, tying her to the fence by her hair."

Wulfric barked with laughter at the memory, then worried what she must think of him.

"And the day the earl came you stopped Tovi from joining the hunt because you left him hanging in a tree!"

Wulfric was relieved to see her smiling. "Aye, I do believe we *were* very bad to them."

They laughed together and Freyda said, "I didn't mind, because all the while you boys were tormenting them, Mother and Father didn't notice me running off to meet Edgar."

"Like the dutiful Christian daughter that you were," Wulfric grinned. He mimicked his mother and they giggled loudly.

"They could be brats some times," Freyda said.

They sat in companionable silence whilst Freyda picked the dead flower heads from the little grave.

After a while Wulfric asked, "Do you think we will be forgiven for our sins?"

"Nay. God won't forgive me. And neither will Æmund."

"Æmund will see that you did not knowingly cause your child's death."

Freyda turned sad eyes to him. The sun reflecting in them made the green shine like bright emeralds, a reminder of Mother's, before they were filled with such bitterness. "It was my fault," she said in a voice full of anguish. "I failed my little boy. I failed Æmund. I should not have left Hechestone. I should not have ridden that damned horse. And I should not have disobeyed my husband."

As she sobbed again, he once more gathered her close and held her, feeling her slight frame tremble against him. Wulfric wondered about the little boy whose bones lay in all that earth. His nephew: a child who had died long before its time. He understood his sister's agony. Just as he'd shared their mother's womb with Wulfwin, she'd also shared hers with the little mite.

A thought came of his twin. He should have known something bad was going happen to him. Hadn't Wulfwin tried to warn them of Helghi's murderous intentions?

In his mind's eye he remembered that portentous draw across his own throat that Wulfwin had made with his hand, showing him the sign that Helghi had made.

"Wulfwin's death was my blame," he announced, breaking the silence between them.

"How so?" She had been leaning her head against his chest but pulled away to look at him.

"I lost Wulfwin in the chaos of battle. When the lines broke... I should have looked for him; found him. Been at his side. Then that bastard, Helghi, would not have got to him."

"Father says it cannot be proven."

"It doesn't need to be proven. He did it. I know it. Everyone knows. And Father knows it too. He just –"

He cut himself off. The breeze caught a few strands of her golden hair that fluttered from the cap his sister wore. Wulfric's whole body went cold. Goosebumps ran across the surface of his arms and legs and the back of his neck went rigid.

"Did you feel that?" He asked.

"Feel what?"

"That chill? Like a cold gust of air just blew through us."

"No? I felt nothing. Just the wind."

"Look! Its him!" Wulfric jumped up. Some feet away, under the big oak tree that spread its ancient limbs out over the horse's paddock, stood an ethereal shape. A faint mist surrounded the figure, and it seemed to be laughing, beckoning.

On her feet beside him, Freyda said, "I can't see anyone."

"Over there, by the horse's paddock." He turned to face her. "Wulfwin."

She swung around to look. "Wulfric, no one is there."

Wulfric turned back to look at his twin, saw him still laughing, a scene out of a memory. He reached out, placed his hands on either side of her shoulders and turned her to face the ghost. "See? There!"

She turned and caught his face between her palms. "Look at me, Wulfric. Wulfwin is not there!"

He moved aside from her and turned his gaze back to where his brother had been. Freyda was right. No one was there.

"But I *saw* him."

"You couldn't have. He is gone. Wulfwin is gone."

"I did see him, there, calling me." Wulfric's eyes welled with tears.

"Listen to me, Wulfric, you're grieving. That is all it is. I used to think I could hear my baby boy crying at night. I just wanted so much for him to be alive that I imagined it."

She drew him to her, arms around him tightly. He sunk into her embrace and silently shed his anger and despair. She was right, hard as it be to accept. He just wanted a chance to make amends for not protecting him – for letting him die. Grief had maddened him.

Wulfwin was not coming back.

That evening, sleeping in the space he'd once shared with his twin, Wulfric struggled to sleep. They'd shared everything, even their dreams. And now, without Wulfwin, he would be spending the first night home from what would have been their first battle together, alone. But this was not the only reason slumber would not come. Mother was still tearing into Father, and what with Freyda and Æmund arguing well into the night, small wonder he could not doze off.

Over the next few days, Wulfric spent much time lying in his bed chamber, curtained off in the hall. If he did get up, it was to wonder about the homestead like a wraith. Sometimes he caught his family staring strangely at him as he slouched around, muttering like a lunatic, forgetting to keep the conversations with Wulfwin in his head.

He liked to search out places where he and his brother once hid together, plotting their devilish antics. Their favourite had been in the space behind the woodshed. There now, he stroked the bench they had fashioned together from a log. The smoothness of the wood through the tips of his fingers drew the memories of them together into his mind. He lowered himself down to sit and leant against the ram-shackle building, imaging that Wulfwin was beside him. A smile formed on his lips as an old conversation came to his mind.

"Tovi always had to come and spoil things, didn't he, Wulfwin?"

His brother nodded, a mischievous glint in his eye. Was Wulfwin's voice and image only in his head? Could it really be him he saw and spoke to? Or could it be just grief, playing tricks with his imagination, as Freyda had said? Nonetheless, he took comfort in knowing he could summon Wulfwin's spirit anytime he felt like it – real or not.

The quiet tranquillity of the warm afternoon away from the noise of the homestead, began to filter into Wulfric's mind. Still laughing with the ghost of his sibling, Wulfric tried to stop the sleep from coming, but his eyes grew heavy and heavier until he fell into slumber.

Wulfric's eyes flash open. Surprised, he finds himself on the ground and quickly springs into action. Had he been sleeping?

The impact as the lines are forced back causes the men to tumble and fall over one another. On one knee, Wulfric crouches behind his shield. The air fills with screams as blades plunge into flesh. The noise of squelching blood and innards terrify him. Now on his feet, he grabs his spear. Where is Wulfwin? Where is his brother? The shieldwall is torn asunder and its warriors are no longer standing side by side.

Heart pounding like a hammer on an anvil, he sees all around is chaos. The Wícinga are big men with giant axes that swipe across the shoulders of his battle companions. Heads, still with their helms at-

tached, fly from their necks and the stumps are left looking like fresh meat.

He searches for Wulfwin but cannot find any familiar faces amidst the clash of weapons. He breathes through his nose and is immediately hit by the stench of blood. He tastes it as globules of gore land in his mouth.

"Wulfwin! Wulfwin!" Wulfric wonders if it is really he that shouts. His voice sounds distant even in his own ears.

The noise of battle diminishes as though he is suddenly leagues away, but still the fighting goes on.

Then the howling comes.

A faint voice calls... "Brother... Come to me! Come... The wolves... They are howling."

Wulfric listens for the voice. He is standing still. All else circles him like a wheel.

He hears it again, very faintly. "Wulfwin?" he calls.

Looking before him, some yards away, he sees Father's banner, Running Wolf. It flaps furiously in the wind. His brother is there, like a maddened boar. He gives good slaughter with his long-shafted spear, protecting the standard and its terrified bearer, Yrmenlaf.

Suddenly Wulfwin is still. He stares, smiles, and then nods to Wulfric who is close enough to see that someone has reached around his brother's neck from behind. There is a blade and Wulfric shouts a warning.

His eyes focus on the knife as it presses into the unprotected skin of Wulfwin's neck. Even from that distance, he can see the trickle of blood that runs into the gully of his brother's collarbone; the skin that is unprotected by his mail.

He closes his eyes and the screaming starts.

With a sharp intake of breath, Wulfric woke. He lay panting, sweat running down his back, the sun hot on his face. He must have slipped from the bench and onto the grass, his heart still racing.

He jolted himself to a sitting position, casting a look around him, gaining his bearings. He saw no sign of Wulfwin – or anyone else for that matter. Almost immediately the dream had begun to fade. He tried to claw it back. What had he seen? But he could recall nothing significant, just an image of his brother with a knife at his neck. Only a nightmare.

*

For the seventh night since arriving home, Wulfric lay, wide-eyed and lonely in bed. The wind whispered through the eaves like the faraway howling of wolves. During the day he longed for sleep, but at night it evaded him, and his head swirled with thoughts of Wulfwin. Most nights they talked, and this night was no different. As always, Wulfric told his brother of the misery he felt without him. Wulfwin, however, did not return his sympathies. He was not happy for some reason. Wulfric shivered with the ominous feeling of hostility that seemed not only to pervade the air, but also his skin, setting the fibres of his nerves on edge.

It was the last of the hot weather months and still humid at night, but the atmosphere abruptly altered from warm to freezing. An aroma of damp, rich soil filled the space around him. The dark grew deeper, and he sank into a murkiness of shadows as if he had fallen into an earthly tomb.

"I know you miss me too brother, but I am not at fault. I told Father we should bring you home. I didn't want to leave you in that hole. I'm sorry... If we had brought you home, then you would be here too...."

The wind rose in a high-pitched wail and suddenly the mattress felt cold as snow, and it shifted, as though someone lay down next to him.

Afraid, Wulfric slowly turned his head and as he did so, an eerie voice spoke, sibilant and serpent-like; demonic, "But I *am* here with you, brother...."

He screamed as a face, white as ash, dispersed into the darkness like splintered glass.

Wulfric sprang upright, shaking, perspiring, and puffing for breath.

The image of Wulfwin, now gone, had been lying on its side, head leaning on the palm of its hand as the real Wulfwin had often done when alive. Wulfric looked around, the darkness was not as strong as before. Leaning forward, he pushed through the curtain and gazed out. In the hall silence reigned.

Lying back against the bolster, he felt calmer. *It must be a nightmare.* He shut his eyes, and after a moment opened them again and looked to where his brother had been. Nothing.

As time went by, the vivid dream of battle continued. So very real; the crash of weapons, the cries of the wounded. And the howling – yes, the howling of wolves. It always ended the same. Every time, just as the blade was about to slide across his brother's neck, Wulfric would wake up screaming, covered in sweat with a feeling of impending doom. And something else? *What are you trying to tell me, my brother?*

Then, as the day wore on, those feelings would diminish. He'd shrug. After all, they were just dreams, weren't they?

Though he never spoke about the nightmares and the conversations with Wulfwin to anyone, he was often seen around the homestead talking to himself – or someone that could not be seen. Both Ealdgytha and Wulfhere believed there was something quite wrong with their son talking to the dead. But Father Paul advised them to leave him be, reassuring them it would help the healing process.

Then one day, his parents surprised him with a different idea of what might aid his recovery.

Growing up, Wulfric had never been able to fathom the inner workings of Mother's mind. He could, if he wanted, recall some magical moments in the past when she'd smiled spontaneously or genuinely laughed at some prank of his and his brother's. These were, however, mostly old reveries. Since returning without Wulfwin, her expression had become grimmer, and mostly now remained that way. But on this particular morning, leading a young woman into the hall from the snowy, wintry afternoon, Mother's features were aglow with pleasure, as if she were about to tell him something wonderful.

Brought to stand before him, the girl pulled back her hood to reveal a mass of unveiled chestnut hair, set aglow by the light of the hearth. He couldn't help but stare. He chided himself as he tried and failed to draw his gaze away from her, only to discover a pair of startling green eyes already fixed on him. The gentle curve of her plump, rosy lips displayed a light smile. Perfect. Her lips were perfect. He briefly looked at his feet, as Mother introduced her as Cynethryth, daughter of a local thegn. Wulfric began to stare again. Catching him out once more, the girl's grin broadened, pricking her freckled cheeks with attractive dimples.

Thus, Wulfric learned he was to be married.

He hated the idea of having this marriage forced on him in order to help him forget the pain of losing his brother. Did they think him a child who could be placated with a puppy when an old dog had died?

"It will do you good to have a son of your own," were Mother's words of wisdom.

And the very thought he might father a brat or two filled Wulfric with terror. Nay, he was not ready for that responsibility. What he really wanted was Wulfwin back.

"As if a mere female could replace you," Wulfric said to his brother in their nightly talk.

"You didn't protest much," came Wulfwin's caustic reply.

Wulfric shrugged. "Mother will get what Mother wants, regardless of what I say."

"She will make a fool of you, that one."

"Mother? Or the girl?"

"The girl."

"Why so?"

"You'll see."

At first, Wulfric found his bride irritating, cloying, expecting affection after their bed romps rather than the indifference she mostly received from him.

At eighteen, Cynethryth was more mature than he. And more so than the lasses he'd previously been with. He could not deny the excitement of having a woman in his bed instead of a mere girl. And she was not unversed in the art of love, teaching him a trick or two he'd not known before. Her naked body in his bed was tempting, but with the deed done, he just wanted to get away, provoking angry outbursts from her which he returned in kind. Eventually the aggression seeped into their lovemaking and he soon discovered that they both held a liking for ferocious bed play.

Occasionally they would arrive at mealtimes with scratches, their faces bruised, inducing some odd looks from Mother and curious ones from Sigfrith. Father though, seemed oblivious to it. He regularly appeared preoccupied of late, often found with an empty horn of mead in his hand.

As much as Wulfric tried to avoid his new wife during the day, he would always find himself in their chamber at night and Cynethryth's loud screams of pleasure meant that they now had their own sleeping hut outside the hall.

But there was a change in him. The more time he spent as a husband, carrying out his husbandly duties, the less he thought of his brother... and the less he dreamt. Until one night...

Wulfric... Wulfric...

Wulfric's eyes opened. He surveyed the darkness, listening to the delicate snore of his sleeping wife. She did not make any movement, lying with her head on his outstretched arm.

Wulfric... His ears pricked. Who had called?

The voice sounded familiar. Was he dreaming again? Sleep forced his eyes closed, before a light brushing on his shoulder disturbed him. His lids flew open as he felt himself shaken. He extricated his arm out from under Cynethryth's shoulders and sat up, careful not to wake her. A dark mass moved as the door creaked open.

"Wulfwin?"

The shadow fled through the opening. Wulfric pulled on his clothes, threw his cloak around himself, slipped into his boots, and followed it into the night.

As he looked out across the green, the figure moved across it coming to a halt by the twin towered gates. "Wulfwin? Is that you?"

The dark human shape waved a beckoning hand, then disappeared through the unopened exit, sinking into the structure as though engulfed by it.

"Follow me..." Wulfwin's disembodied voice called.

Without realising how he got there, Wulfric found himself outside the palisade and down the track into the forest. The rime on the path gave him the sensation of crunching dried leaves and twigs under his feet and the frosty balls of breath floated around him, caressing his cheeks. But he did not feel the cold. He felt detached. There, but not there. In the distance he saw the dark outline that had drawn him out of his warm bed. "Wulfwin is that you?" he cried out and ran after it. "Wulfwin wait! Where are you taking me?"

Soon, the ghostly figure disappeared into a dark part of the woods, where the half moonlight could not penetrate. Wulfric stopped at the edge of the gloom, afraid to go in.

"I am scared, Brother. I don't want to see."

He heard in what could only be a resonance of his twin's voice, "To see what happens in the light, you must venture into the dark..."

"Is that really you, Wulfwin?" Wulfric stared into the black before him. *What will happen to me if I go in?*

"Look, down there..."

Wulfric turned and beheld a shallow ravine.

Moonlight shone as if to purposely show him what lay there. He saw a burial pall covered in vegetation. Within the coverlet of leaves, a bright light glowed, and something pulsated with the rhythmic thump of a heart beating.

His brother's death pall. What was it doing here?

"Christ! Wulfwin, you're alive!"

He scrambled into the ravine and slid down its short slope. He brushed away the dirt and leaves and tore off the shroud to reveal the face of his twin.

What he saw made him scream.

Hollow cheekbones, rotting skin, brown and wrinkled like leather. And the eyes – black in their hollow sockets.

Wulfwin's voice hissed, "Aye, Brother. I am dead but not dead. Real but not real. It is not a dream."

Wulfric leapt up. "Nay, nay, nay!" he cried out, hands over his ears.

He was unable to stop looking at the undead cadaver at his feet. The thing's lips moved. "Look at the hand…"

Fear coursed through his veins, and he scrambled up the bank, the monstrous voice echoing. *Look at the hand… the hand…*

On the ridge he stood panting, staring into the ravine. The enshrouded corpse had gone. The voice quiet. "If you are trying to scare me, it is working!"

"Trying to make you see…"

"See what? What?"

"The hand…"

Wulfric shook his head. It must be a nightmare! He looked down at his dirt-soiled hands and fingernails. He was awake after all.

The darkness still loomed ahead, drew him to it, his eyes growing heavier and heavier, drifting into a deep, penetrating slumber.

Wulfric crouches behind his shield, as the enemy is attacked. He must protect Yrmenlaf and his father's banner, Running Wolf. He lashes out with a spear, stabs anyone that comes near them. Screams of slaughter echo through the air, raw and terrifying as death takes anyone in its path.

A heavy blow by a huge-bladed axe crashes against his shield and causes him to go down. He rolls, slides, and is up again in a thrice. He hopes his brother Wulfwin is safe.

Running Wolf is nearby, and he realises he is not Wulfric, but Wulfwin – or is he?

Suddenly, he is hauled rearwards, his helmet dragged off exposing his head. He struggles but can do nothing as cold steel bites into the skin at his throat. He tries to call for his father and brother, but what comes instead is the high-pitched whine of a wolf cub. The sound of despair.

Shock surges through him as he slips slowly to the ground. The gore-laden grass squelches beneath him. Warm liquid pours from his neck, saturating his mail. He grabs at the wound, hot blood gushes through his fingers. A gurgling sound. He is dying.

Unable to dam the exodus of his life any longer, his hands fall helplessly beside him.

Someone sobs loudly and he looks up as the light wanes. Father looks down from above, beside himself with grief.

"Wulfwin..."

He turns his head towards Father's voice but all that can be seen is a man's shadow. I am not Wulfwin, he thinks, and wants to say it out loud. But the words do not come because he is dead.

Wulfric gasped, panting, hands cover his throat. He inhales deeply, replacing the breath lost. "Christ," Wulfric muttered and sat up.

He had been in the forest all night. The sun was coming up and his bones ached with cold. A deep depression hung over him. What was he doing there? He struggled to remember. Standing up, he thought he must have been sleep walking.

Then Wulfwin's voice came to him like a whisper in the wind: *To see what happened in the light, you must venture into the dark.*

Weeks later

It was a freezing cold *Candelmæsse* eve, late in the afternoon. Wulfric had been ordered out of the hall to help his father with the pruning in the orchard, but just as he usually would, he ignored the summons. He'd made himself comfortable as near to the hearth as he could without getting in the way of the women's cooking. He lounged on a pile of animal skins, supported on one elbow. His dog, Brun, slumped across him, and he stroked the dog's fur. Around him, some of the villagers were taking down the greenery that decorated the hall since *Christmæsse tide* to replace them with new for the coming celebration.

His eye lids grew heavy, and he almost dozed off. He could hear the chatter of the women as they attended to the evening supper. The cauldron pot that hung above the hearth bubbled away, the delicious scent of meat and vegetables wafting about him, tantalising his sense of smell.

His eyes snapped open when through the back doors of the hall, stormed his father. Picking up a spear and shield, Wulfhere stomped out again, this time through the front doors, slamming them behind him. About to return to his relaxed state, Sigfrith's announcement that trouble was at the gate jerked him awake and he sat up. He shifted Brun off of him, and the dog leapt up, tail wagging as Wulfric raised himself to his feet. Brun panted and circled himself with excitement as if it was time for a hunt. Wulfric approached the door just as Mother, her face etched in fury, stormed back in, pushing him aside.

"What is going on?" he asked as she returned to her cooking.

"Tigfi is out there with Helghi of all people and those awful men of his. They have come to discuss your sister," she said. Her tone could have killed all the weeds in the kingdom.

"What?"

"Aye! It seems your dear Father did not attend the hundred moot summons, nor the shire court summons, and now Tigfi has orders to hand Winflæd over to that disgusting foul creature outside as a wife for his equally foul offspring!"

"Winflæd? She is but a bearn still."

Mother rolled her eyes.

"And Eadnoth? Father will never let her marry him."

"He's let them in the gates. He's talking to them now."

The rumbling of voices could be heard outside. Wulfric pulled one of the doors ajar and looked out. Father was arguing with Tigfi as Helghi ranted in the background.

His piss boiling, Wulfric burst through the doors, sorely testing their hinges. There stood his brother's murderer - the enemy - arms folded, watching as Father and Tigfi argued. There were others also, a woman and another man, standing in the background. Though it was Helghi who interested him most.

"Helghi! You lie and you know it! You killed my brother!" Wulfric lunged at the man with his seax drawn.

Tigfi knocked the blade spinning out of his hand. "Oh no you don't."

As Tigfi dragged him away, Wulfric yelled, directing his ire at Helghi, "My brother told me you threatened him like this!" and he made as if his hand was a knife cutting his throat.

"Ælfstan!" Tigfi cried. "Contain this boy on pain of death should he move," then at Wulfric he said menacingly "Wulfric! If you do that again I'll have my men clap you in fetters. Stay there!"

As Ælfstan forced him back, Wulfric stood, sullenly making fists. A perfect opportunity to revenge his brother now lost. He peered out from behind the burly blacksmith. To his annoyance, Winflæd snatched the seax from the ground.

"Don't worry, I'll make sure he doesn't move." The knife quivered as she threatened him with it.

Wulfric hissed. "What are you at, stupid little girl?"

Winflæd scowled and looked away from him at Tigfi and Father. Tigfi had his arm around Father's shoulders. He walked him forward a few steps. "I know this is difficult, Wulfhere, but it could get worse. Is there nothing we can do here? I know that Helghi is an *earsling*, but the boy may not be so bad–" Their heads turned to look at Helghi's son who was picking at an unsightly spot on his nose. Catching everyone gazing at him, Eadnoth looked flustered, then dropped his hand away from his face.

Wulfric felt a moment of disgust. This was the creature they wanted his sister to wed. He still thought her the plain, skinny, wispy thing, so unlike his other sister. He'd not bothered with her much since coming home. They had not spoken as he and Freyda had.

He turned his attention back to Tigfi, hearing him talking animatedly with Father. Wulfhere suddenly turned and jabbed a finger in Eadnoth's direction. "*He* is not getting my daughter!" Father then glared at Helghi, who drew breath deeply, his bearded cheeks lifting into a smile as he let out a sigh of satisfaction. Wulfhere shouted as he stepped forward, "Helghi!"

"What are you doing, Wulfhere?" Tigfi held onto his arm.

"You wanted a solution, I have one," Father said. "Helghi!"

"What?"

"We fight. You and me. If you can get me to submit, then you may have her."

Wulfric heard his sister gasp. "Father! Do not do this! You are still not well," she shouted.

Father pushed her toward the hall. "Winflæd, go – in – side!"

"Don't do this. Please?" she pleaded.

Tigfi took her arm and said softly to her, "Go, Winflæd. This is not the place for you to be right now."

Winflæd shrugged him off. "Tigfi, my father is not fit. You can see how ill he is? He is weak as a kitten."

Father looked indignant. "Why don't you let everyone know how he easily he will pound me into the ground?"

Clenching his fist, Wulfric's rage grew as Helghi, smirking, looked Father up and down as though measuring his chances against him.

Wulfwin goaded, *"Kill him, brother! Kill the bastard!"*

"Very well." The sneer on Helghi's face stretched to a wide grin that was more like a grimace.

Wulfhere nodded. "When you lose, your fat, bulbous, stinking shadow never darkens my door again."

Wulfric could stand it no longer. He forced his way past Ælfstan. "Father, Winflæd is right. Let *me* fight. I will fight Eadnoth. If I win, then Winflæd goes free." He glared at Eadnoth. "And I *will* win."

"Stay back, boy!"

"I am sick of you calling me a boy! I am not a boy anymore, Tigfi. You cannot treat me like I am!"

Wulfric's eyes then flew to where Eadnoth stood. Sneering, Eadnoth crossed his arms and widened his stance.

"What say you, Eadnoth?" Wulfric stepped forward to stand nose to nose with Helghi's son and felt himself whipped away by the large capable hands of Ælfstan.

There was a lot of commotion. Raised voices were giving their opinions on what should happen next.

It was his sister who put a halt to them. She swung around at them all, eyes ablaze with such uncommon fury for her nature. "Stop it, all of you! Have you not had enough of fighting?"

"Nay. *That* is exactly what we are about to do, little girl." Helghi, his voice menacing, gestured at Wulfhere and himself. "Your father and I will fight it out and your fate will be decided."

"Don't, Father," Winflæd pleaded.

She went to him, put her arms around him.

"I'd sooner wed you to Edgar than this godforsaken *wyrmlicin*," Wulfhere said in a low voice, but not so low Wulfric could not hear.

His sister's head jerked up from where she had lain her head against Father's chest. "Then it shall be done."

"What?" exclaimed Tigfi.

Wulfric's heart was thumping. Had his ears heard right? His sister, agreeing to wed Eadnoth's brother Edgar. How could she agree to swap one bastard for the other? And Edgar was outlawed! And what's more, Father had admitted to having…What? Did he hear correctly again? Had Father really rescinded the sentence of outlawry? *Nay, nay! This cannot be happening.* He began to pace, shutting out the noise from his head with his hands.

When he could stand it no more, he released his ears and bellowed at both of them. "Winflæd, if you do this thing, you will no longer be my

their children to wed so that there would be peace between them. Lord Harold hated feuds. But Father had no intention of allowing a daughter of his to marry to a Helghison and went against the earl's wishes and promised her to his friend Leofnoth's son, Aemund. Freyda had kicked against this at first but eventually she preferred her prospects with Aemund, who, unlike Edgar, was a thegn's son, and not a mere ceorl.

A broken-hearted, enraged Edgar, kidnapped Freyda. During the rescue he killed Father's beloved right-hand man, Esegar. But eventually, Freyda was freed, and Edgar outlawed. A furious Helghi, sought out Earl Harold and the earl demanded that Wulfhere offer younger daughter Winflæd to Helghi's other son, Eadnoth, as recompense and so that the truce between them could be restored. Not that it had ever been a peaceful truce.

Father reluctantly gave an undertaking to carry this out, though in truth he was never going to submit to the order. And then, Wulfwin was slain during the fight against the Norse, his demise resembling an execution rather than a battle-death. Father accused Helghi of murdering him. There would never be peace now. Neither would Wulfhere willingly consent to a wedding between his daughter and the insufferable Eadnoth Helghison.

Or so Wulfric had thought.

And Father had let her go without a fight.

Helghi! Wulfric spat as the filth's name left his lips.

Father walked toward him from the gates and Wulfric blocked his way. "Why did you let her go?"

"Leave it, Son. I do not wish to quarrel with you… not now."

"The hell I will leave it!" Wulfric said, mirroring him as he tried to move out of his path. "Come on, Father. Tell me. Why did you let the murdering scum win?"

There was something so defeatist about Wulfhere at that moment. It angered Wulfric.

Rage built up inside him and he pushed Father.

"Don't," Father said.

Don't? "What's wrong with you? Are you turning coward? There was a time when you would have torn Helghi limb from limb rather than let him win this thing."

"I do not have to justify myself to you. Men do not always think of consequences when they do violence. A boy of sixteen-year-old thinks even less of them." He moved to pass, but again Wulfric refused to let him.

77

"I say you have lost your nerve." Wulfric spat. He thumped his father's chest with balled fists, causing him again to stagger backwards. "You *are* a coward. What kind of a man allows his daughter to be carried off by the murderer of his brother, his friend, *and* his son?" Wulfric's voice cracked with emotion. So many lost because of Helghi.

"Don't you think I want the same as you? I want revenge, I want to see Helghi dangling on the end of a rope. To see his eyes bulge and the stain of shit soiling his trousers as he cries for mercy!"

"Spare me the sermon, Father. I've heard it before, remember? In Kings Holme?"

As Wulfric turned to walk away, Father caught his arm. "It will come, Wulfric, I swear it."

"When?"

"That, I cannot say. But it will."

Supressing a sob, Wulfric said, "When Wulfwin and I were little, he used to comfort me when I was afraid of the dark. He used to say to me, 'Do not fear, brother, Father will protect us from the *nihtgenga.*' I wonder what he thinks of you now, to see the weakling you have become. He asks me every night, 'Where is my vengeance, Brother?' And every night I must tell him I do not know."

The muscles in Father's jaw rippled as he clenched them, then, before he knew anything more, Wulfric found himself flung to the ground. He lay winded, head thumping with pain as it hit the earth. Father crouched over him, hands around his throat. Wulfric tried to pull them away, but Wulfhere tightened his grip.

Looming over him, a grimace of rage on his face, Father growled "Do you think it was easy to let her go to that pig? Knowing he was the man responsible for killing my son. Knowing that because of him my brother died – that Esegar died – and there is nothing I can do about it. Do you think it has not torn my heart out? You know nothing of what I have just been through in my head. Fighting is easy! I could swat you like a fly – just like that, I could crush the life out of you, but–"

Father's hands tightened, his eyes blazing like a madman's. Wulfric desperately tried in vain to loosen the hold. He could not breathe; he was going to die.

"Coward, am I?" Father sneered. "It takes more courage to walk away than to fight – aye! It takes more courage than you will ever know, to see your daughter stolen from you and not be able to do anything about it."

Wulfric gasped for air. Father let go and rose to his feet, stepped over Wulfric's prone body, and limped away back toward the hall.

Wulfric leapt to his feet, coughing and spluttering. He ran after Wulfhere, undeterred, as though Father had not almost choked the life out of him.

"Father! You have fought many battles. You fought and won the *cheampa*. Men sang your praises in the warrior's hall – and now you speak words of cowardice, not courage."

Wulfhere halted, faced him and enclosed on him, their foreheads touching. "Do not even think to talk to me of the things you know nothing of. You will regret your words to me one day – by God, you will! Aye, you will learn in the fullness of time, if you get there."

Father walked on and Wulfric hurried alongside him. "You have lost your mind. We are warriors. *Wulfsuna* – a bloodline that stretches back through our family since the first sons of the wolf came to this land."

"Aye, we are warriors. But there are many kinds of battles to fight other than the ones you fight in the fields. As you go through life, you will find out what they are! Now, get out of my way, *lyttel mana!*"

Wulfric hurried after him. His brother's voice nagged him, wanting his vengeance. "Shut up!" Wulfric cried.

Inside the hall, he went to his mother. She was sobbing in Sigfrith's arms.

"Farewell, Mother." He bent and kissed her cheek.

"Where do you go, my son?" she asked as he collected his things. "Am I to lose all my children?"

"I go to Leofnoth. I'd rather eat pig *scite* for the rest of my life than stay here," Wulfric said.

Cynethryth hurried to him. "What about me?"

"You may come, if you wish," he said, joylessly. He went through the doors, carrying his spear and shield, his wife securing her cloak and hurrying to catch him up.

They rode at a slow pace, through the night, his young wife, in pillion behind him. It was freezing. Frost floated on the air around them like smoke.

"Cynethryth?"

Her non-response and gentle breathing suggested she slept. He clung to her hands that were folded about his waist so she did not slip. The road to his foster father's homestead stretched out ahead of him, grim like a black abyss. It was not dissimilar to the dark mass in his dream the other night.

As Wulfric gently nudged his mount forward, the ice he'd seen hovering in the atmosphere disappeared and looking around him he saw nothing but shadows, no moonlight, no frost. Just darkness.

"Wulfric…"

Wulfric gazes into the leaf-laden ravine. Beside him, his brother's ethereal presence stands. He turns sharply to stare at the phantom and shakes his head. "Nay, I don't want to go down there again. Don't want to see…"

"You must…"

The pale death shroud is there in the ravine, he sees it through the covering of dirt, twigs, and leaves. A limb extricates itself from the rotting fabric, its decaying flesh drips off yellowing bone. Slowly other parts of the putrid corpse appear as it begins to climb out of its cocoon in jerking movements.

"Go into the darkness…" Wulfwin commands. His voice is like a demon's, sibilant and snakelike.

Wulfric gazes around himself. The phantom Wulfwin has gone from his side without him seeing. He is there, down in the gully. "Come to me, Brother…"

Wulfric's heart is in his mouth as the corpse of his brother sits up, head turned to look at him. He has hollow eye sockets, and strips of leathery flesh peel and hang from his face. His mouth is stretched into a weird ominous grimace, exposing gumless teeth.

"You are not my brother! Go away!" says Wulfric, his hands over his eyes. He wants to run but feels rooted to the spot.

He peeks from between his fingers and sees the thing is on all fours crawling toward him. The once thick, vibrant red hair now clings to the skull in long hanks shedding as the undead figure clambers to stand. He covers his eyes again, hoping the thing will go away.

Suddenly, a bony hand grasps him round the throat. Fingers digging into his flesh like claws.

"Aghh!" His lids shut tight, blocking out the horror. "Why are you doing this to me?" Wulfric shouts as the skeletal hands tighten their grip.

"I told you to look at the hand!"

Wulfric reopens his eyes. The face of his brother is now that of the one he'd come to know more recently. The white veiny flesh of death had returned to the skull. The fibrous skin of moments ago gone. His brother's voice is no longer like a serpent's and he is shaking him and shouting, "Look at the hand!"

Cold, malodourous breath fans his face. His brother is so close to him, it is as if he is alive and not buried deep in a hole in Somerset. He recognises the familiar mix of woodsmoke, wool, leather, and body odour.

"What hand? Whose hand? What do you want me to look for?"

"Useless piece of scite! What kind of brother are you?"

"You are not my brother. He would not terrify me like this."

"Look at me! Am I not Wulfwin?"

"What do you want from me?" Again, Wulfric closes his eyes, willing himself to wake from this nightmare.

Then the voice of the spectre growls like one of the old gods of yore blowing up a storm. "Vengeance!"

The cry that rings out is subterranean. The strength of it blows the hair back from his brother's deathly pale face and rumbles through Wulfric's body. As his own mouth is forced open by the powerful gust of his brother's roar, he feels his soul sucked out of him, swallowed into the dark mass and thrust into another time, another place…

Wulfric crouches behind his shield. Men around him are being attacked and he knows he must protect Yrmenlaf. He lashes out with his spear, stabbing anyone that comes near them. He hopes to God that his brother is safe.

An arm grabs him around the neck and pulls him backwards, tugs at his helmet until it slips over his head. He is surprised, and there is nothing he can do but let it happen. He looks down and sees a glimpse of a hand holding the handle of a blade. It is the assailant's left hand. There is a blur of red, a blister or birthmark between the thumb and the forefinger. He wonders momentarily why he has never noticed it before. Cold steel rests against his throat.

He tries to call for his father and brother, but the only sound he can make is to howl like a wolf cub as the knife opens his throat.

The ground squelches beneath him. He slips down to lie in the gore of other men. There is a gurgling sound as he grabs his neck, and the blood gushes from the wound through his fingers.

He knows he is dying. His hands have no strength to stop the flow of scarlet and they flop beside him. Around him he hears sobbing and his sight wanes. He looks up hoping to see the sky and glimpses the face of *his brother, hovering above. "Wulfric..." He turns his head towards his brother's voice. Wulfwin is smiling.*

"I saw it, Wulf," Wulfric says. "I saw the hand."

Wulfwin is nodding and he has a look of happiness on his face as he gets smaller, diminishing into darkness.

Wulfric lies there waiting. There must be more.

Then he sees it. An image of that pockfaced son of a filthy swine; Eadnoth.

Wulfric is standing before him as he squares up to him in his father's courtyard as he had earlier that day. As Eadnoth crosses his arms over his chest, Wulfric sees clearly on the left hand, the blood-stained birthmark, like a blister, between Eadnoth's thumb and forefinger.

His brother's killer was Eadnoth.

Wulfric could not remember how he came to arrive at the home of Leofnoth, but when he awoke just before dawn, he found that they had slept in the barn. Looking around him, he did not recognise the place at first, but after some moments of searching for memory of what had gone before, he recalled the night ride up until the nightmare. As it all came back to him, his heart raced at recollections of the demonic brother and his incessant demands for vengeance. *Could you not just have told me who it was that had killed you? Did you have to put the fear of God into me?*

He bent over the girl lying next to him, deep in sleep. He shook her gently, but she did not stir. He lay back in the growing light and closed his eyes in the hope that he would return to the peaceful sleep he longed for and rarely got.

Then his brother spoke to him, as though it were his own thoughts.

"Oh Wulfric, Wulfric. You do not know what it is like to be in this state, between worlds. I could not tell you who, because I did not know. I had to make you see for me. It is you that has shown me who murdered me. And now you must do your duty, my brother. You must give me my vengeance."

"And it shall be done, brother of mine. It shall be done."

Some days later

Wulfric lay in wait as he had done every day for the last week. Much time had been spent learning of Eadnoth's daily movements. The murdering bastard regularly went hunting. After a few unsuccessful attempts to waylay his quarry, Wulfric realised he must have been in the wrong place, or in the right place, at the wrong time. It took him some further days of enquiring to find out the route that Eadnoth seemed to take the most and at what time.

As he crouched, hidden by dense foliage, anticipation pulsed through him. Something told him that today he would avenge Wulfwin. The same rush of blood that had sent exhilaration into his veins at his first battle, washed over him at the thought of killing.

He heard rustling and a tuneful whistling, accompanied by soft footsteps on grass. Moving aside the shrubbery, Wulfric flinched as his hand caught a prickle. Sucking the blood, he peered through the greenery and saw a pair of sturdy legs stride by, encased in grubby green hose and dirt-stained pale *winningas*. He caught a glimpse of a hunting bow beside the legs as they went on their way. Wulfric had no doubt it was Eadnoth.

Peeping out of the bushes, he saw the back of the murderer. Wulfric remembered Eadnoth had worn the same green hood and the same weld dyed tunic the week or so ago in Father's yard. It had to be him.

This was the opportunity he'd been waiting for. He would make it a slow death. He'd make the swine suffer. There would be no mercy for this *horningsunu*. Helghi was about to know the pain of losing a son, just as he and Father had lost Wulfwin.

Wulfric crawled out of the bushes and unravelled the rope he'd held in his vigil. Elation rose within him as he found the length needed and made a noose. Flexing it between his fingers, he hurried along the lane, blood rushing through his veins as he caught up with his target. His heart leapt as he flung the snare over the hooded head, before the poor sod could turn and see who it was that attacked him. Pulling the noose tight, he dragged his terrified victim to a suitable oak tree. Tossing the rope over a strong thick branch that would carry the weight, he thought of what he was doing and was filled with righteousness. It was justice he was serving, and everyone will look up to him for having the guts to act. Well if Father wasn't going to do it, then it fell to him, did it not? He tugged down so the kicking, spluttering Eadnoth rose upwards. When it felt secure, he flung it over the branch again and heaved on it.

Knowing that the life of his brother's nemesis was now in his hands gave him a thrill akin to ecstasy.

But despite the joy, he did not want to see the eyes bulge, the tongue protrude, nor the blackened lips. He suppressed the feeling to vomit and hung on to the twine, stood on the end of it, panting, gritting his teeth as the weight of the struggling Eadnoth threatened to bring the soon-to-be-corpse back down.

He could not say how long he'd stayed like that until he could not hold anymore, and the twitching body of his victim crashed to the ground. Wulfric collapsed and fought for breath, staring at the heap of dead humanity that no longer jerked with life. The deed was done.

Wulfric laughed. It had been easier than he'd thought. "I have avenged you, my brother."

Wulfwin did not answer. Odd, because he thought his brother would have been with him at that moment.

He crawled over to the carcass that only moments ago had been swinging from the tree. His heart pumped with the fear of what he would find. A strange thing to be worried about, for in battle he'd not concerned himself with the thought of slaughter or seeing the enemy with his blood spilled, guts sliced open, and pouring onto the ground.

Wulfric studied the area. He would need to move the body; somewhere where the undergrowth was thickest. He could not leave it there to be found. No one must know. Eadnoth must simply disappear, quickly before anyone came to see what he'd done. But the idea of touching the dead body made goose bumps rise on his flesh. Suddenly, he did not feel so good.

He stood over the corpse, glanced momentarily at the bloated face before swiftly looking away. Bile rose as he glanced at his handiwork, and he vomited to one side, heaving and heaving until his stomach emptied.

"Wulfric? Is that you? What is it you have there?"

Ælfstan? The rest of Wulfric's stomach sprang into his mouth as his father's blacksmith approached. He tried to speak as he swallowed down the hot acidic liquid, "I-I-"

"I came to find my nephew, we were going hunting, but he seems to have grown impatient of waiting for me."

Wulfric felt a stab of fear as Ælfstan came closer. "Yrmenlaf?" He spat the disgusting mucus from his mouth.

The blacksmith's face that had been looking at him curiously, paled as his eyes rested on the body in the grass. "Christ on the Cross!" Ælfstan's gaze went to the rope in Wulfric's hand. "What have you done?"

It was not me! I found him hanging. It was I who c-cut him down!"

Ælfstan buckled over beside the body of his nephew and held the youth to his chest. Tears streaming down his face.

Wulfric's hands went to his ears. "Nay...nay!" he cried. *What have you done?*

Wulfwin mocked him. He was laughing. *What vengeance is this? Stupid fool.*

Wulfric sank to his knees, his heart thudding, his head about to explode with grief. *What have I done?*

The world suddenly caved in on him. There would be no justice for his dead brother.

He had killed the wrong man.

The End

If you enjoyed Wulfric's story then you may want to read more about him and his dysfunctional eleventh century family in the *Sons of the Wolf* series.

- ❖ Book1 *Sons of the Wolf*
- ❖ Book 2 *The Wolf Banner*
- ❖ Book 3 *Wolf's Bane* is a WIP.

About Paula Lofting

Paula achieved a lifelong ambition to write a historical novel when she started on her first attempt, *Sons of the Wolf* which became the first of a series, a family saga about a bloodfeud between two men and the ripple affect it has on their offspring. It is set against the historical events of the period leading up to the Norman Conquest as also follows other historical characters that played their parts in the downfall of Anglo-Saxon England.

Paula Lofting was born in Middlesex, then immigrated to Australia in the 60's as a two-year-old where she grew up and went to school. She gleaned a love of history inherited from her father with whom she spent hours talking on hot summer's nights about the English heritage she'd left behind. Eventually the family moved back to England when she was 16 where she cultivated a love of history and historical fiction and vowed one day she would write the book she promised herself she would write. Subsequently life got in the way and it wasn't until long after three children and a life changing event which left her as a single mum, deciding a future for herself and her children took her to university to train to become a psychiatric nurse.

It was whilst she was studying her nurse training, she decided that she was inspired to write the historical novel which had been her dream. To enhance her research, she joined re-enactment society, Regia Anglorum, and has spent many a weekend running around in fields attacking her fellow reenactors with spears and has even fought and died at the Battle of Hastings re-enactment. Another aspect of her writing career is blogging about the period she writes in and being part of the facebook group, Historical Writers Forum, admin team.

She is still a psychiatric nurse which she loves and enjoys writing in her spare time when she can in her very busy life.

Paula can also be found blogging at 1066: The Road to Hastings and other stories at

www.paulaloftinghistoricalnovelist.wordpress.com
Twitter - https://twitter.com/Paulalofting
Facebook author page - https://www.facebook.com/Wulfsuna

SHADES OF AWAKENING

BY

STEPHANIE CHURCHILL

Slave Village
Croilton Castle, Honor of Cilgaron
Agrius

1

I smoothed the pale blue tunic over my stomach as I fiddled with the loose braid hanging down over my shoulder.

I was considered short by most, and petite. But I was strong from long hours of laboring in the village and at the castle. The blue tunic I wore had been given to one of the villagers by a ladies' maid at the castle many years ago when she had taken a new position. Charged with getting rid of the girl's possessions and deemed too shabby for use by anyone who worked for the Lady Helene, the tunic had found its way to the slave village. It had passed around until it ended up in my family. My pale-blonde hair, bright in the sun, seemed dull in the darkness of the shack I had just entered.

"I've come to tell you that I'll be leaving for Lyseby soon."

Heliarde stopped her needle and looked up at me, confusion plain on her face.

"What? You goin' to the market there? Long way fer the market."

I smiled and slid closer to her, leaning in to whisper. No one else was in the tiny little shack she shared with her father and two brothers.

But my confidence wasn't substantial enough. Louder words would only scare it away. A whisper would do. Louder words might make the dream disappear like smoke in the wind.

"No." I couldn't hide my eagerness. "Anscher nearly has enough money to free me."

Heliarde's eyes widened into moon orbs. "All that just to buy you fer 'imself?"

"Yes."

"What does a gardener need with a slave?"

I jostled her. "Not a slave, Heli, but a wife."

She tilted her head, still confused. She opened her mouth to say more but the rickety door slammed open. A man shoved himself through the door.

"You're to come with me."

We stood. Heliarde grabbed my arm.

"Why? What've we done?" she asked in a voice pitched high with fright.

They didn't reply but stepped aside to give us room to exit. "Now," he said. "The master's orders."

We looked at each other and followed.

Outside we found the muddy street lined with bewildered slaves.

"You diggers is comin' with me."

"But sir," I began, moving to catch up with him. "Sir," I said again, throwing off Heliarde's hand to reach the man. "I am not a digger. I work in the castle, clean the servants…"

"Don't care. You'll do just as well as these."

"For what? They'll miss me if I'm not back…"

He spun on me and slapped a heavy backhand across my face. My head snapped to the side, and I stumbled to the ground. Heliarde stooped beside me, helping me stand.

"We'd better go," she whispered.

I nodded. We followed him deeper into the valley behind Croilton Castle, home of Aksel, Lord Cilgaron, baron of the Honor of Cilgaron whose slaves we were.

Slavery had existed in the Kingdom of Agrius for centuries. Some said that the new queen urged her husband to rid Agrius of the egregious practice, but her husband took a more circumspect position, not wanting to topple the economy of his kingdom in one fell swoop, preferring instead to ease his people away from it. That a decision had not been made pleased Lord Cilgaron immensely, for it meant the Honor of

Cilgaron would not lose its biggest source of coin in the trade human flesh.

Once across the stream separating the village from the lands beyond, we began to arduous climb on the other side. The afternoon sun shone brightly in all its spring glory, highlighting the castle in the distance behind us, and the foothills leading to the mountains beyond. Once our bedraggled company of slaves reached the top, most of us were winded, leaning on one another for support as the lead man into a cave just beyond the lip of the broad ledge we'd reached.

"You lot," he said, pointing at us, "in there. All the way back." Tired feet shuffled, confusion making footsteps hesitant. "Back, I said!" He backhanded a man who wasn't moving fast enough. "That Vitus prick on the throne," he said before stopping to spit out of the side of his mouth, "may the gods despoil him, and his poxy whore of a Sajen wife, have declared you lot free. You're not slaves no more."

The deep cold of the cave made my arms shiver and goose flesh prick, but I felt a flush of hope and warmth wash over me at the news.

"Heliarde! Do you know what this means?" I grabbed at my friend's hand. "Anscher can save his money! As soon as I get back, I can tell him the good news. We can make our plans to be wed and be gone from here!"

"Not being slaves," the man continued, "means you sons of dogs gets paid a wage." Murmurs rose up, excited whispers replacing the questions. I squeezed Heliarde's hand more tightly. The man stared balefully back at us with his good eye, his other unseeing, white and viscous from ruin. A vivid scar ran from his cheekbone up through the useless eye, disappearing into his hairline. But his pernicious look didn't last long. As quickly as the sun peeks out from behind the storm clouds, a grin spread his lips. "But my master'd just as soon kill ya than pay ya." He bared yellow teeth in a sneer then stepped closer. "And we don't need diggers."

He hefted his cudgel, and chaos ensued.

Small and scrawny for my sixteen years, and being at the far back of the group of slaves, I thought we might have a chance. I grabbed Heliarde's hand and pushed around those on my left, ducking low to keep our heads out of sight.

But there were too few of us, and the men were thorough. It was a short-lived hope.

When it was clear we could not escape, I pulled Heliarde down next to me.

"Lie still. Maybe they'll think they got us already." I ground my teeth and squeezed shut my eyes, hoping to avoid what I knew could only inevitably come.

In a moment, I heard a cry just ahead of me, felt a body crumple to the ground. Against my better judgment, I opened my eyes. The man with the cudgel stood before me, his good eye wide with glee, his mouth slack with the abandon of the kill. He raised his cudgel.

I didn't know what it would be like to die. I'd seen my father die, but his death had been silent. It had come upon him in his sleep, a mercy since he had suffered the violent thrashings of a man in utter misery, his gut twisted inside him and wrung inside out from the wasting sickness that had poured through his body. His exhausted body succumbed. Death took him as he lay on his own bed.

What about Anscher? Our plans?

Lyseby awaited us. We needed to be together. How would he live without me?

Heliarde rolled to my side, grabbing me and hugging me close, with her face pressed against my own.

The man swung.

2

The warren of sheds, fences, gates, and doorways felt like an unnecessary maze to Mêlie; like the obstacles put in the way of the heroes from the old stories. Thickets of hedges grown in a specific pattern meant to trap the hero, keeping him from finding the one true thing he sought to save the world.

Only Mêlie didn't want to save the world. She simply wanted to empty the contents of the buckets into the pig troughs so she could head home to her bed.

It was late. Much later than she was used to, even as a slave. Lord Cilgaron's hall had been lively this night, bursting with music and dancing. Or so she'd heard. Slaves never saw such revelries, were only there to clean up after the lords and ladies finished with them. The guest this night was an important man from Prille, a man very high up in the king's graces, or so the hall servants said. Mêlie didn't much care. What happened in Prille had little effect on her. She reckoned it was only a few hours before she would start a new day's work with barely time to sleep before beginning again, and that was much more relevant to her.

She yawned and stumbled as she came to the last gate. Thinking merely to bump it open with her hip before going through, she was surprised when it wouldn't budge. Frowning, she set down the bucket in her right hand to find the latch. As she bent to retrieve the bucket once more, she sensed something behind her and spun around just as a hand reached out for her, settling on her shoulder to steady her.

"You should be more careful," said the face in the shadow. Mêlie took a step backward, trying to make out the voice.

"I'm nearly done."

The shadow moved closer. "It's a bit late, isn't it? Wouldn't be safe for you to make your way back down that hill outside. No, not such a little thing like you." He stepped nearer, and Melie stepped backward again, only to run into the gate behind her. The man stretched out his hand, snaking his arm around her waist. "Wouldn't be safe at all." He pressed nearer, his face near enough to her now that she recognized him.

Stapi, they called him. Slave girls were particularly vulnerable at the castle, but Melie usually managed to avoid the worst offenders. There was the usual, the leers and obscene suggestions, the over-long gazes as she went about her duties. Now and then a hand strayed, brushing against her hip or breast, and only once had one of them pushed her against a barrel and forced a kiss. But Stapi was different. His stares of late had turned meaningful, calculating.

She turned her head to the side, trying to see around him, but there was no one, the shadows to dark, too obscuring, too thick. They were alone, and no help was likely to come. Even if someone did pass by, she was a slave.

Fair game.

"Not so safe for you," he said, his lips curling back to reveal broken teeth. His breath smelled of rotten onions. Melie tried to wrench away, but the arm around her waist only drew closer as he laughed. His other hand traveled up her body, his hand cupping her breasts before moving to her cheek as he moved his lips near her ear. He drew a rough thumb over her lips. "I think it would be best if you came back with me. It's a cold night, and I'd keep you warm. I'll show you a thing or two…"

But before he could finish his thought, a shadow flit behind Stapi, something hard swung at his head. Stapi staggered forward, but Melie shoved him away, and he fell back into the mud.

"This one is mine," the attacker growled.

Stapi eyed the newcomer with a mixture of fear and irritation but said nothing. Instead, he lifted a hand to the side of his head before nodding, rising to his feet, and staggering away.

The shadow that was the newcomer did not move, and Mêlie eyed it as a new threat. She cast her gaze to one side and the other, looking around it for a way to escape. But before she could devise a plan, a hand reached out, taking her wrist. She tried to pull it away, but the grip was too strong. The shadow became a face. Another one she recognized.

"It's okay. You don't have to fear me. It's Mêlie, isn't it?"

There was no sense in struggling, so Mêlie stopped. "Yes." Her eyes focused on his face, and she saw no evidence of evil in the eyes that met hers, steady and calm, like a gentle summer breeze.

"Stapi is a fool," he growled. "Here, let me help you with these." He let go of her hand, and she watched as he picked up the buckets and straightened. "Where do these go?"

Mêlie pointed to the troughs on the other side of the next fence. And then, as if they weighed nothing more than a bucket of goosefeathers, he lifted them, dumping their contents where she'd directed.

"I'm Anscher," he said when he had finished. "And I'm sorry that lout bothered you. I've set him straight, and he won't do it again." Anscher threw a look over his shoulder as if he could see Stapi in the darkness. He flashed a grin. "In fact, no one will. I've said you are mine, and no one is likely to cross me." Mêlie felt a niggle of discomfort at the arrangement, wondering how he expected her to pay him for his protection.

"Thank you," she said, trying and failing to keep her voice from faltering. She swallowed hard and his eyes softened. "I should get home. Morning comes early."

Anscher threw a look up at the sky, as if the darkness could tell time. "You should, and it does. Let me walk you home."

"Why?"

"Because it's late, and even though Stapi will get word out regarding you, I don't trust that word to have traveled very far yet."

"Oh," she said, not sure what to think.

The pair found the path leading away from the castle, down the winding hill toward her village.

"You haven't worked here long," Anscher said after they'd gone some distance.

"No, I've only had duties in the village before. But I'm older, and help was needed here." When she realized she'd said more than she'd intended, her jaw snapped shut.

Anscher didn't seem to mind she'd stopped short and kept walking companionably beside her. When they reached her shack, he paused. She thought he might demand payment, but he merely grinned, touched his imaginary cap, and disappeared into the night.

She smiled.

As he walked away, the full moon broke out from behind the heavy clouds, and a silvery light washed over Anscher's retreating figure.

She knew then that she would wed him.

3

If this was death, it was not at all what I expected. Death felt, sounded, and smelled like life.

I inhaled a gasping breath as I opened my eyes.

Darkness, like heavy woolen blanket, met my gaze, and I wondered for a moment if I had been blinded. How long had I been here? How long ago had the men brought us here, had they corralled us like sheep to the slaughter? I reached up to feel my head, my fingers testing the place the cudgel hit me, and found crusted, dried blood against cold skin.

I pressed my hands into the scree of the cave floor and pushed myself up to sitting. After a long moment, vague shapes came into view, piled about me in a grisly display. Bodies lying where they had fallen. I squeezed my eyes shut and opened them once more, then glanced to my side to find Heliarde crumpled beside me. Heliarde. The closest to a friend I'd ever had before Anscher. I bit back a sob.

I pushed myself to standing, focusing my attention on the cave's mouth which showed a brighter darkness than the cave's interior. I picked my way across the cave's floor, keeping my gaze focused on the entrance so I wouldn't have to see the carnage around me.

I'd as soon kill ya than pay ya.

I heard the weasel-faced man's scratchy voice in my head as I peeked out of the cave, finding the area deserted, the land dark under cover of night. Had my mother worried when I didn't come home, or was she too ill to have noticed? And what about Anscher? Had he grown concerned when I'd not come to meet him as was our usual way? I flew down the side of the mountain as quickly as I dared, the voice of the weasel-faced man chasing me in my mind. His words, the screams of of the dying... Was I going mad?

I fought back the voices and the terror. I didn't want to hear it.

I wanted to live.

Once home, I crept to my mother's pallet, finding her soundly asleep. I brushed the hair away from her face and kissed her before finding my own straw-stuff mattress in the corner, then fell into the sleep of one dead.

The cry of an infant woke me from my sleep. Bright morning light filtered into the single room of our fragile shack. Hadn't I just closed my eyes? It was late, and regardless of what had happened to me in the caves the night before, my tardiness would not be tolerated if noticed. I grabbed my shoes and made for the door, only to pause and turn back. My mother still slept. I bent and kissed her once more before leaving her, secure in the knowledge that the older women of the village would come later to care for her as they had done all this time.

Other than the older women who were too old for hard labor but watched the youngest children of the slave village, few were about. No one made eye contact with me as I passed, and the part of the village where the diggers had lived was empty. No smoke billowed from the eaves, for there was no one left alive to inhabit them. I continued on, climbing the road up the hill toward the castle which passed by the village burial ground. A sensation rippled through me, pulling me toward the sorry ground. I imagined the crumpled bodies littering the cave floor. Would anyone retrieve them and commit them to their final resting place? The rippling sensation grew stronger, but I ignored it and pressed on, nearly running to reach the castle to see if I could lessen the damage my lateness might cause.

And yet... I was no longer a slave. The Vitus king and queen had declared us free.

Though it seemed Lord Cilgaron did not approve, had chosen to kill us off rather than pay us. I screwed up my face into a scowl then forced myself to slow down, not wanting to draw attention to myself. I looked around, but no one paid me any mind. I wasn't a digger, I reminded myself. The man had only come for the diggers. They were the most expendable labor. I thought of poor Heliarde lying cold on the cave floor and pressed on toward the servants' quarters in the east range, under the administrative rooms on the other side of the court beyond the hall. Once in the lower level, where the kitchen and other serving staff had rooms, I paused at the mouth of the corridor to make sure no one was about.

I might be a freed slave, but I was certain my legal status had not changed anyone's attitudes toward me. I would still keep myself from speaking to others, from working closely with others, from being seen at all if I could help it.

The corridor stood empty. I slipped into the first sleeping room to find the chamber pot.

Empty.

As were the pots in the other lodgings.

I had been too late. Someone else had done my work.

A knot of anxiety twisted in my stomach.

I heard footsteps and turned to find a young woman enter, carrying a bundle of fresh sheets for the beds. She didn't glance my way, and I pressed myself against the wall.

"M-my apologies for being late," I stammered.

She seemed not to hear me. Most likely didn't care. She was trained to ignore others as I had been.

I had seen this girl before. She worked in the kitchen as a free woman, not a slave.

She busied herself removing the dirtied sheets and piling them into a basket by the door. Finished with that task, she put fresh ones on the beds. I watched her, uncertain what I should do, not comfortable saying anything more to her.

Taking up the basket of soiled sheets, I hurried away, heading for the laundry yard behind the east range. Women tended their work with little regard for the comings and goings of others. I set down my burden and left.

Tomorrow, I decided, I would arrive early.

4

"I should get back. My mother can only watch Fleurie for a short time, and Zenai can't come today."

"She is getting worse then?"

Mêlie nodded, biting back the bitterness she felt. "She worsens each day. Sleeps more and more. It's been a month since Fleurie was born, and we thought mother's sickness would improve in that time. But it hasn't."

"There are others that watch her sometimes? What of the other women, the ones who sit and watch the other children?"

"I'm not there to find another, am I?" She pursed her lips before flashing a quick smile. Her mood wasn't one to harbor levity, so she sobered as the weight of her situation weighed on her. She turned to go, but Anscher stopped her with a hand on her shoulder, spinning her back around to face him.

He drew her closer, stealing a kiss. "You could go, yes. Or," he said, his sly grin lifting one side of his lips, giving him a rakish look, "you could stay here and dally with me." He nodded with his chin toward a grove of trees at the base of the hill then leaned in to nuzzle her neck. "When no one comes to care for Fleurie, someone else is bound to step in." He kissed her ear, and Melie felt her resolve weaken. "How often does Lord Cilgaron go away like this, and the slave masters give you the day off? You can't use what you've been given to work over-hard. What would be the point of a day off?"

Mêlie giggled, doing her best to squirm out of his grasp, but his arms were too hardened from wielding a hoe and hefting bales. He held her fast. But the truth of the matter was that she did not want to go. She did want to dally with him in the trees, enjoying the soft, grass beneath her as Anscher showed the fullness of his affection.

She reached up and cupped his face in her hands, studying his eyes. Anscher, her protector, the one who had saved her from abuse at the hands of Stapi that night which seemed like another time.

Mêlie hadn't seen him right away after he'd walked her home that first night. She'd hoped he would meet her by the pigs again the next night. Disappointed when he didn't, she'd kept an eye out for him as she went about her chores. Sometimes she'd spy him working in the fields or near the fish ponds. It was by happenstance one day that they'd crossed paths, and as they passed, he smiled. She smiled back and blushed. He went on his way, but the next night— there he was, waiting for her by the pigs. He hadn't spoken, had simply taken the buckets from her, hefting them over the fence to pour the contents into the troughs. And not long after that, he started to come every evening. Though they'd never spoken the words aloud, it became a secret assignation between them, giving her something to look forward to throughout her day's labor.

Not long after that, Mêlie began to dream of a future between them. But Anscher was not a slave; he was a freeman who worked for pay.

What hope was there for them? The thought worried her enough, that one night she found the courage to ask him about it.

"I will buy you, Mêlie. I will buy your freedom, then we can be married."

Mêlie tilted her head, and in an unusual show of uncertainty, he dropped his gaze. "If you would have me, that is."

He need not wait for her reply. She kissed him in answer.

Now as they stood in the light of a sunny afternoon, any draw to her responsibilities wrestled with her desire to be with Anscher.

He waited for her reply, his eyes pleading. "You know you want to stay."

Of course she wanted to stay. She never wanted to leave him, and he knew it. But her mother needed her. Fleurie, her baby sister, needed her.

"When we are married, you will see more of me," she argued.

"Oh-hoh, indeed I will!" He waggled his eyebrows, and Mêlie felt a wash of color and heat rise in her cheeks.

"I meant you'll see me more often. Anscher, I really should get back home."

"Or else..."

"Or else, what?"

"That's what I'm asking you. What would happen if you didn't go? Wouldn't someone else step in to help? Surely there are other women around."

"Yes, possibly."

"Your father sleeps, doesn't he? And Fleurie is but a babe in arms. She can't go anywhere. Even if your mother drifted off to sleep, she could cause no trouble."

Mêlie could not hide her doubt or confusion.

"I need to get home. My mother needs me," she said resolutely.

"But if you stay, and we dally, and you go home late telling your mother you had been detained at the castle... who would know?"

"Who will know?" Mêlie echoed, her resolve fading.

He leaned in and nuzzled her neck again. "Yes, who?"

"My father would know." He leaned back, wide-eyed. Mêlie twitched her lips at his reaction. He looked around as if looking for her father. She laughed and swatted him on the arm.

"How would he know?" he asked again.

"He would know when his daughter came home in a good mood."

He sobered then, even while he twirled a strand of her hair in his fingers. "I will find a way to get your freedom, Mêlie, and we will get away from here."

Mêlie took in the beauty around them, the green of the fields and forests beyond, the purple tinge of the mountains at the edge of the world. Where could they go? Croilton was all she knew.

"We can live near Lyseby," he said, as if hearing her thoughts. "I can find work there."

"Croilton is all either of us knows. What would you do?"

"I'm not sure, but there is bound to be a place for someone willing to work." He shrugged. "If nothing else I could find work aboard ship..."

"No, not that!" she said, suddenly concerned. "Anything but that. You cannot go off on a ship, leaving me with our children." He eyed her at her recommendation of children but did not interrupt. "And what if you never returned? No, there is other work you could do, I am certain of it."

"Then it's settled. We will improve our stations then."

The idea sounded fanciful, probably overly hopeful. But hope was a powerful thing when hope was all you had.

When they'd wasted the afternoon, they turned together to head back to the village. The sun had begun its lazy descent in the west, and many other workers headed in from the fields for their supper.

As they passed the slave burial ground, Anscher stiffened. Mêlie lay her hand on his arm to comfort him. His mother had only just been laid to rest there, and he still felt the sting of it.

"It's the destination of us all," his father had said in despondency after they'd filled in the hole where they'd lowered her body.

And while it may have been true, Anscher and Mêlie had dreams to use what life they had in the time they had left.

"Come, Anscher. That is the past. Our future is ahead."

5

I dipped my hands into the bucket, breaking through a layer of ice on top, splashing frigid water onto my face. The towel was difficult to grab with trembling hands, but I finished my morning ablutions and considered the thin shawl hung on the peg near the door. It would be little protection for me against the cold, and my mother would be slightly warmer for it. I spread it over her thin frame as she lay sleeping then pressed a kiss to her forehead before making my way out into the thin light of early morning.

My feet turned from habit onto the familiar path that wound its way from our village, up the long hill toward the castle, joining the other villagers who did the same. No one spoke, each of us keeping our chins lowered in sullen resignation to a day's hard work. Soon we passed the slave burial ground, and the same sensation I experienced yesterday rippled through me. I shuddered and edged my way to the farthest side of the path, around the villagers and hurried to get past the graves as quickly as I could.

At the top of the path, we reached the garden plots, encountering herdsmen leading their animals to pasture, workers carting implements to begin their work of preparing the soil for planting which was weeks away, and others toting wood, feeding animals, hauling provisions and other essentials to the kitchens from the fields beyond the castle. As I reached the gate into the outer bailey, a man pushing a water wagon approached behind me. Those of us entering moved to allow him access with his wide burden before continuing on.

Once inside the inner bailey, I navigated to the east range, checking to be sure my path across the court was empty. I flew down the stairs and into the accommodations of the kitchen staff who were already away preparing the day's meals. It was with an odd sense of relief that I found the chamber pots full of their night soil. With efficient swiftness, I emptied then cleaned the pots, then returned to tend the linens and sweeping. I did my work undisturbed, and when I finished, I took my usual place in the kitchens, in the dark corner behind the butts of lard where I squatted, waiting for more orders to come.

But the day wore on, and none came.

"Marjory, take this to the lord's steward," the cook called.

The young woman I had seen the day before completing the duties in the accommodation block that were my own rushed in from another room and took the tray and pitcher on offer.

"There's no ghosts there, is there?" she asked?

The cook swatted the back of her head. "Be off with you, and none of that nonsense!"

"What a strange thing to say," the cook said when she'd gone. I settled back in my place as they muttered about Marjory's oddities and went back to work. The sun arced across the sky, and when the time came for supper to be prepared and served, I still waited.

Once the supper had been laid and the kitchens cleaned, and no work had been given me, I rose from my place and left by the side door and into the yard beyond. Even my regular duty of taking the kitchen slops to the piggery had been given to another.

I walked in a daze, lost in thought as I considered the odd direction my day had taken. Work rarely varied, but there were times — particularly when the lord was not in residence — that meals were unusually light, requiring little extra help. But even in those times I was required fetch water or scrub pots.

I skirted the back of the smoke house, along its low stone wall, taking in the fading light of day, and happened to glance down at the fish ponds beyond. A tall, broad shouldered figure with hair the color of clay stood on the far side.

"Anscher!" I called.

He was speaking with three men, too busy to hear me. I had to go down there, had to apologize for not meeting him near the pigs. I hurried through the upper bailey, through the gate, dancing past the workers who were completing the last of their day's work. I flew down the path which led to the fish ponds, threading my way along the gardens, coming to the place I had seen Anscher. But he wasn't there.

"Anscher!" I called. But then I spied a familiar face on the path near the gate leading back into the castle.

"Make way!" A man carrying heavy bales lumbered down the path, and I moved out of his way along with others who were behind me.

When I turned back around to find Anscher, he was gone.

That night I dreamed of a city I had never seen. Situated on the shore of a vast body of water, I saw its buildings in detail; the markets and shops, its houses and central square. The harbor protected enormous ships from the crashing waves of the ocean beyond. Markets which used to trade in human flesh, bartering their lives for money, stood empty. The shackles and poles, the fences and locks of confinement, gone. But life still existed. The streets teemed with activity, even through the night. Taverns spilled light into the streets, carousers stumbling drunkenly amongst thieves and beggars.

Though I had never been there before, I knew this to be Lyseby, the heart of commerce in the Honor of Cilgaron. And this would be my new home, once Anscher and I could be wed.

100

6

"Mêlie, get up."

The voice came as an irritant at first, like the buzzing of a bug in her ear. When it continued, Mêlie, roused, cracking open her eyes to darkness. She rubbed her eyes, wondering why her father had awakened her after keeping her awake for much of it with his incessant cough. It felt on moments ago she'd fallen asleep, and she wanted to go back to her dreams of Anscher.

She mumbled and rolled over, but her father shook her shoulder. "Mêlie, now, or we will be late."

She rolled over and tried to peer at him in the darkness, but she couldn't make out his features. Only the barest outline showed in the brooding, inky night. "Why?"

"You must help me with my work." He bent into a coughing fit. "I cannot do it alone. And without the work done, the masters will cause trouble. It will not go well for you and your mother."

He coughed into his sleeve again. These fits had worsened these last weeks. The village healer called it an ague, but Mêlie and her mother knew better. The illness had been spreading through their village, and very few had survived it.

She sighed, wishing once more that Guérôme was still here.

Guérôme. Her older brother. Dead last winter from falling down the mine shaft. Mêlie was the oldest child now, and when her father was gone, it would be up to her to complete all the work allotted to her family so they could keep their shack and have food to eat. After Guérôme's death, she had been given more work to make up for his loss in the mine. She had her work in the village, but had also been given the task of helping in the kitchens of the castle in the afternoons. And now that her mother was ill, she had to care for baby Fleurie too.

Her father coughed again, and Mêlie pushed away her thin blanket, sat up, and rubbed her eyes. The fullness of night brought the fullness of dark, and she couldn't see. But it didn't matter since her shoes were just beside her bed, and there was nothing else necessary to do before they left. There was no food for her, so no need to prepare it. Her father handed her a cup, warm from the thin tea filling it. She luxuriated in the warmth of it on her fingers then finished it, handing him back the cup.

"Now come. We must hurry."

Mêlie followed him into the dark street where they offered silent nods to others who worked night hours.

Haralt Tosher, Mêlie's father, was a night soil man. Every night he visited the places around the castle and the castle grounds where human waste collected during the day, cleaning it out and hauling it to the cesspit. Mêlie set to work alongside her father, taking up the shovel while her father instructed her. After many hours of heavy work, digging and carrying, carting and unloading, Mêlie's arms and shoulders screamed.

Haralt's coughing increased as the night wore on, growing deeper, as if the work made it worse. Mêlie wondered if it happened every night, but he would never speak of it.

"We must work," he'd say. "No time for talk. Talk uses energy we need to work. And besides," he added, "if they look down from their high towers and see us talking, they punish us."

Being seen was not an option for slaves, and being heard unimaginable.

They finished their work outside the castle then made their way to the gateway into the inner courts. "Careful now, Mêlie. You must do exactly as I do. Once inside the courts, it will be a little harder, but there shouldn't be many about. Only other slaves. You mustn't talk to them or even acknowledge them. They have work to do as we do. It's when we must enter the Isle Court, the lord's private court, that you must be wary. If we are seen…"

He didn't finish his thought. He didn't need to. To be seen by the lord or a member of his household would bring severe punishment, even death.

They passed into the castle grounds, entering the area behind the inner court where Lord Cilgaron, his mistress Roswen, and his daughter, Helene, resided.

Mêlie had seen the Lady Helene a few times. Once when she was very young. And more recently now that she was older. The Lady Helene was old enough to be married, and very beautiful. Mêlie often saw her out riding with only her maid and a single guard to attend her. Her dark hair poked out from under a veil, her round cheeks flushed from the fresh air. Mêlie knew that she was not beautiful like Helene, but Anscher found something appealing in her, despite her thin frame.

Mêlie followed her father through the gateway into the Isle Court on the west side of the hall. The grand staircase leading up and into the lord's residential wing loomed dark and mawing just ahead, like the mouth of a great beast.

They had just begun to edge past it when the heard sound of foot-steps. Someone walking with an unsteady tread descended from the up-per part of the grand stairs. Haralt pressed Mêlie's shoulder, moving them back into the darker recesses of an alcove just before the stairs.

The footsteps grew louder, and soon a figure emerged in the dark-ness. It was a man, dressed as a courtier, and too drunk to notice the figures huddled in the dark. He passed by them then stopped to spew the contents of his stomach onto the ground. He straightened and con-tinued on his way toward the hall. Haralt touched Mêlie's shoulder, and they continued on to the kitchens where they worked to empty the vast grease pots.

The sky had turned a watery pale blue in the east by the time they finished their work. Haralt could now go home and sleep, but Mêlie would have to turn her attention to her regular duties. If she had to help her father again the next night, she wasn't sure how long she could last.

She had her answer soon, for it was only two weeks later that the grueling pace of work ended. Haralt Tosher, night soil man at Croilton Castle, lay dead on his bed, the illness that has plagued him finally claiming him.

Jacotte Tosher and Fleurie Tosher were now left in the care of Mê-lie. But even that task would not be hers for much longer. Fleurie had taken ill with the same fever as her father and soon followed her father to his grave.

7

I pondered my sighting of Anscher near the fish pond as I drifted off to sleep that night, dreaming once more of Lyseby, soaring over the city, it's empty markets and dark alleyways. The next morning I awoke, dis-concerted and wondering where I was. My mother slept on her pallet, anchoring me to the moment, to the village of former slaves and the terror of the night in the cave. She rested, as she usually did, undis-turbed by my rising. It was with reluctance I left her to attend my duties at the castle.

It was as I made my way through the outer bailey that I saw him again.

Anscher.

I left the path and ran toward him. He did not see me coming, did not stop his work, and did not acknowledge my approach.

"Anscher!" I cried as I neared him. "Did you hear? We are slaves no more! We are free!"

Still he continued to work and did not look at me.

I came to a stop before him. "Anscher, we can leave, we can go to Lyseby now and be married. Isn't that good news?"

He straightened from his work with the hoe and looked at me, but his face held no warmth, no expression at all. I could have been a tree or any other inanimate object for all his reaction expressed. If anything, he looked sad.

"Anscher? All the money you've saved, you don't need to use it to buy my freedom." My smile dropped. A knot twisted in my stomach. "Anscher?"

He inhaled a great breath and bent back to his work, his movements heavy, sluggish as if he worked in a great bog.

"Anscher, have I done something to upset you?"

He began to hum, and I reached out a hand, laying it on his arm. It felt cold, and I recoiled, pulling back my hand as if I'd been stung by a bee.

Tears flooded my eyes. I turned and ran, not stopping until I reached the back of the smoking shed where I stopped and collapsed to the ground, sobbing. I could not explain Anscher's strange reaction. We had not spoken since before the slaves were freed, but our last leave-taking had been pleasant. I could not recall anything I had said or done that would have changed his opinion of me. Yes, in the past, when we had argued or some silly thing, he would descend into brooding silence toward me, acting as if I was not there. But after a time, he would forget our argument, and all would be right between us again. Could I have upset him without realizing it? Perhaps he needed time, and then I could ask him what it was I had done.

Another thought occurred to me. Could my freedom have anything to do with it? Just because he had always told me he was saving his wages to buy my freedom didn't mean he was really doing it. Perhaps he had been lying all along? Perhaps he wanted nothing more from me than to steal my kisses and offer me false promises, had never had any intention to buy my freedom. Or to wed me.

I sank into a deeper despondency, but realized I could not stay here. My duties would not tend themselves, and I could not neglect them as I had done earlier. If Anscher was faithless, I could not risk my position at Croilton, as meager and mean as they were. It was all I had.

I retrieved my bucket from the supply lean-to and began my duties. It was as I reached the long corridor in the darkness of the lower servants' quarters, that I saw a figure coming toward me in the gloom. I stopped and set down my bucket, pushing myself against the wall. Peering up through my eyelids, I saw Marjory. She paused, glancing down at my bucket on the floor, giving it an odd look, before hurrying along. Neither of us spoke, and as a matter of habit, I kept my chin down until she was gone.

I rushed into the first chamber and found the pots empty. The last room where the men slept had yet to be cleaned, so I proceeded to finish the work before Marjory could return. Back in the kitchens, I found my corner and waited.

"…strange things since the slaughter, I tell you. The stable boys reported it, and so did the guards on the curtain wall."

"You can grant them that, though, surely? The guards were likely deep in their cups."

Their chatter rolled off me at first. I huddled in my corner, miserable over Anscher's treatment of me. I had to find a way to get him to speak to me but knew there was nothing I could do until later. Would he come see me, as was our habit, when I took the pigs their slops?

"What would the gain from such tales though?"

The one called Hauise laughed. "Always trying to one up the rest, you know."

"But Marjory says she's seen something too."

"The new girl? She was on about ghosts yesterday."

"She'd only heard stories. But she says she's seen something herself. She says some of her work was done already when she went to do it."

"Well, that explains it, don't it? She don't know what she's about." They laughed. "She's young. She don't know no other way to do it and makes excuses."

"Could be. But I swear its ghosts, Hauise."

Hauise put down the pot she was carrying and pressed her hands into her hips. "Ghosts. At Croilton Castle?" She laughed. "It's as good a story as I ever heard, I tell you. But I'd not thought you to be the one telling them."

Agathe hurumphed and blew air from her cheeks. "I tell you, them slaves that was killed are angry. They're getting their revenge on us for it."

"And King Casmir's me husband," Hauise scowled. "Get on with ya. That's just tales." She set down a flagon and hollered, "for the larder!" over her shoulder. I leapt up and grabbed the vessel, taking it away before anyone else could do it as the cooks continued to bicker.

Ghosts in Croilton Castle. I thought of the feelings I'd felt near the burial site and shuddered, wondering if the notion wasn't too far wrong. Could that be what I had sensed when I walked the road to the castle? The idea of loose spirits wandering the castle grounds was almost too much for me to fathom.

8

It seemed an odd thing, feeling relief after burying a loved one. But it was all Mêlie felt after the rigor and hardship of the past month. She slumped down on the damp grass, holding the memory of her infant sister in her weary heart. Her mother stood at her side, head down. Neither of them spoke as a dreary drizzle fell from gray clouds, soaking them.

They had received a dispensation by the master to leave their work early so they could bury little Fleurie. At first, Mêlie wasn't sure if her mother would be able to come, as weak as she was. But just when their neighbor Turchil had come by, telling them the little grave was dug and ready for them, Jacotte stood on unsteady legs and came along, joining her only remaining child to bury her youngest.

When the deed was done, and the assembly had gone back to the village, Jacotte moved away as Anscher approached and took Mêlie's hand. "Come away, Mêlie. There is nothing for you here now."

She heard his words but did not move. Unshed tears broke free of her lashes, spilling down her cheeks. Anscher took her in his arms.

"She never had the chance to live life," she sobbed.

Anscher stroked her hair. "But we have ours."

"But I am a slave, Anscher. That is no life."

He gentled her away from him, holding her at arm's length to look into her eyes. "Soon, Mêlie. Soon I will have enough for us."

"I don't need you to have enough for us. I only need to be together."

He slanted her a look then turned her, taking her arm, to walk back to the village. "You say that now, but how much after we get your freedom and our new lives and nothing to live on? I can't take up a trade with no money, Mêlie. We must live somewhere, we must eat. And if we will care for your mother too—"

"I know, but…"

"Trust me," he said, pausing and turning toward her, taking her hands in his own, "the time will come soon enough."

Mêlie nodded. The drizzle had stopped, and along the horizon, the sun poked out from behind the clouds. The sight made her feel better, and having Anscher near her made everything feel somehow hopeful. He was right.

"How are you doing it, Anscher? You are just a gardener. You can hardly make enough of a wage to save enough to buy a slave."

Mêlie knew that Anscher had friends. Old men who knew the life he wanted and showed kindness by giving him extra work to do, and extra coin from time to time if they could spare it. Sometimes they took pity on him and let him win at dice. But how was that enough? Anscher had never given her a good answer.

"Trust me." He squeezed her hand. "I promise you it will be soon."

His voice held an edge, something sly, something cunning. "What do you have planned?"

He gave her a mysterious wink but would not answer. "I must leave now, Mêlie."

"What, so soon? I had hoped you would stay."

"I have to meet some people." Mêlie gave him an inquiring look and he relented. "They say there is a place over the foothills before the point. A shack where men go to play games of chance, and those who are good can win a lot of money. It's more than the masters allow at the castle."

"Anscher, you don't need to do this."

He lifted his hand and brushed away a loose strand of hair from her face.

"Yes, I do. The life of a slave is no life for you. The sooner I can get you away from it the better."

Mêlie furrowed her brow. "Can you trust these men?"

"What is there to trust? They play games. They bet money."

"And with that combination, there is much that can go wrong. Anscher, please…"

He leaned over and kissed her, silencing any argument.

"Hush, Mêlie. All will be well. I will do this thing, and then we will have a life together."

*****

"I've come to tell you that I'll be leaving for Lyseby soon."

Heliarde stopped her needle and looked up at Mêlie, confusion plain on her face.

"What? You goin' to the market?"

Mêlie smiled and slid closer to her, leaning in to whisper. No one else was in the tiny little shack Heliarde shared with her father and two brothers. But Mêlie's confidence wasn't substantial enough. Louder words would only scare it away. A whisper would do. Louder words might make the dream disappear like smoke in the wind.

"No." Mêlie smiled more broadly. "Anscher. He nearly has enough money to free me."

Heliarde's eyes widened into moon orbs. "All that just to buy you fer 'imself?"

"Yes."

"What does a gardener need with a slave?"

Mêlie jostled her. "Not a slave, Heli, but a wife."

She tilted her head, still confused. She opened her mouth to say more when the rickety door slammed open, and a man shoved himself through the door.

"You're to come with me."

They stood. Heliarde grabbed Mêlie's arm. "Why? What've we done?" she asked in a voice pitched high with fright.

He didn't reply but stepped aside to give them room to exit. "Now," he said. "The master's orders."

Outside the street was lined with others who stood in bewilderment.

"You diggers is comin' with me."

"But sir," Mêlie began, moving to catch up with him. "I am not a digger. I work in the castle, clean the servants'…"

"Don't care. You'll do just as well as these."

"For what? They'll miss me if I'm not back…"

He spun on her and slapped her, knocking her to the ground. Heliarde stooped and helped her stand.

"We'd better go," she whispered.

9

Heliarde. We were only mites when we'd met, both ill with something. The healer's wife told our mothers she would keep us until we were better because we were too young and our mothers needed to work. We'd played as often as we could after that, but those opportunities be-

108

came more and more rare with each passing year. Children old enough to carry were put to carrying, and there was no more time to play.

I thought of the cooks and their conversation about ghosts as I took up the buckets for the pigs. Was it Heliarde I sensed as I passed the burial ground? I had no idea how people became ghosts. Had her spirit left her body the moment she was killed, or was she not a ghost until her body was found? Maybe she was a ghost *until* her body was found. I shuddered again, wishing I had never overheard the women and their gossip. The bodies in the cave above the village likely still lay where they had fallen. Perhaps, if I was brave enough, I would venture back again, could find Heliarde's body, and give her a proper burial. Maybe then the odd sensations I felt passing the burial ground would subside.

I paused as I took my usual circuit behind the smoke house, hating to pass around the front as it skirted so close to the smithy on the other side, where men stood waiting for work done. In the time I had been Anscher's woman, I hadn't had to deal with the stray hands and lewd comments from anyone. Even so, I was still careful.

The evening's light was fading into the west, and I glanced down at the garden plots below, to the place I had seen Anscher yesterday, and was startled to see a group of men hauling something from the water of the fish pond. My steps halted, and I froze in place, watching with dreadful fascination. The men lay the body on the ground. It lay inert, and the men who had done the deed stood around in conversation. No one seemed urgent about the task, as if the man was dead.

A heavy lump descended into my stomach as I watched them bring a cart, lifting the dripping body into it.

His clothing looked familiar.

Anscher? Could it be?

Forcing my feet to move, I wound my way around the smoke house and into the yard behind the pigs. From the far side of the building, I heard the meaty thud of a stick hitting flesh. Someone was receiving a beating, and I shivered, not wanting to round the corner and see it.

But I continued on. I needed to meet Anscher. An image of the body pulled from the water invaded my mind's eye. I shoved it aside. It was so dark that it could have been anyone. Anscher was waiting for me in the usual place. I knew he was.

I rounded the corner and pushed my way through the first gate. Another group of men filled the yard beyond. Wrists tied and arms stretched over his head, a young man stood shirtless in the center, his back running red with blood. Another man stood behind him, bringing his arm back for another strike with the wooden rod. It connected with the young man's back once more, and he let out a cry of pain. I dumped the slops into the trough, dropped my chin, and hurried away past the pig yard without even thinking to wait for Anscher. I rounded the corner and came upon three men who sat with their hands tied, leaning their backs against the wall. I recognized them as the ones Anscher was talking to the other day.

They appeared angry with each other, but I couldn't hear what they argued about until I drew nearer.

"…should have left his body where I told yas, not in the water. They float, the bodies do."

"I weighted it. No reason that gardener should have come up like that. After two days, I thought we's was safe."

"Well it came up, didn't it? I'd smack your head if I wasn't tied!"

"Shouldn't a cheated, that one. Cheatin' at dice an all when we's were usin' bad ones already…"

"Quiet, you!" one of their guards yelled. "You murder one of the lord's workers and you get punished. When the first one's done, it's your turn."

The man scowled at the prisoners, but I was past them and didn't hear more.

A gardener who played dice? *Not Anscher*, I told myself. It couldn't have been him. But he had just been with them, and he played dice, betting money to buy my freedom.

But the man said he'd done the deed two days ago.

I had seen Anscher only just that morning. It couldn't have been Anscher.

It couldn't have been.

With a start, I came up short. Just ahead of me, coming in through the gate into the upper bailey, came the cart, pulled by the men I had seen pulling the body from the pond.

And there, in the back of the cart, was the body.

10

Two torches blazed in their sconces just inside the small gateway leading into the inner bailey. The wind picked up, and the flames danced in a diabolical flutter, sending shadows weaving and waving across the stone wall, along the faces of the somber men as they accompanied the cart with its load. A piece of debris skittered across the cobbles as the men pulled the cart into the yard.

I approached the men and the cart, needing to pass them in order to leave. I wanted nothing more than to get back to the village, to my bed, to ignore all I'd seen and heard this day and start a new search for Anscher in the morning.

None of the men looked at me as I neared them. The body in the back was uncovered, and I could see a leg shifted off to the side of the cart, the dripping pant leg pushed up to reveal pale, bloated flesh. I wanted to look away, but I could not. Something about the sight pinned my gaze to it.

But there was more than just macabre fascination. The logical side of my brain wanted to keep walking, to keep my gaze averted and go along my way. The fading light of the evening would make the path home harder to navigate if I tarried longer. But instinct told me I needed to see who was in that cart. Instinct had told me it was Anscher even if I didn't want to believe it. Truth was truth, regardless of my feelings toward it.

The cart came closer, the body in view. I peered through the dim light, relying on the overhead torches to provide illumination.

My legs threatened to give way. The face was bloated from having been in the water, but there was no doubt in my mind that the body in the cart was Anscher.

"Anscher!" I cried out, running toward him. The men pulling the cart paid me no notice. "Anscher, oh my love… what happened!" I grabbed his hand, oblivious of the condition of it. "What happened? How did you find him?"

My questions came in frenzied succession, one following the next without waiting for an answer to the previous. And yet the man continued, ignoring my hysterical interrogation.

"Why don't you answer me?" I dropped Anscher's hand and ran up to the man pulling the cart. "This is my husband-to-be! You must tell me what has happened."

The man kept his chin down, his expression somber. "Where should we put him tonight? He'll have to be buried or burned at dawn tomorrow. The masters will want the matter dealt with before he becomes putrid."

"Oh, aye," his companion answered. "The poor lout shouldn'ta been gambling with that lot. Trouble they is, and a good thing they's gettin' what's been coming, I says."

111

I couldn't believe my ears. They discussed the man I loved as if I wasn't standing there, crying and begging for answers. "Answer me! Who did this?"

The men continued to ignore me. "Put him in the shed behind the pigs for now. Don't bother taking him out. We'd just have to load him up again."

I moved to stand directly in the path of the men. They would have to run me down if they continued to ignore me.

And yet, they continued to walk toward me. I pounded the man's chest.

But he passed through me.

*****

I had seen Anscher that morning. And the day before that. He hadn't seen me, hadn't heard me.

And neither had Marjory. Or the cooks. Or these men.

No one had seen me. No one had talked to me.

And then the man pulling the cart…

All these thoughts raced through my mind as I ran headlong down the path to the village. I flew in through the door, stumbling to a stop when I saw my mother sitting up in bed, her elbows resting on her knees with her head resting in her hands. She sobbed uncontrollably as Inge, the elderly woman who lived next to us, sat beside her with an arm around her shoulders. Neither of them glanced at the door which had banged against the wall behind it when I'd come in.

"Mother!" I cried.

"Jacotte, you must calm yourself and think to your future."

"They're all gone! All of them!" my mother sobbed. "First my Guérôme, and then my Haralt. Then my baby, and now my Mêlie!" She wailed, rocking forward and backward.

"Mother, mother, I am here! Right here in front of you!" I dropped to my knees before her, grabbing her arms, trying to pull her hands away from her face so she could see me. But I could not move them.

"The men will go to the caves tomorrow and bring the bodies down for burial. You can put your Mêlie by her father, brother, and sister. I will help you. We all will."

"But mother! Mother!" I screamed. "I'm right here! Why can't you see me?"

112

I pounded on her legs, tears blinding my vision, but she did not look at me.

I rose and stood over her, shaking my head. "No! No, no, no, noooooo!"

A cold wind blew in through the open door as I backed away from them, nearly tripping over the threshold as I passed over it.

Once outside, I turned and ran.

I stumbled up the long hill, tripping over rocks and dips on the terrain as I scrambled toward the top, to the cave where the bodies lay.

I had to find out.

I needed answers.

Fullness of night descended over the land as I neared the entrance to the cave, but a full moon emerged from behind the clouds just as I passed into the cave, revealing the gruesome scene.

I made my way toward the back of the cave where the men had come upon me. I recognized Heliarde's form immediately. She still lay where she had fallen, unmoved.

And there, beside her, lay another form.

I was considered short by most, and petite. But I was strong from long hours of laboring in the village and at the castle. The blue tunic I wore had been given to one of the villagers by a ladies' maid at the castle many years ago when she had taken a new position. Charged with getting rid of the girl's possessions and deemed too shabby for use by anyone who worked for the Lady Helene, the tunic had found its way to the slave village. It had passed around until it ended up in my family. My pale-blonde hair, bright in the sun, seemed dull in the darkness of the cave.

I gazed at my inert form, my face bloodied from the cudgel which had struck me.

I smoothed the pale, blue tunic and left.

Near the burial ground, the familiar, odd sensation rippled through me again, calling and urging me to follow it. This time, I obeyed.

About Stephanie Churchill

Being first and foremost a lover of history, Stephanie's writing draws on her knowledge of history even while set in purely fictional places existing only in her imagination. Inspired by classic literature, epic fantasy, as well as the historical fiction of authors like Sharon Kay Penman, Anya Seton, and Bernard Cornwell, Stephanie's books are filled with action and romance, loyalty and betrayal. Her writing takes on a cadence that is sometimes literary, sometimes genre fiction, relying on deeply-drawn and complex characters while exploring the subtleties of imperfect people living in a gritty, sometimes dark world. Her unique blend of non-magical fantasy fiction inspired by true history ensures that her books are sure to please of historical fiction and epic fantasy literature alike.

She grew up in Lincoln, Nebraska. After graduating college, she worked as an international trade and antitrust paralegal in Washington, D.C. and then in Minneapolis, Minnesota. She now lives with her husband, their two children, and two dogs in the suburbs of Minneapolis.

Stephanie has written three novels loosely inspired by the Wars of the Roses: The Scribe's Daughter, The King's Daughter, The King's Furies

Media:

Website: www.stephaniechurchillauthor.com
Facebook: www.facebook.com/StephanieChurchillAuthor
Twitter: https://twitter.com/WriterChurchill

THE HAUNTING OF EDENBRIDGE CASTLE

BY

JUDITH ARNOPP

Edenbridge – 1951

"Morning Sir; anything new?" Arnold tosses his bicycle clips onto his desk and loosens his tie.

Inspector Callow sits back, scratches his head and yawns, revealing large yellow teeth and a coated tongue. "Not much. It's been a quiet night. I'll be glad to get off home. I want you to go back to the castle this morning, try to get a word with the housekeeper. Her last statement just didn't add up; she claimed not to know half the staff who work there alongside her. Mrs … erm …"

He shuffles through paperwork, picks up a dog-eared form. "… Ah, Cook. Mrs Cook. Read through this and you'll see what I mean." He passes Arnold the document. "It's as if she dropped from the sky. Claims to remember W.P.C. Bambridge arriving but can't recall seeing her leave. The powers that be are calling for the case to be closed but I smell a rat, Arnold, a rat that's been dead for some time."

He rises from his chair, shrugs into his raincoat, picks up his lunchbox and escapes into the freshness of the morning. Arnold frowns at the form while he waits for the kettle to boil. On opening the fridge, he discovers they are out of milk. Five minutes later, back at his desk, the first sip of tea takes the skin from his lips.

"Arghh!" Hot liquid soaks the front of his shirt.

"You ok, Arnie?"

Woman Police Constable Grace appears at his elbow with a fistful of paper towels and begins to mop ineffectively at his damp chest. "That will stain horribly." The cheap blue paper towel disintegrates and rolls into elongated wet balls.

"Leave it, leave it. I've a spare shirt in my locker. I'm going up to the castle shortly to follow up on that cold case, the disappearance of Bambridge."

"Oh, that was so strange. She disappeared just after I arrived. I was supposed to go with her but ..."

"It is odd, to disappear on a routine follow up on a minor traffic incident."

Grace stares wistfully through the window.

"And she never came back. You don't think anything ... I mean, she just ran off, didn't she? Spur of the moment thing ... maybe she met someone and scarpered, or maybe she'd been planning it for ages."

"If you are planning to abscond with your lover, you don't sign on for duty on the day of your departure, you go on the weekend, or after work, not in the middle of an investigation, and you don't leave your cat alone in the flat to starve to death."

Grace nods, stares into space, her brow furrowed as if she is trying to find the answer in the dark corner.

"You suspect foul play then, sir?"

"Well, Inspector Callow has some misgivings about the housekeeper, Mrs Cook. He suspects she knows more than she is letting on, as we will no doubt discover once I've spoken to her."

It is a bright day, the sun dazzling as Arnold peddles up the hill to the castle. It is the sort of day better spent fishing or boating or walking his dog for miles across the countryside. Instead, he is pedalling slowly uphill, the sun in his eyes, and sweat dripping down his collar.

The castle gates are standing open, lank nettles sprawled at their base proving that they have not been closed for years. He pedals into the forecourt, dismounts, and rests his bike against an ivy-covered wall. He takes off his hat, drags his sleeve across his brow. The place is deserted, a light mist rising from the moat. From the depths of the castle a dog barks frantically. He looks up at the towering walls, suddenly conscious of how many have stood here before him.

The huge wooden doors are locked and barred, but he discovers a path and follows it, circumnavigating the building until he reaches the back of the castle. A low gate blocks his way; he steps over it into a small yard, vastly different to the stiff formality of the knot gardens at the front. It is a domestic setting, humble even. His policeman's eyes take note of the grass growing between the cracked paving, a clump of tall daisies by the fence, the orange splash of marigolds, herbs growing in a broken pot by the open back door.

He places one foot over the threshold.

"Hello?"

"Oh, my Good God in Heaven!"

A stout woman of indeterminate age jumps in surprise, collapses into a chair, her hand to her chest. "I nearly had kittens!" she exclaims. "What do you mean, just barging in 'ere without so much as a …"

"Edenbridge Police, Madam. I mean no harm. Just following up enquiries."

She stands up, picks up a teapot and tosses grouts into the sink.

"And what can I do for you then, Inspector? I take it you haven't come for tea and cake."

Arnold removes his hat, places it on the table, bicycle clips inside.

"Erm, its Sergeant actually. You will recall … Erm, before we begin, can you confirm your name please."

"Amelia Cook. Housekeeper."

"Ah, good day, Mrs Cook. My name is Sergeant John Arnold. I am here to look into an old case that you will no doubt remember. The disappearance of W.P.C. Bambridge in …" He flips through the pages of his notebook. "July 1941"

Using the back of her hand, she pushes a grey hank of hair from her eyes.

"Oh, that. After all this time? I'd have thought you lot would've cleared that up by now. I told the policeman everything I knew when she disappeared. I expected them to keep coming back but after a while all the questions just stopped. I thought you'd all forgotten about it or she'd turned up again."

"The war years were difficult; people were dispersed all over the country. Edenbridge was full of child refugees, troops, people disappeared all the time during the war. Many cases were side-lined. Now, if we can get down to the day in question. You said at the time you remembered W.P.C. Bambridge arriving but didn't see her leave; is that correct?"

"Yes, as I said several times before. She turned up here wanting to talk to … now who was it? I can't recall. But I do remember that I took her into the castle myself, up to the private apartments. It was a war hospital at the time, you see so the family kept just two or three rooms for themselves. I showed her to the solar, but I didn't see her leave."

"But you are sure she left?"

"Well, she must have. She isn't here now, is she? I remember there was a commotion, and someone had left the kitchen door wide open and let all the dogs into the garden to run amok in the cabbages. I had a devil of a time to catch 'em."

Arnold scratches in his notebook. Looks up, catches Mrs Cook dabbing sweat from her forehead. She smiles at him, crooked teeth, missing upper incisor. She smooths her apron. He gives a tight smile in return.

"Mrs Cook, could you show me the room you took her to?"

"Yes, of course. Oh, and while you're at it, you could take this back to the station with you. She left it here, do you see? I kept meaning to bring it to Edenbridge but never got round to it."

She waddles to a tall cupboard, stands on tip toe to reach the top shelf, and lifts down a package, wrapped in yellowing newspaper.

"I 'ad it all ready to bring." She holds out the package to Arnold, who takes it warily and tears back the paper.

"Her hat? She left her police uniform hat here? All this time and you told nobody?"

"It just slipped my mind, Officer. Now, do you want to see the upper rooms?"

Arnold places the parcel on the table beside his own hat and follows Mrs Cook from the kitchen, into the castle interior.

It is markedly colder, the thick stone walls excluding the heat of the day. As he follows her across the chequered floor, their steps echo around the vaulted ceiling. Arnold shivers as oil-painted eyes follow their journey to the upper reaches of the house.

Mrs Cook bustles ahead, leading him down a corridor. At the end she pauses, opens a door into a solar and he follows her in.

The sun streams through the windows, tiny specs of dust dance in the brightness, but the air is frigid. Arnold shudders, turns up his collar.

"I'll leave you to look around, Inspector. Feel free to poke about where you will. We are closed to the public on Mondays, so you won't be disturbing anyone."

She backs out. Closes the door.

Floorboards creak as he moves. At the window he looks down on the garden, a cunningly wrought pattern of box and gravel. Two brightly clad figures are walking arm in arm, but the glass is old and warped, obscuring his vision and he is unable to make out any detail. He turns away, sniffs air that is rich with age, smelling of musty hangings, damp plaster, and the smoke of centuries of fires.

Arnold crosses the uneven floor, reaches out to pass into the next room when a small sound makes him pause. As he turns, the cold intensifies and the hair on the back of his neck prickles.

A woman who had not been there a moment before, is standing by the hearth, her face white, her eyes wide and staring. She is dressed in a blue uniform, the sort worn by policewomen a decade or so ago. He steps forward, and when he speaks, his voice issues in a squeak.

"W.P.C. Bambridge?"

Her empty face turns slowly toward him. She frowns as if trying to remember.

"I – I used to be…"

He shuffles forward, stops just short of taking her hands. His head is heavy, hard to think, hard to …

"You've been here, all this time? Whatever … I do not understand? How is this possible? What happened? We've been looking for you for …."

"No, you haven't." Her eyes narrow, misery in every bone of her face. "You forgot all about me. Everyone forgot all about me."

He stammers and stutters. Shakes his head to clear his mind.

"Tell me what happened."

She frowns and blinks, shakes her head as she wets her lips.

"I came here, to this room, to speak to someone … a woman. The housekeeper said … she had information about the traffic accident I was investigating. The housekeeper … "

"Mrs Cook?"

"Yes …Mrs Cook … she told me to sit by the window. She said the woman would tell me all about it."

"And?" His head is pounding, his pulse loud in his ears.

"And I sat down and the woman with the empty eyes told me …."

"The woman with the empty eyes? What do you mean? Who was she? What did she tell you?"

He fumbles for his notebook, drops his pencil, scrabbles at her feet to retrieve it.

"Oh, a story of witchcraft and … ghostly things. Sit here with me and I will tell you all I can remember."

119

Arnold and Bambridge sit in the window. Arnold waits while Bambridge clasps and unclasps her hands, wrestling them in her lap as if resisting an unpleasant truth.

"We were sitting here, like this. The woman was old. Her skin transparent, like a lace curtain, her eyes were staring and empty. I sensed her sadness and wanted to make it end. I wanted to help her.

'The dead don't rest here, in this place,' she told me. 'Oblivious to our human joys and sorrows, they wander the grounds, trapped in the heaviness of their own lost lives.

I've been here since birth. I was born in the year 1642 yet they've been here for far longer than that. I used to think everyone could see them. I thought it was just how things were. I knew they were not like us, but I didn't think they were wicked. There was nothing evil about them, nothing to be afraid of ... not then. I was just a child. I thought they were merely a part of the castle's memories, you see. I imagined that one day, when my time on Earth was done, I'd join them in their hazy repetitive after world. I never imagined I would come to this.

The first time I ever spoke of them I was helping mother in the kitchens. Mother often sent me on errands, small tasks that took me all over the castle and gardens. On the day I first told anyone about it, she'd sent me to deliver a tray of dainties to the young mistress. I climbed the stairs and hurried along the upper hall and tentatively opened the chamber door. When I peeped inside, I saw a woman weeping by the window. I'd seen her before but on that day, when I asked her what was wrong, she just looked through me, as if I wasn't there. So, I left her.

On the way back, I took my time, retracing my steps down the winding stone stair and scaring the cat by leaping from the third step into the hall.

After the coolness of the upper part of the house, the kitchen felt hot; the windows were thrown wide, but a great fire burnt in the hearth, where a boy was slowly turning a spit. A handful of maids ringed the table, preparing vegetables, and Dorothy who worked in the dairy, had just brought in a slab of butter. Mother held a bowl in the crook of her arm, remorselessly beating cream into stiff little peaks. Her face was red; her forehead slick with sweat and her cap was slipping slowly off the back of her head.

"Mother," I said, climbing onto a stool. "Who is that woman weeping in the solar?"

Mother's arm stilled. She looked up slowly, frowned and shook her head.

"What woman?"

I pointed toward the upper floor. "She is up there now, she ignored me even though I spoke quite loudly. She was groaning and weeping. When I asked her what was wrong she just looked right through me and continued to wail, so I left her."

Mother's face paled. Her lips tightened. She put down the bowl and grabbed my upper arm; I cried out in pain as her fingers dug into my flesh. She thrust me backwards, away from the ears of the gawping servants, and into the empty scullery.

"You must never speak of this again, do you hear me?" she hissed. "You must not say these things, or they'll take you away and burn you as a witch, do you hear me? You know what has been happening in East Anglia – women taken on the slightest suspicion."

I shook my head. I didn't know. For me, the world was the Castle – I'd never travelled further than the water meadow. I'd heard the older girls whisper of witches, love charms and cures but …

'I am not a witch.'

I screwed up my nose while she searched my face.

"Aren't you? Are you sure?"

I wanted to ask what she meant but I daren't. Instead, I just nodded, my chin quivering as I rubbed my bruised arm. When she released me, I hastily widened the space between us. How was I to know it was wrong to see the 'people' and besides, how could I help it?

They were just there.

Swallowing my tears, I crossed my fingers behind my back and nodded.

"I won't, Mother. I will never speak of it."

"You just imagined it," she hissed as she backed from the room. Before she opened the door, she wagged a warning finger and I nodded again to confirm my vow of secrecy.

I would never speak of it.

So, I never told a soul that on warm days the 'people' were all around, strolling between the flowers in the garden, lounging on the sward, minstrels, and ladies, and sometimes a big man with a laugh that seemed to fill the sky. These people altered. Sometimes they were young, sometimes they were old; sometimes happy, sometimes sad. Often they were bored and in search of mischief.

One afternoon, as I took a short cut through the garden, I came across a child a few years older than I. She had long dark hair, a gown finer than anything I owned yet it was stained green from the meadow. She brushed irritably at her skirt.

"I will have my vengeance on you for this, George," she cried without looking up. "Mother is going to have me whipped!"

It didn't seem fair that such a pretty girl should be beaten. I often made my own clothes dirty and there have always been ways and means to clean them before mother noticed.

"Ellen knows how to clean grass stains from fine linen." I said, and my sudden voice made her jump. She sprung up, her mouth open, her eyes wide.

"I thought you were George," she said. Then, growing suddenly tense, "You can see me?"

She leant forward, as curious and afraid of me as I was of her.

"Yes," I replied. "Of course, I can see you. I wasn't sure if you'd be able to see me thoughor hear me. I don't think the others can."

She abandoned her attempt to brush the stain away from her clothes and straightened up.

"Well. I can see you. I've watched you before, going about your business like a busy little mouse but … I never thought I could be seen or heard. George says there is an invisible shield … that separates us from your … I am unsure if yours is a different world or a different time. You aren't always there so I have wondered if you are a gh… My brother tries to frighten me with stories but I've never been afraid. I'm not afraid now." She lifted her chin, tossed her head.

"What is your name?" I asked.

"Anne," she said.

"And your brother is called George?" An idea as to her possible identity blossomed in my mind. They told stories of 'headless Anne' in the kitchen.

"That's right and I have a sister, Mary, but she is away."

"You are Anne Boleyn, the queen who …"

She laughed suddenly, high pitched and melodic.

"A queen? You are funny. You wait until George hears that!"

She turned and ran away, her laughter echoing back along the path. I stood for a long time in the garden, hoping she would return.

I waited until the light began to fade and Mother called impatiently from the kitchen door.

I didn't see Anne again for many weeks, and when I did it was in the same part of the garden as before. She was older and no longer ran about the garden but glided sedately along the path, her hand in the crook of her brother's arm. The hoyden child had transformed into a lady, yet I looked down at myself and discovered I was just the same as the last time we met. I shrunk into the arbour and hoped not to be noticed but they stopped and, although she gave no sign of it, I knew she had seen me.

"Do you ever feel watched, George?"

He slumped onto the arbour seat.

"At court I do, the place is full of spies."

"Do you remember when we were children and you used to try to frighten me with stories of 'the others'?"

He laughed. "I had forgotten. Fancy you remembering that. We were little then. Who were 'the others' do you think? I never see them now. We must have imagined them."

"Perhaps."

She was looking directly at me, a slight smile quirking her lips. "While I was in France, I didn't think of them at all. There was too much else to think of; dances to learn, songs to sing but now I am back, I sometimes think ..."

She was lying to him. I knew she could see me, and she knew I could see her. Why did she not speak of it?

"You will soon be at court with Mary and me. There will be far too much to do then for idle imaginings."

George leant back, crossed one leg over the other. "Until you marry Cousin James. Then you'll be whisked away to Ireland and I will probably never see you again."

She sat down heavily beside him.

"Oh, do not speak of it, George. I can't bear to think of leaving England. I am not ready to marry. I want a place at court before I am forced to settle and be mother to a stable of little Irish boys."

George's laugh was loud until he noted Anne's lowered head, the beginnings of tears on her lashes. He reached out, placed a finger beneath her chin and lifted it.

"Anne, you never cry. Don't let it trouble you. Do you see me crying about marrying Jane Parker?"

She snatched the kerchief he offered and dabbed her eyes.

"That is just like you, George. You never worry over anything. I swear, you will go to your death laughing."

No, no he won't! I closed my eyes, squeezed them tight and willed them both away.

Leave me! Go back to your time and leave me alone!

When I opened my eyes, I was alone in the arbour and it was raining, my hood and gown soaked. I'd not noticed the weather changing, the clouds looming in to drench the garden. I ran between dripping flowerbeds, splashed through puddles, and barged into the kitchen.

"Where have you been?" Mother frowned at my wet clothes. "Go and get changed and make sure you hang your things where they will dry properly."

I turned on my heel and fled to the tiny chamber at the back of the house and as I struggled from my wet skirts, I thought back on my latest encounter.

This time, Anne and George were young and full of optimism. Suppose I'd told Anne how it would end? Was it possible to change the future? Was the woman I encountered in the garden the real Anne, in her own time, or was she a shade of what once was, somehow strayed into mine? So many questions. Questions I could never voice aloud because, as mother kept reminding me, *they are hanging witches in Huntingdon.*

I was twelve the next time I saw her. I was in the garden; it was always in the garden that I encountered Anne. The others appeared in every part of the house, but Anne was always outside, in the sunshine. I had almost given up seeing her again. I was not looking for or even thinking of her when I heard her unmistakeable laugh floating on the wind. I stood waiting for several minutes before she turned the corner and I realised she was not alone.

She was arm in arm with a giant. A tall gentleman in a fine velvet doublet, sporting a jewelled hat with a white feather plume. My legs were suddenly as frail as string. I knew him at once and didn't know what to do. We'd all heard tales of King Henry.

Could he see me? Would she point me out as a witch? *They are hanging witches in Huntingdon.*

I scarcely dared to look but one glimpse at Anne and I knew she had seen me and was showing off the fine company she was keeping. My heart hammered like a woodpecker knocking but the king did not notice me. As they drew near, Anne stopped, lifted her foot.

"There is a something in my shoe, Your Majesty," she said. She perched on the arbour seat, displayed a fine ankle and obligingly, the king knelt at her feet and removed her slipper.

She smiled at me behind his back while the king shook out the invisible stone. She'd grown into a woman, not as pretty as childhood had promised but her face was unforgettable. Enchanting.

Wincing a little, the king stood up again and she nestled against his arm.

"Thank you, Your Majesty. Do you know, when I was a child, I met a little girl in this garden – a witch-child who told me that one day I would be a queen. Such an extraordinary thing for her to say. Do you believe in witches, Sire?"

"Witches?" The king looked warily about the garden. "No – maybe ... I am unsure. I've never encountered one. Why?"

"Oh, no reason. Just suppose, if you would, that one was able to 'see' people from another time, another place ... another realm, if you like; would that make them witches, do you think, or evil spirits?"

The king fell silent, lost in contemplation, then he shook himself and fumbled for an answer.

"Possibly, Sweetheart, but why this sudden talk of dark things?"

"Well, if she were a witch, transported from some other place and could see me but I could see her too. Which of us would be the witch? How could we tell?"

He shuddered, glanced at the sky to see if the sun had gone in.

"Stop it, Anne. You brought me out here to show me the roses. Come, come ..."

They hurried away and as they turned the corner and were out of the view of the house, he drew her close, and she raised her face to be kissed.

My heart leapt. I had to do something, something to stop it from happening, but perhaps I was too late. It had already happened ... long ago ... hadn't it? There was nothing I could do.

Anne and George and Henry were all long dead. It was merely their shadows who walked in the castle garden. Or were they caught, perhaps are still caught, in an endless circle of happiness and death; death and life, and happiness and death again and again ... forever?

If that was so, then I was trapped in it too.

125

I could never tell my mother. I could never tell anyone. I carried the burden of the others with me day and night. Sometimes, whispering voices hindered my sleep or interfered with my tasks and I was beaten for tardiness. Lack of sleep made me slow, apprehension stole away my joy.

"Look at you. You will never catch a husband," Mother scolded. "No man wants to wake up next to a sour face in the morning."

She was right. No man ever so much as glanced my way unless to remark on my strangeness. "What a peculiar child," people said, "What an oddity," but I wasn't peculiar, it was the perpetual presence of the others that made me seem so.

How could I concentrate on slicing carrots or skinning a rabbit when the kitchen was teeming with servants from other times? The past spun constantly around me. My head was full of their business, their lives; it left me no time for my own.

I'd jump when the voice of John Cobham called for his long dead servants. I'd halt when Stephen Scrope marched through the house with his architects, or a party of royal Tudor horseman rode into the yard, setting the dogs barking. Once Mary Boleyn came running through the house, searching for Anne, calling for George, while their infant brothers screamed for attention in the darkness. She barged into me, sent my pail crashing to the floor before running off again. All that, together with the maddening, relentless weeping of that woman in the solar was driving me mad.

As I grew older, the louder the voices became, and the clearer I saw their faces. I never quite knew if I was intruding on their lives, or if they were intruding on mine.

Was it madness, or witchcraft? Were they evil, or was I?

I lived with it. I grew into a woman, a spinster. My ripe years shrivelled and then I was old, my bones as dry as dust, my joints stiff. One night I awoke in the dark, and something drew me upstairs to the forbidden parts of the house.

I was not supposed to leave the servant's quarters where I had lived out my life in service to both the living and the dead inhabitants of the castle. I should have stayed curled in my hard cot, but the incessant weeping was so loud that night, it allowed me no rest. Keeping my head down, making myself as invisible as I could, I made slow painful passage through the castle and pushed open the creaking door.

Cool blue moonlight illuminated the woman who rocked to and fro, a letter clasped to her chest. Once she had seemed old but now, I was the elderly one. Slipping from the long shadows, I shuffled to her side and looked into a face ravaged by a century of weeping.

Her fingers plucked at the fine velvet of her skirt. She was insubstantial. I could see through her body to the chair she rested in. She was nothing but a shade, made up of shadow and sorrow.

Her hand fell, the letter lay open on her lap, but I could not read the heavy black scrawl.

"Why do you weep?"

She laid back her head and closed her eyes. Her cheeks were hollow, her mouth turned down; misery seeped from her and spilled to the floor, into the bones of the castle. I reached out and tried to take her hand.

"What has wounded you?"

The weeping ceased. She turned fearful eyes upon me.

"Witchery!"

I flinched from the accusation, shied away from her terrible eyes.

"I am no witch," I whimpered. "Or if I am, I mean you no harm. Please, tell me why you weep?"

Her mouth opened, her voice screeching in my head, battering me with bitter belching despair.

"I weep for the children; for the victims; for the wives. I weep for all of us."

Her despair engulfed me. I put my hands to my head, tore at my hair as I was absorbed into her anguish. Now, we are one and we must wail together as you must now mourn too. We are an eternal vessel of uncontainable sorrow.

Silently the others enter the chamber, their united voices anointing the air. W.P.C. Bambridge lifts her hand that Arnold suddenly realises is skeletal, the bleakness of her eyes fill his heart.

"You should never have come," she says. "Those who come here asking questions are never permitted to leave."

Downstairs, in the kitchen, Mrs Cook finishes her biscuit and removes the singing kettle from the hob. Then she replaces the tin and taking Arnold's hat, she wraps it in yesterday's newspaper and places it on the top shelf ... with the others.

Is it ever The End?

127

About Judith Arnopp

A lifelong history enthusiast and avid reader, Judith holds a BA in English/Creative writing and an MA in Medieval Studies.

She lives on the coast of West Wales where she writes both fiction and non-fiction based in the Medieval and Tudor period. Her main focus is on the perspective of historical women but more recently is writing from the perspective of Henry VIII himself.

Her novels include:

- ❖ **A Matter of Conscience**: Henry VIII: the Aragon Years
- ❖ **The Heretic Wind**: the life of Mary Tudor, Queen of England
- ❖ **Sisters of Arden**: on the Pilgrimage of Grace
- ❖ **The Beaufort Bride**: Book one of The Beaufort Chronicle
- ❖ **The Beaufort Woman**: Book two of The Beaufort Chronicle
- ❖ **The King's Mother**: Book three of The Beaufort Chronicle
- ❖ **The Winchester Goose:** at the Court of Henry VIII
- ❖ **A Song of Sixpence**: the story of Elizabeth of York
- ❖ **Intractable Heart**: the story of Katheryn Parr
- ❖ **The Kiss of the Concubine**: a story of Anne Boleyn
- ❖ **The Song of Heledd**
- ❖ **The Forest Dwellers**

Judith is also a founder member of a re-enactment group called *The Fyne Companye of Cambria* and makes historical garments both for the group and others. She is not professionally trained but through trial, error and determination has learned how to make authentic looking, if not strictly HA, clothing. You can find her group *Tudor Handmaid* on Facebook. You can also find her on Twitter and Instagram.

Webpage: www.judithmarnopp.com
Author page: author.to/juditharnoppbooks
Blog: http://juditharnoppnovelist.blogspot.co.uk/

KINDRED SPIRITS: THE MONSTER OF MACHECOUL

BY

JENNIFER C WILSON

You want a horror story, do you? Well, by the end of this, you might just have changed your mind.

It starts as a shiver.

A tiny, meaningless shiver, the type you imagine people have suffered when you hear them say somebody's walked over their grave. Funny that you only feel those when you're alive. I've stood and watched hundreds, thousands even, walk over my grave, and never felt a thing. Have you? I suppose it doesn't help that my grave doesn't look like a grave. Or that nobody ever really noticed I was gone. Not for me, the grand monuments of royalty, or even a humble gravestone that my relatives could have visited after my passing.

But still, I felt that shiver.

Of course, it could have been anyone. Fadings happen all the time, after all, ghosts vanishing away to nothing at all, either suddenly or over time. And yet, there's nowhere with quite so high a concentration as here along the Loire. I mean yes, he travels, but he always comes home in the end, even if it is in ruins. He's been seen at the Castle Machecoul at least twice a year since he died; ask anyone.

And I had been visiting the castle the very day I felt the shiver.

It had to be him. You know, in some parts of France, ghosts still daren't say his name. But I'm not afraid. Gilles de Rais, Baron de Rais.

It's strange to think he was such a hero in his prime. Fought alongside the wonderful Jeanne d'Arc. He was at her side during the Siege of Orleans, and even took part in the glorious coronation of King Charles, named as a Marshal of France, one of the most powerful men in the country. Who knows what happens to make a man like that fall so badly? I mean, yes, he didn't have the easiest of lives; talk of scandal amongst the ruling classes always spreads like wild-fire, doesn't it? But having been held in such high esteem, he could easily have survived the downfall of poor Jeanne. He *was* surviving her downfall. He hurried away to Brittany, and with all that money, he could have had it all. A magnificent inheritance, a wealthy heiress for a bride, and a child in the cradle, albeit a girl – he should have been happy.

But he wouldn't settle. Threw all his wealth away just trying to show he was better than the king himself, no less. All those servants, the heralds, the building work around here. It was a sort of madness, an obsession.

And then the king stepped in. Had to. De Rais was ruining his family. They would have been left with nothing if he had continued. So, they sought a ruling from Charles, who banned anyone from entering into a contract with de Rais. Well, with all his expenditure on theatrical productions and showing off, being unable to sell anything else off to fund his lavish lifestyle, he went down, let's say, a darker path.

None of us knows exactly when or where it started, not even now, but there are always rumours after the fact. People get brave when the person they fear is dead. An easy mistake, but definitely one to avoid.

Poor young Jeodon, son of the fur-merchant, was the first murder we all knew about, but there were plenty before him, I'm sure of it. Just twelve years old, never seen again, no body ever found. And so it went on. For more than eight years, it's believed, de Rais kept up his reign of terror.

If only it had stopped when they killed him.

When you think about it, there are so many things which just don't make sense, when you really start to analyse things. He uses a knife, they say, to commit his Fadings. He must have got it from one of his executioners; there was no way he would be allowed to carry a weapon to his own execution. You hear the children laughing, teasing one another, when they first enter our world, that strange afterlife, somewhere between the living and the forever dead. They joke about it when they first hear of a Fading, that it's de Rais, wielding the knife the hangman used to cut him down once the devil of a man had stopped kicking, but surely a professional like that would have noticed his knife being stolen? And once de Rais had that knife, where and how did he stay hidden for so long? The first fresh Fadings didn't happen until a full five years after his death. Some say he remained hidden here at Machecoul, I remember hearing the tales myself. Even in death – those poor children – were they still being tortured by that monster? There were never any bodies to be buried or mourned by their families. So many nameless, lost children.

It was 1445 when the stories began to spread in earnest. Like I say, there had always been tales that yes, a ghost can be killed. Then killed again. And again. That the remnants of a spirit can be worn down, over and over, until there's nothing left.

It's different for different ghosts.

For some, Fading can be instantaneous. One cut, one shot, one injury, and they're gone. Although in truth, that's rare. For most, it's like a war of attrition, each injury making them just a fraction fainter, a little bit harder to see, to feel, to sense. Even they don't always notice at first. If a ghost keeps to themselves, then they may not even notice until it's too late, and they're gone.

Well, somehow in those missing five years, that 'thing', for we cannot name him as a man, not anymore, discovered his ill-deeds could carry on far beyond the grave.

That's what happened to Collette.

She had escaped him, you know? One of the few children who entered his castle not to suffer a horrendous fate. The poor girl was sent with a message, alongside her brother. He… he wasn't so lucky. But Collette realised quickly enough she would be in danger if she stayed. As soon as they were offered a meal as a reward for undertaking their task, she saw something was wrong. Nobody rewarded children like them for carrying messages. A couple of coins from the likes of Prelati or de Sillé, that's all they could ever expect. Her brother, he wouldn't listen. He was entranced, seduced by the offer of roasted meats, sumptuous clothing, and the chance of a comfortable bed for the night. I suppose he got two out of the three.

They never found his body.

One of almost one hundred and fifty children torn from families. This region lost so many. All those poor children, never having the chance to grow, to reach their potential.

I was there in the crowd the day of de Rais' execution. There was no joy amongst us. Just mothers, fathers, siblings, wishing they were able to pay their respects to their own lost ones. You know what he did with their bodies, don't you? Threw them onto the fire like pieces of rubbish, along with all the stunning clothing he'd clothed them in. Didn't want any evidence of the poor things ever having been in that monstrous place.

But back to Collette.

She may have escaped de Rais, but that was in January 1440, just months before his arrest. The poor girl didn't live long enough to join us in the crowd, or not for us to see anyway. A flux spread through the town the same month, taking her, and I followed not long after.

It's a strange feeling, the moment you realise you're a ghost, destined to walk this earth for potentially the rest of eternity. Mind, in truth, there were so many of us from Machecoul that it felt the village hadn't changed a bit. Too many parents still hoping to find their children. Too many siblings and friends missing their playmates. For a while, as the flux took hold, we out-numbered the living. If it wasn't for the sadness, we might almost have been happy, all still together, the same gossip, the same relationships, even 'living' in the same houses we always had.

And that's when I saw Collette again.

She had been devoted to her brother, little Jacques, had known something must have happened to him up at the castle, just hadn't known what, could never find out, and hadn't been brave enough to return to try and find out.

One night, when Collette was up at the castle with a few of the other young spirits, she felt the shiver. Put it down to fear at first. After all, who wouldn't feel something when entering the lair of such a vile creature? But it kept happening. None of us noticed anything wrong at first, just assumed she was making something of nothing, possibly even telling tales to scare the younger children, keep them from venturing too close to the place. Then one day, I looked at her hand, and couldn't help but gasp.

"What is it, Tante Marie, what do you see?" Despite her bravado, there was still a hint of anxiety in her voice.

"Nothing, Ma Petite, nothing," I tried to assure her, and I was being truthful. Around the edges of her hands, and the tips of her fingers, there was simply nothing there. She was fading away.

I had only been dead a few months back then. I didn't realise it at the time, but looking back, I was witnessing my first Fading. Suddenly, Collette's stories of feeling a shiver running down her spine took on a different meaning once I could see what effect they seemed to be having.

We tried to protect her, told her to be careful, stay away from the castle, but it was no use. See, she was lonely without her brother, even when around the other children's spirits, and she kept becoming fully visible and tangible to the living, just wanting find a friend. We realised it was during those times she had been feeling the shivers, that whatever was causing them had cruelly perfect timing.

I don't remember now who first suggested it was de Rais.

We should have realised sooner, once news of similar Fadings began to spread. The longer we were all dead, the more we found out about how such things happened, and it was clear the local children were being targeted. Again. Yes, plenty of Fadings happened elsewhere, but these things can be accidental, after all. There were tales of knights inadvertently taking others out during mock battles, trying to keep themselves fit during the afterlife, or people attempting to save the living from meeting their fates, thereby putting themselves in harm's way. And there will always be a malicious sector of every community, those who deliberately seek to hurt people, whether strangers or those they believe wronged them in some way, in life or death. But we were seeing too many, and as I say, it was always the children.

Those poor families. It's bad enough to lose your child once, in life, but for so many, they were being lost again, in death. And once more, no body to bury, no chance to mourn.

The final Fading can be brutal. There's no chance to run anywhere, to find anyone for a final goodbye; you just go. It isn't like a white light. I've seen both, and believe me, there's a peace about a spirit finding their white light. It's positive, calming, full of love, somehow. Fading is anything but.

I saw the start of Collette's, and I witnessed the end. She was so pale the last time I saw her, but she was still 'her', just. We were alone, mere feet from the castle's grounds, and she'd forced herself into as full a being as she could, so that I could see her properly. Out of nowhere, a shadow swept across the ground, silent as an owl, and just as deadly once it had locked in on its prey. A flash of silver amidst the blackness, the shape of a hand across Collette's mouth, her face contorted in pain as though she were trying to scream, and yet, nothing but silence.

Then, nothing.

In the shock of the moment I had staggered back. I'm ashamed to say my instinct was to run, to hide from whatever it was I was witnessing. If our hearts still beat, then it must have lasted no more than three heartbeats, and I swear I never took my eyes off the spot where Collette had been standing. But that was all it took. She was gone, never to be seen or heard again.

Nobody believed me at first. It all sounded too dramatic, too forced, but it didn't stop. He couldn't stop.

And of course, that's the problem with death, isn't it? Comes to everyone in the end. There was a constant stream of victims for him. Centuries, it's been going on, and on, generations of children meeting their end at the hands of that monster.

We tried, oh, we tried. Those of us who survived, we did our best. Told the children to stay away from the castle, thinking that was the centre of his depravity, but that's the thing about us ghosts, isn't it? We can go anywhere, do anything, unseen, undetected. Handy in so many ways. Who amongst us hasn't visited a family member, to see how our descendants have fared? I've done it myself. I'm lucky; my family hasn't travelled far, and none have died young. I haven't had to watch him destroy any of my flesh and blood.

In the end, we encouraged the children to keep the story going, to tell the tale of de Rais and his evil, thinking that would deter anyone going up to the castle, or being out alone after dark. We forgot how the minds of the young work, being too far away from it ourselves, and that strange attraction they feel towards the things that should terrify them.

I'll never forget one All Hallows Eve, we found a gang of about thirty of them, from across the years, gathered up at the castle. It had started falling into disrepair by that stage, not many of the living visiting anymore, so it was irresistible to our ghostly children.

That's when we knew we had to act.

By then, we had a good number of ghosts, all equally determined that we needed to do something about de Rais. There had started to be sightings, you see. It wasn't just hearsay anymore. Perhaps he was getting braver, perhaps he was getting careless; we'll never know. I sometimes think it was because he thought nobody would recognise him anymore. Perhaps he thought he'd killed enough that nobody from his own time were left anymore, that we'd moved on, in one way or another. And a lot had. Either through his Fadings, following their white light, or simply giving up and leaving the area. The monster had been seen, fully visible, fully tangible, and not just within the bounds of his castle. Throughout the town, throughout the Loire, throughout France. Talk spreads, as you know, through the dead as much as through the living.

More remembered him than he thought, and we weren't going to let him get away with it anymore.

Like I say, there were more of us now, and not just feeble villagers. This was the late-1900s after all; we had plenty of young, fit, fighting men at our disposal, sadly for them. Combining their military cunning and strategy with our local knowledge, we believed we could finally bring about the end of de Rais' reign of terror. Over five hundred years is too long for anyone to cause such horror to a region. And Fadings can happen to anyone.

I'll always remember the day we made our first move. Up at the castle, that was where we began. It was his lair, we thought – only right that we took the fight to him, rather than sitting, waiting for him to strike down more innocents.

The bravery of those young soldiers is something I'll never forget. I'd seen de Rais in action, after all, and those men were going right into the heart of danger. The plan, if you hadn't gathered already, was to coax him out, force him into trying to attack, then ensure we made the first move. We knew there would be injuries, possibly even full Fadings, as a result, but if we could get even a few hits in first, at least weaken him, then eventually, we knew we could wear him down, push him further and further, until thankfully, there would be nothing left. Nothing left to torment the souls of our children, nothing left to destroy the hearts of local families, nothing left to fear.

It worked. We were almost surprised at our success. We had hoped, of course, but never entirely believed that we could do it.

In the ruined hall of the castle, two young soldiers, brothers, were the first to get a strike at him. They'd made their way back to us after the hell of the trenches, only to discover their parents hadn't survived, and had already moved on by the time the boys reached the town. Having waited a couple of decades, they were ready to risk it, no longer cared if de Rais took one or both of them with him, and they volunteered their lives once again, for the greater good.

I was watching, hidden in invisibility, as they approached, shouting to him, taunting to de Rais, calling him a coward for only attacking the young, that he hadn't the stomach to take on anyone who could fight back, whether in life or death.

Clearly, somewhere in the depths of the monster he had become, there was still a trace of the honourable, chivalric man that de Rais had once been. He heard their mocking, and came out of the darkness to them; the same shadow I had seen the night Collette was attacked, the same sweeping movement, the same sense of dread overcoming everything for a few seconds. But he couldn't attack two men in one movement. Not even centuries of practise could make him that good. Or evil. And he wasn't the only one with a knife. Our boys were fore-warned, and fore-armed, and safely away from the eyes of the town, they appeared in full, both carrying weapons they'd snatched from the old town museum – one bayonet, one mace. An odd combination, but it worked. De Rais managed to land one blow on the younger brother, but his elder sibling predicted his action, and launched at the shadow, bayonet in hand.

If the scream had come from anyone else, it would have had all the mothers in the land hurrying to his aid. It had a rawness to it, as though these lads were the first in all those years to have fought back. Perhaps they were. True or not, de Rais clutched at his chest with one hand, and stared in horror at the other. Even I could see the effect of the wound, from fifty feet away. The monster was almost glowing as the edges around him flickered in and out of visibility for a moment. Nobody moved. We were all waiting, on tenterhooks, to see what would happen. Even de Rais didn't seem to know. The three of them stood for what felt like an eternity, but could only have been less than half a minute, before something in de Rais snapped, and he vanished back into the shadows.

Not much, then, but for a first attempt, we had a victory. The success of that first attack made us brave, and we knew we had to keep striking at the very heart of him, keep pushing home every advantage we were able to obtain. Now, the man is no fool. Nobody can torture and kill so many and not get caught without a degree of wit and intelligence, after all. We couldn't use the same approach more than once, or at least not close together; he would grow wise to us, refuse to be drawn out by any more taunting.

That's when young Michel stepped in. Such a brave lad; we'll never forget him around here. He'd been with us since the middle of the

1600s, poor lad, after a failed journey to Paris. He wanted to become a musketeer, but he didn't quite have the skills with a blade or fire-arm. He had the courage though, a fact we never questioned. That was what got him killed. He'd been so determined to prove himself, he got involved in a street-fight in the heart of the capital, trying to help the men he thought would soon become his comrades. He did his best, he swore, but training with local lads here in Machecoul is no comparison for being in the middle of a brawl like that. He ended up being cut down within minutes, and so returned to us, his heart full of sorrow, but also with a determination to do what he could to help the community he'd grown up in.

He might have just turned sixteen, but he was small for his age, and could easily pass for younger. If I'm honest, the thought of using children to lure out de Rais had struck a few of us, but we had immediately decided against it. There had been enough children to die at the monster's hand when he lived, and we couldn't bring ourselves to risk losing any more. We may have been plotting a Fading, but we still had our morals.

Still, Michel convinced us. He wanted a chance of glory, to win that respect and admiration he had never achieved in life. And who were we to argue? Each time we were able to land a blow might be the last time anyone saw de Rais, the last time anyone needed to suffer. We needed to take every opportunity open to us.

This time, we chose the winter solstice. The longest night, to give us maximum time to prepare. De Rais had been seen in the town just the night before, watching a local Christmas parade the way a cat would watch a party of mice. Just thinking about the look on his face sends a shiver through me as bad as any Fading. We had selected our timing well – he was clearly in a predatory frame of mind. There was something about those eyes. He had always had charm, that was part of his danger in life. He could get anything out of anyone, through either coax or threat.

There had been a constant, heavy snowfall. It was one of those days that never really gets light, when the sun isn't able to break through the clouds, for even an hour. There wasn't a single footprint up at the castle; nobody had ventured up there in days, living or dead. We kept it as haunted as we could, you see, to try and scare the living away, protect their souls. It didn't always work.

As true night fell, we headed to the castle, around two dozen of us in total, determined to bear witness to the creation of another chink in de Rais' armour.

"You're cowards!" Michel called to the other young men who had agreed to accompany him in his quest, his shouts giving any onlookers the impression of a falling-out. "Honestly, you think de Rais scares me? I'll spend all night here, alone, just you watch me!"

They laughed at him, as planned, at his mock bravado. I could see he was shaking beneath the borrowed finery we had dressed him in for the night, knowing the monster's love for beautiful things. Paul, a local nobleman, had donated his beautiful silk doublet, and was even now watching on, standing at my side, wearing Michel's scruffy leather jacket.

"Don't be a fool, Michel, just come back to town; there are fancy-dress parties, we can really enjoy ourselves. Live a little, in our deaths."

"I'll feel alive enough up here! But do give my regards to the lovely ladies of the town, and I'll recount my daring deeds to them at the next one. All the girls love a hero, after all." With that, he strolled into the centre of the old ruins, looking the epitome of calm collection. "You hear me, de Rais? I'm going to be staying here overnight, and there's a not a thing anyone can do to deter me. I'm not afraid of any rumours." He said the last to the backs of his friends, as they headed towards town.

One ghost did Fade through a single injury in the ensuing attack. But it wasn't de Rais.

Despite the darkness, somehow, the shadow, when it appeared, cast even more light out of the castle. The moon was doing its best, but the clouds that had hung low in the sky all day were still heavy, and all we could see were streaks of silver where tiny fragments of sky showed between the grey.

"Ah, come on, darkness, you really think you can scare me?" Michel kept up his chatter throughout, seemingly to the moon, the night, the very stones of the castle itself, taunting the darkness, the sense of doom we could all feel now. "I fought alongside musketeers in the heart of Paris, a little shade can't affect me."

A little shade maybe not, but we all saw the flash of silver as he launched himself towards his victim. This time though, we were ready. Not only Michel, but others, all leapt forward, pouncing on the shape which appeared within our midst. Looking back, we think we landed a dozen blows, each of us armed with our own blade this time, not leaving anything to chance. Even I managed to strike him.

My weapon of choice had been with me since my death. You'll know, of course, that if we are able to gather things within those first few hours of death, they stay with us, taking on the form we choose, whether visible, invisible, tangible or not. Well, it wasn't much, but I grabbed my knitting needles. There was nobody to greet me into the afterlife, nobody to explain what I would and wouldn't be able to do, so I went for the thing which had always brought me such pleasure in life. I was never without my basket of wool, I was well-known for it, and my warm creations were worn by half the neighbourhood. They served me well again that night. One blow, to the top of his right arm. I was proud of that – striking a fighting man on his sword arm – not bad work for somebody everyone sees as nothing but an aging widow. I know he felt it too, hearing the intake of breath as I pushed them home as hard as I could. Not the devastating injury of a sword blade, and one of the soldiers even managed to discharge his pistol, but we must all do our bit in times such as these.

In the chaos, for a few moments, none of us noticed the pale glow on the floor at our feet. The snow was no longer the tranquil beauty it had been just minutes before. The trampled mud showed the clear evidence of our attack, a mixture of footprints, boots and bare feet, shoes from each of our centuries. And Paul. His face mirrored poor Collette's, contorted in agony, a mix of pain and sorrow, for the few moments he remained in front of us. As he left us, our eyes met, and I swear at the end, he smiled. Branded a fop in life, in death he had been part of the great sacrifice to bring down de Rais. None of us would forget him for that. I know I won't.

And then he was gone, and we were once again surrounded by nothing more than the night air, de Rais still free to roam.

Free to roam, and now very much aware of what we were trying to do.

Michel, devastated that his bravery had caused the Fading of another, took it as a sign that it should be his own destiny to bring down de Rais, however long it might take. And he no longer limited his campaign to Machecoul, castle or town. The monster knew too well what our intention was now, and wouldn't be so easily fooled again. So Michel began tracking him. Throughout the Loire, throughout western France, and then the rest of the country. Wherever stories of abnormal Fadings or strikes on ghosts came to light, off he would go, to listen, learn, and plot.

For all these decades since, he's been working so hard. He's not always been on his own either – he's had all the help we can offer him, from Machecoul and further afield, wherever possible, not to mention local support. It's been a lonely journey for him, but he's never failed us. Strike after strike, he's found his way close to de Rais, working towards what he hoped would be the final Fading.

Which brings me nicely to this year. It was always going to end here, at Machecoul castle. It was where de Rais' reign of terror began, only fitting it's where we brought it to an end.

It had been years since de Rais had been struck at within his own four walls, we thought sufficient time had passed that he would have dropped his guard. This time, we lay in wait, as soon as Michel reported rumours of his presence back in the Loire. De Rais had spent the summer in Paris itself, by all accounts, in the heart of the city, loitering around Père Lachaise Cemetery, trying to ingratiate himself back amongst the great and the good, according to what Michel had learned. Thankfully, the spirits there had heard of his misdeeds, and weren't to be fooled. Nor were those of Montparnasse or Montmartre, to everyone's relief. We have friends in high places, who have been following our attempts these last years, and ensuring word is spread of de Rais. As a result, we haven't been the only ones to try and stop him. Peter Abelard and his wife, Héloïse d'Argenteuil, have been key amongst them, but even British royalty have helped carry news of Fadings, and supported our cause.

All Hallows Eve was our chosen date this time.

We've read the stories, or seen the depictions on the televisions of the homes we now reside in, of the furious villagers storming the monster's hideaway, torches blazing, baying for blood – we may not have been carrying torches, but there was no hiding this time. We spirits stormed the castle, calling him out, knowing that he must have been feeling invincible after all this time, and wouldn't be able to resist taking us on.

Sure enough, once we were there, the familiar darkness fell over the place, even in the twilight of the hours before dusk.

And there he was. He'd been visible in the past, yes, but never quite like he was that night. It was clear that Michel and our allies had taken their toll; he was paler than any ghost I'd ever seen. As he approached, I refused to take my eyes off him, and I swear I could see the outline of the stones in the wall behind him, even in the gloom. It was eerie, let me tell you that. Collette, Paul, the others, they vanished into nothing, yes, but it didn't look like this. With de Rais, he looked just like the spirits you see in films sometimes, almost an outline, nothing more. I wasn't sure whether he would be able to present in full visibility, even if he wanted to. Then he laughed. He shouldn't have laughed. It was as though, in that moment, he conjured all the hatred, anger and sorrow of the centuries and condensed them into a single moment. There were still parents of the lost children amongst us, and they weren't going to let him get away with that.

Before our code-word could be uttered, before Michel and the other leaders had chance to strategise, the mob went for him. We all went for him.

Even in his half-visibility, half-tangibility, his weakened state meant we could do more damage than we anticipated, than he likely anticipated. I know there were innocents harmed in the attack, me amongst them. Michel's own blade cut through my lower arm as I threw myself into the fray, but I was lucky. A hint of a glow, a moment of pain, and carried on. Not everyone was so lucky. Three village Fadings happened that night, three souls lost to eternity in agony.

Despite the chaos, it must have been over in less than a minute.

If we'd had breath in our body, we would have been holding it, waiting, hoping, to see what would happen next. Could we have been successful? Was he defeated?

"Look." Michel's voice brought us all back to the present.

The infamous hangman's dagger.

For what seemed an eternity, none of us dared move, dared to touch it. But it had to be done. Finally, Michel stepped forward and carefully picked it up, as though afraid the evil would somehow rub off on him.

"We should bury it." To this day, I have no idea where the idea came from, or what made me speak up, but suddenly, it seemed the obvious thing to do. "But not here. Not where his Fading happened. There could be a power to it."

Waiting until darkness proper fell was the hardest thing any of us have ever had to do. Almost without thinking, we formed a group, facing outward, Michel in the centre of us, clutching that knife as though his death depended on it. Perhaps it did. Finally, there was silence from the town, and we began our journey.

"The church," Michel called out to us all, as we walked in formation through the streets.

A murmur spread through the group, but in the end, transferring the bloodied blade was straightforward. It had belonged to a ghost, after all, and to our relief, took on the form of the spirit carrying it, in this case, Michel. Whilst most of us waited nervously outside the great building, he and a small guard slipped through the heavy wooden doors, and took the knife down into the crypt. When they returned, we all prayed that there it would remain, undiscovered and undisturbed.

We had done it.

We had defeated de Rais.

The children of Machecoul, of the Loire, of France, were safe. We could all sleep easy in our beds again.

The town became a different place for us spirits, almost overnight, as word spread of our victory. Ghosts more inclined to travel spread the word through our region, through France; we were heroes, we had saved the children of France.

Nights were drawing in, closer and closer, as winter began to take its hold on Machecoul, with dark clouds casting their strange shadows over the church. We kept a vague watch on the place, but as the days, then weeks, passed without incident, the patrols of the streets became less regular. When Pierre, one of the young soldiers who had formed the guard that transported the knife, went missing, we didn't worry. Well, we didn't notice immediately. He was a bit of a wild one, after all. We assumed he had gone travelling. But Dominique, she was never one to show signs of wanderlust. She vanished the week after Pierre.

Despite myself, I couldn't but wonder, had we been successful in forcing the Fading of de Rais, or did we just grant him the gift of permanent invisibility?

A month later, out of the darkness, we all heard the scream.

Author's Note

I've been wanting to write a darker Kindred Spirits story for years, when a writing friend suggested Gilles de Rais, Baron de Rais. Reading his story, sadly, he was perfect.

A commander under Joan of Arc, he was a celebrated military leader, and honoured with a role at the consecration of Charles VII, as well as being created a Marshal of France.

But he bankrupted himself and ruined his family through pursuit of his own glorification, and began using the dark arts. What started as alchemy turned into trying to summon demons, and ultimately the horrific assault and murder of potentially hundreds of children.

Finally discovered in 1440, he was executed in October of the same year.

143

Jennifer C. Wilson stalks dead people (usually monarchs, mostly Mary Queen of Scots and Richard III). Inspired by childhood visits to as many castles and historical sites her parents could find, and losing herself in their stories (not to mention quite often the castles themselves!), at least now her daydreams make it onto the page.

After returning to the north-east of England for work, she joined a creative writing class, and has been filling notebooks ever since. Jennifer won North Tyneside Libraries' Story Tyne short story competition in 2014, and in 2015, her debut novel, Kindred Spirits: Tower of London was published by Crooked Cat Books. The full series was re-released by Darkstroke in January 2020.

Jennifer is a founder and host of the award-winning North Tyneside Writers' Circle, and has been running writing workshops in North Tyneside since 2015. She also publishes historical fiction novels with Ocelot Press. She lives in Whitley Bay, and is very proud of her two-inch view of the North Sea.

You can connect with Jennifer online:

Facebook: https://www.facebook.com/jennifercwilsonwriter/
Twitter: https://twitter.com/inkjunkie1984
Blog: https://jennifercwilsonwriter.wordpress.com/
Instagram: https://www.instagram.com/jennifercwilsonwriter/
Amazon: https://www.amazon.co.uk/Jennifer-C-Wilson/e/B018UBP1ZO/

Her books include:

❖The Kindred Spirits series
❖The Raided Heart
❖The Last Plantagenet?

AN UNQUIET DREAM

BY

LYNN BRYANT

Elvas, Portugal, 1812

The dreams were the worst.

They came relentlessly every night, so that after two months of waking trembling and bathed in sweat in the early hours of the morning, Sean O'Connor dreaded going to bed. He knew that he cried out in his sleep from the awkward enquiries of his room-mates, and Sean was embarrassed. He was immensely relieved when Dr Adam Norris, who was in charge of the general hospital, approached him as he was leaving the mess one afternoon and suggested a change of room.

"It's very small, Captain, one of the attic rooms. I've had Colonel Stephens in it, but he left us on Thursday. There's a convoy leaving for Lisbon, he's going home."

"Do I warrant a single room, Dr Norris? I thought you usually reserved those for more senior officers."

"We don't have any senior officers left, Captain O'Connor. And I thought you might prefer it."

Sean felt himself flush. "I think my poor room-mates might prefer it. Have they been complaining?"

"They're worried about you, Captain. As am I."

"Thank you, Doctor. There's no need, I'm doing very well."

"No, you're not."

"I'm fine. The infection has gone and I'm getting stronger…"

"Captain O'Connor, you spent eighteen hours lying under a pile of dead bodies with your abdomen slashed open, it's astonishing that you're still alive."

"Don't," Sean snarled, and Norris fell silent. After a long pause, he said:

"I'm sorry. I know you prefer not to talk about it, but…"

"I can't talk about it," Sean said. He could feel his muscles beginning to tense. There were beads of sweat on his brow and he longed to turn and run. It happened all the time. He could manage short, simple conversations about the weather or the quality of the food, but anything that touched on the long hours of his ordeal at Badajoz set off a collection of incomprehensible physical symptoms which terrified him.

"All right, Captain," Norris said soothingly. "Don't worry about it. I'll get one of the orderlies to move your kit to the new room…"

"I don't need help," Sean snapped. "I may not be capable of doing my job any more but I'm quite capable of shifting a few bags up a couple of flights of stairs. Thank you, Doctor. I appreciate your concern."

Sean had made it to the door of his current room before he remembered there would be no solitude there. Captain Hendy and Lieutenant Brooke were still downstairs in the mess room, but Captain Smith would probably be in their shared room as he could not yet make it downstairs without assistance. Sean changed direction and went down the back stairs and outside. He was sorry that he had snapped at Dr Norris because he liked the man and he knew that Norris was genuinely concerned for him, but it did not help Sean to talk any more than it helped him to be silent.

Sean had been moved from the general hospital on the edge of Badajoz to the attractive little town of Elvas. There was no accommodation for officers within any of the three hospitals there. It was one of the ironies of Wellington's army that the privilege of holding an officer's commission turned into a significant disadvantage when an officer was sick or wounded. It was considered unsuitable for them to be treated alongside the common soldiers, so they were billeted in individual houses and left to fend for themselves. Those officers with private servants, or who had the means to pay for help, might do well enough. Others, who had nobody to tend them, were left to the mercy of whichever householder they had been billeted on and Sean had heard of men dying alone and untended.

Sean was surprised and relieved on his arrival in Elvas, to be offered space in a tall house in a narrow street behind the cathedral. It was under the supervision of Dr Adam Norris who ran one of the hospitals and was also responsible for the care of a dozen sick or wounded officers billeted in the Casa Mendes. The house was plainly furnished but scrupulously clean and food and basic nursing care was provided by Señora Avila the stout housekeeper who spoke little English but ran an efficient household. The officers combined their pay and rations, and Captain Hendy's servant ran errands and assisted with the heavier nursing tasks. The arrangement was very effective.

"Better than being in one of those hospitals, old boy," Hendy said to Sean at their first meal together. "They're hellish."

"I've never heard of an arrangement like this for officers."

"It's not common, although Norris and Guthrie and a few of the other surgeons have been writing to the medical board to ask for better provision for the officers. This was set up by the regimental surgeon from the 110th but most of their wounded have been moved out, so Dr Norris has taken it over."

"Thank God for the 110th," Sean said with real feeling.

For ten days after his arrival, Sean was confined to bed, still burning with fever. There was a small isolation room on the first floor and having established that Sean could pay, Norris found a skinny twelve year old to take care of him, ensuring that he was fed when he could eat and kept reasonably clean. Eventually he examined the appalling wound across Sean's midriff and gave an approving nod.

"It's doing well, Captain, and the fever has gone. I thought we might lose you, but it appears you'll live to fight another day."

Sean tried not to shudder at the thought. He could not explain to Norris or anybody else how that day haunted his dreams. Badajoz had not been his first battle and not even the first time he had been wounded but the long hours that he had lain trapped under dead and dying men in the breach had left him with wounds that could not be seen and could not be treated. Around him, his fellow officers moved on. Some were sent back to England to recuperate while others went back to join their regiments with real enthusiasm.

Sean could do neither. Physically he was becoming stronger every day and Norris continued to give positive reports on the healing of his horrific wound. Mentally, he was a broken man. He started at every sound, cried out in his sleep and awoke sweating and terrified after dreams of blood and death. He was morbidly anxious about his health, and that of his fellow officers, checking on them compulsively and asking Norris worried questions about anything that seemed unusual. Sean knew that his fellows regarded him with a mixture of compassion and embarrassment and had begun to avoid his company.

Outside in the narrow street, Sean walked quickly down to the cathedral. The doors were open, and he slipped inside and made his way to a pew. There were several other people around, all of them locals who were either praying or sitting in quiet contemplation. One or two shot Sean a curious glance but did not speak to him. The priest was at the lectern, flicking through a huge bound bible and he looked over and gave a faint smile. Sean nodded in response then sat back and closed his eyes. Father Nani had become accustomed to his daily visits during these past weeks. He spoke a little English, and had even discreetly heard Sean's confession when the cathedral was empty and there was no danger of an unexpected visit from a red-coated tourist. The religious preferences of Irish officers were never discussed in the mess. Sean kept silent on the matter and practised his childhood Catholicism in secret when he could.

He found the church both a comfort and a refuge in his current misery although so far his impassioned prayers had brought no answer. Sean knew that his continued, steady recovery was putting Dr Norris in a difficult position. Within a few weeks, he was going to have to declare Sean fit for duty again and that would place the onus of making a decision squarely upon Sean's shoulders. Sean knew that Norris was trying to avoid that for as long as possible. If Sean was physically fit, he needed either to return to his regiment, resign his commission and go home, or at the very least, request a spell on half-pay.

Sean could not decide. Theoretically, an officer could sell out at any time, but few did during wartime unless they were too sick or too badly wounded to carry on. Sean's wound had healed well, and he suspected that at least some of his fellow officers would think that fear, rather than necessity, had made him leave the army and despise him for it. He rather despised himself.

There was no comfort today in religion. Arriving back at the Casa Mendes Sean was both relieved and irritated to find that Norris had ignored his wishes and that Private Coulson was already arranging his possessions in his new room. He saluted as Sean arrived and Sean found a coin and handed it to him.

"I can unpack for you if you like, sir."

"No need. I'm not that helpless, Private. Go on, off you go."

The room was small and clean with a narrow bed, a wooden table and chair and a small wash stand with a ceramic bowl and jug. Sean had few possessions, and it did not take him long to arrange them, using one of his boxes as a table beside his bed and the other as storage for his clothes. He set out writing materials on the table alongside a bottle of brandy and a pewter cup. It had been two weeks since his last letter to his wife and he knew she would be frantic for news, but somehow he could not bring himself to write until he had a decision to give her. Janey would want him to come home. Were it not for the children, she would have been on a transport to nurse him herself. Sean ached to see her but was glad she was not here. At some point she would have to know how badly his ordeal had affected him, but he was happy to delay it until he had made his choice. He sat staring at the blank page and had written nothing when the call came for dinner.

Meals, for those who were able to attend, were served in what must have been a parlour and which the officers had turned into an informal mess room. After dinner a few officers generally lingered on in the room playing cards, sharing wine and swapping battle stories. Sean rarely joined them. He desperately missed the camaraderie and banter of late nights playing whist for pennies and making bad jokes, but he could not risk making a fool of himself by flinching at a slammed door or getting a bout of the shakes at the mention of Badajoz. His mess mates were kind, but Sean did not expect them to understand.

Sean spoke little during dinner. He managed a conversation about the departure of Colonel Stephens and his new quarters and listened to a squabble between two subalterns about the best fishing spots on the Guadiana River. When the table was cleared and the cards were produced, Sean made his excuses and went up to his room. The others no longer tried to persuade him to linger.

Sean had recently received a parcel of books from Jane, and he sat on his bed under the sloping attic window and read until the light faded. He could hear the others going to bed, the opening and closing of doors and a muffled curse as Captain Gregg missed a step and stumbled, with his newly fitted wooden leg. Eventually it was quiet, and Sean got into bed and lay there, both longing for and dreading sleep.

It came eventually but when he awoke it was still dark. For a moment he was disoriented, expecting to see the shape of his room-mates on their narrow bunks and the litter of their possessions scattered around the room. Instead there were the few items of furniture and the closed ill-fitting door. Sean lay still for a few minutes with a sense of bewilderment, although he did not immediately know why. Finally it dawned on him that he was awake but perfectly calm. There was none of the usual panic and he could not recall dreaming.

The realisation almost sent him into panic and Sean unexpectedly wanted to laugh at how stupid that was. His usually lively sense of humour had been one of the first casualties of Badajoz and it was very good to see that it had not gone forever. Sean sat up, listening, and realised that he had been woken, not by his usual terrifying dreams, but by a sound.

Sean sat listening for a while. It sounded like footsteps, pacing backwards and forwards across a room. Occasionally it would stop, as though the person had paused in their restless movement, but then it would start up again.

Sean could not work out where the sounds were coming from. They could not be above him as his room was at the top of the house. There were other rooms on this floor, but as far as he knew they were not occupied by patients. Dr Norris definitely had the room next to his, and Sean had an idea that the other rooms belonged to the medical orderly and two or three officers' servants' as well as the Portuguese maid who was employed to clean the house and to help in the kitchen. Norris had not returned from the hospital by the time the other officers went to bed. Sean supposed it could be him, but somehow he could not reconcile this restless pacing with the doctor's calm demeanour. When he had told Norris about his sleep problems, the doctor had replied that his long hours of work left him so exhausted that he slept the moment he got into bed.

Sean got up and padded to the door, listening. After a moment, he opened it cautiously and stepped out onto the landing. Out here, the sounds were quieter. Sean tiptoed to the door to the next room and listened again. He could still hear them but not as distinctly. For a moment, he hesitated, then shrugged and went back into his room, closing the door. He was curious but he could hardly knock on the doctor's door in the early hours. Given the noise he frequently made in his own room during the night, he did not have the right to complain about anybody else. Sean got back into bed, closed his eyes, and resigned himself to a sleepless night, hearing the steady tramp of the footsteps.

It was light when he awoke, dawn coming early on these summer days, and he lay there for a while feeling very relaxed. The bed, although narrower than the wide bunk in his previous room, was very comfortable. It was covered by an old patchwork quilt which must have been part of the original furnishings of the house. It reminded Sean of home, where his mother and sisters had worked at quilting through the long winter evenings. This one was faded but very soft and Sean ran his fingers over it and wondered about the women who had made it and whether they had lived in this house.

Eventually there were signs of life below, and Sean got up. He had no servant with him so he had got into the habit of bringing up water each evening so that he could wash in the mornings. It was cold, but that hardly mattered at this time of year. Sean washed, shaved, and dressed. He was sitting down to pull on his boots before he realised what had brought on this unaccustomed sense of well-being.

He had not dreamed.

The realisation shocked him, and he remained seated on the wooden chair, gazing up at a blue sky through the high window without really seeing it. Sean could not remember the last night he had slept without the awful nightmares. Nothing had happened to bring about the startling change and Sean was almost afraid to hope that this was more than a temporary respite. All the same, it had cheered him up considerably and he arrived at the breakfast table and collected his portion of bread and spiced sausage in an excellent mood. The arrival of a supply convoy meant that there was sugar for his tea and Sean ate with a good appetite, listening to the usual conversations.

Letters had arrived from Wellington's army, marching towards Salamanca and Madrid to engage the French, and there was a lively discussion about his Lordship's probable plans which Sean found himself able to endure surprisingly well. There was also news of a convoy travelling to Lisbon within a fortnight to convey some of the sick and wounded either to convalescent hospitals in the capital or back to England. A hunting party had brought down several deer which promised a feast of venison that evening and Captain Hendy, who was almost fully recovered and expected to be able to rejoin his regiment in a week or so, offered to supply the wine for a celebration.

As the other officers left, Dr Norris appeared in search of a belated breakfast. Sean sat down again and poured more tea into two cups. Norris thanked him and began to eat.

"You seem better this morning, Captain O'Connor."

"I had a better night," Sean admitted. "At least, I didn't dream. I did wake up though. It was very odd, I thought I could hear somebody walking about in the early hours, but when I checked the corridor there was nobody there. Did you hear anything, Doctor?"

"I wasn't there," Norris said, around a mouthful of bread. "I was called out at about eleven and ended up having to perform an emergency operation on a German cavalry officer. I've only just come back. Once I'm at the hospital, there are always patients to see and I'm never back before morning. I was going to eat and go up to see if I can get a couple of hours sleep. God, I'd forgotten what tea with sugar in tasted like. Is there any more in the pot?"

"I'll get some," Sean said, getting up. He took the pot through into the kitchen, ignored Jenkins' rolled eyes at the request and went back to the table to find Norris regarding him with some amusement.

"You really are a lot better, Captain. Who knew that a night without dreaming could bring about this effect?"

"It probably seems stupid," Sean said. "It's just that I think I'd convinced myself it was never going to happen. That I'd be like this forever."

"The reassuring thing for me is that you're talking about it," Norris said. "You've been trying to hide from it."

"We don't discuss fear in the officer's mess, Doctor."

"No, because you're all too frightened to," Norris said without irony. "But that doesn't mean men don't talk about it at all, among friends. And it affects most soldiers at some point or another, even those who haven't been through such a horrific ordeal as you. I've a friend, a fairly senior officer these days, who freely admits that in the early days he used to throw up after every battle and that his hands shook for half a year after Assaye. You're not unique."

"I bet he doesn't talk about that in front of his junior officers, though."

"I've no idea, although knowing him, I wouldn't place a bet on it. But congratulations for taking the first step. Don't panic when it comes back – because it will – and don't run and hide again. Now that we've spoken, believe that I can be trusted. I'm not going to share your confidences with the rest of the army."

"I know you won't. Doctor – thank you. You've been the soul of patience and I know you've delayed signing off my sick leave for longer than you should."

"I have, and I'm going to extend it for longer. You shouldn't rush into a decision either way, just yet. In fact, I've a proposal for you. We've no commandant in charge since poor Major Clarke died of typhus. Eventually they'll assign somebody, but how do you feel about helping me out with the running of the place until they do? I'll write to

Dr McGrigor, and he can speak to Lord Wellington and your commanding officer about it."

Sean was taken aback. "I know nothing about medicine, Doctor."

"That's why I'm here. The medical staff are my responsibility, but there should be a regimental officer as commandant, in charge of the orderlies and ward-masters and to take care of general discipline. It won't be a formal appointment, but it would be a big help, and it might give you more time to decide."

"All right," Sean said. "Doctor, I'm not sure I've ever said this, but I'd like…it was always my aim to get back into combat again."

Norris smiled and poured tea from the replenished pot. "I know, Captain. If it hadn't been, you'd have allowed me to send you home on those first transports. Let's give it some time, shall we? Now what was this about footsteps in the night?"

"I thought it was you, at first," Sean admitted. "They sounded so close, like a man pacing up and down the room."

"Not me. By the time I get to my bed, I've no energy to pace the floor. I wonder if it could have been in the room below? Sounds can carry in an odd way in these old houses."

"Who has the room under mine?"

"Ashby and Newton. It won't be Newton, though, I've had to move him out, he's down at the fever ward."

"God, I'm sorry, I didn't realise that."

"I must say I've never heard Ashby moving about in the night, but that doesn't mean much, I sleep like the dead and besides, my room isn't above his."

"I wish I knew," Sean said. "If it is him, then there's a reason behind it. I don't know Ashby well. I don't know any of them that well, but perhaps something's troubling him."

"He never seems that troubled to me," Norris said frankly. "But in any case, he's got a clean bill of health and he's off back to his regiment."

"I'll be the only one left soon," Sean said.

"Not for long, Captain. There'll be another battle and another wave of wounded men coming in by wagon and it will all start up again. That's why I need your help."

Sean was doubtful about his new role as temporary hospital commandant, but he quickly found that his new responsibilities kept him very busy and kept his mind occupied. Over the following week he met with the commandants of the other two hospitals in Elvas and began to familiarise himself with his new duties. There was a lot to learn but Norris was a patient and informative teacher.

There were no more dreams. Most nights, Sean slept through, tired out after a long and busy day. Twice he awoke in the night to the sound of pacing footsteps, and lay listening to them in growing bewilderment. He broached the matter with Lieutenant Ashby just before his departure and Ashby stared at him so blankly that it was clear that he knew nothing about the matter. It was a mystery, but Sean had no time to dwell on it.

The dream came after ten days and was so unexpected that it shook Sean, who had begun to think that his troubles were over. He awoke after hours of peaceful sleep into a room bathed in silvery moonlight. He had left the window slightly open against the stuffy heat of the summer night and a breeze had sprung up, wafting cool air into the room. At the foot of his bed, a woman stood immobile.

The moon made it possible to see her clearly. She was dressed in a shapeless white garment, her long dark hair loose around her shoulders. Sean thought that she looked very young but also very unwell. She was thin and gaunt, her arms almost skeletal and the bones of what should have been a very lovely face standing out in sharp relief. Her eyes were pools of darkness.

The shock make Sean yell. He closed his eyes tightly and pulled the quilt up over his head. There was no sound in the room. Sean lay curled up for some time, sweating in fear, with his heart pounding. Eventually, reluctantly, he forced himself to move. Peering over the top of the quilt, he saw the room, neat and unremarkable as it had been when he went to bed. The girl was not there, and Sean decided that she never had been.

Sean got up and went for the brandy. Pouring a generous measure, he went back to bed and sat sipping it, waiting for his heart to slow down. He realised it must have been another dream and that his first waking had been part of the illusion. It was disheartening, but Sean sternly forbade himself to overreact. He had gone for almost two weeks without dreaming and this dream, although terrifying, was nothing like the repetitive nightmares of Badajoz. At the very least, that cycle had been broken.

Sean mentioned it to Norris when they were going over some supply requisitions the following day. His instinct had been to keep quiet about his relapse, but he remembered what Norris had said and decided that talking about it might be a good idea. Norris heard him out without interruption.

"Well done for talking to me," he said, when Sean had finished. "And it's certainly different from your previous nightmares. I wonder why this woman? You didn't recognise her, did you?"

"No. She looked ill…half-dead to be honest. I did wonder…"

"Go on."

Sean took a deep breath. "I could hear them screaming," he said abruptly. "When I was lying there all those hours, thinking I was about to die. I could hear the people screaming when the soldiers sacked the town. Especially the women. I heard afterwards what they did to them. How many of them were raped. And I felt guilty that I was lying there listening to it happening and I couldn't get up to help."

"Dear God, I didn't realise that," Norris said softly. "No wonder you have nightmares, Captain. Look, try not to worry about it too much. You've come so far in the past few weeks. Do you want me to give you a sleeping draught?"

"No. I tried that at the beginning, and it made me feel terrible. I'll be all right."

"Well let me know how it goes over the next few days," Norris said. "Are you still hearing the footsteps?"

Sean laughed. "Yes. Although not last night, oddly enough. They don't bother me, I think it's just the house falling down around us. They don't even keep me awake for long, although I always wake up. I do wonder what it is, though."

"Rats scampering around and chewing on the plasterwork, probably. We'll know when a section of the roof caves in," Norris said philosophically. "I'm glad that you're taking a more light-hearted attitude Captain, it'll do you good."

Sean agreed with him. While he was unable to deny his disappointment at the return of his nightmares, he was pleased that his mood remained optimistic. He was enjoying having a job to do and he realised it was improving his confidence. As many of the convalescents left and others arrived, he had no need to explain his continuing presence at the hospital. Norris merely introduced him as the temporary hospital commandant and his new mess mates did not hesitate to come to him with questions and complaints. While it was not the same as being in command of a company of the line, it made Sean feel useful and for the most part it kept the nightmares at bay.

He saw the woman again a few nights later. This time, the dream caught him just on the edge of wakefulness and he made himself lie still, his heart pounding with the shock, staring at the slender form. Without the panic he had felt at his first sight of her, he was able to observe details that he had not noticed before. She was definitely wearing some kind of nightgown, stained in places and with a ragged hem. Her hair looked dishevelled and the sunken misery of the dark eyes unexpectedly wrung Sean's heart. His eyes hurt as he forced himself to stare at her, trying hard not to blink. He could not help himself, and in that flicker of an eyelid, she was gone.

Sean sat up. The dream puzzled him because he had no sense of when he had slipped between sleep and wakefulness. The first time he had seen her, it might have happened at any point when he was huddling under the bedclothes, but tonight he would have sworn that he had been awake the whole time. It was clear that he could not have been. If he had, then his illness had taken an unexpectedly sinister turn. Sean settled down, then lay awake for several hours worrying about brain injury.

He took his concerns to Norris the following day. Norris had asked Sean to join him on an expedition to inspect a building which might be suitable for a new fever hospital. Fever patients were currently lodged in one of the convent buildings, but it was not large enough. Sickness was rife in Wellington's army and far more men died of fever or dysentery than in battle. Norris had been searching for a new location for his fever patients for some time and walking through the dusty sheds of an abandoned winery, Sean thought he might have found it.

They were at the site for several hours, making lists and notes and talking to the owner, an elderly farmer who had lost his son to war and clearly had very little interest in what became of the unused farm buildings. Repairs would be needed and a thorough cleaning before bunks could be installed, but Sean thought that there were probably enough walking wounded to do much of the work. His new position had quickly introduced him to the idlers and malingerers who haunted every army hospital and he suspected that giving them an honest day's work would convince many of them that it was time to return to their regiments.

It was evening before they rode back towards the hospital, and Norris suggested that they stop at one of the taverns in the square for a meal and a drink. It was the first time since Badajoz that Sean had done anything like this, and he enjoyed it enormously. They sat outside on wooden benches after they had eaten, sharing a jug of wine and swapping stories.

156

"How are your nightmares?" Norris asked finally, as they poured the last of the wine.

"I'm not sure. Yesterday, I started to wonder if it's a dream at all or if I'm going a bit mad. I saw that girl again, but it felt as though I was wide awake. Is it possible that I'm seeing things?"

"Hallucinations?"

"Are they real? I've heard of them, but I've no idea."

"Oh yes. It's not unusual with a brain injury, I've known men who have seen the oddest things. I suppose it's possible, but if you hurt your head in that mess I'd have expected to see signs of it weeks ago. If you want my honest opinion, I think it's another of your dreams and you just didn't realise it. But this one doesn't seem to be upsetting you as much, and you're definitely less jumpy now."

"That's the wine," Sean said, lifting his cup. Norris laughed and raised his in a toast.

Sean felt pleasantly mellow as they went back to the house and up the stairs to their rooms.

"If they need me in the middle of the night you'll have to shake me awake, Captain, or I'll never hear them," Norris said. "I'd invite you in for a last brandy, but I've run out."

"I've got some," Sean said. "Come in. It'll help you sleep."

They laughed together as Sean poured the drink, slightly tipsy and shushing each other loudly. Sean sat on the bed, giving Norris the chair. It was a bright clear night, a sliver of moon and a canvas of brilliant stars shining through the window. Sean lit two candles and sat back, sipping the brandy and enjoying the companionable silence. He realised he was becoming sleepy and closed his eyes. Norris had fallen silent as well and Sean wondered suddenly if he had dozed off on the hard wooden chair and opened his eyes to look.

She was there, as on the previous occasion, wholly immobile, with the dark eyes staring sightlessly towards him. She was so close to where Norris sat that he could have reached out and touched her. The shock of it drew a squawk of alarm from Sean. He scuttled backwards on the bed into the corner by the wall, spilling the dregs of his brandy onto the quilt, and closed his eyes tight.

"Captain! Captain! Are you all right?"

"No," Sean said, shaking his head violently. "No. Oh no, no, no, no, no. I can't stand it. I'm going bloody mad. Bad enough with the dreams, but now I'm seeing things when I'm wide awake and I can't take it."

A hand grasped his arm. "Up," Norris said in peremptory tones. "Come on, into my room. Don't argue with me, move."

He bundled Sean into the next room and pushed him into a folding camp chair. Sean realised Norris had brought the brandy with him and watched, silent and trembling, as the doctor poured two cups. He carefully put one into Sean's shaking hand and made sure that he drank some before sitting in an identical chair opposite him and drinking a large gulp from his own cup.

"Better?"

Sean nodded and drank more. "I'm sorry. Look, I know you've tried, but I need to resign my commission. I'm never going to…"

"Sean, will you shut up for five minutes and let me speak. Don't say anything at all."

Sean was surprised into obedience. He suddenly realised that there were beads of sweat of Norris's forehead and his hand holding the cup was not entirely steady either.

"You're not going mad and you're not seeing things," Norris said quietly. "Or at least if you are, it's contagious. I saw her too."

Sean stared at him. It was at least a minute before he really understood the words and when he did, he could not say anything, frozen with shock and sudden terror. His voice when he finally spoke was a croak.

"You saw her. You mean…"

"No, don't say anything," Norris said quickly. He was on his feet, rummaging around on his desk. His room was considerably larger than Sean's with a wide old fashioned bed and a collection of battered furniture. Norris came back to him with paper and a pencil. He handed Sean a large book to lean on.

"Write, he said briefly. "It doesn't have to be neat. That's why I wanted you to keep quiet. I want to compare what we saw. You've seen her several times, so yours should be a lot more detailed than mine. Get on with it."

Sean put down his glass on the floor and took the pencil while Norris went to the desk. Having something to do helped to calm his fear and he found that after a moment he was able to write fluently. As he wrote, Sean reflected that it was an advantage to have a scientific mind. It would not have occurred to him to compare notes in this way.

Eventually, Sean ran out of things to write. He read what he had written and put down his pencil. He got up and handed Norris the paper and Norris scanned it, his lips quirking into a smile.

"Yours is a lot neater than mine. I suppose you've had time to get used to her."

Sean looked over his shoulder. "Or it could be because you're a doctor. I've never yet met one who could write legibly."

Adam gave him a look. "Perhaps I should hand over more of my paperwork to you, Captain O'Connor, as you're so proud of your penmanship. As I thought, yours is a lot more detailed. I didn't notice the embroidery on the shift although I did see the stain, mainly because I thought it might be blood. I didn't see as much of her face as you did, and I didn't notice that her feet were bare. But I wrote a lot about her physical condition because she looked as though she was half starved."

"That might also be because you're a doctor. It makes sense that we noticed different things."

"But generally, the accounts tally remarkably well. I'd say we saw the same thing."

"I can't believe it," Sean said. "I thought I was going mad. But Doctor…"

"My name is Adam. I think we've gone beyond formality."

Sean smiled faintly. He was beginning to feel a lot better. There was something very reassuring in Norris's practical approach to the vision. "Adam, how did she appear? Every time I've seen her, I've had my eyes closed and I've just opened them and she's there."

"It's difficult to say. I was looking at you, laughing to myself, thinking you were going to fall asleep in front of me. And then I saw something to my left, like a flutter of movement, so I turned my head, and she was right there. I nearly died of fright."

Sean could not help laughing at his frank admission. "It probably sounds rude to say that I'm glad, but I bloody am. Look, Adam…have you ever come across anything like this before? I mean what is it? What is she? Is she…have we seen…?"

"A ghost? How the hell would I know? No, I've never seen anything like it before, although I've met men who say they have. To be honest I've generally put it down to too much drink and a dark night on sentry duty."

"We've been drinking."

"That's why I wanted to write it down," Norris said. "I think it's entirely possible for two men in drink to egg each other on to the point that they're convinced they've seen a ghost. But I don't think they'd be capable of the kind of detail we just produced independently. Admittedly you did tell me previously that you'd seen a woman, but you gave me no details at all."

Sean regarded him for a moment. He felt very sober, with the beginnings of a headache. "So who the hell is she? Or was she?"

"I've no idea. Look, why don't you sleep in here tonight, Sean, I've…"

"No, it's all right. I'm not afraid of her, Adam, it's just a shock when I see her. But she never appears more than once a night. I wonder if it's always the same time, I've never looked."

"Well it was around midnight when she turned up this evening because I'd just taken out my watch. I was going to wake you up to say goodnight."

"I'll add that to the notes," Sean said, and his companion grinned.

"We'll make a scientist of you yet. Get some sleep, Sean. I need to do my early rounds tomorrow, but we'll meet up during the afternoon and talk about it. If you want to."

"I do. There must be some explanation for this."

***

Adam Norris slept late the following morning and dragged himself through his rounds with an effort. He was usually a moderate drinker, and it was not until midday that his headache subsided, and he began to feel better. The evening was one of the strangest he had ever experienced, but Adam found himself thinking about the early part as much as its dramatic conclusion. He had enjoyed spending time with Sean O'Connor, and it reminded him how much he missed his friends who were up at the lines. It had been a promotion to be placed in charge of a general hospital, but there were some disadvantages of being away from the main army and isolation was one of them.

Sean's ghost was entirely another matter. Adam considered himself a rational man and had made it a principle during his medical career to weigh the evidence as far as he could before making a decision about diagnosis or treatment. In the heat of battle, there was no time to do anything other than react to every emergency and Adam knew that he sometimes made mistakes, but it was part of the job to accept that many patients could not be saved and live with it. Generally, however, he took his job seriously, studied whenever he could to keep up to date and was willing to accept new ideas.

160

Adam had never expected his open-mindedness to be tested by the appearance of a ghost, but no matter how hard he tried, he could not come up with any rational explanation for the figure he had seen the previous evening. There was no possible way the girl could have entered the room without him seeing her do so, or indeed hearing her as Sean's door creaked horrendously. She had looked, for those few moments, as real and solid as Sean, but then she had vanished as Adam blinked and left no trace behind.

The apparition had alarmed Adam at the time, but there had been no sense of menace about the woman. She seemed sad and possibly desperate, but not threatening. Making his way through the hot, stinking wards of the hospital, Adam found himself wondering about her. Having never believed in ghosts, he knew nothing about them apart from stories around the fireside during his boyhood, but all the tales of hauntings he had ever come across involved a person once living.

He mentioned this to Sean when he joined him in the commandant's office that afternoon before dinner. Sean looked surprisingly well and grinned when Adam said so.

"Ten years of army life will give you an awfully hard head for the drink, Adam. Sit down. I've a very nice madeira or I can send Private Edwards for some tea if you'd prefer."

Adam laughed. "Let's try the madeira, although if this goes on I'll be dead of the drink before the end of this war. I've been thinking about your ghost all day."

"My ghost, is it now? I did wonder about that, you know, because I'm assuming that Colonel Stephens never mentioned seeing anything. So is it the room she's haunting, or is it me?"

"I don't know," Adam admitted. "To be fair, Stephens was in a lot of pain. He'd lost his right arm and I had him dosed on as much laudanum as I could. Which he later supplemented with wine. He'd have slept through an army of ghosts marching through that room, and this one was fairly silent."

"Was she though? I admit she's never made a sound when I've seen her, but I've heard those footsteps pacing many times."

Adam was startled. "Good God, I'd forgotten about that. So you never found out who it was?"

"No. I've asked around, but they all looked at me as if I was mad. As you know, I put it down to rodents of some kind but I'm not so sure now. It didn't sound much like rats or mice, it's too regular and too loud. And honestly, it didn't sound as if it came from below me. I'd have said either next door or above, but there's nothing up there that I'm aware of."

"Or in the same room," Adam said quietly.

"Now isn't that a delightful thought."

"Well it's one you don't need to dwell upon. I've had them clearing out Major Clarke's room for you, I wanted it well scrubbed because of his illness, but it's ready now. It's on the floor below mine and it's a lot more comfortable than the room you're in. You could move your kit before we go into dinner. I'll help you if you like."

"I'm not arguing with you," Sean said. "It's not that it's frightening exactly, but it's a little unnerving now that I know she's not just in my head, not knowing when she'll make an appearance. And we can treat it as a piece of research. At least that way, we'll find out if it's me or the room."

Adam laughed aloud. "Whatever the cause of this, Captain O'Connor, it's been the making of you. You're a changed man, between ghosts and your new responsibilities."

"And a man I can call a friend," Sean said, echoing closely what Adam had been thinking earlier.

"That as well."

"About those dreams, though. I actually think she did help me out with that infernal pacing. It woke me up so many nights, that I think it interrupted the dreaming. By the time I went back to sleep, I was thinking of something else and once I stopped worrying about the dreams, they stopped coming so much. Although I still jump like a nervous colt if a door slams close by."

"One thing at a time, Sean, you're doing very well. Have you written to your poor wife yet?"

"I have, so. I told her I'm staying out here for the present, in a temporary posting and that I'll make my decision when they find a replacement for me."

"Good for you." Adam paused. He had a question, but he was not entirely sure how to phrase it. "Look, Sean, we can leave it here if you like. If you move into another room and the whole thing stops. I'll close that room down, use it for storage."

He could see the Irishman considering it. "We could do that," he said. "But I rather like the notion of a hospital for officers, I think we should have more of it not less. And besides, now that I've seen her, I want to know."

"Know what?"

"Who she was. What happened to her. Why in God's name she's wandering the rooms of this house."

"And how are you going to find that out?" Adam asked with genuine curiosity. Sean grinned and raised his glass.

"Research, laddie. I learned the value of it quite recently from a scientific mind that I very much respect. Your good health."

***

Sean slept well and dreamlessly in his new room. He was kept busy for a few days because of a selection of disciplinary matters among the convalescing soldiers. It was well known that idle soldiers were the most troublesome to manage and Sean was finding that discipline was the biggest challenge of his new post. He had been trying to steer a course between firmness and compassion, but a report from the Portuguese authorities in Elvas about a raid on a local farmhouse pushed him beyond his limit. The owners of the house had been robbed and beaten, but what infuriated Sean was the tearful aspect and bruised face of the farmer's daughter. No complaint of sexual assault was made and Sean was not surprised, since the farmer would not wish to broadcast his daughter's shame, but he was determined to make an example. Too many of the more active convalescents assumed that their status on the sick roll made them immune from punishment and Sean summoned a court martial, determined to prove them wrong. He could not flog them for rape, but their other crimes were well documented and although the punishment was relatively light, Sean could sense their shock that he had administered it at all, and in front of every man fit to witness it in the entire hospital.

When it was over, Sean informed Dr Norris that the men involved had effectively proved their fitness for duty and would be sent back to the lines with the next convoy, along with a letter to their commanding officer about their crimes. Adam made no attempt to argue, and with the matter concluded, Sean had time to turn his attention to the matter of spectres. He knew nothing about how the Casa Mendes came to be part of the general hospital and took his initial queries to Adam, who shook his head regretfully.

"I wish I could tell you, but I had nothing to do with it. We were struggling with the wounded after Badajoz and the officers were billeted all over the place and then Mrs van Daan informed me that she had found this place and that we could have the use of

163

it. Señora Avila and her staff came with the house, but I know nothing of the owners."

"Mrs van Daan?" Sean said blankly.

"The wife of Colonel van Daan of the 110th. He commands the third brigade of the light division. She helps out with the wounded, and…"

"I've heard of Mrs van Daan," Sean said, and then saw the expression on Adam's face and hastily revised a large amount of gossip he had been about to repeat. "I mean…isn't she the lady who has worked with the surgeons and who does rather more than nursing?"

Adam Norris studied him for a long moment then gave a faint smile. "Anne van Daan and her husband are two of my closest friends, Sean. She came to work with me as a volunteer in Lisbon three years ago and I trained her, against enormous opposition from my fellow surgeons. She's extraordinary. She's also a very good organiser and she found this place. I'll write to her to see what she knows. In the meantime, I've had another idea. We need an excellent source of local gossip and I know just the place to find it."

"Where?"

Norris grinned. "At the local brothel, of course."

Sean stared at him. He realised his mouth was hanging open like a callow boy who had never heard of a brothel and closed it quickly. "I wonder why I didn't think of that."

Norris laughed aloud. "Sorry, I couldn't resist. There's a young woman by the name of Pereira who runs a very pleasant tavern on the edge of town. I have been there, but not as a customer. One of the girls was very unwell during the time we were here, and Senorita Pereira had no faith in the local apothecary so I was asked as a personal favour if I would attend."

"A personal favour for whom?" Sean asked.

"A young officer who is a particular friend of the lovely lady. I'm not giving you his name, it wouldn't be right. We can walk over tomorrow if you wish. It's not far, just near the Santa Luzia Fort."

"Convenient for the garrison, then. If my wife knew I was planning a visit to a brothel, she'd never speak to me again. I'm assuming you aren't intending to tell yours either?"

"Oh, I'm not married. I can't imagine how your wife would find out, but I promise to bear witness to your good behaviour if ever I'm asked. You'll like Diana Pereira, she's not at all what you'd expect."

It was less than two miles to the tavern, and they walked through quiet streets as the people of Elvas generally took a siesta during hot summer afternoons. Sean wondered if they would be admitted but the tavern door was wide open. They went in and found the tap room almost empty apart from two elderly men seated on a bench with a jug of wine and a chess board between them. A stocky dark-haired man was seated on a high wooden stool behind the bar with what looked like an account book in front of him, but he stood up as they entered and gave a little bow.

"It's Emilio, isn't it?" Adam asked pleasantly. "Dr Norris, I was here last year, to tend Lotta, I'm not sure if you remember me?"

The man nodded but did not speak. Adam ordered wine. As he was paying, a door at the back opened and a woman came into the room. She was dressed in yellow muslin and she wore her hair pulled back at the sides with decorated combs but otherwise loose down her back. Sean thought she was probably in her twenties and was very attractive and very self-assured.

"Welcome, gentlemen. A pleasant change to see a red coat, we don't see so many of them these days. Have you just arrived...?"

She stopped, her eyes on Adam's face, and then she smiled again and there was warmth in it. "I'm sorry, Doctor, I didn't recognise you immediately. You're even more welcome as an old friend. Please, put your purse away. You wouldn't take a penny for your services to Lotta, the least you can do is allow me to buy you a drink."

Adam took her outstretched hand and raised it to his lips. "Miss Pereira. May I introduce the acting Commandant of my hospital and my good friend, Captain Sean O'Connor."

"My pleasure, ma'am."

"Mine too, Captain. Are you just here for a drink, Doctor, because I'll willingly leave you in peace?"

"I was hoping to speak to you, ma'am. We're in search of some information about the Casa Mendes and the family who lived there before the army medical service took it over. An administrative matter."

Bright brown eyes surveyed them with amusement. "Well I can't help much with that, Doctor, because I understand the place is rented through an agent. Although I imagine you knew that."

Adam grinned. "I do, ma'am, and you have caught me out. I'm in search of gossip."

The woman gave a broad smile. "Ordinarily, I would tell you that you have come to the wrong place, Doctor. Discretion is, after all, my business. In this case, however, there is no need for discretion since none of the Mendes family have ever patronised my establishment.

Come through to my sitting room and I will give you a rather better wine."

The sitting room was a comfortably cluttered room at the back of the house. Diana offered chairs and wine then seated herself in a comfortable armchair. Sean tried hard not to stare. It was many years since he had last visited a brothel as a very young officer but he was sure that it had been nothing like this. He looked around the room curiously and looked back to see that his hostess had caught him staring. She smiled.

"It is my place of work, Captain, but it is also my home. And since you are probably wondering, my English is so good because my father was English."

"I'm sorry, ma'am, I was being rude."

"No, just curious. What do you want to know?"

"Did you ever meet the Mendes family, ma'am?"

"Heavens, no. Dom Alfonso was a gentleman in his fifties, a widower for several years. There is a son, who serves at court in some capacity or other, so he went to Brazil when the royal family fled Lisbon. I believe the house is rented out through an agent."

"You said 'was', ma'am."

"Yes. Dom Alfonso died several years ago which means the house belongs to his son. I must tell you that I was not in Elvas at the time of these events, by the way, so I am repeating gossip. But I have heard the story often enough from a variety of local gentlemen, and I think it is largely true."

"Go on."

"When the French invaded in 1808, the house was occupied by Dom Alfonso and his sixteen year old daughter Juana. She was convent educated and I am told she had only recently been brought home because a marriage was being arranged for her. Her mother was already dead.

"Dom Alfonso could have fled south to Lisbon and joined his son, but he did not wish to leave his various properties to the mercy of the French, so he remained. He was apparently furious when they took the town, and very quickly commandeered his house as billets for French officers. He loathed the invaders and made no secret of it.

"They were here for six months and when they marched out after Lord Wellington's victory at Vimeiro and the peace treaty, Dom Alfonso was left in the house again, without the invading officers but also without his daughter."

"You mean she left? Or did she die?"

"Well that, of course, is the question. Here, I am afraid, there are several different versions, and I cannot tell you which is true. Dom Alfonso gave out the story that his daughter had been abducted and murdered by a French officer. He behaved from that day on as though she was dead, and very soon made arrangements to leave for Brazil to join his son. He never arrived, however, but died of some illness aboard ship."

"But was the murder never investigated?" Sean asked. He had forgotten his awkwardness in her presence in his interest in her story. "Surely if he reported this to the local French commander, there would have been a court martial?"

"One would think so, but the French had gone before he ever told the tale," Diana said. "This of course, led to a number of different theories which quickly spread through the town and probably contributed to his sudden decision to go to Brazil. Some people suggested that Juana's father found her dead and killed the officer then hid his body. Another story was that the girl fell in love with the officer and left with him, either married or in disgrace. Either way, Mendes would never have forgiven an alliance with the enemy, so he cut her off entirely. I would like to believe that one."

"Any others?"

"Many people seem to think that Mendes found out about the affair and killed the girl himself. I do not think he could possibly have killed her lover, since the French would have arrested him and the whole story would have come out. But his daughter? From what I've heard of him, I think he might have done it."

"Do you think anybody suspected?" Adam asked.

"As I said, I wasn't here then, but Elvas is a small place and Mendes had boasted about the grand Court marriage he planned for the girl. I think he might have considered she had dishonoured him. He was a minor member of the nobility and he had high hopes for the alliance."

"What of her brother?"

"Still in Brazil as far as I am aware. When Dom Alfonso packed up and left for Brazil to join the royal family he employed Señora Avila with a small staff to take care of the house until a tenant could be found. I believe it was briefly used to billet some of the light division officers last year and then Mrs van Daan took it over for the 110th regimental hospital."

"That poor girl," Sean said softly. The woman studied him thoughtfully for a long moment.

167

"Yes, I've always thought it a very tragic story. As I said, I would love to believe she managed to leave with her French lover, but I am rather afraid she did not. I am longing to know why two English officers have such an interest in a long-buried local scandal."

Sean could think of no answer that would not leave Miss Pereira thinking them mad, but Adam was better prepared. "There is a question over the lease," he said. "If we are to make further improvements to the hospital, we would like to know that the family are not about to return, demanding their house back. The agent was odd about it, but it sounds as though he was concealing a scandal rather than avoiding a business arrangement. Thank you, Miss Pereira, you've been very helpful."

Sean drank deeply. He was vaguely aware that the wine was excellent, but he found it hard to think of anything other than the thin, tragic figure of the girl in his room. He endured the rest of the visit as best he could and waited until they were well away from the tavern before he said:

"It has to be her."

Adam glanced at him. "Our ghost?"

"Yes. It must be Juana Mendes. He killed her."

"Her father or her lover?"

"Either of them. Or both of them, one way or another. She was just a child, straight out of the convent. Whatever they did to her between them, somebody should have been there to look after her."

"Well if they didn't, there's nothing you can do about it now, Sean. She's dead. She died four years ago."

"Is that what you think? You don't think she went off with her French lover?"

Adam glanced at him. "We're probably never going to know for sure," he said gently. "Honestly, we've found out more than I thought we would. I still don't really know what it was that I saw that night in your room, but it's clear we saw the same thing and if you add that to the story we've just heard, then I think it was some kind of ghost or spirit – the spirit of Juana Mendes. I wish there were something more we could do, but there isn't. Unless you feel like talking to the local priest about an exorcism, and I must say…"

"No. Oh God, no," Sean said, revolted. "You're right, I need to let it go. I'm glad we found out what we did, though. Adam, thank you for this. For all of it. Wherever I end up, I'll always be glad I had this opportunity to get to know you."

168

High summer brought news from the front, of a spectacular victory at Salamanca and a march further into Spain. Wagons full of wounded and convalescent men made their way back to the general hospitals in Portugal and Adam Norris was so busy that he had no time to ponder the sad little story of Juana Mendes. The usual autumn sickness arrived early that year and Adam was grateful for Sean O'Connor's capable presence as the hospitals were overrun and new premises became essential.

In November, they received word that Lord Wellington's glorious campaign had come to an abrupt halt against the implacable walls of the citadel of Burgos and his Lordship's army was retreating through appalling weather back to the safety of the Portuguese border, with the French snapping at their heels. Adam was supervising the unloading of a convoy of medical supplies outside the hospital when Sean joined him.

"The post is in. Endless letters telling us to expect a flood of sick and wounded. It sounds as though they've had another Corunna, poor bastards."

"I know, I had a couple of letters from friends. Something went badly wrong with the supply chain." Adam noticed that Sean was holding a letter. "What's that?"

"A job offer," Sean said. "Did you know about this?"

"Yes," Adam said. "They wrote to ask if I would recommend you for the job. I said I would."

"It comes with a promotion to major."

"I also told them that I thought you were fully recovered and ready to return to combat if you should wish to do so, Sean."

"I know. It's my choice." Sean looked around him. "It didn't occur to me that I'd end up doing this permanently."

Adam eyed him hopefully. "That sounds promising."

"I ought to make you sweat, you underhanded bastard, you've been working at this, haven't you?"

"Sean, it's my job to make sure this place is well run. The improvement since you took over is astonishing, I'd have been mad not to ask them to make you permanent. But you can go if you want to. We'll still be friends."

"I'm staying. There's so much to do here. In addition to running this place, they've made me district superintendent, which means I can inspect and make recommendations about the other hospitals."

"Thank God for that," Adam said. "The large convent is a bloody disgrace, I wouldn't send an animal to stay there."

They dined together in celebration and Adam felt pleasantly mellow as he settled to sleep. It had rained for almost a week and many of the town streets had turned to quagmires, the mud churned up by wagons and carts bringing in supplies and the first sick men from the retreat. Adam fell asleep thinking of the men currently marching into Ciudad Rodrigo with empty stomachs, camp fever and unhealed battle wounds and felt very fortunate.

He woke in darkness to an unfamiliar sound and sat up in bed. For a moment, disoriented, his mind flew to the apparition of the young girl and he wondered if this was some new manifestation of the ghost, but a moment later, he realised that what he was hearing was very much of this world. The rain was still falling, a strong wind driving it against the wooden shutters but there were sounds in the corridor outside, loud voices and footsteps and an alarming crashing sound.

Adam scrambled out of bed and into his clothing, then opened the door. Every occupant of the top floor of the Casa Mendes was there, the housekeeper and maids with cloaks and shawls over their nightclothes, and the clamour of voices was deafening.

"Sean, is that you? What the bloody hell is going on?" Adam called, and a voice floated up the stairs.

"The roof has caved in. Must have been a leak and the plaster has rotted. Thank God it's above the empty room. Don't go in there, Adam, it's not safe. The rooms below are flooded though. Can you get everyone downstairs? I'm helping Fellowes down, he can't make it on his own. The ground floor is dry, they'll have to camp out down there until the morning, then we can get somebody to take a look."

Adam groaned inwardly and turned his attention to the staff. Fortunately, after her initial panic, Señora Avila had regained her usual calm and was shepherding them downstairs with armfuls of bed-clothes to find refuge in the dry part of the house. Adam made his way to the next floor down, where eight sick or wounded officers had their quarters. Sean had managed to light two oil lamps and was guiding the men, wrapped in blankets, down the narrow stairs, their feet splashing through water on the bare boards.

It was dawn before they were finally settled. The kitchen was in the basement and thankfully unaffected and as a grey light began to filter between the shutters, Señora Avila roused her staff and chased them upstairs to dress properly then down to the kitchen to begin preparing hot drinks and food for the exhausted invalids. Adam drank coffee with Sean in the mess room then rose with a sigh.

"Shall we have a look?"

"Might as well get it over with. The rain seems to have stopped, so I'd like to get someone out as soon as possible to start clearing up this mess so that Da Costa can have a proper look at it. I don't want to have to give this place up if I can help it, Adam, not now. We'll be back to having sick and injured officers scattered all over the damned place and with so many men coming in from this bloody retreat, we don't need that. I want that roof repaired. We can round up enough convalescent men to do the clear up and if that's not enough, I'll write to Lord Wellington asking for a work party. There must be some men still on their feet in his army."

"If it comes to that, I'll write to Colonel van Daan. It will avoid a lot of unnecessary argument, he'll just march them down here and claim it's a training exercise," Adam said with a tired grin. "But let's see what we've got first."

They made their way up the stairs, inspecting the damage. The south facing wall of the house was drenched, but not damaged and Adam thought that it could be dried out, as could the floorboards. They sounded walls and moved furniture and tested floorboards.

"I think we'll have to keep an eye on that corner of the ceiling, but this is not as bad as I thought," Sean said. "I wonder why it came down in such a deluge?"

"At a guess, I'd say the water has been pooling somewhere, it's been raining for weeks. We'd better have a look in that empty room. Are you all right about that?"

"I'm fine, Adam. Come on."

It was the first time Adam had been in the corner room since he had helped Sean move his possessions to his new quarters. The room was empty apart from some crates of medical supplies, the meagre furniture having been put to good use elsewhere. Fortunately, the equipment had been piled against the internal wall because the ceiling against the outside wall had completely collapsed. A pile of soaking, unpleasant

171

smelling rubble was piled beneath a gaping hole and the room was covered in sticky plaster dust.

"What a mess."

"It is. We'll need to get this room cleared out as soon as possible and get the builder over to have a look. The first priority is to fix the roof, since it's clear that's how the water has been coming in. I'd guess it's been collecting in the roof space above this room and soaking the plaster until it just gave."

"Yes, the roof comes first. We could just board this up since nobody is using the room."

Sean walked over to the pile of rubble and peered upwards into the dark hole. "I can see daylight up there," he said. "I think a couple of tiles are missing."

He paused and stood staring. Adam waited but his friend said nothing. After a while, Adam said:

"Sean? Are you all right?"

"Yes." Sean turned. "Adam, this doesn't make sense."

"What doesn't?"

"This house. The roof of this house. Come with me."

Adam followed him downstairs and out into the street. Although it was still early, there was a good deal of activity as the people of Elvas emerged after the storm. A few doors down, an elderly man stood on a ladder wielding a hammer, the nails held between yellow teeth as he repaired a broken shutter. Sean looked up at the house and Adam followed his gaze.

"Look at the slope of that roof. That's the window of the small room. If you move this way a bit, you can see the missing tiles. That's where the rain came in, it's probably been collecting there for months."

"Very likely, it will have rotted the boards through."

"But what's above there? It must be an enormous space."

"You mean under the eaves? Attic space, I presume. There's nothing odd in that, Sean, loads of houses have a decent amount of space under the eaves, most people use it for storage."

"How do they get up there?"

"A loft hatch, usually. I've seen them with wooden pull down ladders in some old houses, or they just keep a ladder nearby to be used when they need it."

"So why is there no hatch in this house?"

Adam stared at him blankly. "I don't know. Isn't there?"

"No. I've been in and out of all the rooms on the top floor since I took over as commandant and none of them has a hatch. In most of the houses I know, it's above the corridor but there's nothing there. Why wouldn't there be? Everybody needs storage space. Even if the house was built without a hatch, it's an old building. You'd think one of the owners at some point would have seen the need for it and put one in."

Adam stared at him. Sean was right and for some reason the thought made him uneasy, although he was not sure why. "I can see your point," he said slowly. "It is unusual. But why does it matter?"

Sean's eyes were troubled. "Because I think there was a hatch," he said softly. "Looking up where the ceiling came through, I can see the remains of a wooden square hanging down. I think there was a loft space and it's been boarded up. That's why the rain pooled so specifically in that area."

"You mean…in that room?"

"Yes," Sean said. "Is there a ladder about the place somewhere?"

"I think there's one in the wood shed although I don't know its condition. Sean are you sure?"

Sean turned back. "I have to," he said, almost apologetically. "I have to know."

***

They found the ladder attached to the wall in the wood shed. It looked in good condition and as they carried it up the stairs between them under the curious eyes of a number of the other occupants, Sean reflected that the last time he had climbed a ladder had been at Badajoz. He did not mention the fact to Adam, however, as he wanted to be the one to go up into the roof space and he did not want Adam fussing over his emotional state. Sean did feel emotional and a little shaky but that had nothing to do with his experience at Badajoz.

It took several minutes to work out the safest place to set the ladder. Adam looked at him, but Sean shook his head firmly. He could not have said why it was so important to him, but he needed to be the first to enter the roof space. Adam nodded and took firm hold of the ladder and Sean climbed up.

As his head and shoulders emerged above the ragged hole in the ceiling, he could see immediately that he had been right. Part of the wood had rotted away and been pulled down when the ceiling fell, but the remains of the square loft hatch were unmistakable. There had been no sign of it from below, Sean was sure. He had spent plenty of time looking up at that ceiling when he could not sleep, and he would have seen the outline. Somebody had not only boarded up the loft but plastered over it.

The space was enormous. It must stretch the full length of the top floor of the house and had clearly been used for storage at some point, since it was fully boarded with wooden planks laid over the rafters. A variety of objects were scattered about the room, all covered in a thick blanket of dust. The light was good, owing to the missing roof tiles, and Sean could see several chests, a pile of mouldy fabric which may have been curtains, a broken mirror and a battered table with miscellaneous objects piled on top of it. Further down the space were two stacked wooden chairs, a wicker basket and a sturdy box of the kind Sean had seen used to store letters and paperwork. At the far end was an old mattress with straw poking out from its torn cover. There was something lying on top of it which looked very much like another hand stitched quilt although this one was covered, like everything else, with a thick layer of dust.

Sean stepped off the ladder. The roof was steeply sloped and at its highest point down the middle of the attic, he could stand upright. He took two or three steps forward then stopped. After a moment he set off again. The sound of his steps was unmistakeable. Sean felt that it should have been obvious that the footsteps could have been from a room above his head, but then he had not known this space existed.

He stopped before he reached the mattress and stood looking down. Nothing could be seen other than the quilt, but Sean had absolutely no doubt that she was there. He waited for a moment, steeling himself, then bent and lifted the edge of the quilt very gently, coughing in the cloud of dust that arose.

Sean had been dreading some horror, some sign of the agony of her last days, but he supposed at the end, after long hours of pacing the room, probably of crying out for help, she had grown progressively weaker and had just lain down. The bones were white, resting within the tattered fabric of her shift. The most upsetting thing was her hair, which had not yet rotted away and lay dark against the white of her skull. Sean felt tears start to his eyes and he settled the quilt back over her as she had been before and turned away.

As he turned, he thought Adam had followed him up the ladder, but he quickly realised his mistake. The girl stood before him and in the bright daylight spilling through the broken roof, Sean saw her more

174

clearly than ever before. Her eyes were a deep brown and must have been lovely before dehydration and starvation had hollowed out the sockets. There were the tragic remnants of beauty in the bone structure of her face.

Something was different though, and Sean felt a sudden chill as he realised what it was. For the first time, the girl was looking at him. Before, in the room below, she had been an image, like a portrait with eyes staring into nothing. Now the eyes were on his face and he was sure that she could see him. For a moment, he was terrified, and then the fear receded and instead he felt a deep and abiding sorrow.

"He left then, did he?" he said very softly. "Your lover? He probably had no idea what that evil bastard did to you. I don't know what happened on that ship, but however he died I hope it was long and painful. I'm sorry, Juana. All I can do is see you properly buried, but that I'll gladly do. Then you can rest, I hope."

She said nothing, but Sean had an odd sense that she could hear him although he did not know if she would have understood since he had no idea if the living Juana understood any English. He could feel tears on his cheeks and as he blinked and then wiped them away, she was gone and there was no mark in the dust where she had stood.

***

The burial service was private, with only the priest, Sean, and Adam present. Sean used bribery, when persuasion had failed, to pay for a simple stone with Juana's name and the dates of her birth and probable death. Adam listened in shocked silence to his friend's account of his experience in the loft and did not question his insistence that Juana have a memorial. She was buried in an army coffin, wrapped in the dusty quilt from the attic and afterwards, Adam arranged for dinner to be served in his room and opened a bottle of wine.

"Are you ready to hear the rest?" he asked.

"The rest of what?"

"We've been clearing out the loft ready for the repairs. The carpenter is going to restore the hatch and put a proper ladder in so that it can be used for storage again."

"Not while we're here."

"No, but in the future. The point is that they found some papers in a box and brought them to me as they'd no idea what else to do with them. They should go to the family agent but given how that girl was

175

murdered by her own father, I felt no scruples about going through them, and I'm glad I did."

"What did you find?"

"Letters. Her lover wrote several of them in the weeks after his immediate departure, asking her why she didn't keep their appointment and begging her to join him. That bastard Mendes must have put them up there with her deliberately before he walled her up and left her to die. He probably thought it was fitting. I hope she found comfort in them."

"Oh God, Adam. You mean there really was a French lover?"

"More like a French suitor, as far as I can see. He wanted to marry her and when the old man refused, they planned to elope. When the French marched out after Cintra she should have been with him as his wife."

"I wonder if he's still alive?"

"I don't know, Sean, but I'm going to write to him to tell him that she died and where she's buried. Not the details of how, he doesn't need to know that. But if he's still alive and still out there, I'd like him to know that she didn't mean to let him down."

"Can we do that?"

"Oh yes. There are regular channels of communication regarding prisoners and if we enclose a note explaining it's about a family matter, they'll see he gets it. It's surprisingly reliable, I was a prisoner myself for eight months."

"Do you mind if I do it?"

"Not at all. I have the letters here, you can read them. It gives his regiment four years ago, but if he's moved on for promotion they'll know how to find him."

They finished dinner in companionable silence, then Adam produced the letters and finished his wine as Sean sat reading them. Afterwards, Adam was called to a patient in the main hospital. Sean walked part of the way with him then made his way through the town to the churchyard and stood in the gathering dusk before the fresh grave in the churchyard.

Sean could give no reason for his certainty that Juana Mendes was finally at peace. He thought about the young Frenchman who had fallen in love with her during those months at the Casa Mendes. The man's letters had upset him with their increasing desperation at receiving no word from Juana. It was clear that he had loved her very much and Sean wondered if there were other letters, written after her

176

death and destroyed by her vengeful father. Adam was right, the man deserved to know at least part of the truth.

It was full dark now, and Sean could barely see the grave. He bent his head and spoke a short prayer for Juana and for the young man she had loved, then he crossed himself and turned to walk back up to the hospital. He had paperwork to do, then he would open another bottle of wine in case Adam was back early enough to share a drink. While he was waiting, he would write a letter to his wife to remind her of how much he loved her, and another to a young French officer called Louis Bernard, to tell him that he too had been loved.

Author's Note

The idea for this ghost story came from somebody I met locally who was reading my Peninsular War Saga and told me the story of his ancestor. Lieutenant Waldron Kelly, an Irish officer who served in Wellington's army eloped with a well-born Portuguese girl and married her against furious opposition from her family. Mrs Kelly went back to Ireland, partly because her family threatened to kill her for disgracing them. The story is told in some detail in Charles Esdaile's *Women in the Peninsular War* and is one of a number of tales of local women becoming involved with British soldiers. It occurred to me that this probably also happened during the French occupation, and that a Portuguese or Spanish family might have been even more angry if their daughter became involved with a hated invader.

While both Adam Norris and Sean O'Connor are fictional characters, there really were several general hospitals in Elvas and they would have been jointly run by a senior doctor and an officer commandant. Hospitals for officers were rare, although in 1813 the voluntary provision of a separate hospital for sick and wounded officers was finally included in regulations. It was hugely inconvenient for medical staff to have to travel to wherever a sick or wounded officer happened to be billeted, and there are several accounts of what appear to be informal hospitals for officers throughout the war. It seems madness to us today that considerations of rank were placed above good medical care, but Wellington's army existed in a very different world.

About the Author

Lynn Bryant was born and raised in London's East End. She studied History at University and had dreams of being a writer from a young age. Since this was clearly not something a working class girl made good could aspire to, she had a variety of careers including a librarian, NHS administrator, relationship counsellor, manager of an art gallery and running an Irish dance school before she realised that most of these were just as unlikely as being a writer and took the step of publishing her first book.

She now lives in the Isle of Man and is married to a man who understands technology, which saves her a job, and has two grown-up children and two Labradors. She is passionate about history, with a particular enthusiasm for the Napoleonic era. She is the author of twelve books. When not writing, she walks her dogs, reads anything that's put in front of her and makes periodic and unsuccessful attempts to keep a tidy house.

The Peninsular War Saga
An Unconventional Officer
An Irregular Regiment
An Uncommon Campaign
A Redoubtable Citadel
An Untrustworthy Army
An Unmerciful Incursion

The Manxman Series
An Unwilling Alliance
This Blighted Expedition

Regency Romances
A Regrettable Reputation
The Reluctant Debutante

A Respectable Woman (a novel of Victorian London)
A Marcher Lord (A novel of the Border Reivers)

https://www.amazon.co.uk/Lynn-Bryant/e/B06X9VVHHV%3Fref=dbs_a_mng_rwt_scns_share

HERE THERE WERE DRAGONS

BY

KATE JEWELL

Castle Neroche Farm
Spring, 1848

T he squawking, flapping birds set up a good racket, but it wasn't enough to outdo Little Tommy's squeals and shouts. Chasing the hens was Little Tommy's favourite game this week. Last week it had been dropping snails in his big brothers' boots and the week before it had been squiffling all the apron strings together as they flapped on the washing line.

John Rowsell stuck his head out of the workshop door and yelled for his wife. 'Mistress Rowsell, where the blazes are you? This scamp's going to be the death of your hens if you don't get out here now.'

His wife, flour up to her elbows, stood on the kitchen step, surveying the chaos. 'Don't you get in a flap, mister! You can send him scaring the crows off the fields as soon as you like. He's old enough. Annie, Annie, where are you, girl? I told you to mind Tommy.'

Annie dropped from the wall she had retreated to when the chickens had exploded out of the barn.

'I'm here. I'll see to him. We'll go exploring.' She anticipated what her mother was going to say next. 'Not long, just long enough to wear him out a bit.' She grabbed at her youngest brother as he scooted past. 'Come on you little scoundrel, let's go hunting beasties.'

They abandoned the yard and ran along the steep track that skirted the hill. Annie picked up a stick to flush out monsters for Tommy to chase. With some luck, there would be a mouse or two, or maybe even a weasel. This time of year, young rabbits were fair game, and Little Tommy dived through the bushes after a bobbing white scat. Annie wandered down the path, keeping pace with her brother's whooping and crashing. Then it went quiet. She called and pushed through the undergrowth.

In the clearing at the base of the hill, Little Tommy, all dishevelled hair and muddy trousers up to his knees, stood with his mouth gaping and eyes wide-open. He pointed at the rocky slope behind him.

'I found a big one,' he shrieked. 'A monster. In there.'

Annie went to look, but the small opening in the hillside was hardly wide enough for Tommy, let alone a monster.

'There's nothing here, Tommy. Come on, it's time to go back.'

'But I poked it. With my stick,' Tommy insisted and continued to prattle all the way to the yard. In front of Mother he was smug, his arms folded just like his father when he was not to be crossed. 'I seen a dragon,' he proudly announced.

They had heard this all before. Apart from chasing hens, dragons were of the utmost interest to Tommy.

'Oh, don't be silly,' Annie and her mother chanted together. 'There are no such things as dragons.'

Mornings were busy. Under her mother's stern eye, Annie went back to her chores; fetching and carrying, dipping for water in the well, collecting eggs from the corner of the shippen where the hens had decided to lay, and making sure her youngest brothers didn't get into mischief in the madhouse that was her mother's kitchen.

'Annie, you mind these nippers,' her mother would call, shoving Mick and Little Tommy away from the big fat slices of bacon jumping and spitting on the griddle. 'I can't have them *ellers* poking their grubby fingers in that bread, neither.'

In winter, breakfast was a steaming, heavy, sociable affair. As the grandfather clock in the hallway struck nine, the farm labourers crowded into the large open back kitchen after one or two hours of arduous work. Chairs scraped on the stone floor and the thick, salted oat and barley porridge was ladled out, supplemented with the bacon or whatever meat scraps mother had in the pantry. Big mugs of strong tea arrived before each man, sweetened with a mountain of sugar. If they

180

were lucky, there, in the centre of the table, would be a plate overflowing with slices of Bridgwater manchip, the flaky jam-filled lard pastry that was her mother's speciality. The men would linger in front of the fire, warming their butts, with their hands round the mugs, begging a second slice of pastry, teasing the boys and casting longing gazes in Annie's direction.

But now it was late spring, and the season was slipping into summer. The bacon was hastily stuffed into thick muffins and cider swiftly slaked the thirst. There was little time for banter. Annie gave each man muslin-wrapped parcels of bread, hard-boiled eggs and generous portions of cheese to take out to the fields. For as the days grew longer, the hour of dinner slid later. The farm hands would not sit round the scrubbed kitchen table until well past seven o'clock.

Her father was already loading a firkin of small ale on the cart, so Annie took his portion into the yard.

'You're a good girl, Annie.' He went to ruffle her hair.

She ducked out of reach. 'Don't, Pa! I'm not a child anymore,' she said and gave the horse a scrap of apple.

'I know, I know. But you've still got a deal of growing to do yet.' He pulled himself onto the cart's bench. 'There's a new book for you in my library. Reverend Warre sent it over. But make sure you finish all your chores first.' As the cart swung out of the home-field gate, he shouted back. 'And be sure you're here to help your mother in good time. We'll be in for dinner well before dusk.'

Annie's father had built the farmhouse as a marriage portion for her mother on untilled land. Ancient earthworks surrounded the house and yard on the very edge of a great scarp overlooking a steep valley and distant forested hills. He revelled in tales of historical goings-on and was always ready to boast that no one would oust him from the land; 'I got me-self a fine castle with a moat, an' there's not anyone can breach these walls.' That the walls were just ridges of crumbling mud and stone, and the moat only a deep dry ditch round a substantial mound on top of the escarpment, didn't seem to quell his enthusiasm one jot.

The 'library', an extra room backing on to the parlour, was lined with miss-matched shelves laden with books and odd things he had unearthed around the farm. It was Annie's favourite room. She loved to sit there, listening to Pa's tales and poring over old volumes with him. She eagerly tagged along when his friend, the Reverend Warre, came to poke about.

It wasn't so long ago she had been party to the discovery of the ancient sword they had dug out of crumbling ramparts. Her mother, even though exasperated by 'more rusty old hodgepodge diggings', brushed it free of earth and wiped it with an oily rag. Pa had hung it above the library fireplace with much ceremony while the reverend applauded. Little Tommy was convinced it had been used to slay a dragon. 'Look, look, there's the dragon's blood.' he said, pointing at the rust stains. Her eldest brothers, Jonnie and Peter, tittered behind their fingers.

After that, the reverend took Annie under his wing. He explained her home was on the site of a motte-and-bailey castle.

'It's an old defensive place where villagers found shelter in times of conflict.' he said. 'There was much conflict in those far-off days. That's the motte,' He pointed at the mound rising above the farmyard. 'And this…,' he extravagantly waved his arms around at everything else, '…this is the bailey, and your home is slap-bang in the middle of the bailey yard.'

Annie regarded the lay of the land. 'They must have been lucky to find somewhere with all these ups and downs,' she said. 'Otherwise they would have had to haul a load of stone up here to build walls.'

The reverend laughed. 'Well, young miss, that's where you're wrong and why your Pa keeps finding old tools and bits of pottery when he digs through the ridges. He even showed me some ancient coins last week. The lord who built this place,' he continued, 'would set his warriors to hauling carts of earth and stones from the fields to raise these banks and mighty fine banks they are. Quite a climb for an enemy warrior. Just picture what it was like with archers loosing arrows at you. Now, why do you think they built that?' He pointed at the motte.

'It's a good place to watch the valley,' Annie said. 'You can see for miles from up there; keep an eye out for your enemies. Especially if you have a tower up there as well.'

The reverend vigorously patted her on the back. 'Well done, Miss Annie, well done,' he exclaimed, and Pa had come out of the big barn to discover what all the fuss was about.

Reverend Warre reassured him. 'You have a budding antiquarian here, John. I do believe Annie has a natural talent for it.'

Subsequently, when visiting, the reverend would bring some artefact or other to show to her father, but the discussions and inquiries about antiquity and cultural provenance were with Annie. Recently, he had been lending her novels.

Annie tried to ignore the flutter of anticipation as she swept the yard and polished the step. What had the reverend sent her this time? Another romance story by Miss Austin? Or a daring adventure by Mr Scott? She hoped it was the latter; Mr Scott's tales of times long past were far more exciting. But first there were pudding cloths to boil and hang out in the garden, cream pans and strainers to be scoured, laid out to dry and sweeten in the open-sided lean-too by the dairy. She scattered grain for the hens and sought permission from her mother to please herself until it was time to prepare dinner.

She sped to the library. On the rent table was a slim package addressed in the reverend's meticulous hand. She slit the wrapper with her father's paper knife and eased the book out. It looked unremarkable, with nothing but a simple heraldic device on the cover. On a bookplate affixed to the flyleaf was a neat inscription.

For Miss Ann Rowsell
May this small volume entertain and intrigue
From your partner in archaeological adventures
Francis Warre
May 1848

Annie flipped through a few pages. The little book wasn't a novel but something else entirely, a collection of short illustrated pieces. She stopped at one and read the entry below a finely drawn illustration of a wild looking man perched on an ancient wagon, driving his team of horses round a leaning stone.

The Caratacus Stone
Near Spire Cross, Winsford Hill, Exmoor

This stone is said to have treasure beneath it. A greedy wagoner tried to uproot and drag the stone away to get at the wealth it concealed. The stone overturned, upending the waggon and team, crushing the foolhardy driver. Villagers believe their ghostly presence can still be heard and met on the moor, protecting the treasure on foggy nights.

'Well', she said, 'I *am* intrigued,' and turned a few more pages until pulled up short. The drawing was unmistakable, even though there was no farmhouse or yard. A series of ramparts defended a large open space with a squat stone tower atop a high mound on the edge of a cliff. At the foot of the hill, a fierce looking winged creature faced up to a group of terrified men clutching picks and spades.

Castle Neroche - An Ancient Hill Fort in the Parish of Curland, Somerset

A Wyvern's hoard of treasure is believed to be hidden in caves under the escarpment at Castle Neroche. There are tales of labouring men urged on by the love of filthy lucre, armed with spades and pickaxes, who violated the sanctity of this mysterious place. But before they found a single coin, they were seized with a fearful panic and renounced their search. It is awful to relate that within one month from the commencement of their covetous and most presumptuous enterprise, all paid with their lives by accident, sudden death or virulent fever.

This motte-and-bailey castle was most likely built on the remains of a Roman camp. The name, Neroche, could be a contraction of the Old English words 'nierra' and 'rachich', meaning the 'camp where hunting dogs were kept'. Rache were a type of scent-hound used in Britain in the Dark Ages. The site is still known as Castle Rache by local villagers.

Annie turned back to the title page.

Here there were Dragons
An Inventory of West Country Myths, Legends
& Other Improbable Tales
collected by
Rev. F Warre
Bishops Lydeard, Somerset
1840

184

She glanced through the window at the thinning clouds and decided it would be warm enough to take the book up to the great mound.

As she settled herself by the ruined wall at the top of the motte, Annie looked across the wide vale to the hills beyond and considered the prospect of an afternoon of uninterrupted solitude. *If the best time in winter is between a dinner at two o'clock and an early supper,* she mused, *then the summer hours that stretch out the day between breakfast and an evening dinner are the best of all.*

It took Annie nearly a fortnight to read all the stories in the reverend's book. He must have spent months, even years, to gather all these tales. All these mythical beings; the sprites, faeries, pixies and the poor dancing maidens turned to stone circles on Dartmoor, all sketched in pen and ink. He had been as far west as Cornwall and north east to the Forest of Dean. But of all the counties he'd visited, their own Somerset laid claim to the most dragons; her home, it appeared, hosting one of them if she was to believe the reverend's drawing.

When she had finished the book, she turned back to the Castle Neroche entry and knew she had to find out more. Where had the dragon found his treasure? What had it done to scare those labourers to death? And who were they? Just plain robbers, or menfolk from the villages? And what sort of dragon was a Wyvern anyway? There must be something in her father's library about it all.

She stifled a laugh; she was starting to sound like Little Tommy. 'Don't be silly Annie,' she admonished herself, 'dragons don't exist.'

Annie walked through the gap in the high bank and onto the rough track, Dog running back and forth, worried his mistress wouldn't keep up. She knew exactly where she wanted to go with her book and her drawing paraphernalia, and it wasn't chasing after a useless hound trying to flush out rabbits. Once out of the shadow cast by the escarpment, she stopped to look back, squinting into the sun. Undergrowth softened the stony cliff and the few trees clinging to the thin soil barely disguised the pitted and treacherous slope. Was there a mysterious cavern there? It didn't look like it, but the base of the scarp definitely invited more exploration.

Not today, though. Today she planned to go down to the pond in the valley and record the old drove road that snaked away north towards Bristol. Near the water's edge, she settled on a weathered boulder and spread her ink bottle, pens and pencils out beside her. Dog began

185

snuffling around, disturbing leaves and investigating the water. A chaffinch threw its alarm call, but the birds soon calmed down, recognising the hound wasn't a threat as he shook himself off and went to sleep in the sun. A slight breeze rustled the leaves, hardly lifting her notebook page as she sketched. It was altogether the perfect day, and she leaned back and let the sounds and scents wash over her.

A deep-throated growl disturbed her reverie. She looked around but saw no one and assumed Dog was dreaming of unobtainable rabbits. She heard someone chopping wood, a rustle in the trees and a scurry of animal feet, but nothing more.

Dog stirred and growled again.

'Shush, you silly thing. It's only someone collecting firewood.'

But although the dog dropped his head to the ground, his ears twitched, and his hackles were raised.

Annie stood up. She could hear the woodsman but couldn't see him. There was a very low rumble in Dog's throat.

'For goodness' sake, what's the matter with you? I'm only going to take a look.'

She set off and Dog slunk along behind her.

The trees thinned and a man, tall and lean, his white hair shining in the sunlight like silver, wielded an axe with a force belying his slight body and thin arms. A coarse shirt was open to his waist, the sleeves pushed above his elbows. Although the day was warm, there was no sweat on his skin. Skin too pale; not the colour she expected to see on someone working outdoors. Effortlessly, he felled a birch and took up a billhook to strip the smaller branches. There was a methodic grace to his actions, a practised skill. As he bent to retrieve his axe, he lifted his head and saw her. He straightened.

He was taller than her by a hand or two but seemed more so because of his extreme thinness, and she was surprised he was so young; not much older than herself. It was hard to believe he had the strength to cleave the wood with such force, but she had seen him do just that. He had reduced the fallen timber into logs and kindling with less effort than Jessie, her father's hired woodsman, had ever done.

He looked straight at her and raked his fingers through his hair, as if he were stripping off silver tissue, revealing a pale mottled brown, like shadows dancing across the forest floor. With one smooth movement, he was right in front of her, wiping his fingertips on his trousers to remove the last traces of…last traces of what? She couldn't help but stare at the silver streaks evaporating before her eyes.

186

'How did you do that?' she blurted out and blushed scarlet. What on earth did she think, to speak out of turn?

'It was nothing, miss.' He made a formal bow. 'Edwin Whisholme, miss. At your service.'

Embarrassed, Annie took a step back. 'I'm sorry, I didn't mean to…I…' His eyes were the most vibrant green she had ever seen. '…I was out drawing, and the sound of your chopping disturbed my hound.' She went to ruffle the animal's fur, but Dog's low growl turned into a whimper and he backed away, his belly close to the ground.

'You silly thing. There's nothing to worry about.' She looked up. 'I'd better take him home. I'm sorry…'

'That's all right. Dogs don't seem to like me much. Have you far to go?' There was a slight lilt to his voice which she couldn't place, almost as if English wasn't his native tongue.

'Only to the farm up the top of the scarp.'

'Named for the castle.' It was a statement, not a question.

'Yes. You know of it?'

He smiled, the creases at the corner of his eyes deeper than she anticipated.

'I'm around this place for a while,' he said. 'Maybe we'll cross paths again.' And he went back to his work.

A week later, tucked against the old wall on the motte somewhat sheltered from a warm but unseasonably mischievous wind, Annie struggled to keep her paper still as she sketched. The clouds sent shadows scudding across the patchwork of fields, and the landscape became too changeable to portray. As she tied up her pencil roll, a sudden gust grabbed her drawing and tumbled it over the grass.

'Oh, drat.' She tried to catch up with the paper, sliding to a halt right at the edge as it flew into the abyss. She peered down, but she couldn't see the sketch at all. 'Drat and double drat!'

'I think,' said a quiet voice, 'you should step away. This wind might blow you right over.'

Caught unawares, she spun round and Edwin Whisholme reached out a steadying hand. All she could sense was how hot her face had become and, before he let go, how cold his hand felt.

'No dog today?'

'I…I was just… No, no Dog. He refused to come.'

'I think this is yours.' He held out a crimpled piece of paper.

187

'How…how did you…' Words failed her. She hadn't heard a thing, and here he was. Where had he come from? How had he got her drawing? She pointed over the edge of the scarp. 'But it blew over there. How…'

'It snagged in a tree as I came up the path.'

She stared at him. 'But there *is* no path this side. It's too steep…' Her voice trailed away. The trees on the periphery of her vision undeniably reached out to intertwine with brambles, concealing an opening in the dense undergrowth.

'Miss, I think you've had a bit of a scare. Come and sit here.'

Annie jolted her attention towards the strange young man. He had perched on a fallen tree, the ties on his tunic loosened almost to the waist and his head flung back. He was drenched in sunlight. *Like a lizard on the yard wall*, she thought, *soaking up the heat*. The wind eased to a gentle breeze and Annie fetched her satchel and sat down.

She watched his long fingers skim across her drawing, along the creases, over scuffs of dirt, while he gazed far into the distance. It was as if he was reading the view from her pencil marks by touch. When he handed the sheet back to her, the paper was as smooth and the drawing as unsullied as it had been before the wind had stolen it. Wide eyed and not daring to comment, she slipped it between the pages of her notebook.

'You have skill,' he said. 'You were drawing when we met before.'

'I'm thinking to make a record of this place. Something for the people hereabouts to read and see some of the history of where they live.'

'That's very laudable of you.' There was a crease of humour round his mouth and she raised her hands to cover the flush threatening her cheeks again.

'No, no, don't be reticent. It's a sterling idea.' He reached for her wrists in a reassuring sort of way, easing her arms down. His smile broadened. He appeared to be genuinely interested, so it felt safe to continue.

'My father's friend explained all the history to me. Pa says he's a very clever archaeological expert, but his writings wouldn't interest most people. It's so fascinating I thought to show it through pictures and simple facts.' She reached into her satchel. 'Look at this. This is the sort of thing.'

She passed him the reverend's book, and he paused at the bookplate, then at the title. He smiled at the stories, seemed amused at the drawings.

'These myths,' he said, 'they are all based on truth.'

Annie pondered. 'I suppose so. But truth twisted and spun until it's hidden. Castle Neroche is here.' She leant forward, found the entry. 'Pa claims it is his personal fortress, but Reverend Warre says it is ancient. It seems it has its own dragon.' She began to thumb through the pages, then looked up. 'All these dragons… why so many dragons?'

'Don't you believe in dragons?'

She laughed. 'Of course not. Now, my little brother Tommy, he believes in anything. He's forever seeing monsters and dragons in the clouds.'

Edwin Whisholme stretched. 'Everywhere I hear different tales. Why, at Aller Hill there are many versions of their dragon myth. Look…' He retrieved the book from her and turned up the page. 'Even your Reverend Warre has listed some of them.' He returned to the Castle Neroche entry. 'But here there is only one. Let me tell you a story I heard.'

He slipped to the grass, leaned back against the tree trunk, and patted the ground to his left. Annie dropped down to face him, drew her legs up under her skirt and wrapped her arms round her knees.

'Can you imagine what this place was like, seven centuries past?'

She nodded. 'A tower, on top of the earth mound. A good lookout over the road from the north. A place ringed by ramparts. Wooden palisades. Reverend Warre told me all about it.'

'But how would it be for the ordinary people who lived here and worked for the lord of this castle? What do you know about them? And how did the treasure come to be concealed in the first place?' He paused, shut his eyes against the brightness of the sun. 'This is what I heard. There *was* a dragon that lived deep in a hole beneath the fort. It used to come out at night to attack travellers on the road and take their treasure back to its lair. This went on year after year, the villagers far too scared to do anything about it. At last, a brave farmhand plucked up the courage to investigate and, sneaking up on the dragon, found it dozing on a great mound of gold. Creeping away, the man came up with a plan. He persuaded the villagers to divert a nearby stream to flood the cavern, and the dragon drowned.'

'Did the villagers find the treasure afterwards?' Annie asked.

'Who knows? Some say they did, but others say the hoard has never been discovered.'

'What do you think, Mr Whisholme?'

He stood, laced his tunic. 'What I think is another tale altogether, Miss Rowsell.'

She jumped up. 'Do tell. Please.'

He inclined his head. 'I fear the wind is getting up again, and I hear someone calling you.' He formally shook her hand. 'So that tale must be for another day.'

She bent to pick up her bag and glanced over her shoulder to ask him which day, but he had gone. She rubbed at her palm, then wiped it down her skirt. For all the lounging in the warm sun, his hand, when it had gripped hers, had still been icy cold.

By the weekend, everyone was busy in the fields scaring crows and weeding between rows of beans and turnips, untangling cleavers from the wheat. Even Mother abandoned her kitchen, though she carried a wide basket to collect the fat hen that grew along the field margins. Donning a broad straw hat, she had hitched her skirt almost to her knees, so the hem wouldn't drag in the dust. If Annie did that, Pa would scold her for being unseemly.

Then it was Sunday and church. Annie was left to shepherd Mick and Little Tommy into Miss Hembury's Sunday school, as Pa decided Jonnie and Peter had education enough and would go into morning service. More likely, her eldest brothers had played truant once too often and Pa wanted to keep his eye on them. After church, there was Bible reading in the library. It didn't take long for Pa to declare that reconciliation with the Lord had been satisfactorily achieved and it was time for a midday dinner. Then they went out to the fields again until supper.

All afternoon Annie kept thinking about Edwin Whisholme, how strange he was and how he appeared out of nowhere. She wondered where he was living, but nobody she asked seemed to know; an itinerant labourer, they suggested. And if his story was based on truth, there must be interesting things to find; some old coins perhaps, a bracelet maybe, even the entrance to an old cave. She hoped she might spot something as she pulled at the groundsel and mayweed between the turnips, but there was nothing.

Monday morning Annie had to assist with the cheese-making. It seemed the whole day was passing her by; milk was heated, rennet added, and left to coagulate before Annie was set to cutting the curds. Then there were other household tasks to complete while the whey separated, ready to be strained off. At last she helped her mother squeeze out the remaining liquid, add the salt and lift the curds in their cheesecloth into the mould and load it into the press. There were pans to wash, cloths to boil, surfaces to wipe down and the dairy floor to be sluiced. It was not until well past noon she was let go.

Annie found a trowel in her father's toolbox and a canvas sack for finds, tucked her notebook in her pocket and escaped down the old drove road to the base of the escarpment. She intended to record everything she unearthed, to report back when Reverend Warre came visiting again. She collected a few things, but nothing of importance. No golden treasures, not even any coins. Only a couple of worked flints and some pottery shards much like her mother's old crockery. The nearer the cliff she got, the more difficult it was to turn the earth over. Water trickling from the scarp seeped into the ground all around, and the trowel just squelched in and out of the mossy soil. Her shoes started to leak.

She took her finds to a large flat stone, laid them out in the sun, ready to record them in her book when she caught sight of something white and smooth sticking out of the grass. She started to scrape away the dirt. A shadow fell across her arm and cool fingers barely touched hers as they took possession of the trowel.

'May I?'

It seemed the most natural thing in the world to stand by and watch him kneel on the ground and release the pointed object from the earth.

'I do believe it is a tooth, Miss Rowsell.'

'Annie, please. Just Annie.'

'Then you must call me Edwin.' He concentrated on brushing earth off the find. 'Definitely an incisor. Maybe even be a dragon's incisor?' Still on his knees, he held out the large item for her perusal.

She gasped. The loose sleeve of his smock had slipped back to reveal a ridged weal on his forearm.

'You've hurt yourself, let me look.' She scrambled to help him up and twisted his arm into the light. The puckered flesh was livid against the pale skin. 'How —'

'It's old, from long ago.' He backed away, pulling at his sleeve. 'It's nothing.'

'But it looks painful. I could get my mother to make a poultice. Something to —'

191

'I said it was nothing.' He swung around and, without another word, walked into the forest.

Annie crumpled, all enthusiasm for her exploration gone.

When the reverend next visited, Annie displayed her finds and sketches; explained his little book had inspired her project. He was most impressed by the tooth but didn't think it was from a dragon.

'More likely a tusk from one of those wild boars that roamed the woodland hereabouts; highly prized in the hunt because of their ferocity.' He took great interest in her drawings, staring a long time at the view from the top of the motte.

'This drawing,' he said, 'what did you use?'

'Just my ordinary pencils. Here, I'll show you,' and she spread her pencil roll out before him.

A puzzled frown creased his forehead. 'Nothing else? Just these?'

'Sometimes I take ink and a pen, but not that day. It was too windy, and I didn't want the ink bottle to blow over.'

'That is strange. I could attest these marks were made with silverpoint if you hadn't told me otherwise. Have you ever done any silverpoint drawing?'

She shook her head.

'Very strange.' He gave the drawing another close inspection.

Annie decided it was a good time to divert the reverend's interest before he asked any more awkward questions. 'I thought to look for cave entrances the day I found the tooth, but the ground was so wet I had to give up. Even further along, it seems impossible to get through all the bushes and scrub. I'd have to take a long route round to get past. Do you know if there's a way down that steep side?'

'Possibly. Your father and I came across some spear heads along that edge of the escarpment, just strewn around, half hidden in the grass. If lost in a skirmish, how would the enemy have got up there unless there was a path to follow?'

'I could ask Mr Whisholme. He seems to know a lot about the dragon stories. Do you know him?'

The reverend shook his head. 'Never heard of him, but these old village folks are full of tales.'

'Oh, he's not old. Nobody seems to know much about him except he's working in the forest. I think he must have lived here a while ago. Maybe his family moved away.'

'We could investigate hidden paths the next time I come by. You could ask your Mr Whisholme if he might like to join us. Now, where's your mother? I must thank her for the pie recipe she gave Mrs Warre. It was delicious,' and he hurried off towards the kitchen.

Not knowing when the reverend would come again, Annie set off to discover Edwin Whisholme's secret path at the first opportunity. She took Dog with her to ferret out any tracks that rabbits or foxes might have used. Brambles caught in her clothes, scratched her arms, snagged at her hair, but she pushed on. There must be a way down through this thicket to the base of the scarp. How else could Edwin have retrieved her drawing that day? Or disappear so suddenly?

The brambles thinned out, and she stepped onto a ledge not more than five feet across. Dog sniffed at the short, cropped grass, his tail wagging furiously. Beyond was an uninterrupted view of the Quantock Hills far off to the north and she was sure the glittering horizon to the west was the sea. She went to the edge to find a way down, but the slope was just a jumble of rocks and loose stones. The scarp was no different further along; it was more treacherous if anything.

Without warning, Dog set up a loud barking and backed away until he shot off up towards the farm. 'Stupid animal,' she muttered, and went to see what had intimidated him. At the edge of the ledge was a steep flight of steps. There was a handrail that looked fairly new and the way down was clear. She gripped the rail and descended with care. A recently trodden trail snaked to the left, leading to a slight depression in the ground. She looked up the cliff, but there was no cave, not even a fissure in the stone. She turned back towards the stairway and something glinted in the light. A coin? Or a medallion? There was a chain of some sort. She leant down, reached for it.

***

There is no breeze, no movement, no summer scents. No sound except an echo bouncing off the cliff.
—*Don't touch*—
She spins round, but nobody is here.
'Hello?' she says, then a little louder, 'Hello?'
No one answers.
She pokes at the object with a stick, loosens the chain, pulls it up. The small medallion, spinning round and round, sheds glistening light

into the air. She waits for it to slow and, as she lowers the shining disc to her hand, a voice screams through her mind.

—*That is mine. Thieve it and regret*—

She cannot help but close her fingers over blazing, white-hot metal and a searing agony surges up her arm.

Another voice, real and urgent.

'Drop it. Drop it — NOW.'

It is Edwin, catching her wrist, prising her fingers apart, forcing her hand over.

As the medallion swings free, he gathers the chain, slips it over his head. The disc loses its brilliance, settles on his breast.

She stares at the blistering skin on her palm, then up at Edwin.

'Let me see.' He reaches forward, but she recoils, cradles one arm with the other, tries to deny the anguish. Uncontrollable shaking overtakes her body. Her throat opens on a whimper. Arms enfold her, holding her still.

'Let me see,' Edwin says again. 'I can ease the hurt.'

She surrenders. Stares, dumfounded, as he wipes away the burn and the pain with his thumbs. They are chill and damp, as if washed in a winter river. His touch leaves a silvery shadow over the fading wound.

And all the time his silent words fill the space around them.

—*Leave her alone. She is our final hope. LEAVE...HER...ALONE*—

***

Edwin carried her through the understory to a deeper hollow in the rock and settled her on a sun-bleached bench. He disappeared into the gloom and she realised the opening must go much further back into the cliff. He re-emerged and passed her a metal flask. 'It's just water.'

She drank deeply of the pure, cold liquid. The vessel was heavy and covered in a raised design made of wire. In places there were scraps of coloured glass. Annie brushed away a little of the dust clinging to the surface to reveal a soft gold edge to the ornamentation. Sunlight transformed the glass fragments into sparkling gemstones.

'Once it was extremely fine,' he said, 'but time has robbed its beauty.'

'It must have been splendid. I cannot imagine how splendid.'

Abruptly he took her injured hand, brushed it with his own. The silver residue intensified and her skin throbbed. He swept her fingers just above the surface of the flask and it came alive, almost as if she was restoring the design with a polishing cloth, every space filled with glowing colour.

This is impossible, she thought. *This can't be happening.* She dropped the object into her lap and the tracery began to revert to its damaged state. She grabbed it with both hands and thrust it back at Edwin.

'Imagination is a powerful thing,' he said. 'It can lead to grief and misunderstanding, greed and hostility. But mixed with intellect, foresight and, above all else, belief in the beauty of life, imagination can bring great serenity.' He dropped the flask to the ground and settled back against the rock face. The shifting light cast green shadows across his skin; his eyes, watching her so intently, were shot with threads of carmine.

'You have just discovered an ability to see beyond the ordinary. I think now is the time to recount the true events at the castle of the hunting dogs. Sit back and hear the story of one young man...'

Annie closed her eyes and let Edwin Whisholme's soft, lilting voice enfold her.

Castle Rache
Spring, 1148

The lord of this place, where the hounds were lodged, had built the stone and timber tower on the motte; a symbol of power to keep a watch for enemies from the north. Edric knew he shouldn't come up here, but the watchmen had grown used to his escapades and would nod and smile and pretend they didn't see. He balanced on the parapet looking over the forest, oblivious to the sheer drop down the scarp. Up here he felt free; free from the noise and the chaos in the bailey yard. For where else could he escape from reality?

'Edric, Edric!'

His master's harsh voice drifted up and the nearest watchman cleared his throat in a meaningful sort of way. Edric swung his legs over and dropped to the wooden wall-walk, slick green with moss. He bent and pulled at a birch seedling lodged between the planks. He delved into his pocket for a rag and used it to secure some moss round the long spindly root. Tucking the bundle into his apron, he scrambled down the tower stairs and raced along the palisaded bridge over the motte ditch. By the kitchen range, he found a broken jar thrown out with the remains of last night's feast. Just right for a growing tree. He stooped to prise the jar out of the soggy mess of turnip, meat and bones, lodging it next to the seedling birch in his pocket.

'You God-forsaken wastrel.'

Edric was yanked upright, his ear almost torn from his head. His master shoved his face so close their noses almost touched.

'Little idler,' the man growled, 'the fire needs stoking. Now!'

Frog-marched back to the smithy, Edric's only thought was if he would have a chance to collect some wood ash and dirt to nestle the tree seeding before he was let go for the evening.

The master blacksmith kept Edric back to make sure he banked down the forge fire correctly. At last he joined the other apprentices round the smouldering logs in the pit at the centre of the hall.

'Heard the latest?' The baker's prentice shuffled up to make space, holding out a chunk of bread still warm from the ovens. The clamour of conversation and laughter bounced off the roof beams and Edric leant forward to hear better what Malin was saying. 'There's been another robbery. A merchant from Bricstow. Says a wild woodsman attacked him along the Harepath. Took all his metal goods. Pewter plates, silver gewgaws for the ladies, and a gold enamelled flask ordered by my Lord of Dunster.'

'Wild woodsman!' Hamo chipped in. 'It's a dragon more like. Dragons collect gold.' He nodded towards a huddle of guardsmen and archers by the dais 'That's what they will be saying.'

Malin dug the stable boy in the ribs. 'And how do you know that, Hamo?' he asked.

'When they brought the merchant's horse in, its mane was all singed. The merchant's cloak is burnt as well. He said he had been attacked with fiery breath and —'

'Oh, what tush!' Malin interjected.

Edric stretched out to warm his toes. 'It's always blamed on dragons,' he said, 'but never proven. Let's ask Alard, He'll know.'

A tall, skinny lad moved from group to group, topping up mugs and tankards.

'Over here, Alard,' Malin waved his beaker above his head. There was a grumble from a nearby group of soldiers. Malin shot them a fierce look. 'Our cups are dry too,' he said.

Alard arrived and started filling the beakers.

'You must have overheard the talk,' said Malin. 'What's going on?'

'Not much. Speculating who the robbers are and where they've hidden the treasure.' Alard wiped the edge of his heavy jug with a cloth. 'Some of the archers said they were going to take a look tomorrow. At the foot of the scarp.' He offered ale to the soldiers. 'Will you be going with them, sirs? They could do with some strong arms, I reckon.'

'Hamo believes it's a dragon, so they'll be better off with a knight and his sword.' Amid rising hilarity, Edric clapped the cringing Hamo on the shoulder. 'May I present Sir Hamo, the mighty dragon slayer!'

But, before it was truly light, curiosity sent Edric down to the Harepath where it joined the drove road to Bricstow. There were signs of a scuffle, churned up earth and a strange charring of the verges. The tall stalks of cow parsley fell to ash in his fingers. With his back to the brightening sky, he followed a trail of trampled grass until it abruptly ended at the foot of the scarp. There was a sudden commotion in the undergrowth and five men blundered past him, eyes wide with terror.

Edric pushed through the scrub into a clearing. Smouldering weapons and tools lay around, and the smell of scorched flesh caught in his throat. With a sense of foreboding he squeezed through a deep cleft in the cliff into a vast columned cavern. Overhead, light filtered through elevated fissures, shedding a strange cathedralesque lucency across the space.

In places the walls were smooth and polished as if something brushed against them every day. Elsewhere, the surfaces were rougher, covered in simple drawings, economical in line but still full of movement. Men with long spears surrounded a magnificent beast with huge ears and long curving tusks, and a deer seemed to fly through the air as it leaped from a high ledge. The most wondrous drawing was of a creature standing on two legs, powerful shoulders supporting huge out-flung wings and an arrow tipped tail trailing behind. A long neck supported the horned head, and spines ran all the length of its back. The beast looked almost real, its eyes staring directly at him. He stepped nearer, reached out a finger to touch the rock surface.

In that moment sunlight streamed through a gap in the wall and bathed the drawing in fantastical greens and golds and deep, deep carmine. The image shifted, seeping from recesses in the stone to slink around Edric; a great scaled creature, assessing with catlike, bloodshot eyes.

197

Amazed, Edric felt no fear. He wondered what the creature's scaly skin felt like; would it be warm or cold? If this was a dragon, would it spew out fire?

—You can touch if you want—

Edric pulled back. He knew he hadn't spoken aloud, yet here was an answer floating around in his head. The dragon, if that was what it was, stretched down its neck, inhaled a huge great breath and pushed its spiny nose against his.

—I only breath fire on those who want to harm. Go on, touch—

The creature dropped its head and let out a slow, laborious gust of air. Edric placed his hand just below what looked like ears. The scales were firm but soft, like the finest Cordovan leather.

'How did you know I wanted to touch you?' he asked.

The beast tipped its head to one side as if trying to understand.

'I never said anything, so how did…?'

—I see you are making words, but I only interpret thoughts. Think your words and I will understand. Yes, I am a dragon, but we come in many forms. Your kind call me a Wyvern—

Edric started to speak again but halted. The dragon looked expectant; waved its tail almost like a dog. A clattering some way off caught Edric's attention. The tail-point was dislodging objects from a mound of gold and silver in the depths of the cavern.

'It's you,' he blurted out. 'It *is* you that's…' He stopped and started again.

—You're attacking travellers and stealing their things—

—Yes—

—Why?—

—We are so charged. To only take from those possessed of greed and vice. Those who lust after riches. We hold it for those with greater need. Those more deserving —

'But Milo Sparrable, you attacked him.' Edric shook his head. This thinking instead of talking was too hard. He tried again.

—Milo Sparrable, all he was doing was coming back from delivering new boots. You took the six silver pence he was to give to his wife—

—Fourteen pennies I took from him; the six for his wife and the eight he overcharged for his work. He had such plans for those eight, such a night of debauchery—

The dragon snorted a great belch of foul air and its whole body shook. Edric could only surmise it was laughing.

He walked towards the hoard of treasure, bent down to retrieve an enamelled flask displaced by the dragon's tail. As he turned it over and over, the decoration sent spangles of sunlight quivering through the air.

—*You appreciate the beauty. You can keep it*—

Edric looked at the dragon, then back at the flask.

—*I can't. It would brand me the thief if anyone saw it*—

Edric replaced the glittering flask on the pile, walked past the creature and out into the normality of the early morning, the dragon's last words embedded in his mind.

—*The flask is yours. I will guard it. For your return*—

No one noticed him as he slipped into the bailey yard, not even his master, for the place was in uproar. The garrison serjeant cursed the archers and soldiers for losing their weapons, and another victim had been brought in. Not so lucky this one, for the thief had plundered his life as well as his goods.

Castle Neroche Farm
Early summer, 1848

'And did he return?' Annie asked.

'Oh, I had no…' The words faded away and Edwin shielded his eyes from the sun.

Annie leant forward, insistent. 'Did he? Go back?'

Edwin shook his head as if clearing cobwebs. 'It's getting late,' he said. 'Your mother will need your help and I can finish the telling another time.'

It rained for what seemed like days, and Annie was kept busy darning socks and turning sheets side-to-middle. Afterwards it was too wet underfoot to go scrambling down the escarpment, so she took the long way round to look for Edwin. She found the bench in the hollow, but there was no answer when she called. She ventured through the opening in the rock face and into a light filled cave.

It was exactly as Edwin had described except for a platform with a straw mattress and a coarse blanket, a few items of clothing hanging from a wooden peg forced into a gap in the stone, and a tin mug and plate on a pile of apple crates. Everything was tidy and in order; the cave floor was swept, and a small food safe stood in a corner. She looked around. There were the faded outlines of a leaping stag and huntsman trapping a mammoth. She went closer and tentatively reached out to the mythical creature outlined in the other drawing.

'It's all right, it's sleeping.'

Annie whirled round.

Edwin was right behind her. 'I'm sorry but I haven't any chairs. You can use the bed and I'll sit down there.' He pointed at a nearby rock. 'There's no tea either, but there's water.' He put a second cup on the crate and filled it from the old flask.

'Please, sit.' He indicated the mattress. 'There's a slab of gingerbread if you want some.' He busied himself at the food safe and fetched another plate for the cake. It was almost as if he was expecting her. Annie sat down.

'I asked around,' she said, 'but no one knew where you were staying. This is a strange place to live. I'm sure Pa wouldn't mind if you slept in the barn for the return of some labouring.'

'It serves me well enough. No one to bother me and plenty of work in the forest.'

'But it must be lonely, out here on your own.'

'What, with these huntsmen to keep me company?' He was teasing her. 'And someone has to make sure the dragon behaves.'

Annie glanced at the strange drawing, inhaled sharply. Surely the creature's eyelid hadn't moved. 'Do dragons wink?' she said.

'I don't think so. At least it's never winked at me. Now, listen and I'll continue with the story.' And he told of more attacks and robberies on the road, of villagers frightened to go out and cowering indoors at night. 'The trouble dragged on for months and travellers and merchants began to avoid the area. Nobody knew what to do, not even the priest.'

'But couldn't the lord's garrison have stopped it?' asked Annie. 'Sent a band of spearmen and skilled archers to ambush the thieves? The lord could have called on his neighbours to help.'

'Maybe, but most of the military-minded men were following the civil unrest as it shifted north, taking many skilled craftsmen and trades with them. Edric would have followed if his master hadn't remained at the castle. There were a few years left of his apprenticeship with an expectation of paid work afterwards. It was even suggested the blacksmith's young daughter would soon be —'

'Ah hah,' she exclaimed. 'That's the way to tie a young man to his employer. Offer him the daughter!'

Edwin sprang up and grabbed the flask. 'Would you like more cake? Or there're some apples. I'll just fill this up.' He rushed towards the back of the cave.

Annie stared after him. *Why's he so flustered? And that hint of...good heavens, he blushed!*

Castle Rache
Autumn, 1148

Nan went missing while foraging for mushrooms. The other girls had no explanation; one minute she was there and the next she had gone. With no hesitation, Edric downed tools with the rest to form a search party.

His master thrust a stout spade handle at him. 'We'll find her, lad. Don't you worry. We'll bring her home and she'll be yours.' The blacksmith's voice rang out, 'A proper wedding mind, not just a handfasting.' Edric ran to join the other younger men, bright colour flushing his cheeks for all to see.

They searched in circles all afternoon, but Nan was not to be found. Dusk came with lingering wood-smoke, and torches flickering along the ramparts. Malin suggested they try again in the morning. 'We've been over this ground before,' he said. 'It's impossible to see anything in this gloom. Especially under the trees.'

Edric kicked at the ground. 'I'll look a little longer.'

Someone spoke, raising a laugh and the blacksmith growled at them. He put out a restraining hand.

'Edric, leave it. They are as vexed as you. I would stay but I must go to Nan's mother. She'll be worried out of her mind.' Edric felt a weight on his shoulders as a thick coat dropped over him.

'Just don't stay out too long, lad,' said his master.

She couldn't have left no trace at all, Edric thought. *There must be a clue somewhere.* He swung his arm out in frustration and a stand of nettles just fell away to ash. A memory stirred, and he knew where to look. Somewhere he hadn't been since...

He ran, brambles grabbing at his clothes, impeding his progress. It was getting so dark he couldn't make out where he should go.

—*You will fall. Slow down*—

Edric stumbled and cried out, 'If you've hurt her, I'll...' *This can't be happening*, he thought.

—*It is. Look up*—

201

He looked up and the scarp loomed over him. Pin pricks of fading light glowed through the cliff face and he at once knew where to tread. He deflected his words into conscious thought.

—*If you've hurt her—*

—*She is safe—*

Edric pushed through the gap into the cave, and there she was, cowering against a fold in the rock. He rushed up to her and she curled up tighter.

'Nan, Nan, it's me. It's all right. I'll take you home.' He reached out, but she flinched, her eyes fixated on the far reaches of the cave.

There was a low rumble and she screamed. Embers in the depths flared up and warmth surged around them.

Edric's thoughts erupted.

—*What are you doing?—*

—*She is cold—*

—*You're frightening her. Why don't you explain?—*

—*Her mind is closed. The words bounce off—*

—*How did she get here?—*

—*She was carried off—*

—*By you—*

—*No. Men from the castle. She broke away. They chased. I drove them off, told her to run—*

Edric walked right up to the dark shadow on the wall.

—*What have you done?—*

—*She didn't hear me. Didn't run. I had to make her safe. I carried her here. Called to you—*

The dragon pushed its head forward, its mouth outlined in flickering orange.

—*It took you long enough to get here—*

'I didn't...' Edric faltered as glowing nostrils flared.

—*I didn't hear you—*

—*You weren't listening. You should always be listening—*

Nan's distress was growing, her breath coming in laboured gasps. The creature's head pulled back.

—*Take her home—*

—*I'll need something to wrap round her—*

The dragon moved to one side and Edric pulled a thick cloak from the treasure hoard. The lining was of squirrel, the hood deep. He lifted Nan from her niche and wrapped her in the sumptuous fabric, speaking quiet words all the while.

'You're safe now. There's nothing to fear.'

The dragon took a step forward and Nan whimpered, went rigid. Edric held up his hand, flinging thoughts out.

—*Stop. She doesn't understand*—

—*Explain to her, she need not fear. Not for herself, nor her family*—

—*I will try*—

—*Her assailants will suffer*—

—*I'll kill them. Cast a light to guide us*—

The dragon dipped its head, then stretched its great neck up to a crevice high in the wall.

Edric cradled Nan's face in his hands. 'There is nothing to fear. We are going to walk out of here and I will take you home. The dragon will light our way with its fire. Nan? Do you understand? I am taking you home.'

As he led her out of the cave, there was an escalating discordance and a sharp metallic tang in the air. A fiery light filled the whole clearing. Edric tucked the cloak tightly round Nan's shaking body, scooped her up and carried her back to the castle.

Castle Neroche Farm
Early summer, 1848

They walked towards the farm

'Did they marry?' Annie asked.

'No. Nan was forever silent. Would not venture outdoors. Could not sit by a fire, even in the dead of winter. It was kinder to leave her in the care of the nuns.'

'I wonder if Edric managed to explain to her about the dragon, and if she understood.'

'After all the time…the time Edric spent with her, I always hoped she did.'

'What about the men who attacked her?'

Edwin shook his head. 'Will and Hugh? Thought they had got away with it. Even concocted a tale that they discovered Nan a prisoner of the terrible monster hoarding the treasure and were just about to rally a rescue party when Edric brought her back. The rogues even devised the plan to block up the entrances to the cave, divert the river to flood it and drown the beast. And of course, they would be the perfect candidates to take charge of the stolen goods and make sure the items were all returned to the rightful owners.'

'I can't believe they intended to do that. Didn't Edric say what actually happened?'

'Do you think anyone would have believed him? Talking to friendly dragons wasn't on the agenda back then.' Edwin looked askance at Annie. 'I'm not sure it is now.'

She strode ahead and twirled around to face him. 'Well, I think it would be quite enlightening, talking to a dragon.' *Or just talk to a dragon's friend*, she thought. *Isn't that what I'm doing now?*

Edwin seemed to miss a step, almost stumbled, then walked on. Annie felt her chest tighten with excitement. *Oh, this is stupid. I'm imagining things. Just like Tommy.*

Annie rushed to catch up. 'What happened next? Did Edric warn the dragon so it could flee?'

'Oh, yes. But there was a problem. The dragon was tied to this place to guard the hoard. There was only one way to escape; give all the treasure to those who earned it through a kindly act or were in genuine need. But if before this was accomplished, the dragon was slaughtered its being would be forever imprisoned in the cave. And there was a final condition; the last piece could only be awarded to someone who also believed the dragon's tale.'

They had arrived at the entrance into the yard.

'That would be nigh on unachievable,' Annie said. 'The dragon would have to find someone to tell the story. Someone to convince the intended recipient that...' She faltered, as the unimaginable took hold. *But the dragon did find someone. You.* Edwin was staring right at her. *But that's impossible.*

He raised an eyebrow.

—*Is it?*—

She broke the gaze, and to hide the confusion, hitched herself up on the milk churn stand.

He leaned over the gate.

'So, what did Edric do?' She hoped she sounded calmer than she felt.

'Edric had to join forces with the dragon to trick the villains, then make sure the treasure got to the right people until they gave away the very last piece, however long it took. To be strong enough to follow this through, the dragon had to become Edric and Edric, the dragon.'

'How could they do that? How *did* they do that?' Annie asked.

Edwin gripped his forearm, rubbed it as if chilled. 'A transaction in blood.'

'Blood brothers. My big brothers did that. Mingling their blood. I told them they were being silly because they were actual brothers and didn't need to cut their... Oh, that's what's on your arm.' She reached out to still his hand. 'Doing it like that was a bit drastic, wasn't it?'

'Maybe slightly over dramatic, but it felt necessary at the time. I was much younger then.'

Mother was at the kitchen door, waving. Edwin handed Annie down from the stand.

'And did... Did Edric keep his bargain with the dragon?'

'Almost, almost. It is almost completed.' He relinquished her hand. 'Your mother's calling you. She must be wondering who this man is you've been spending time with, so you'd better go.'

'I told them you're helping me. With the stories.'

'Yes. It has to be finished. Before I move on.' He made her a casual bow and walked back down the track.

Castle Rache
Autumn, 1148

The lord's sword, newly forged, was at the rear of the workshop waiting for collection. Edric carefully wrapped it in sacking, picked up a shovel and went out into the bailey yard. He slipped into the shadows behind the stables and walked beside the rampart towards the eastern gate. Nan's abductors were still arguing over who was to breach the new damn holding back the diverted river. The serjeant was favoured by most of the villagers, but some thought it should be the blacksmith. It was his daughter the dragon had stolen, after all. Edric froze as his name was put forward, but the lord took the task on himself and decreed it would be done an hour ahead of sunset, before the beast woke to terrorise any more travellers.

At the gatehouse, Edric was bold, as if on official business.

'Where are you off to, lad?'

'Been told to check all the exits are securely blocked.' Edric held up the shovel.

'Not planning to break out the gold for yourself, I hope.'

'From what they're saying,' he nodded back towards the crowd in the yard, 'there'll be plenty for everyone once we drain the flood.'

The guardsman waved him through and Edric sauntered along until he was out of sight, then ran the rest of the way to the cave.

—I'm here. Where are you?—

—On the west side. Pushing through. Where the broken ash is—

Edric scrambled round and saw a fall of small stones.

—Don't push too hard. Just enough to get through—

They worked without communication, shielding their thoughts. The dragon squeezed and wriggled its way between the rocks, stood tall and shook its wings right out. It was the first time Edric had seen the dragon's full size. It was magnificent.

—Stop gaping. Fill the hole in—

Edric shovelled the soil back, pressing it hard into the rock wall. The dragon disturbed the leaf litter and used its feet and body to mould the ground into a deep depression. It settled down, tucked in folded wings, and started to drag leaves and twigs across with its tail.

—I need help. Throw some earth over me—

Edric had almost finished filling in the dragon's hide when the sound of frantic activity reached them from further along the scarp.

—What's that? Have they come early?—

Edric went to look. Just beyond a stand of ash, the two rogues were breaking into the cavern with mattocks. There were sacks piled on the ground and a donkey was hitched to a covered cart.

—We have company. Trying to get into the cave. Did you bury the treasure?—

—Of course. Those villains won't find it. Return here and finish burying me—

—When I've dealt with these two—

Edric unwrapped the sword. The leather-bound grip felt comfortable in his hand. He ran his fingers over the exquisitely engraved letters on the blade; letters he could not read, but whose power he could sense. He tested the edge. He knew it was keen; his master had kept him a whole day honing it to the lord's exacting requirements.

He watched, waiting for his moment.

One brigand went into the cave, leaving the other cheerily whistling, unfolding sacks. Edric walked forward, held the sword point level over where the heart should be, and leant in with all his strength. The man fell beneath the thrust before he had a chance to call out.

Edric went through the entrance, the weapon by his side and called soft and low, 'Hugh, are you there?'

The second man came out of the darkness holding a torch. 'Will? Is that you? There's nothing here.' Edric stepped in front of him. The two-handed stroke was fast across the man's legs, taking him to the ground. 'That's for the people you are defrauding, and this…,' Edric lifted the weapon above his shoulder, '...this is for Nan.' The blade edge sliced the soft flesh of the throat and through the bone.

Edric dragged the first body inside, sealed the opening, finished settling the dragon, and took the donkey cart back to the castle. When the lord led the men out to break open the damn, Edric buried the sword deep in the motte rampart. The wound on his arm, where the dragon had forged their pact, didn't hurt; it just looked awful, so he had Nan's mother bind it up tight while he sat with her daughter. When asked, he said he had torn the skin on a thorn bush, but knew he wasn't believed. Just before sunset, he kissed Nan's pale cheek, fetched his few belongings and left for the forest to wait until their work could begin.

Castle Neroche Farm
Early summer, 1848

She knew Edwin had nothing more to tell when he buried his head in his arms. She put her hand on his shoulder and waited.

When he finally looked up, he said, 'There is one last thing to do. Tomorrow. If you will come.'

'I don't know. I...'

'I'll wait at the Rylands ford.'

'My Pa has a sword,' she said, in a rush. 'Just a sword blade, really. It's very old. It must be...Edwin, you need to see it.'

She took him up to the farm and into the library. He seemed hesitant at first, unsure crossing the threshold, but he followed her and stood staring at the rust pitted iron blade above the mantle.

She dragged a chair over and climbed to lift the sword off its hook. As she placed it in his outstretched palms, the room grew dim, and his hand went towards where she supposed the hilt would have been. She watched, enthralled. The pommel and cross-guard materialised, with a finely decorated leather binding round the grip under his fingers, and he stroked the metal of the blade; lifted the weapon high. Mercurial light outlined letters engraved along polished steel, and a strange iridescence misted the air.

A distant shout came across the yard and from the kitchen her mother answered, 'She's in the library.'

Edwin let go of the sword as if scalded and it was all Annie could do to catch it. She felt the honed edge cut deep and the ethereal light snuffed out.

'Oh, there you are.' It was her father. 'What *are* you doing up there?'

'I wanted to sh…' She turned. The Reverend Ware was smiling at her over Pa's shoulder. There was no sign of Edwin. It was as if he had never been in the room at all.

'I wanted to…to look at the blade. I had a notion there could be words along here. A motto, a good luck charm.' She lifted the sword back into place. There was no evidence of blood or a deep wound on her fingers, merely a blackened mark from the age scarred metal. 'I was wrong, it's only a rusty old bit of iron.' She clambered down, stared at her hand, then went to follow her father into the kitchen. The reverend stopped her, guided her to a chair.

'Go ahead John, I want to ask Annie something. We'll be along in a moment.' He sat on the other side of the rent table. 'Are you feeling well? You seem quite out of sorts. Your mother asked me to have a word.'

Annie didn't know what to say. Was this bewilderment she felt being 'out of sorts', or was she suffering from romantic delusions? A childish hankering after adventure?

'I…I'm well, thank you, just a little confused about something. It's the stories Edwin — Mr Whisholme — has been telling me. They were quite ordinary at first but after the…after a while they got more tangled.' She untwisted her fingers and spread them out on the table. 'Not tangled exactly, more interwoven. Like those old paintings; the more you look, the more you see.' Annie leant forward. 'I think Mr Whisholme is leaving, and he said there's one last thing he has to do to finish his story. He asked me to meet him tomorrow. I don't know what to do.'

'Your Mr Whisholme, Annie; what do you think he is? A skilled storyteller or something more?'

'I'm not sure. He tells it as if he was there. It's like he was remembering.'

'Maybe he was there.'

'I don't know, Reverend. I don't know what to think. And if I don't go, I won't know what happens.'

'So, meet him. Otherwise you'll always be wondering about the end.' The reverend looked up at the sword. 'It must have been a fine blade once, deserving of a motto.' He stood up, smiling. 'The stuff of legends! Now that's all sorted, what about a cup of tea? Your mother had some of those pastries of hers in the oven when I arrived.'

'One other thing,' she said. 'Little Tommy…I keep thinking, maybe he's been telling the truth all along. Perhaps he actually did see a dragon.'

'Have you seen one?'

'Not really, only the drawing in the cave. I went to look again, but it wasn't as clear as I thought, only a few scratches on the wall. Maybe I imagined it, wanted it to be more than it is. Reverend Warre? Do you believe in dragons?'

'Well, Miss Annie, where would all these stories come from if dragons didn't exist?'

Annie walked with Edwin to the edge of the wood and would have gone further, but he put out a hand to stop her. The dappled sunlight cast a strange green glow over his skin and the scar on his forearm was rough to her touch. 'It doesn't seem to fade,' she said.

'Don't worry. Soon it won't be noticeable.' He tugged impatiently at his shirt sleeve to cover his arm. There was a sudden commotion above, and two pigeons tumbled through the branches. The disturbance sent a shimmer of light over the rough cloth and for a moment she thought it looked like silk shot through with gold. She reached out to touch, but the vision was gone.

'I won't be here tomorrow,' he said.

'Why ever not? You can come back with me. Pa will find you work. He's always complaining there's too much to do.' She was trying very hard to act normally.

'I can't stay. I think you know that would be impossible.'

The catch in his voice was almost as if he would break into tears, but she knew that was silly. Men didn't cry even if they wanted to. She raised her hands to his cheeks and thumbed the shadowed skin under his eyes. It was slightly damp.

She dropped her hands to his shoulders.

'Edwin, I'm trying to understand, but it's not —'

He kissed her.

It was nothing like the stupid village boys who tried to grab a handful of skirt as they came out of the schoolroom. Nothing like the casual labourers who thought they could steal favours behind the barn.

His lips barely touched hers. It was a gossamer breath of wind and surprisingly warm from someone who always felt so cold. She spread her hands and ran her fingers down the prominent bones of his spine. And when he strained away from her, she did not want to let him go.

She began to speak, but he pressed fingers to her mouth and stepped away.

'There is something I would give you, if you will accept it.' He lifted the gold chain from around his neck, freed the small medallion from his shirt, and started to fold her fingers over it. She pulled her hand back and knew instantly she'd been overhasty. He was disengaging from her; his eyes glazed over and his skin lost what little colour it had.

'I'm sorry. It wouldn't harm you, not now.' Even his voice seemed distant. 'We…I…I shouldn't have assumed so much. Forgive me.'

'Edwin, there is nothing to forgive. It's just that I'd rather wear it than hide it away.'

His fingers lingered as he fumbled with the clasp and his nails pricked when he dropped the disc into the hollow beneath her blouse. It throbbed against her skin like an extra heartbeat.

He tipped her chin up. 'You are just like her, you know. The same eyes, the same hair, the same curiosity. Almost the same name. And you are the first person in all these years who accepted what I had to tell was credible. You didn't laugh or threaten or tell me I was an idiot. Because you opened your mind to me, I am no longer tied to this place. I am free to travel where I will. You, Ann, have released me.' He stayed close for a moment longer, then stepped back. 'You do understand, don't you?'

He moved even further back. 'Ann, I don't belong here. I am not of this time, nor of your world.' His voice cracked, the words rasping the space between them, 'I cannot stay.'

He walked away; his hands bunched into fists, and she saw the subtle changes. She knew it wasn't just the sunlight through the leaves that washed his skin with green, knew the raked flesh on his arm was not just a scratch, knew his spine had become more pronounced, that the staining in his bloodshot eyes would no longer fade.

She called out, 'Stop. Edric, stop.' And when he halted, she went towards him until she was just short of an arm's length away.

'You called me Edric.' he said.

'Yes.' She paused. 'The young man in the story you wove for me, that was you. On the day the dragon drawing winked at me, you were listening to my thoughts. I heard some of yours. And your gift; it's the last piece. So, Edric, turn around and see that I truly believe who and what you are. For I don't think either of you will be free to leave unless you do.' She took the last step forward. 'Edric, turn round. Please.'

He turned and he was laughing. 'Oh, Annie, Annie, you don't know how happy that makes me.'

She said, 'Give me your hands.' As she suspected, claw-like fingernails had dug into the flesh. She tore a strip of linen from her underskirt and bound his blooded palms. 'Unless you want to be totally helpless, remember not to make a fist. On the other hand, I could always come with you. To clip your nails and...and...what exactly would you need me to do?' She looked up just in time to catch an expression of horror cross his face. She grinned. 'Maybe not. Somehow I don't think I'd fit into your world either.'

'There is one thing you could do. Help me with this shirt. It would be such a pity to destroy it when I have to discard it.'

As she undid the buttons, material finer than any labourer's fustian slid through her fingers. She ran her palm down the front; felt, not a smooth, honed body, but overlapping ridges and snags. She squeezed her eyes shut and hesitated before she guided the fabric over his shoulders.

'You can look if you want,' he said.

'No.' She turned her back to him. 'I'd rather remember you as you were. Can I ask you something?'

Taking his silence as permission, she said, 'If you come back, will I know you are there? Will I be able to touch you?'

The silence stretched out. 'Edric?'

When she looked over her shoulder, he was walking into the forest, not making a sound. It was so quiet she realised the birds had stopped singing and the wind had completely dropped. Everything was still, even the stream in the valley bottom was silent. As she watched, he started to fade into the wildwood, the hanging mosses and lichens enfolding him.

'Remember me on your travels, Edric,' she whispered. 'I won't ever forget you.'

The words seemed to unfold and float through the silence towards the trees until the spectre halted, turned and raised a long, webbed arm in salute. Then there was the sound of the stream and birdsong and no trace anything else had been there at all.

As she climbed back up to the farmyard, the wind rose, and she looked back. The tops of the trees across the valley shuddered and flattened as if under a sudden onslaught.

Her mother called out, 'Annie, come in. You'll get soaked. It's going to pour.'

She looked up at the swirling clouds and big fat raindrops bounced in the dust. She ran to the house.

'Look, look.' Little Tommy was tugging at her skirt, pointing at the cloud shapes. 'Look, Annie, look. A dragon.'

'Don't be silly, Tommy,' she and her mother said in unison, but Annie faltered, could not say the rest. Her mother, alone, finished it. 'There are no such things as dragons.'

Across the sun, the dark cloud spread its wings and lifted its head, the long tail trailing behind. A gust of hot air seared Ann's cheek and a stream of consciousness filled her mind.

—You will know, but maybe not touch. Our name is Âzæ'zŷâl. We will never forget—

Although there is no grand stone edifice at Castle Neroche, it is a magical place to visit in any season. When my story opens, it was believed to have originated as a Roman encampment, but 20th century research places it as an Iron Age hill fort going back to 700 BCE. The Norman motte-and-bailey castle was built around 1067 and was enlarged during the Anarchy, a period of civil unrest between 1138 and 1153. During the 13th century it fell into disrepair. Castle Neroche Farm was founded in the old bailey enclosure in the early 1800s. The forest to the north and east, acquired by the Forestry Commission in the early 20th century, has been commercially managed as a diverse mixed woodland since 2006. There are many footpaths and tracks to follow and all the visitor is asked to do is respect the landscape and the farm's privacy.

Somerset is renowned for having more dragon myths than any other county in England, Scotland or Wales. Not only are there numerous tales about these fascinating creatures, but physical evidence, notably in churches, can be found throughout the county. In fact, dragon spotting is a popular pastime.

The Rev. Francis Warre, (1807-1869), vicar of Bishops Lydeard, was a locally respected archaeological historian. In 1849, he was one of the founding members of the Somerset Archaeological and Natural History Society and was their General Secretary until he retired in 1867. His detailed paper on the Castle Neroche site was presented to the Society and published in their journal in 1854.

I have taken a couple of liberties with the Rev. Warre's academic career. There is no evidence that he wrote a book on the myths and legends of the West Country although his 1854 paper ends with an anecdotal account of one of the tales surrounding Castle Neroche and I have based the entry in the 'fictional' book on his actual words. Although he mentions the discovery of the sword and marks where it was found on the plan in his paper, he doesn't lay claim to finding it himself. That is purely conjecture on my part.

Annie Rowsell, her mother, father and brothers are the creation of my imagination and have no relationship with anyone farming the land at Castle Neroche in the past or today.

I can vouch for the authenticity of the Castle Neroche dragon. As for the truth of Edric/Edwin's relationship with the Wyvern…that is for you to decide.

Kate Jewell was brought up in Portsmouth and educated at boarding school in Bournemouth. Unsuccessfully applying to Brighton Art School, she ended up at her pin-in-the-list second choice: Coventry, graduating in Graphic Design. She has worked in advertising, as a book designer for a children's book publisher, in a busy Local Government graphic design studio, and as a Creative Arts lecturer in Further Education.

An avid reader, Kate was grabbed by historical fiction at an early age, reading Rosemary Sutcliff's *The Eagle of the Ninth* with a torch under the bedcovers late into the night. Her passion for the 15th and 16th century was ignited by a history teacher who, on hearing complaints about having to do more 'boring Napoleonic battles', suggested she join an archaeology summer camp run by medievalist Colin Platt.

Kate's short story, *The Daisy Fisher*, won the 2019 Historic Writers Association/ Dorothy Dunnett Society Short Story Competition, and her long-running series of articles on the Dorothy Dunnett book cover art is published in *Whispering Gallery*, the society's journal. She is currently working on a fiction project, following a group of adventurers through the turbulent transition from the Plantagenets to the Tudors.

After over thirty years she has finally escaped from landlocked Leicestershire to pastures new in West Dorset, a welcome return to the south coast. She has two daughters and four grandchildren. When not writing, she can be found in the garden, painting and drawing in her studio, or exploring the countryside with her camera.

Here there were Dragons, Kate's first foray into spooky fiction, is a ghost story with a difference, a dual era tale with a 700-year time gap.

AMONG THE LOST

BY

SAMANTHA WILCOXSON

Traverse City, Michigan - 1927

I will never forget the day I arrived at the Northern Michigan Asylum. Plain giddy with excitement, I was already envisioning how I would be the best nurse they had ever encountered – compassionate with the aged, able to draw out the silent, and a delight to the children. I was nineteen and still full of ideas about how wonderful life was if only you were determined to make it so.

Autumn was the best time to arrive in Traverse City. The splendor of the rolling hills covered with a kaleidoscope of trees left one quite breathless. And if that were not enough, gorgeous blue lakes hid around every corner. The smell of the season was crisp and clean, splendidly healthy for the patients I looked forward to serving.

When my car approached the facility, I was struck by the beauty of it. The creamy brick and countless spires gave the hospital the appearance of a castle in the midst of this wild northern beauty. I could scarcely believe that anyone could remain ill or morose long within this setting.

I practically skipped across the lawn and through the front entrance.

~

The first time I entered a patient's room, I was struck not so much by the person but his surroundings. It was neat and cozy, as were many of the rooms, but it had an astonishing view through the narrow win-

215

dow of the lawn where Dr Munson, the facility's founder, kept his collection of trees from his world travels. I had asked about the strange grove where no two trees seemed to be alike. It was like a collection of snowflakes, and the differences were even more pronounced in October when golds, bronzes, rusts, and bright ambers dotted the lawn.

It was only after gazing at this scenery for longer than was polite that I took notice of the gentle resident of the room. He was thin to the point of appearing fragile with wispy hair the color of snow. His eager smile told me that he was one of the patients who looked forward to their few moments with the nurses.

"Well, you must be new. How lovely!"

My heart warmed toward this patient instantly as I considered the loneliness of a life wherein a new acquaintance brightened one's day so.

"My name is Lotte. You must love sitting at this window," I said, gesturing toward it.

"Oh, yes," he nodded enthusiastically. "My name is Marvin."

Of course, I knew this from his chart, but the introduction was welcoming all the same. His chart also informed me that he had been born during the Civil War, and I couldn't help but reflect upon what that must have been like.

He rambled on about the trees, his family, and his former nurse throughout my ministrations, but I must admit that I stopped listening in order to focus on my tasks. I had been assured that the work would quickly become second nature, but I was not yet at a point where I could converse and administer medications at the same time.

~

The next time I approached Marvin's room, I heard his voice before turning the knob. I felt my eyebrow rise but forced it down. Although he seemed quite sane, many of the patients spoke aloud to themselves. I allowed myself a condescending smile and opened the door.

"Oh, how lovely! You've just missed Nurse Nancy. I'm sure you'd like to meet her."

I searched my memory for any mentions of Nancy, but I had been introduced to so many new people recently that I could not be sure if I had met her. I nodded and offered a smile but made no comment. I was

216

curious what another nurse would be doing in a room that I was scheduled to attend.

"No matter. I am here to see you," I said, dismissing all thoughts of the mysterious Nancy as I saw to Marvin's medications and comfort.

As I left his room, I could hear the man across the hall raving again. *"Through every city shall he hunt her down, until he shall have driven her back to Hell, there from whence envy first did let her loose!"*

The poor man spent his days loudly reciting lines from Dante. It was impressive, in a way, how his mind had firmly trapped the medieval prose. Sad that it hadn't done the same with the names of his family. Such a strange selection to hold on to. I wondered that his mind hadn't retained something more comforting for the old man, a hymn perhaps, but no. He resided within the Inferno. I paused and listened, but I had not paid attention enough in literature class to determine which circle currently claimed him.

What was surprisingly delightful about him was that his face cleared and the devil's plans drifted away as soon as anyone entered his room. When I opened the door, the dear thing would complete whatever line he was uttering – no line was ever cut short – but then he would smile and chat as if a switch had been flipped. He was perfectly kind and pleasant but couldn't seem to remember anything besides the Italian text.

The women's wing had some intriguing patients as well. My favorite, not that nurses are to have favorite patients any more than mothers have favorite children, sat at a window with a view filled with ivory brick of the children's building rather than trees. It was beautiful in its own way but wearying in its sameness. However, sweet Ms Ginny didn't seem to mind. She spent many afternoons gazing at a painting hung on the wall across from her bed. It was a fairly nice landscape but clearly amateurish work. I did not notice anything special about it until I looked in on Ms Ginny during a night shift.

My breath caught in my throat when an unexpected luminescence greeted me in the darkness. My shock was noise enough to wake poor Ms Ginny, and I apologized for disturbing her.

She chuckled, "It is no worry. This must be your first time noticing my painting."

"It is," I stated. Hearing an infantile awe in my voice, I struggled to regain my professional composure. "It is rather unique . . ."

217

I hoped to quickly change the subject, but she interrupted, "My niece painted that for me." Her voice lowered conspiratorially, "She used paint from work. That is what makes it glow."

Despite my hope to avoid seeming naïve, I couldn't help but satisfy my curiosity. "Is that so? What makes it glow? I do not believe I have ever seen the like."

Chuckling again, Ms Ginny shook her head. "Neither had I, and I doubted her word when she warned me of what would happen. I guess she didn't want to be the cause of her old auntie's heart failure. I sat here and kept my eye on that painting as the sun went down that first night, and wouldn't you know? The stars on that canvas started shining right along with those outside!"

I couldn't resist drawing closer to the painting, examining the pinpoints of light that were not visible during the day. They shone over a river lined with trees that I assumed to be a setting familiar to aunt and niece.

"It's quite marvelous."

Ms Ginny appeared content with that praise and accepted my ministrations without further comment. I was still pondering what kind of paint made things glow in the dark as I carried out my rounds.

Most of the other patients were asleep, and I woke only those who required nighttime medicines. Some, lonely even in the middle of the night, carried on whispered conversations for as long as I was willing to stay in their rooms. Some of them asked about current events, and one believed Woodrow Wilson was still president. She shook her head at me in bemusement when I tried to tell her about President Coolidge. It made me feel more important than I had a right to feel, offering them this simple companionship.

The asylum was pleasant at night. Dim illumination made the hall feel cozy and safe, and the rounded corners of each room's threshold were welcoming. What moonlight there was shone through the patients' windows and stretched out as far as it could reach across the hall thanks to high transom windows above each door. Some people commented that it must be eerie to be the night nurse at an asylum, but I found it rather peaceful.

Leaving one room, I noticed another nurse in the hallway. I thought this was curious, since there was little need for a single night attendant in this ward, let alone two. Not wishing to disturb anyone's slumber, I tried to whisper down the hall with my hands cupped around my mouth, but I failed to gain her attention. Shrugging, I carried on to the room in which my Dante slept.

~

The next day dawned bright and crisp with chilliness. Frost had formed on the autumn leaves and blades of grass in a cold, hard beauty. When the coal train stopped and dumped its load – straight from the train car into a deep underground bin – I felt the boom might crack the icy scenery. I was thankful that few of my duties took me out of doors. The more experienced nurses laughed when I said so and implied that I would be too delicate for a Traverse City winter. I accepted their teasing with good humor, partly through the softening presence of Bernice.

She had begun taking me under her wing in a matronly but not condescending fashion that I appreciated. It was difficult for me to admit, as a young woman wishing to appear independent, that I missed my mother horribly. Bernice not only filled that gap a bit, she also gave me priceless tips on becoming an excellent nurse.

When I asked her who else was assigned to my ward the night before, she looked at me curiously. "Why, just you. Were you not able to visit all the rooms?"

She looked worried that I had failed to fill my responsibilities, so I quickly reassured her. Confident that she was satisfied with my work, I pressed on. "But I'm certain I saw another nurse walking down the hall."

Bernice looked up to search her mind for a response. "Maybe someone from another ward had to come collect some supplies or whatnot." She shrugged, and I decided that she was likely correct.

"I believe I'll have you work down a ward for you next shift. You've done well with the easy cases, but you should have experience with the more serious ailments as well."

I nodded in assent. It was an understood but mostly unspoken truth that the patients grew more deluded and difficult as one moved through the wards of Building 50. The center held doctors' offices and living quarters. From there, each long wing, one for men and one for women, stretched out with mild cases nearest the staff and getting worse as one progressed down the long halls. I had never been to the end of either wing, but I was eager to test and improve my skills.

My excitement in anticipation of this assignment evinced the naivety I had brought with me to the asylum.

219

Yet, at this point, I only moved down a couple of wards, nowhere near the end of the wing where nurses were challenged to control difficult patients without restraints according to the asylum rules. No straitjackets. No handcuffs. Patients were treated with love and respect in the hope that gentle treatment and the beauty of the surroundings would serve as cure. Dr Munson famously preached to his staff at every opportunity that beauty was the best therapy for our patients, but I couldn't help but think that a straitjacket might sometimes be necessary as well.

I was surprised to find a relatively young man in this ward among others who seemed much more troubled than he. His shaggy head was bowed low over a notebook each time I entered his room. He scribbled so frantically that I wondered if he had been a writer or if he were one of those who simply took comfort in journaling or describing their surroundings. Never glancing up, the distressed man scarcely seemed to notice my presence as he wrote and wrote.

Intrigued, I asked Bernice about him. "What is his ailment? And do you know what he is writing? Does he speak to you?"

Bernice's face pursed in an unsettled way that it hadn't when I had asked about other – more difficult – patients. "That poor dear," she finally murmured. "Bobby is one of very few who have deteriorated since arriving here." Shaking her head in disappointment, she continued, "Dear thing seemed a prime candidate for healing in a calm, restorative setting, but he suddenly got worse not long before your arrival. He had been on your regular ward but had to be moved as he became nonverbal."

"So, he did used to speak?" I asked eagerly. Something about him stirred up wistful feelings of hope in me. Could Bobby be a patient for whom I could make a great difference? I longed to be a dramatic part of the healing that took place here.

"Oh, yes, quite normally, in fact," Bernice was responding to my question as my own mind wandered. "I do believe he was more depressed than ill. Bobby has a sensitive way about him."

I nodded slowly, trying to picture him calmly conversing rather than furiously writing. "How interesting," I murmured.

Sighing, Bernice closed the subject as she moved to see to her own duties. "I have hope for him yet. If only we knew what caused the fracture in his mind."

I watched Bernice walk away with the feeling that I had been given a mission. I imagined Bobby's rust colored hair hanging down to curtain his face as he endlessly wrote. Could I encourage him to speak again? "I wonder," I whispered to no one in particular.

~

I did not immediately have the opportunity to try my skills on poor Bobby. Back on the first ward, I took comfort in the familiar prattle of Dante. All the nurses referred to the patient by the name of the Renaissance poet to the extent that I had forgotten his real name.

"No sadness is greater than in misery to rehearse memories of joy," I heard him recite as I stepped across the hall and closed the door of Marvin's room behind me.

"I was talking to Nurse Nancy about you," he said with a smile. "I do think the two of you would get on."

"That's sweet of you to say," I murmured, trying to remember who Nancy was. Marvin had mentioned her before, but I still didn't recall anyone by that name. "She works this ward?" I asked.

"Oh, she did, but now she just comes to visit," Marvin said with a shrug. He sipped his tea and looked out the window. When he next spoke, it was on unrelated matters.

"Who is Nurse Nancy?" I asked Bernice the next time I saw her.

Her eyebrows shot up. "How do you know about her?"

I frowned, not expecting this to be a scandalous inquiry. "I don't. Marvin talks about her."

Bernice seemed to relax, her face softening and her shoulders lowering. "He was rather fond of Nancy," she said sadly.

"But who is she?" I pressed on.

"No one special," Bernice waved away vaguely. "She was a nurse here, but she left suddenly not long before you came. It was somewhat of a surprise, I suppose, since a few of us thought she might marry Doctor Arnold."

She shrugged and said no more.

Questions piled up in my mind, but Bernice was moving down the hall away from me. I could take no more of her time at the moment. One, I had to ask.

"Does she still come to visit?"

I'd had to raise my voice a bit because Bernice's quick stride had already taken her a fair way down the hall. She stopped abruptly and turned around.

"Well, isn't that a funny question." She tilted her head in reflection. "She disappeared during her shift one night, and I haven't seen her since. Rumor is she was homesick and just decided to leave." Bernice leaned her head the other way. "I don't know if I believe that, but she left, whatever her reason."

With that she turned and walked away again. I sighed. Marvin must be a bit muddled in his mind if Nancy hadn't been seen at the asylum since before my arrival. Ah well, I was more interested in the challenge of broken Bobby anyhow.

Once I had seen to the tasks of my assigned ward, I padded down the hall to visit Bobby. I strolled into his room as if I were appointed to be there. Someone had put on a jazz record at low volume, and I was curious if it improved his mood. He, as was his habit, remained bent over his notebook. I was astonished that he never seemed to need to pause and think. Words must come to him faster than he was able to record them.

"Pardon me, Bobby." I tried to make my voice sweet and inviting, but he reacted not at all. I bit the inside of my cheek. "Is there anything I could get for you? Cocoa?"

I watched as he kept up his frantic pace without appearing to hear me. Instead of trying to force him to react, I decided to settle for getting him accustomed to the sound of my voice. I prattled on about my parents and siblings, realizing what a mundane life I had led before arriving in Traverse City. Bobby did not respond, but I felt I had done something and left his room with a feeling of satisfaction in my work.

~

Not more than a few days passed before I found myself assisting Doctor Arnold with a patient, and I remembered Bernice mentioning his connection to Nancy. Instead of paying as close attention as I should, my mind wandered, trying to figure out how I might ask him about her in an innocent sort of way. He was a handsome man, some fifteen years or so my senior. His manner with the patients was competent if not overly friendly. He was not cruel, but neither was he approachable. I was dismissed from his presence without having formed a proper question about Nancy.

It was not necessary to be clever with Marvin. He mentioned Nancy as soon as I next entered his presence.

"Oh, how lovely. I was just talking about you with Nurse Nancy. She is anxious to meet you."

"Is that so?" I asked with what must have been a condescending smile and tone.

"Yes, she needs help, and you're just the one to assist her."

At this I furrowed my brow. Then Dante's voice echoed down the hall.

"The path to paradise begins in Hell!"

I grinned at the reminder that much crazier things were spoken within these walls.

To Marvin, I simply said, "I would like to meet her, too. I wonder when she might visit again."

Looking perfectly sane, Marvin stated, "She will see you the next time you work the night shift."

I must admit that a shiver passed through me as his cool eyes studied me with greater clarity than I recalled seeing in them before, but I forced myself to give a little laugh and say, "Alright, that sounds quite nice, Marvin."

However much I tried to shake off the feeling, I was a bit nervous when my next night shift came. I couldn't think why Marvin's promise of a visiting nurse left me more unsettled than Dante's constantly promising hell to all within hearing. When most of my shift went by without any unexpected occurrences, I naturally relaxed and had a bit of a laugh at myself.

Then, as I approached Marvin's room, I was surprised to hear voices in conversation, and one of them most certainly female. I tried to listen with my ear close to the door, but the murmuring was low and failed to carry on the still night air. Taking a bracing breath, I plunged in with a quickness that made me wonder to myself about my objective.

Marvin sat up in bed, speaking calmly with a young woman who was dressed exactly as I was, her starched uniform crisp and white. Her pale skin was almost undiscernible from her dress, but her face was turned away from me. Marvin, however, noticed my entrance and grinned broadly.

"How lovely! You're here in time to meet Nurse Nancy." He clapped almost like a child as he looked back and forth between his visitors.

I cleared my throat and tried to sound confident. "Hello. We don't usually have visitors at night."

Nancy brushed past me and out into the hall without speaking. Although she hadn't seemed to move quickly, I felt that I hadn't had time to speak or stop her. I looked at Marvin, who gave me an encouraging nod, and then stepped back out into the hall.

"Nancy?" I called quietly, reminding myself that the other patients were sleeping. I saw her form walking away just as I had seen it that first time, I thought, realizing that it had indeed been her then as well.

"Nurse Nancy?" I cried out more loudly than I should, but it was no use. She was gone. The long, dimly lit hall was empty and silent.

I kept my eyes on the passageway where she had disappeared as if I anticipated her return until Marvin's voice reached me. I returned to him disappointed, but he was in good cheer.

"Isn't she lovely? I just knew the two of you would get on. Very alike the two of you are."

My voice was caught firmly in my throat, and I found myself entirely incapable of responding. I simply administered Marvin's medicines and left his room without uttering another word.

~

In the bright sunlight of the next day, it was easy to dismiss the odd incident of the night before. While sitting over coffee with Caroline, one of my coworkers, I casually mentioned that Nurse Nancy had been visiting.

"Well, that can't possibly be," she stated with a firmness that gave me pause.

"Whatever do you mean?"

Caroline shook her head and leaned closer. I had already learned that she was one who thrived on gossip. "First, you tell me what you mean by saying she's been visiting."

A stuttered over my words. I was always one to be embarrassed when proven wrong. "Well, what I mean is that Marvin said she had visited him." I could feel the fire of blush on my cheeks, which only served to increase my nervousness.

My companion relaxed with a laugh. "Ah, is that all now? Marvin is a bit batty, isn't he? Well, that's alright, but he surely hasn't seen Nancy."

"Why is that?" I asked, trying to appear as though the answer concerned me not in the least. I sipped my coffee and glanced toward the window. Still, I could see Caroline's devilish grin out the corner of my eye.

"Well, mainly because Nancy is dead."

Blood froze in my veins, and I was thankful I had turned my face away for it must have fallen deadly white. I slowly placed my coffee cup on the table, ordering my hands not to shake. I was impressed by my acting when I casually responded.

"What happened to her? I don't believe I've heard of her."

"Well, she died – sorry, disappeared – before you came now, didn't she?" Running her fingers through dirty blond hair, Caroline considered her memories. "She was supposed to marry Doctor Arnold, I believe – or at least some people believed. I wasn't quite sure, though he was clearly sweet on her. Then she was gone."

She shrugged as if the young woman was of no consequence.

"But you said she was dead."

Caroline shrugged again and took a gulp of coffee before responding. Here she was now trying to appear all innocence. "Well, I suppose that's just what some of us assumed when she disappeared so suddenly as she did. And in the middle of the night, too. Now, if she were going home, as some would have us believe, why on earth would she go in the middle of the night?" Caroline's countenance had shifted from uncaring to smug.

"Maybe she was dreadfully homesick," I countered with my own impressive façade of unconcern.

"Maybe," she conceded with her voice full of doubt. Then she sighed, Nancy forgotten. "Well, I've got to get to it. I've got the scribbler today."

"Do you?" I brightened. "Would you like to switch? I've been trying to draw him out."

"Have you now?" she laughed at the very idea that I might be successful where others had failed, but it appealed to her to take the easier ward. "Alright then," she shrugged. "I rather like Dante."

I nodded with a smile and forgot all about Nancy as thoroughly as Caroline had. The challenge to be a key component in Bobby's healing was more interesting to me as I was sure that it would increase my standing with my superiors if I were successful. So far, my efforts to speak to him had accomplished nothing, but I wasn't discouraged. He had grown used to my presence and the sound of my voice. It was a start.

My spirits were high as I strode past my ward of minorly afflicted patients. I was concentrating so on thoughts of the patient who would be my breakthrough that I didn't even notice which circle of hell Dante was threatening us with. In my mind, I envisioned Bobby looking up from his writing today and responding to one of my questions or asking me about my mother.

He was as he ever was when I entered his room. Dark auburn hair flopped down to conceal his face as his pencil flew across the page.

"Hello, Bobby. I'm especially happy to see you today," I greeted him as I straitened up the room and moved toward him. "I thought you might like to share what you are writing."

I felt daring as I moved close enough to peer over his shoulder. Stopping short of touching him, I leaned forward, struggling to make out the words. A weight dropped heavily into my stomach when my eyes focused on the lines. "The scribbler," I whispered, recalling Caroline's words. Bobby did not look up from his pages and pages of incoherent scribbles. I could not discern a single legible letter.

Quickly completing the tasks required in his room, I left feeling foolish and disappointed. Did I truly think I would make the difference in a patient whom far better trained doctors had failed to cure? I laughed harshly at my own ridiculousness and was glad that no one had witnessed my humiliation.

In my efforts to put Bobby out of my mind for the rest of the day, I naturally thought of him even more. Hadn't Bernice said that he had recently been on the ward where the worst ailment was an affinity for strange, old literature? Why did he now spend hours a day scrawling nonsense? What happened to the unfortunate man? It may be said that I was doing a rather poor job of letting go.

Even as I found my bed that night, I was thinking of anxious Bobby. A trigger. Something must have prompted his slide into madness, but what? Sleep claimed me as I pictured his large hands scribbling, scribbling, scribbling.....

~

A knock awoke me, and I worried that I had overslept and missed part of my next shift. That concern was soon abolished as I realized that no sunlight yet illuminated my small room. The nurses' rooms were much the same as those of the patients, except that we had the freedom to leave them at our will. I listened for the sound to come again, hoping that it fell upon someone else's door for I was cozy under my duvet and the wind sounded harsh. The floor would be frigid, and morning would dawn cold.

The rapping did come again, and indeed was not at my door. However, I was certain the sound came from my window. Fully awake against my fervent wishes, I furrowed my brow toward the curtains. That couldn't be, being that I resided on the third level and couldn't think of a single soul who would need to sneak to my window rather than use the traditional entryway.

Yet, the knock came again.

A ridiculous fear rose in my chest and caused my heartbeat to skip. I reminded myself again that my room was not within reach of someone outside. Surely, there must be a reasonable explanation, I worked to convince myself as I mentally put my nurse's cap on. I was a woman of science. I almost exclaimed it aloud.

When the sound continued in spite of my insistence that it was impossible, I angrily threw back my toasty covers and forced my bare feet to the icy floor. Best to get it done quickly, I told myself. I marched across the room and pulled the curtain back as though expecting to startle someone on the opposite side of the glass.

Of course, no one was there. A tree branch blew in the wind, hitting several windows and likely disturbing the slumber of a number of asylum employees. I laughed at myself and wished that I might rid us of this nuisance. None of the windows in Building 50 opened. It was not considered prudent in a structure filled with mental patients. Therefore, the limb would continue its rhythm until we could get a groundskeeper to climb up and cut it.

Just as I was about to return to the warmth of my bed, I saw someone crossing the lawn. Nurses rarely had cause to leave their building during the day, let alone at night, but there was a woman casually strolling along. I was amazed that she wasn't freezing and didn't have to lean into the wind to make her way. Then I realized that it was Nancy.

I couldn't explain just how I knew, except by the ridiculous notion that I *felt it*. She was too far away, and it was too dark for me to truly identify her, but, all the same, I was certain that it was her. I watched her make her way across the grounds and considered if I should follow, then wondered why on earth I would. Stepping back from the icy glass, I shook my head at myself. Go running outside after someone in the middle of the night. What an absurd idea!

Excusing my melodrama as a symptom of being roused from my slumber at an untimely hour, I snuggled back into my covers and was promptly reclaimed by sleep.

~

The next day, I was scheduled on Bobby's ward, and I was excited to see him again, although I admonished myself for a fool. Something about him made me sure that he was as sane as any one of the rest of us, though that might not be a great recommendation when one lives in a mental asylum.

He, of course, was scribbling in his notebook when I entered the room, and I began babbling on. Before I knew it, I was even telling him about the night before and seeing who I believed to be Nancy. I could have sworn that he paused in his nonsensical writing, but when I peered closer at him, his pen was dashing across the paper as furiously as ever. Feeling bold, I took an unprecedented step with Bobby. I kept up my constant stream of one-sided conversation as my tasks brought me closer to him, and as I reached the side of his chair, I touched his shoulder.

He flinched away, as I had expected he would, but he also spoke. "Only Annie!"

My eyes grew as large as saucers as he resumed his writing. I had never heard him speak and was curious how long it had been since anyone else had.

"Please, accept my apology," I murmured, kneeling beside his chair in an attempt to look into his face. "Is Annie the only one you like touching you?"

His eyes flickered in my direction, seemingly against his will. A quick nod, almost imperceptible.

I smiled as if he had granted me a generous gift and plowed on. "And is Annie a nurse?"

The scrawling stopped. He put his pencil down and closed his eyes.

I waited eagerly, though my legs were beginning to cramp. What would he say when he opened his eyes? Would he look at me, confide in me? I was growing giddy again.

While I waited, I examined his face, which had never been exposed so thoroughly to me. He had an inviting countenance, except that it appeared so weary. He had the look of one who might as easily have been twenty-five or forty, and I wondered at his true age and what had made him look so worn. The faint wrinkles around his eyes and worry line between his brow seemed new, like a young man who had recently encountered great trouble. Freckles were sprinkled across his nose and cheekbones, adding to his boyish air. The stubble on his chin was a lighter shade of red than his hair.

At this point in my examination, I realized that my legs were growing numb and he was not opening his eyes. I stood awkwardly and shook out my tingling limbs, considering if I should check his vitals. The thought of touching him that way felt like an intrusion, though I did it many times a day to other patients. Something about Bobby was off limits.

Before I could decide on my best course of action, he jolted into alertness and was writing again as if I weren't even present. I took a deep breath and decided to move on for now, but I was very proud of our shared moment.

"Annie," I whispered as I closed the door. "Who is Annie?"

Grinning like an idiot, I carried out the remainder of my rounds.

My excitement faded as I inquired of several of my fellow nurses and got no closer to the enigmatic Annie. It did make her ever more intriguing though. I decided I had little recourse but to return to Bobby. I tried to plan out what I would say, what would elicit him to say more in return.

I had no duties that evening, so I made my way to Bobby's ward. Timing my visit to avoid an encounter with the nurse on duty, I slipped into his room and was surprised to find him sitting before the window rather than his desk. This I took as an encouraging sign, and I strode purposely to his side.

Pulling up a chair, I gazed at his sunset view briefly before looking at him. When I did turn to Bobby, I gasped a little to find that he was examining my face as I had his. I wondered, not about Annie, but what he thought as he took in my features. I tried to remain impassive and allow him to look as long as he liked. When he met my eye, he shifted his gaze back to the scene outside.

Not to be denied, I leaned closer to him and touched his forearm. He slid it away slowly, not jerking violently as he had earlier.

I waited.

"Only Annie," he murmured with such pain in his voice I felt tears threaten my eyes. And me a woman of science. How absurd.

"Who is Annie?" I asked calmly, keeping my hand on the arm of his chair. I bit my lip, hoping he wouldn't become catatonic once again.

He did close his eyes, but only for a moment this time. I felt my anticipation rise as he opened them, but he just repeated, "Only Annie."

I pressed my lips together and held in a sigh.

"Alright then." I stood and brushed his shoulder with my hand before walking out. I had no more answers, but I felt that we had still made progress. I forced myself to be content with that.

I tried to imagine who Annie might be as I burrowed deep into my covers that cold night. A girlfriend or wife? A sister? I was convinced after my inquiries that she wasn't a nurse, for the name seemed unfamiliar to everyone I questioned. What had happened to her? For some reason, I tried to envision what she looked like. If a girlfriend, I felt sure that she would have sweet girl-next-door sort of looks to match his homespun appeal. If a sister or other relative, she might share his auburn hair and splattering of freckles. Sleep took me as these figments of my imagination danced through my head.

~

The knocking disturbed my slumber, and I was annoyed this time rather than afraid. I would make my complaint first thing in the morning regarding the rebel branch. Turning over with a groan, I pulled the pillow over my head to block it out.

It was no use. My mind was fixated on the sound, so, unsure what else to do, I stomped to the window and pulled back the curtain to glare at the offender.

It was gone.

The branch had been neatly cut by a groundskeeper, and my view of the lawn was clear. The chill I felt could not be fully attributed to the cold floor or breath of winter seeping through the wall.

A figure moved steadily across the frosty grass, and I leaned forward to squint at her. For it was a woman in a nurse's uniform. "Nancy?" I whispered in fascination. But it couldn't be, or at least shouldn't be. By all accounts Nancy had left the asylum weeks ago, so why did I keep seeing her?

While I did not have the urge to follow her as I had the night before, I did remain at my window watching her progress until she reached an odd little outbuilding. Pausing before the door, I would have sworn on my Bible that Nancy looked right up at me, but that's a ridiculous notion. She entered the shed and was gone.

I waited a few minutes for her to emerge. The structure was no larger than a broom closet, so I felt certain that she wouldn't remain inside for long. My hands and feet were numb with cold when I climbed back into bed having failed to see Nancy again.

~

In the morning, I was groggy from lack of sleep and curious dreams. I took coffee but did not make conversations with my coworkers as was my habit. I was thankful to be back on my original ward where the patients were not too demanding.

"In the middle of the journey of our life I came to myself within a dark wood where the straight way was lost."

The sound of Dante threatening the tortures of hell was strangely comforting, and I hummed 'My Blue Heaven' to counter him as I made my rounds. Marvin was thrilled as he always was to have any kind of visitor. When he asked where I had been, I informed him that I had worked a few shifts on another ward.

"Oh, how lovely! Then you must have met Bobby. He's a good guy. So sad to see him in such a way as he is…"

Before he could change the subject, I interjected, "You know Bobby?"

"Why, of course, dear. He used to be in the room just across the hall before . . . well, before his fit." His voice had lowered as one afraid of being caught in the sin of gossip.

"Of course," I sighed to myself. I knew that Bobby had been previously on this ward but hadn't considered asking other patients about him. "He is a poor thing," I agreed sympathetically. "What happened to the dear man?"

Marvin shook his head, his eyes wide. "I wish I knew." He shrugged. "It really was too bad that Nurse Nancy left when she did. She had such a way with him."

The way he said it brought me up short. A thought began forming in my mind, but I wasn't sure how to investigate its worth. Marvin had moved on to other topics anyway, and I completed my duties murmuring the expected responses.

~

231

At the midday break, I almost fell into my chair so exhausted was I. Caroline laughed at me in greeting.

"Long day already?"

"No, but a sleepless night," I admitted. "Marvin still seems to think he's had visits from Nurse Nancy. What did you say happened to her?"

She shrugged. "I don't know, but it definitely had something to do with Doctor Arnold." She bent toward me with the smile of one who prides themselves on having the juiciest tidbits. "Maybe he killed her."

Caroline said it so casually before walking away, but pieces continued falling together in my mind. I left the rest of my lunch untouched, the beginning of a plan forming in my head.

~

Readying for bed that night, I wondered if Nancy would still alert me to her crossing of the lawn if I didn't fall asleep. Part of my mind reminded me that this was ridiculous. She had no way to be rapping at my window or to know whether or not I was asleep, but I told that part of my mind to hush up.

I decided to try to sleep but had achieved no more than a restless doze when I sprang up at the first *rat-a-tat-tat*. I almost ran for the exit before peering through the glass, but I gave a quick glance to be sure. Nancy made her way toward the tiny outbuilding, and I rushed to follow her.

As I practically fell down the narrow steps, I considered if I should be afraid. I was following a girl who everyone claimed shouldn't be here and who at least one person believed was dead, but I couldn't help myself. What was the worst that could happen?

A harsh northern Michigan breeze blew off the dark waters of the bay and turned autumn leaves into missiles as I raced across the frozen lawn. Nancy seemed to have waited for me but didn't quite allow me to catch up. I didn't pause until I reached the entrance to the shed. She had entered it, as I knew she would, but I began to consider what was inside and why I never saw her come back out.

Freezing and irritated by leaves smacking me in the face, I took a deep breath and pulled the door open.

She wasn't there.

I found myself at the top of a steep stairway that led underground into an indiscernible dark gloom.

I gulped and closed the door behind me. At least the wind stopped. I peered down the steps, trying to decide if I should descend them. I heard my Dante's voice in my head.

"Abandon hope all who enter here."

Knowing I would be angry with myself in the morning if I stopped now, I forced my feet forward.

As I reached the bottom of the short staircase and my eyes adjusted to the dimness, I realized that I was in a tunnel. It was tall enough to stand in and walled with bricks. Evenly spaced lanterns illuminated my surroundings just enough to see Nancy ahead. Dark patches between the fixtures made it appear as though the ground gave way at regular intervals.

Again, I forced myself forward, telling myself that it must be safe if Nancy came here each night.

My shoes click-clacked on the bricks and echoed down the underground passage, and I realized that I couldn't hear Nancy's footfalls even at such a distance. Her figure disappeared and reappeared as she alternated between shadow and light. I hurried my pace, worried that I could get lost underground all alone.

It didn't occur to me to call out to her until I reached a branch in the tunnel and wasn't sure which path she had taken.

"Nancy?" I called out tentatively, and the echo came back to me. It faded slowly, giving me chills as it did so. It almost sounded like…

She didn't speak, but Nancy appeared some distance down one of the shafts, so I sprinted after her. She took several steps toward me and held up her hands as if encouraging me to slow down, and I did so, relieved that she was waiting for me. The lights flickered, keeping me from slowing my pace too dramatically. I began to puzzle over what I would do should I find myself left in utter darkness.

"Don't think about that," I admonished myself in a whisper that still managed to echo quietly.

I was gaining on her, and the excitement of it spurred me on more quickly. It didn't even cross my mind to ponder why she was leading me along underground or what I would say to her once I caught up.

Suddenly, I was upon her. She was standing over a figure lying prone on the curved passage floor. Her eyes locked on mine as if wishing to impart an urgent message. As I opened my mouth to speak, she began to fade before my eyes, never looking away. Somehow this didn't shock me, as if some part of me had known all along that the poor woman was a restless ghost.

I looked at the figure upon the ground.

It was the young woman I had seen in the halls of Building 50 and wandering across the lawn. I was struck by how lifeless her physical body appeared compared to her apparition. But she was gone. I was alone with the decomposing shell she had left behind and directed me to find.

"You poor thing," I whispered. It hadn't occurred to me to be afraid until the next question formed in my mind. "What happened to you?"

Kneeling down, I took up my examination of the corpse. Even for one trained as a nurse, this was a disturbing employment. The process of decomposition did not fully disguise the fact that Nancy had died of a severe head wound. Her skull was cracked like an egg, which I knew would take great force.

Before fear could absorb me, my curiosity bullied its way forward. A paper was tucked into Nancy's pocket, and I had the sensation that this, even more so than her body, was what she had desired found.

I took hold of it and moved closer to the nearest light to peer at familiar scrawl. It was a doctor's order, and the physician's name was familiar, as was the patient's. I gasped when the purpose of the order was illuminated.

"A lobotomy? On Bobby?"

My objective complete, fear washed over me. The fact that I was underground with a corpse and information that at least one person would not want publicized struck me like a physical blow. I scanned my surroundings, certain that Doctor Arnold would suddenly appear at my side.

I began to run.

Guilt pestered me for leaving Nancy as I had found her, but she would keep a little longer. Puzzle pieces clicked together in my cursedly slow brain as my footfalls echoed like thunder through the brick tunnel.

I couldn't be sure about the connection with Doctor Arnold, but I knew one thing about Nancy. She was Bobby's Annie.

I could have smacked myself for taking so long to work it out. He was saying Nancy in his fevered state, sounding just like her name echoing off the curving walls. He knew something terrible had happened to her, and it was more than his sensitive mind could cope with.

What had happened between Nancy and Doctor Arnold? The lobotomy had not been performed, that much was clear. Did Doctor Arnold know then that Nancy was dead? Had he killed her?

The steps to the world above came into my vision, and relief flooded over me. I ran across the frozen lawn with leaves whipping around me and the sound of waves crashing in the distance. Only when I reached my room did I steady my heart and look more closely at the paper I had removed from Nancy's body. I took a deep breath, convinced of what I had to do.

~

I strode into Doctor Arnold's office first thing in the morning, evidence that the night before had actually happened clutched firmly in my hand. My first impulse had been to go straight to the police, but it seemed unfair to accuse the good doctor of participating in a crime when I wasn't certain that anything illegal had occurred. Perhaps Nancy had fallen in the dark tunnels, tripping over the uneven bricks, and this order was pure coincidence. I needed more information.

Doctor Arnold glanced at me with disinterest when I tapped on his door and entered in the same movement. He continued writing for a moment before shifting his gaze to me. His upraised brow invited me to speak.

"I would like to ask you about the young woman who served in my position before my arrival," I began and was pleased with the confidence in my voice. "Nancy. Did you know her?"

He leaned back, sucking in a deep breath as he considered his reply.

"I did." After a brief examination of my face, he added, "I was planning to marry her."

"Is that so?"

I waited. I did not believe Nancy planned to marry him, but silence seemed the best way to force him to say more.

"It is fairly common knowledge among the staff, but she left." He shrugged as though that settled matters.

'Over There' played on his record player, and I wondered if he had served in the Great War. I decided to plunge in. "Did you ever meet her in the tunnels?"

The change in his countenance was subtle and unreadable.

"Why do you ask?"

235

"I found this." I held out the order he had written for Bobby's lobotomy, and he paled.

Without taking the paper from my hand, he asked, "Where did you find that?"

I met his eye but did not answer, because I could tell he knew. His cheeks reddened despite his otherwise astounding self-control. I waited again.

Finally, he sighed and rubbed his hands over his face, clearly hoping I might have disappeared before he had to continue, but I remained.

"I did meet Nancy." He relaxed a little, appearing quite confident in his explanation. "You've not worked here long, so you may not be aware that many couples use the steam tunnels for private meetings." He leaned forward conspiratorially, "I planned to marry Nancy."

I couldn't help myself. As much as I knew I should steer directly toward my objective, I had to ask, "Steam tunnels?"

He seemed pleased by my question and smiled. "Yes, the underground passages were built in conjunction with the Edison power plant. It is how heat is forced into the asylum buildings. It's much safer than fireplaces, as I'm sure you can imagine."

I almost got wrapped up in this intriguing tidbit, but I shook my head and reminded myself that Nancy awaited justice.

"Did Nancy reciprocate your feelings?" I asked, fairly certain she did not.

His eyes moved away from me to peer into the recent past. I thought he would continue spinning his tale, but he admitted, "She claimed she loved someone else." He gestured toward the paper but refused to speak Bobby's name. "We argued about it, and she stole that order."

He looked at me, hoping he had said enough. I thrust my chin forward to indicate he should continue. My shock could not have been greater when his next confession came out in a rush.

"She ran away from me in the tunnels and fell. She struck her head." Tears filled his eyes. "I am a doctor, but there was nothing I could do."

He hid his face in his hands as his shoulders shook, and I began to doubt my next move.

"You did not hurt her." It was a whispered statement, more to myself than Dr Arnold. I had allowed my imagination to run away with me and believe that I might have uncovered a scandalous crime, but it was just as I had thought during my more reasonable moments. An unfortunate accident, nothing more.

He looked up at me, his features raw with pain and eyes swimming in tears. "Of course, I did not hurt her. I could never . . ." His face was buried again.

"We cannot leave her there," I murmured. "She must be allowed to rest in peace."

He nodded weakly without raising his head but did not speak.

The poor man, I thought.

"Please, Doctor Arnold," I whispered, holding a tentative hand in his direction. "Let us see that dear Nancy is properly laid to rest."

He pressed his lips tightly together, nodded slightly, and took my hand.

~

The ward was still quiet when I began my rounds. Marvin slept, though I could hear the quiet murmuring of Dante.

"Death is not the end of these souls' lives."

I decided to check on Bobby.

Other nurses were at work on that ward, but they paid me no mind. Bobby's door was open, so I peeked in to see if he was alone. A nurse stood over him, and I moved to leave and return once her duties were complete. Then I noticed her hand was resting gently on his shoulder.

A strange feeling came over me as I took a step inside the room. I heard murmured conversation and marveled, for Bobby neither spoke nor welcomed touch. The woman turned toward me.

"Nancy?" I whispered. I had believed for some reason that her apparition would stop visiting once I had completed her quest for me.

She looked at me with deep compassion, appearing more alive than ever before. Then, for the first time, she spoke.

"Oh no. Not you, too."

~

Historical Note

The Northern Michigan Asylum in Traverse City was built in 1883-1885, including Building 50, the main structure which is almost a quarter of a mile long. More buildings were added over the years to serve patients that were sent from around the state of Michigan. Men, women, and children were segregated in addition to patients being separated according to condition. 'Beauty is therapy' was a famous slogan, referring to founding Medical Superintendent Dr James Munson's belief that the gorgeous natural surroundings of the area would help the patients heal. The grove of extraordinary trees that Lotte sees was really planted by Dr Munson, however, the rest of the characters and events of *Among the Lost* are figments of my imagination. The asylum closed in 1989 and was left to ruin. Of course, an asylum is rich soil for ghost stories, and you can even take tours of the dilapidated structures and the steam tunnels if you ever visit Traverse City. Recent efforts have saved some of the buildings and the process of redevelopment is underway. Now called The Village at Grand Traverse Commons, the old asylum retains the beauty that made it a place of healing, but one can also sense an aura of mystery as if old ghosts are near and waiting for someone to tell their stories.

About Samantha Wilcoxson

Samantha Wilcoxson is an American author living in southwest Michigan with her husband and three children. She has been obsessed with history for as long as she can remember and loves sharing this passion through historical fiction. Her published works include the Plantagenet Embers series, a set of biographical novels and novellas that take place during the Wars of the Roses through the early Tudor era. *Luminous: The Story of a Radium Girl* is her most recent novel, featuring real life dial painter, Catherine Donohue. Samantha is currently working on *Women of the American Revolution*, scheduled for release in 2022 through Pen & Sword Publishing, and looks forward to diving deeper into American history.

Amazon link: amazon.com/author/samanthawilcoxson

HOTEL VANITY

BY

D. APPLE

1960. A financially strapped hotel owner struggles to corral annoying ghosts so he can sell the hotel, but his ethereal friends are not the only ones who need to find peace.

*T*ap tap tap.

Humphrey's eye twitched each time the pen clanged against his coffee mug. Seizing it before the buyer noticed, he set the cursed pen on his desk and veered his chair toward the coffeepot behind him. He reached for the sugar but grasped only air. *Could have sworn it was closer.* The spoon lay just out of reach, too. He'd have to get a word with a certain somebody.

He spoke into the void. "Mr. Grant, I think you will find our hotel very charming. The locals love this place but would hate to see it change."

"I've heard as much." The man before him reached for the mug. "However, one million is quite a bit of money for a dump like this."

Humphrey cringed, waiting. The inevitable happened each time a prospective buyer lamented about the outdated furniture, lack of television, radio, or any number of other troubles old hotels have. Air conditioning? Out of the question for the five-dollar price of one night.

Sure enough, the coffee mug jolted from his hand, right onto Mr. Grant's lap. *Dammit, Nancy.*

Mr. Grant jumped from the chair, pulled at his pants and waved his hands over his crotch. "Ooooohhhh," he seethed. "What on earth?"

241

"I... I'm sorry, I must have lost my grip. I'll get a towel. So sorry!" Humphrey hurried toward the closet. *"Nancy... leave the man alone,"* he said under his breath.

"I'll do no such thing." A familiar chill blew against the back of his neck as Nancy materialized behind him. "I don't like him." She crossed her arms. "He reminds me of somebody I used to know. Cocky."

"Well, I happen to know a few ghosts here that are just as annoying."

Nancy scowled and tilted her head, pulling a velvet cigarette case out of her brassiere. "I don't know what you are on about, but I happen to remember many a man who enjoyed my company."

"*These* days I rather doubt it. Why do you keep taking all my lighters, really?" Rolling his eyes, Humphrey seized the lighter from her hands and pocketed it as he walked back with the towel. Of all the hotel's former inhabitants, Nancy had scared away the most guests, and consequently the money to run it.

Nancy's high-heeled boots clopped behind him, but only he could hear her. Only he could see her. Until she wanted to be heard or seen. What a blessing. *Or a curse.* He bit his lip as he contemplated what to do with the towel.

"Oh, give it here." Mr. Grant snatched it and patted at his crotch. "Where is the bathroom? I'd like to make sure I don't need to go to the hospital."

"Aw, yes." Humphrey strode to the nearest room and instructed the still seething Mr. Grant how to use the pull handle to flush the toilet, just in case. When he had left the man, he sank into his chair with a sigh. The stack of bills next to him glared back. "Oh, fudge it all, Nance. He bought this place sight unseen, so we had better not make him regret it."

"My dear..." Nancy sat on the edge of his desk. Her red dress spilled over the collection notices and nudged them aside. "Perhaps he can be formed into a model owner. Like you. You also needed some molding, or have you forgotten?" She brushed her fingers over his cheek.

That mild heat that came with her touch always left him confused. Her skin never made physical contact. It couldn't. "Nance, I've told you before. Stop flirting with me." He cleared his throat at her pursed lips, rotating his wedding ring round and round.

"Susan can't see us, there are no mirrors here."

"I am uncomfortable."

242

"So fire me." As if that would keep her from appearing randomly and harassing anyone else.

"Anyway… we need a person who can make this place some money. Not another me." He sighed.

Nancy shrugged. "Maybe I'll play the man some tunes. Men love a woman who plays." Her smirk was just enough to make Humphrey uneasy.

"No, no piano playing just yet. We can't spook him."

"Fine. You make things so dull." Nancy sauntered away, crossing her legs in an oh, so alluring gait he knew she didn't do for him. It was just the way she'd learned to walk, in her former life.

"No smoking, either!" Humphrey hissed to her turned up middle finger, a gesture she'd taken to readily.

#

Humphrey set down the suitcases and checked the room while Mr. Grant browsed in the largest upstairs suite.

Mr. Grant looked out the window and smiled. "A wonderful view. Very simple. Quiet. The vines look a bit hazardous, though." He wandered about, touching tapestries, gazing at the faded carpet, and brushing his fingers over dusty furniture. "This property will be perfect for the resort if we can get them under control."

"Resort? Who under control?" Humphrey tugged at his shirt collar and glanced around the room for anything out of place. Any… *person* out of place. He couldn't afford to screw this up. The roof needed repairs, the water pipes replacing, and each year vines crept closer and closer to choking the life out of the hotel. They didn't call Kudzu the "vine that ate the South" for no reason, and it was well on its way to eating the hotel, thanks to the previous owner planting it to control soil erosion.

"Yes, anyway…" Mr. Grant's voice cut into Humphrey's thoughts. "Did you know my grandfather used to own this place? It had been in the family for a long, long time, but he lost it in a card game in '53. Wretched old man, he was. Always a hothead, but word has it he started drinking when my uncle disappeared. One never really gets over the loss of a child, eh? You don't happen to know about that, do you?"

"What?" A voice belted from the mirror tilted face to the wall.

Eyes wide, Humphrey covered it with a blanket. "Oh, sorry, I just realized this was in here. It's very expensive but the wrong one, and I

243

have to send it back." He tried to parse what Grant had just revealed, and why he felt comfortable saying it to a stranger.

"I see..." Mr. Grant raised his brows and turned in a circle, giving everything one last look. "What time is supper?"

#

"Supper?" Nancy rolled her eyes. "What sort of place does he think this is?"

"I don't know... a hotel?" Humphrey grimaced. He had to lay off the cook months ago and hoped the meal wouldn't be too difficult to put together. "Can you at least help me? You've moved enough furniture to make the last guest wet his pants, so I think you can handle something."

"No, that was Tom." Nancy rolled her shoulder to Tom, who sat by the window as usual, book in hand. Humphrey often wondered how many times the ghost had gone through the library from top to bottom.

Tom raised his bushy, white brows and sighed the way he always did when he had his favorite book. A sly smile tugged at the corners of his thin lips.

"Well, what *can* you do, Nance?" Humphrey interrupted another of Tom's long sighs.

Her smirk could have melted butter. "I could... you know." She twirled her hair around a finger and bit her lip. "Help our guest feel comfortable."

"No! No." Humphrey waved the spatula. "Do not go in his room. Do not touch him. And keep Tom and Susan here in the kitchen."

Tom glared at him over a page and adjusted his spectacles. If the ghost ever spoke, he'd surely have something snappy to say.

"Don't worry." Susan's muffled voice emerged from the mirror by the door. "We aren't going anywhere." She pressed her brown, pleated hair as she slid from one mirror to the next, just above his head where she could look down on him. "I don't particularly desire to see another naked man. The last one was positively ghastly."

Humphrey choked and coughed, trying to push the thought of Susan seeing anyone else out of his mind. "How many have you seen, exactly? Wait, don't answer that. Just keep an eye out for him in the hall so he doesn't surprise us. Please, dear."

Susan glided to the hallway mirror, muttering. "We need to talk later. You know why."

244

Humphrey took a deep breath. Of all the things on his to-do list, facing Susan was the last he wanted to check off. Her comment made his toes curl. They hadn't even gotten to the marriage bed before her accident, and he should have been there to stop it.

Mr. Grant sure enough came sauntering down the hall, footsteps loud on the hardwood floor, and pocket watch open. Humphrey emerged from the pantry with arms full of potatoes, just in time to see Mr. Grant stop at the hall mirror and stare at Susan, Humphrey's most beloved being on earth.

Humphrey's throat caught. He dropped the potatoes. Shaking his head to clear it, he grabbed a large bowl from the counter and gathered them up.

"Quite the picture you have here." Mr. Grant squinted at Susan and touched the impression of her white bodice. "How are these made?" As he looked back for an answer, Susan used the reprieve to blink her beautiful green eyes and adjust her dress.

"Nobody knows, it's um... imported from France, I think. That's what the last owner told me." Humphrey shuddered at his memories of the first days here. Oh, what a shock to return after the card game, to find his bride consumed by a mirror, and realize he was still not alone. Never alone. Couldn't even go to the toilet without a ghost or two materializing. They never knocked, the cold bastards.

"You mean my grandfather?"

"What?"

"The last owner."

"Oh, right. Sure. I do think his name was Grant, yes. Quite advanced in age; I was impressed at his ability to run the place." Humphrey glanced at the Wedgewood stove, eggs sizzling and spatula flung haphazardly to the side. Tom's book lay on the table, though not quite right. An imprint of Tom's fingers holding his place gave everything away to the discerning eye. "Just um... have a seat in the parlor and I'll bring supper down."

"No other guests today? Mind if I take a look at the paper while I wait?"

"We've had a slight shortage this week." Humphrey did a quick glance around to make sure all his ghosts were in the room. "Yes, here, take the paper with you. I'll be ready in ten minutes."

Mr. Grant nodded, and glanced down the columns. "You think Kennedy will win the election?"

"I um—I don't know." Humphrey took a deep breath. "He's fairly young."

"I mean this in the most congenial way. Your hotel and your name are from another century, you know? But that's not always a bad thing. It's peaceful in a place like this." Mr. Grant chuckled and tucked the paper under his arm, strolling out of the room.

Tom stared at the man's retreating back so intently that his finger slipped out of his place as he cradled the book to his chest. Finally glancing back down at his prized possession, his face fell.

"That's an odd way of saying 'you're an old soul'." Nancy tapped her chin thoughtfully.

"I thought he would never leave. Do you know how hard it is to not blink?" Susan rolled her eyes and glided back to the kitchen mirror. "Definitely wouldn't want to see him naked, either."

"Well, I don't know… How do you youngsters say…" Nancy lifted a brow. "I'd nail that."

Tom shot her a scowl and set his book on the table.

#

Supper flew by in a haze. Humphrey brought out the hastily prepared eggs, mashed potatoes, and bacon. Same as breakfast would be, but he wasn't about to admit it. He preferred to let Mr. Grant believe everything was under control for as long as possible. Perhaps if he did a good enough job, the man would let him manage the place, or stay on in some other capacity.

"Thank you. What do you have to drink?" Mr. Grant asked as he stabbed at the eggs with his silver fork. Certainly it was the wrong fork. Nancy would tell him that. She knew little about cooking, but she knew which fork and spoon to eat what with. Or… at least anything to do with consuming food, drink, and… other indulgences.

Humphrey eyed a piece of eggshell flickering on the edge of an egg clump and willed it to disintegrate before the man saw it, or choked on it. Thankfully, a ghostly finger must have picked it off the plate because when he looked back after wracking his mind about drink options, it was gone. His shoulders relaxed. Maybe Nancy was watching out for him today instead of her usual tomfoolery.

"I've got milk and whiskey. I have to bring water in, you know… because of the old pipes."

"Oh." Mr. Grant furrowed his brows and stroked his mustache. "Whiskey it is, thank you."

"Right away." Humphrey ducked out of the parlor and cursed under his breath. Nancy would surely be interested now, and her presence in the parlor near any liquids might ruin the delicate fabrics.

"Did you see what I did?" Nancy leaned against the cellar door as Humphrey rummaged around for a lantern to better see his alcohol collection.

"You took the egg shell from his plate?"

"No, must have been Tom."

"Dear Lord, I don't need both of you in there. In fact, I don't need any of you there." Humphrey grumbled. Hopefully Tom had done nothing out of place yet. "Can you keep Tom out of the parlor?"

"He does what he wants." Nancy swiped at the whiskey bottle, but Humphrey held it behind his back. She pursed her lips. "All right, I'll lure Tom into the library."

"Good."

"Good."

Humphrey cleared his throat and walked back to the parlor. He swept up Tom's book from the table and stuffed it under his armpit as he poured the whiskey into the glass. "Here you are."

"Leave it, please." Mr. Grant put a hand on the bottle's neck and pressed firmly until Humphrey let it drop the inch back to table.

Giving a fierce glance around the room to ensure any ghostly presence behaved, Humphrey left the parlor with nerves on fire. *Curse those cursed beings.* They would be the death of this place someday. He shuffled to the library and, seeing nobody, almost deposited Tom's book with the rest of them.

There were many fine books, classics he remembered reading as a youth. What did the old ghost find so wonderful about this dog-eared one?

He sat in one of the ornate chairs, dust billowing around him as his rear hit the cushion. He'd have to dust this room more often, apparently. Ghost butts did little to keep the place looking used.

He crossed his ankle over his knee and opened the curious book. The title had long since worn away from the spine, and the crumbling title page had been torn out. He flipped through the thick pages and realized they had been pasted over with other paper. Each page was a portion of letter painstakingly cut out and adhered over the top of the actual story.

January 1st, 1900

My dearest Rose,

I wanted to send you a letter from my heart to yours. Can our souls speak to each other across time and place? Or perhaps you can hear me in heaven when I cry for you. So I am doing both. I am sending my soul to you and writing this letter. I don't think there is much time before he finishes me off. Seventeen years is not enough life, and the few glorious weeks in your arms before being ripped away will never suffice.

The writing went on and on about love, and vines constricting the writer's heart as much as they did the house. Humphrey flipped to the next one and raised his brow at the jump in time. Especially the year. That was the year he and Susan arrived.

July 6th, 1953

My dearest Rose,

I sit here in the heat to write this letter. It seems the very air should make the coldest surface sweat, if not drown in humidity, but I do not sweat. I have aged, and yet I feel free. Nancy tells me this is when time stops, though. I won't age, or sweat, or fear. I think the trade was worth it, so I can see you again while I still have my memory. Can you forgive me for giving up? I hope to find a way to pass to you soon. I know if Father were here I'd certainly sweat anyway, but he is gone. He lost the hotel in a bet, I hear, to a new couple. I don't think they will last. They are too worried about themselves.

Humphrey passed a hand over his eyes and blinked. Surely this had to be the uncle that Mr. Grant spoke of—the one who disappeared when his grandfather owned the hotel. Humphrey would have to show the book to the man, but it was late. He needed to make the rounds before bed. Perhaps he'd read more later, if Tom ever let the book out of his sight again. *Curious old man. I wonder what he sees in this writing.*

As if on command, Tom and Nancy entered the library. Nancy swished her way to the nearest chair and harrumphed into it. Tom scanned the room until his eyes rested on the book in Humphrey's hand. He edged over without a word and snatched it to his chest. Both ghosts stared at him dully.

"I think Mr. Grant is cute." Nancy flung her curls behind her shoulder and shoved her bosom out.

"How so?" Humphrey cocked his head. "Earlier you said you didn't like him."

"I don't have to like him to jump his bones."

"Dear Lord, Nance. What did I say about spooking him?"

248

Nancy spread her hands in exasperation. "I didn't say I was going to." She rolled her eyes up. "But he does have better manners than I took him for at first. Maybe in another life. Say... what are your plans tonight?"

"I'm hanging out with Susan in the room." Humphrey spoke a little too abruptly for his own taste.

"Is that what you kids call it these days? I suspect only one of you will be doing the hanging." Nancy winked and sprawled out in her chair, taking up as much space as possible. "Unless..."

"OK, that's where I draw the line, Nance. I don't want to talk about this."

Tom sniggered from his seat by the windowsill and palmed his book open again.

Good grief, these beings were the most irritating souls on the planet. It could be worse. *I could have angry ghosts,* Humphrey reminded himself. He got up from his chair, joints stiff. "You two try and behave, all right? I don't want anyone knocking on my door, banging around—"

Nancy snorted.

"That's it." Humphrey strode, nearly slamming the door before he remembered they had company. He eased it closed and drew a deep breath, holding it for five seconds, imagining all the built-up pressure leaving his body. Soon these unruly beings would be somebody else's problem. But was that really OK with him?

As he walked down the hall to his room, he thought about it. What would life be like without Nancy to keep him on his toes, and Tom to keep him grounded?

Even more than that, what would they think about losing him? Would they be happy to get rid of his gloomy mornings and gruff evenings? Would Nancy finally burn down the building with one of her coveted indoor cigarette breaks? Would Tom do... anything different? Likely he would have to figure out Mr. Grant's patterns and find a new place to sit and read, depending on how Mr. Grant felt about company. How would Mr. Grant feel about company? He cringed, thinking about how best to break the news that the hotel was haunted with the most annoying ghosts he'd ever met. Then again, he hadn't met any other ghosts. Maybe they were all this way. Dammit, he'd miss them.

What about Susan? She was fairly mobile. He assumed that all he had to do was get her in one mirror long enough to transport her. Would she go with him if she had the chance?

He put his hand on the door latch and drew in another deep breath, which seemed to help less and less these days. How was he supposed to live like this? Maybe he needed peace of his own.

#

Night was always the worse part of living with ghosts. They tended to get bored without his attention, and Humphrey often stuffed cotton in his ears to shut out the scraping chairs, clinking glasses, and occasional crashes in the library. Tom had a way of reading until he fell asleep—if one could call it sleep—and letting books drop to the floor. Some nights he woke up again and grabbed another book instead of recovering the last one, ending up with an empty shelf at shoulder height, and a heap of books piled on the floor. Each morning, Humphrey collected and put them back in their places.

Nancy relished in pretending she could still taste whiskey and cigarettes. Humphrey spent an extraordinary amount of time cleaning up splashes of whiskey that spilled right down her ghostly gullet to the chairs. He was ever collecting lighters from random places—ones that he should never have ordered for guests because Nancy took them all, and they never had guests anyway. He had to make a deal that she could use the best crystal glasses if she limited her smoking to waking hours. That way he could watch for fire. Fire in an old hotel would surely be the end of it and their whole, comfortable existence.

And Susan. *Oh, Susan.* The unencumbered sound of her voice sometimes flitted through his dreams. She used to sing in the mornings, but her spirit these days was less enthusiastic. What was there to do inside a mirror? The others had their vices, their books, their various gadgets to pick up and for Humphrey to put back as soon as he noticed them missing. If she occupied the mirror over the vanity, she could just see the rolling hills and oak trees, spotted with tiny ponds and cattails. The vanity was her favorite place, her safe place that she only left when she missed human company.

Susan liked the night. She reveled in the chorus of frogs outside their window and smiled when night birds called warnings to any passers-by. An occasional raccoon or an opossum on the roof would cause her to laugh, and those were the moments Humphrey lived for. He'd taken to putting scraps on the roof just so she could watch the critters come by and swipe with their greedy paws. Just how her beautiful laughter came out of that mirror, he'd never figured.

250

At night Susan sometimes stared at him from her sleeping mirror. The one right above his bed. She'd pretend to lie next to him, and he could see himself in her arms if he looked up. How he missed her touch, her warmth.

This night was no exception.

He'd grabbed the best silk sheets, stripped down, and drank enough whiskey that he could swear he actually felt Susan's gloved hands on his chest. She never took those gloves off, and he'd given up trying to glimpse her delicate wrists. What she wanted to hide this far into their contactless marriage was beyond him, but he accepted it.

"Remember our honeymoon, before everything went bad?" he mumbled. Of course she did. She looked just like she did in the mirror, only younger and less sure of herself. He imagined if she ever got out, she would have a thing or two to say about how the world had changed. "We laughed all the way up to this room." Humphrey stared at the lines creasing her face. He loved every single part of her, and these lines were only more things to love.

A slight pink hue rose on her cheeks. Maybe tonight he'd get lucky.

"I remember." She sighed, moved away from his reflection, and his hopes fell. "You wanted to play cards and drink instead of make love."

Humphrey blanched. "And you told me to go ahead. I—I had it on good authority I could win this hotel, and I did, didn't I? We had a place for ourselves."

"You chose money over me. What was I supposed to say?" She narrowed her brows. "I'd never encountered a man who didn't want to indulge in lovemaking. I had no idea what to do, and it wasn't just that day. You were so distant, so often. I don't know what I was thinking."

A painful lump formed in Humphrey's throat. He closed his eyes and took a deep breath. "I wish I had that time back. I'd show you how much I love you. Every damned day."

Susan wiped her eye with a handkerchief and glided into another mirror.

"Where are you going?"

"I need to be alone," she whispered.

"No! Talk to me!" Humphrey jumped off the bed, but Susan kept gliding. Where in the hotel she planned to go next was beyond him, so he had to move fast and keep up. Why, oh why did he put so many mirrors in this place? At least her paths were like a maze. She could only go where another mirror hung within sight. Had he hung them in certain places, thinking of where she *should* go? Or had he hung them

251

where he thought she *might* go? Had she *told* him where to put them? He couldn't remember now.

Susan glanced over her shoulder. "Stop following me."

"No, we need to talk."

"Stop!" The pitch of her voice cracked the mirror she occupied.

Humphrey halted with his naked backside against the hall and stared at his distorted reflection next to her cracked one. Her lungs were powerful when she was in her actual body, but the mirror amplified them.

"That man's grandfather was the idiot you played cards with and left me alone on our wedding night. He's talking about a resort? He won't let this building stand. At least have the decency of letting us all gain peace enough to move on." Susan crossed her arms.

Move on? He had hoped she wouldn't bring up her moving on. Or him. "I don't want to lose you," Humphrey croaked. "Why do you want to lose me?" To lose Susan meant that these past years had been in vain. His hanging onto her memory, to her image in this mirror—to keeping the hotel because debt was what he deserved for leaving her alone that night—meant nothing.

"I want to be happy, with or without you." Susan glided down the hallway mirrors, leaving Humphrey with a pit in his stomach.

He sucked in a breath and closed his eyes as he let it out. *What a fool. What a stupid fool.* He shivered in the breeze from the open window. When had he opened it, anyway? He walked to it, intending to shut the cold out, but the freedom outside beckoned him.

He stuck his head out and breathed the scent of lavender from the porch. Susan smelled like lavender when she was here with him, in the flesh. He sometimes caught a whiff of it when she cried in the mirror. Her tears tore his heart to pieces and drowned him in them. There was nothing he could do to comfort her from here.

Was she dead or alive? Was he dead or alive? Maybe all of this was a dream and he would wake up in the honeymoon suite with Susan in his arms.

Vines covering the window threatened to grow inward and stretch their talons inside the house. He shoved their still tender leaves back outside and twisted them around each other so that they would grow a different way. The thought of trimming them seemed too much.

\#

The next morning Nancy had started the meal cooking, and when Humphrey walked in, she cursed needlessly over bacon grease splatter. Tom, as usual, sat with a book in hand, eyes roving the pages with vigor younger than his bones could have mustered when alive. Humphrey squinted at the spine and smiled, noting it was the same blank-spined one he'd deposited back in the library. *An old ghost reading love letters.*

"Morning Nance... you seen Susan?" Humphrey got himself some milk from the icebox.

"No, but I'm willing to bet my cigarettes she is unhappy."

"How on earth would you know if you haven't seen her?" He grimaced at the thought he was that close, yet so far from ridding Nancy of her house fire starters.

Nancy tilted her head and gave him a look that could wilt a flower. As usual her face was flawless and red lipstick perfect, but even with all her excessive makeup she still commanded authenticity. "She's a part of this place, you know. She's inside it. The whole thing cries with her."

Yes... yes it does. All night the hotel had creaked and groaned, sending ghastly noises through the radiator and the water pipes. He'd left the window open too.

"What did you do to upset her this time, Hump?"

"What? Nothing."

Nancy shook her head.

"Oh, fudge it all." Humphrey slumped next to Tom and tenderly took the book from the old ghost's hands. "I have to tell you two something."

Tom's eyes flashed for a moment before he settled into his normal, calm self. Nancy strolled over with hands on her hips.

"Mr. Grant's grandfather used to own this hotel. He's the one that lost it to me in a card game, which is probably why young Mr. Grant snapped it up so fast the moment it hit the market. I think he intends to tear down the place and build a resort instead."

Both ghosts stared at him as if they'd seen... well, who knew what was worse than seeing themselves. Humphrey continued.

"You will have to decide if you want to stay, or find peace. I—"

"We know how it works." Nancy's hands dropped to her sides. "This is our home, though. I think it's enough. I don't particularly desire peace, never have."

Tom simply continued to stare, albeit with a slight tremor in his hand.

"You want to stay and occupy the resort?"

"Sure, I could use some more eye candy." Nancy smirked and licked her lips. "Tom will always find a good book or two. That's assuming you don't want to move on, Tom?"

Tom bit his lip so hard Humphrey swore he saw blood. Not much rattled Tom, ever, but this news certainly seemed to take its toll.

"What about Susan?" Humphrey groaned. "I could take her favorite mirror down with her in it, I suppose, but I don't think she wants me anymore."

"She needs out of that mirror. You remember how she got in it?"

Humphrey would never forget that night. He'd foolishly spent his honeymoon night gambling while poor Susan slept. Or so it seemed. Earlier that evening she had claimed to see a figure in their bedroom mirror, and he'd laughed it off, leaving her to wallow in misery. He should have been there.

"It wasn't an accident. It wasn't some curse. She broke the mirror in anger, and traded places with Tom." Nancy leaned forward, her bosom spilling just a little over her low neckline.

Humphrey narrowed his brows and looked to Tom, who sat with his head down, inspecting the worn book's binding. It was hard to be angry with him, especially when the ugly scar on Tom's forehead wrinkled. If one looked hard enough, many more scars poked out from various places: under his sleeves; in-between his shirt collar and neck. The forehead wound must have been the last in a long line of abuses. "It doesn't make sense; how does one get in a mirror to begin with?"

Nancy sighed and shook her head. "I don't see the point in hiding this from you any longer. Susan tried to end her life, but she changed her mind. The mirror… it keeps desperate people in a transitory place. Tom accepted his time was up and let her have the mirror. So here he is."

Tom shifted in his chair.

"Hump…"

"Humphrey." He raked his fingers through his hair.

"Hum*phrey*. You chose this hotel over your wife, and you didn't have to. She's still responsible for being in the mirror. You only need to realize how to love her, and she herself, if the two of you will ever find peace."

"I wanted a place for us! I wanted to set us up and..." the lump in his throat refused to go down. "What do you know about love, anyway?"

Nancy reared back, and the spatula wavered in her hand. "I might not have a love of my own, but I know it when I see it. I know a mistake when I see it too, and you've shit the bed."

Humphrey buried his face in his hands. "I can't fix it if she is stuck in the mirror! Whatever did I do with that broken mirror? Do you think that is the only way out?"

"You tossed it, long gone by now." Nancy handed him the spatula. "I suggest breaking all the mirrors. Maybe that would be strong enough."

"You're insane."

She shrugged. "Then let her go."

"What if she disappears? What if she finds peace, and she leaves?"

"Stop shitting the bed, *Humphrey*. Her happiness, or lack thereof, is not about you. But you aren't helping."

The entire house shuddered. Gripping the table with one hand and instinctively swiping the air for Tom with the other, Humphrey gaped at the empty space. Either Tom had decided to go invisible, or he really had left the room without his book of coveted love letters. What kind of havoc could one quiet, bookish ghost wreak on a hotel about to be flattened?

The house shuddered again, wood creaking and windows rattling. *Susan. Susan is part of the house.*

Glass crashed. A loud moan reached his ears, and he knew.

Humphrey handed off the cooking tools and dashed to the hallway. His heart caught in his throat.

Mr. Grant stalked along the hall, fire poker in hand, smashing mirror after mirror as Susan's rushing white blur fled to the very last one. She had no escape route at the end of the hall, and the whites of her eyes showed.

Not Susan!

"Stop this at once!" Humphrey bellowed as Mr. Grant swung with all his might at the mirror next to Susan.

Mr. Grant glanced up, eyes wild and sweat pouring from his armpits. "I came to prove you killed my uncle, and that you stole this hotel. I found this creature watching me sleep! Some picture from France you have, here!"

"Creature? That's my wife!" Humphrey's fists curled.

"You're a lot crazier than I thought, then."

The mayhem brought Nancy to the hallway, standing beside Humphrey. Her spatula must appear to be floating to Mr. Grant.

Mr. Grant raised the fire poker. "And that! Whatever that is tried to set my room on fire with that damned lighter last night!"

"Nancy!" Humphrey snatched the lighter from Nancy's brazier, gaining a quick slap. He'd assumed she used it to start the stove. Not being hers originally, it must appear to hover in the air, too.

"I was just offering him a smoke! Not my fault he's so handsome he doesn't understand how to light it."

"Jaysus, smoking in daylight hours only, and I told you not to touch him!" Humphrey shook his head. Nancy had gone from hating the man, to thinking he was cute, to objectifying him—which shouldn't surprise him in the least.

"You're insane!" Mr. Grant crouched, ready to swing at anyone or anything that got close enough. His rolled-up sleeves slowly unfolded, and his nightshirt billowed in a slight breeze from the window. "Don't you come near me."

"Set down the fire poker. We'll talk it out. Who is this uncle of yours?"

"You lie… you killed him. I'm going to sue the daylights out of you, after I smash every last mirror in this godforsaken place and burn it to the ground." Mr. Grant pulled back for one last, mighty swing.

"No!" Humphrey lurched toward Mr. Grant.

Before the swing could hit, one of the broken mirrors crashed to the flour, sending everyone jumping back from each other. Humphrey's heart pounded in the momentary silence.

Two more mirror frames flew off the wall, their glass remnants scattering at Mr. Grant's feet. The man's eyes grew impossibly wide as they darted from Humphrey to Nancy's spatula, to the floor. Sweat beaded on his forehead. Could he see Tom?

Humphrey saw him clear as day. Tom, with his normally relaxed frame, stood ridged, his determined stride crunching through the glass. He pulled down one more broken mirror in a rush of momentary youthful energy before coming to a stop a few feet from the threat.

Mr. Grant dropped the fire poker. His hands shook. He took a step back.

Humphrey ran forward, snatched Susan's mirror off the wall, and held her to his chest. He had to save her.

Mr. Grant pulled out a pistol from inside his coat and aimed it blindly through the ghost at Humphrey. No, the man couldn't see Tom. Not yet. "Drop the mirror," he said. "Anyone comes near me I'll shoot, dammit."

Humphrey brought the mirror away from his chest and looked into Susan's eyes. She stared back at him and shook her head.

No. No, I won't let him do that. I need you. Could his soul speak to her? Like in the love letters. Could he reach across time and place and speak to her in the past, or just here? She had to know his sorrow, his regret. Or maybe she only had to be free.

"You have to let me go." Susan spoke low and slow.

"I can't."

"Let me go."

Humphrey shook his head.

"Let me go!" Susan let out an ear-piercing scream that shook the hall and rattled windows. Even the vines outside trembled, and one strand crept into the open window at Humphrey's side.

As Susan continued to scream, Mr. Grant lost his footing and stumbled backwards, falling against the wall.

Humphrey wanted to shut his ears, but he had to hold the mirror. He clutched it desperately to his chest and cried out at the prolonged sound. Hair on his arms raised. His mind raced. His skin tingled, and the glass on the floor lifted an inch before it fell.

The pain in his ears ended abruptly and pure, dead silence settled over the hall. Mr. Grant's pistol dropped with a thud, sending echoes through the impossibly still air.

Humphrey pulled the mirror from his chest and Susan's cracked image stared back at him.

He'd hurt her this much. He'd been that careless. What would happen if he dropped the mirror and let her go? Would her soul be at peace and she'd leave him? His lungs struggled painfully. How could he live without her? How could she live *with* him? "I love you. I didn't know how to show it. I was such a fool…"

"Let me go." Susan commanded.

She deserved to be happy, with or without him. Nancy was right. He'd shit the bed. Damn, that woman was always right. His heart clawed at his chest with the decision.

"I'm so sorry." Hands shaking, he let the mirror slip through his fingers like the thousand pounds of his heavy heart.

Glass shattered and flew in all directions, over his shoes, pelting the beautiful hardwood floor. His heart shattered with it. She deserved better than him. Always had.

They stared at the mirror's empty frame. The whole house stood quiet, dead, like the place where his heart used to live. Humphrey fought back the urge to drop to the floor.

"I knew you could do it."

Susan's soothing voice sounded in his ear, her actual breath hot against his neck.

Humphrey whipped around.

By God she was there, in the flesh, safe and sound, and perfectly aged to match him. Her gloves lay on the floor and her scarred wrists circled his neck. She smelled of the same lavender perfume she always used, and had the same soft arms and sweeping hair. *Oh, Susan.* He would never take her for granted, not even for a second. Hopefully she would let him close to her heart again. He wept in her embrace. *How are you real? How are you really here?*

"U-Uncle?" Mr. Grant's voice trembled.

Tom stood before them, ghostly as ever, but now Mr. Grant took him in from head to toe. Tom never showed himself to guests, and he did so now with his head high. He closed the gap between them and pulled the weeping Mr. Grant to his chest.

Tom spoke for the first time in decades, or ever. "It's alright, nephew."

Mr. Grant closed his eyes and relaxed into his uncle's arms. "I tried, I tried to find you for so long. Before Grandfather died, he told me that Humphrey was keeping you here. And I, I thought..."

"It was your grandfather who killed me. But I've been happy here with Humphrey." Tom glanced over his shoulder. "And Nancy."

Nancy snorted, but a single tear rolled down her cheek. She grimaced at her own show of emotion.

"I have so many questions." Mr. Grant wiped his eyes and his chest heaved.

"I've written down the answers." Tom held Mr. Grant at arm's length and pressed his book to the man's chest. "I'm going to see Rose, now. Do right by my friends."

Mr. Grant nodded.

Tom's face smoothed into a contentment, and his form flickered. A slight breeze pushed against their faces from the open window. In the fullness of dawn, Tom began to fade. First his feet dissipated like fog in the wind. Then, particles from his hands floated to the window, coaxing his body with them until the only thing left was Tom's memory.

#

Humphrey poured champagne with a flourish, watching the bubbles snap as they rose. He corked the bottle and settled in next to Susan, who had just polished off her first post-ghost steak. It was wonderful having a person who understood fine cuisine, even if she did demand that he do the cooking. He was good with it. He'd cook every day for the rest of his life if it meant holding her hand one more time.

Susan smiled from across the table. They had agreed to start dating again, and he could hardly keep his eyes off her. And she'd made him wait until the moment was right for another stab at their honeymoon. He would wait, albeit not without giving her pleading glances. He'd waited this long.

"I always knew my grandfather was a bastard... but I hadn't thought he was the killer. I'm so glad I got to meet my uncle. I never thought I would...such an age difference between him and my father. It's good he is at peace now, though." Mr. Grant lifted his glass.

"We all miss him. The library is quite lonely these days." Humphrey glanced at Tom's favorite book still sitting on the table. He opened it to one of the dog-eared pages and his heart filled, remembering the love letters pasted inside it.

"How did Susan end up staying? Alive, no less?"

Nancy gave Mr. Grant a satisfied, matter-of-fact smile. "The mirror keeps desperate people in a transitory state until they make up their minds. Susan chose to live."

Humphrey grasped Susan's hands and kissed them all the way up her scarred wrists until she pulled them back. Her scars were beautiful, just like every part of her. "I'm so glad you wanted to live."

"Are you saying my uncle didn't want to live?"

"Look at the book." Susan nodded to Tom's book.

Mr. Grant leafed through it and stopped at the same dog-eared page that first caught Humphrey's attention. "My God, he pasted love letters in here. These must be to my... *almost* aunt Rose." A smile cracked his face, and he shook his head. "She had Tuberculosis and when Grandfather found out they were going to elope, he forbade it. Said there was no point to doomed love. And that's when Tom disappeared. My father said the hotel staff had Rose on their doorstep asking about

Tom every so often, but Father doesn't remember him...too young. I can't believe there are so many letters here..."

"Well, there was a rather large gap from when he was inside the mirror. But there you have it. He's got places to be, women to woo in the afterlife." Nancy brushed her fingers over Mr. Grant's hand and he gaped much the same way Humphrey had the first time—shocked that any sensation came from her almost touch. "He's happy now."

Susan sipped only a tiny bit of champagne and set her glass on the table with a satisfied smile. She'd always been a lightweight, and even more now that she'd not had alcohol for years. Humphrey made a mental note not to try to push her too hard to drink.

Nancy snatched up the discarded glass and tilted it down her ghostly gullet, letting its contents splash to her chair.

Mr. Grant stared, open-mouthed. Even after the week he had spent with them going over papers, journals, old books, and anything else Tom had kept around, he still hadn't gotten used to Nancy's lust for life's pleasures that death denied her. At least she let him see her now, which often sent him blustering away in red-faced confusion.

"I'm glad we could be of service to your uncle, and to you. So, what's next for this place?" Humphrey drummed his fingers on the table. He'd hate to see the hotel destroyed after all they had been through together. The very walls had so many stories.

"Well, I've decided not to knock the place down. I'd like to turn it into a haunted resort instead. That is, if you agree to participate." Mr. Grant cast a sly look around the room. "What say all of you?"

"A haunted resort." Nancy clasped her hands together, eyes shining just a bit brighter before her lips twisted into a delighted grin. "Does it come with you in it?"

Mr. Grant regarded her with arched brows. A corner of his moustache tilted up. "It might."

"Fully clothed or..."

"Nancy!" Humphrey and Susan slammed their hands on the table in unison.

Mr. Grant turned scarlet from neck to ears. His shoulders shook and eyes flew to the rafters as he laughed. When he was done, he grinned like a fool.

"I—well—I'm just asking a practical question." Nancy crossed her arms and leaned back in her chair. Two seconds later she fumbled for her cigarettes and, despite deep searches, came up with no lighter. She never stumbled over words, never broke her confident demeanor—especially not with men.

"I… don't see why either of us have to be clothed the *entire* time I live here." Mr. Grant raised a brow. He stared until Nancy lifted her eyes to meet his. "Will you allow me to pour you another drink?"

Author Bio:

When she's not pursuing research bunny trails, Danielle is reading. Her happy place is cozying up on the couch with her dog and a 19th-century gothic mystery novel, but you'll also find her hiking and exploring ghost towns and forgotten graveyards. An avid photographer and language learner, Danielle finds it difficult not to see the story potential in every place or turn of phrase. Sometimes the muses are humorous, and sometimes they are dark, but they always come from an integral place. Her upcoming novel takes place in Northern Alabama, 1834. It's about a boy and his new, standoffish friends who come of age during a decade long blood feud that leaves him digging graves—perhaps even his own. You can follow the progress here:

https://linktr.ee/Dapplewrites

THE END

Many thanks for reading this collection and we hope that you enjoyed it. If you did, we would be very grateful if you would consider leaving a review on the site from which you purchased it, or alternatively on Goodreads. Reviews help books reach new readers, which in turn encourages authors to write on.

We hope you have enjoyed our stories and that this has inspired you to read more of our work.

If you are a writer of historical fiction and would like to join our Facebook group, please search for us on Facebook at https://www.facebook.com/groups/writersofhistoryforum